One Love,
Two Stories

Anna

Amanda Prowse

HEAD
of ZEUS

First published in the UK in 2018 by Head of Zeus Ltd

Copyright © Amanda Prowse, 2018

9 7 5 3 1 2 4 6 8

A catalogue record for this book is available from
the British Library.

ISBN (FTP): 9781788542067
ISBN (E): 9781788542098

Typeset by Adrian McLaughlin

Printed and bound in Great Britain by
CPI Group (UK) Ltd, Croydon CR0 4YY

Head of Zeus Ltd
First Floor East
5–8 Hardwick Street
London EC1R 4RG

WWW.HEADOFZEUS.COM

Anna

AMANDA PROWSE is the author of sixteen novels including the number 1 bestsellers *What Have I Done?*, *Perfect Daughter* and *My Husband's Wife*. Her books have sold millions of copies worldwide, and she is published in dozens of languages.

Amanda lives in the West Country with her husband and two sons.

www.amandaprowse.org

I would like to dedicate both *Anna* and *Theo* to Mr Tim Binding. Without Tim's words of encouragement and advice these books would not have seen the light of day. There are times when everyone needs someone to take them by the shoulders and gently steer them back on course.

Thank you Tim.

Thank you.

Anna and *Theo* are for you.

I did it.

X

One

1974

'Mummy?' Anna called ahead, as was her habit, making her way along the hallway of their flat, stepping over her school shoes that were lined up side by side underneath the radiator. Their laces had been looped on the outside, making it a doddle for her to slip them on. This was just one of the small things her mummy did to make her life easier. She also cut Anna's toast into soldiers so she could hold a slice in her fingers and still colour in with her free hand. And she turned down Anna's bed at night so when her teeth had been cleaned, Anna could, with no more than a hop, a skip and a jump from the bathroom across the narrow hallway, land in her bed and onto the stripey, bobbly, flannelette sheet.

'Mum?' She pushed open the lounge door and stared at the scene that greeted her. 'What're you doing?'

Anna watched curiously from the doorway as her mum, Karen, waggled the long, unattached flexy Hoover hose above her head, darting forward and then jumping back, twisting this way and that, jabbing it into thin air.

'I'm trying to catch this spider without hurting it!'

'With a piece of the Hoover?'

'I thought it was a good idea until you arrived to watch!' Her mum laughed, leapt onto the worn, sagging sofa and poked again at the speedy spider, who darted away across the ceiling, quicker than she could react and further than she could reach. 'I think I need a plan B.' She chuckled, jumped down off the sofa, dropped the hose and placed her hands on her hips. She often did this when she was trying to figure something out.

'Why don't you just open the big window and let him crawl out?' Anna said.

'Or her.' Her mum smiled at her briefly and then did a double-take, before making her way to the window to do just that. 'My clever girl, let's try it. You know I like the fresh air. Darling, I must ask, what have you got on your head?'

Anna liked to make her mum laugh and she delighted in the giggle that now bounced off the walls of the little square lounge.

'I'm getting married!' she announced, adjusting the white pillowslip that sat loosely on her head and cascaded down her back like a cotton veil.

'Ah, I see. And where's my invite?'

'It got lost in the post.'

This retort was enough to send her mum into pleasing fits of laughter once again.

'That's why I've come to get you.'

'Ah, quick thinking.' Her mum tapped the side of her nose with her finger. 'Where are you getting married?'

'In my bedroom. Meet me there in three minutes!' And Anna rushed off to continue with her important preparations.

As instructed, her mum loped in and sat down on the edge of the single bed, folding her hands in her lap.

'Well, it's a good job I was only in the lounge. I would hate to have missed my girl's big day. No girl wants to get married without her mum there.' She smiled. 'But I do wish I'd had a bit more notice, I'd have got my hair done and probably put a frock on.' She ran her fingers through her long fringe.

'You look fine,' Anna said reassuringly, in the way she had heard her mum and Maura do on many an occasion as they checked their reflections in the hall mirror before leaving the flat. She flicked the pillowcase over her shoulder, as if swishing her long locks.

Her mum picked up the pale green, cloth-covered copy of *The Jungle Book* by Rudyard Kipling. Anna wasn't entirely sure where the book had come from, but she couldn't remember a time when it didn't have a place among her things. She was too little to read it for herself, but her mum read her bits of it when the fancy took her, often after a glass of wine. For some reason, holding the book and reading aloud always made her mum sad, which was odd as it always made Anna very happy.

Her mum put the book down sharply and turned to face her. 'So who are you marrying? Someone nice, I hope?'

'I'm going to marry Joe.'

'Oh, how lovely!' Her mum clapped.

'Joe is my bestest friend, he gives me a piggyback when we come back from the park and I know if anyone was mean to me, Joe would get them for me.'

Her mum laughed, nervously. 'Yes, I suspect he would.'

It made perfect sense to Anna. There was no one in the whole wide world she loved as much as her big brother.

'You might have a bit of a wait for your ceremony, Anna.'

Her mum glanced at the little watch on her wrist. 'He's not in from school for another hour or so.'

'I know! This is just a practice and I wanted to line all my teddies up.' She pointed at the row of soft toys propped against the wardrobe door on the narrow strip of carpet in the tiny room.

'And I see they have all dressed for the occasion.' Her mum nodded at the toys, who were adorned with hair clips and necklaces; one even sported a hat made out of a red paper napkin.

Anna beamed, delighted that her efforts hadn't gone unnoticed.

'Where are you having your wedding breakfast?'

'Breakfast?'

'That's what they call it,' her mum explained, 'a wedding breakfast. That's the meal you have after you get married, even if it's at teatime.'

'Do you have cornflakes and toast?'

'No, you can have whatever you want, because you are the bride and it's your special day. It's like being a princess for a day and everybody will do what you want them to.'

Anna liked the idea of this very much. As princess for a day, she'd probably get everyone to make her jam sandwiches and help her come up with dance routines. 'I am going to get married and have two babies, a boy and a girl.'

Her mum reached down and ran her palm over the top of Anna's head. 'Well, that sounds like a plan. My mum had two girls – Lizzie, my older sister, and me. I always thought I was very smart to have one of each and I highly recommend it! I didn't mind what I got, a boy or a girl.'

'So' – Anna considered this – 'if I had come first, I would have been a boy called Joe!'

'Yes, you would.'

'And Joe would have been a girl called Anna!' She wrinkled her nose at this absurd idea.

Her mum paused. 'I was always dead set on the name Joe. And truth be told, I didn't really know what my little girl was going to be called, but then I took one look at you and you were definitely an Anna. My little Anna.'

'I think I will have my little girl first and then my boy.' She nodded, making the decision right there and then.

'Good choice.' Her mum smiled. 'And what will you call them?'

There was a moment while Anna let out a long, low hum, tapping her finger on her mouth and thinking of the names that most appealed. 'I will call my little girl Fifi and my boy will be called Fox.'

'Fifi and Fox?' Her mum leant back and laughed. 'Anna, I love the names Fifi and Fox!'

Anna laughed too, happy that her mum approved of her choices. 'Do you think someone will want to marry me?'

'Oh, baby girl, I think everyone will want to marry you! They'd be mad not to. You are wonderful and you are only going to get more wonderful. You are my little gift that I never expected and it was the best present the universe could ever have given me.'

Anna beamed, showing the gap in her front teeth where one had fallen out; its replacement had yet to appear. She also liked the idea of being presented as a gift. Her smile faltered at the earnest expression that flashed across her mum's face.

'But you know, what you eat on your wedding day isn't really that important. In fact whether you get married or not isn't really important. The thing that matters most is that you spend your time with someone who loves you very much and who you love right back, someone who is kind to you and who you in return want to be kind to.'

Anna stared at her mum, figuring this required further investigation.

'But… But how do you know, Mum, if it's the right person?' The idea of getting it wrong felt more than a little scary.

'Ah, you don't have to worry, that's the easy bit.' Her mum blinked slowly and smiled with her lips in a thin line, the way she did when she was talking about one thing but thinking about another. 'It will be someone who makes it seem as if it's sunny, even on a rainy day.'

'Did you get married, Mum?'

'No.' She bit her bottom lip. 'No, I have never been married.' She shook her hair from her eyes.

'Did you want to marry Joe's dad?' Anna fidgeted with the button eyes on a teddy usher, welcoming the distraction, aware that this topic was usually off limits. The words sitting like something bitter in her mouth.

'No, love. No, I didn't. I am thankful for Joe, but his dad…?' She exhaled. 'He was a proper handful. I thought I could fix him, but life doesn't really work like that and it took me a while to figure that one out. I think I always knew we were on a timer.' She clicked her tongue against the roof of her mouth. 'Long while ago now.'

Anna nodded, as if she had the faintest idea what a proper handful was and what it meant to be on a timer.

'Did you want to marry my daddy?' This she whispered.

There was a beat of silence before her mum answered. Anna heard her sharp intake of breath.

'Truthfully, of all the people I have ever loved, he is the one

I think I could have married. He was a lovely man. Is a lovely man,' she corrected. 'He made my life sunny and then he gave me you.'

'He drives a black cab, doesn't he?' Anna filled in the small detail that she carried around inside her head, a precious snippet of information that she used to try and build a picture of her daddy. Since this fact had come to light, whenever she got the chance she stared at cabbies who had dark, straight hair like hers, waiting to see if any of them might roll their tongue. This, Joe had told her, was a skill inherited from your mum or dad, and as her mum couldn't do it...

'Yes, he does,' her mum said with an obvious lump in her throat. 'And his name is Michael.'

She stared at her mum, who looked dreamily towards the window. This news had been offered so casually, almost as an afterthought, and yet for Anna it was a bright jewel of information that would glow inside her head for ever. *My daddy is called Michael! Michael...*

'So...' Anna proceeded with caution, desperate for details but nervous all the same, her voice barely more than a whisper. 'If you thought Michael was lovely and he took away your rain, why didn't you marry him?'

'Because...'

Anna looked up at the unmistakeable sound of her mum crying. She instantly felt guilty, knowing that more likely than not it was her questions that had caused this. She had a sad, sicky feeling in her tum and wished they could go back to laughing.

'Because he was married to someone else,' her mum managed. Fat tears rolled down her cheeks, which she wiped away with the tips of her fingers.

Anna took a step closer and placed her small hand on the side of her mum's face. 'It's okay, Mummy.'

This had the surprising result of making her mum cry harder. Anna toyed with the idea of calling off her wedding, but she had gone to a lot of trouble and her teddies would be most disappointed. It was as if her mum had read her thoughts.

'But please don't let my tears spoil your wedding day. In fact, tears are almost obligatory on your wedding day, so I'm told.' She sniffed loudly and smiled, a fake smile intended to reassure but which had the opposite effect.

Anna's mum had cried last week too, and this memory was enough to make Anna hold back her own sudden urge to cry. They had been walking down the high street from Honor Oak Park station and as they'd stood on the side of the road by the crossing, waiting for the traffic to stop, her mum had suddenly grabbed her by the arm and yanked her back towards the wall. She'd bent down low, taking Anna with her, as if she wanted them both to fall right into it and disappear. When she spoke, her voice had been shaky and her eyes had swum with little pools of tears.

'What's wrong, Mummy?' Anna had asked, afraid of this odd situation. Her mum was squeezing her arm so tightly it hurt.

'It's okay.' Her mum had smiled broadly, even though her lips quivered in a way that told her the exact opposite was true. 'We are just going to crouch down and stay here for a second or two...' She swallowed. 'It's a game! Like statues. How still and quiet can you be?'

Anna stared at her, being as still and quiet as she could. Her mum usually counted her in when a game began, but she understood that this game had started the moment they'd jumped back from the crossing.

Her mum raised her chin, twisted her neck and watched the row of cars roar past, then stood up. 'Come on, Pickle.' She reached down and calmly took Anna's hand and they had walked home as if nothing had happened.

This felt just like that – odd and as if her mum was fibbing a bit.

'Joe will be home soon and we need everything to be just so. What do you fancy for your tea?' her mum asked with new enthusiasm.

Anna jigged on the spot, happy at the change to her mum's mood. 'I don't mind.'

'And I don't know why I bother asking you and Joe – you both always say "Don't mind!". I might give you something really disgusting one night and I bet the next night you'd be full of good suggestions.'

'Like what?'

'Ooh, I don't know, snail stew or cooked tomatoes!' She laughed, knowing the latter was on her daughter's banned list.

'I hate cooked tomatoes!'

'What? More than snail stew? Eeuuuw!' They both laughed. 'What did you do today at school, anything good?'

Anna nodded. 'We did a bit more on our project, "Under the Sea".'

'That sounds brilliant. How's the collage coming along?'

'Really good!' Anna nodded energetically. 'Mrs Jackson picked my squid to go in the middle.' She adjusted her pillowcase head-dress, which was in danger of slipping off her rather fine, shiny hair.

'Good for you, baby girl. That's wonderful! It's given me an idea – maybe we could have squid for tea?' Grabbing her daughter's hand, she kissed her knuckles, entwining Anna's fingers with her own.

'Oh no, Mum! I could never eat squid. They are too cute. Plus I bet they'd be all slimy and rubbery, some of them look like plastic bags.'

'You're right. I think we'll stick to sausage and chips.'

'That's my fav-ou-rite!' Anna jumped up and down, as if this coincidence was more excitement than she could take at this time of day.

'Well, I never did!' Her mum laughed.

Anna felt an extra-strong rush of love for her mum, who made everything feel okay.

'I've just had an epic idea! We could make a wedding cake if you like? I think I have the ingredients for a lovely Victoria sandwich and you could make a decoration for the top!'

'Yes! Yes!' Anna squealed her delight, rushing from the bedroom and into the kitchen, eager to get started.

It was half an hour later, as they sat at the kitchen table with two golden rounds of sponge slowly rising into domes in the oven, that they heard the sound of Joe's key in the door.

'He's home!' Anna gasped with delight, her eyes bright. Her brother was always the best playmate, jumping into any part with gusto.

She heard Joe slam the front door behind him and make his way into the bedroom next to the kitchen, slamming that door too.

Her mum blinked rapidly and gave a small cough to clear her throat. 'You wait here, darling. I'll go and give the groom a shout.'

'Okay.'

Her mum hesitated in the doorway. 'While I chat to Joe, I want you to do something for me.'

'Okay.' Anna nodded.

'I want you to go round the room with your eyes and try to think of something in here for every letter of the alphabet. Don't worry if you get the alphabet wrong, but do as many as you can! I'll start you off. A... apples!' She pointed at the fruit bowl.

Anna got the gist. 'B...' she said aloud. 'Bananas.' Also in the fruit bowl.

'That's it!' She gave her daughter a less than convincing wink that all was well and left Anna at the table.

C... *cup*. Anna used her index finger to draw shapes in the fine dusting of flour that now coated the shiny work surface. *D... dishes. E... eggs. G... G... No, wait a minute, it's not G next... I'll skip to I...*

It was impossible not to hear the loud shouts being exchanged only feet from where she sat, even though she tried hard not to listen. She tried to sing in her head, tried to concentrate on the image of the fabulous blue squid she'd painted and that Mrs Jackson had picked as the best in the class, but it was no good. Anna was forced to listen to the angry words being hurled back and forth like sharp things between the two people she loved most in the whole wide world. It made her heart beat quickly and her face felt warm.

I think I might write a letter to Fifi and Fox. I can do it in my rough book and rip the page out. I'll do my best writing...

'Only weed?' her mum was saying sarcastically. 'Do you have any idea how stupid you sound? You are fifteen! Fifteen! Christ, when I was your age—'

'Oh God, here we go… When you were my age you were practically a nun, studying and being perfect, living a perfect life and being the perfect child. Well, I'm not you, Mum!'

'No, you're not, because I would never have spoken to my mum like that, and for the record, I don't expect you to be me and, actually, my life was far from perfect.'

Anna heard Joe snort. She drew jagged lines in the flour with her fingertip.

L… leg. N… nits. What comes next – is it P? I think it might be. Petals…

'I am so worried about you, Joe. And to make me worry like this is just not fair! You are only fifteen and I am responsible for you. I hate how you care so little what you put me through. Believe it or not, there are some things in life that I know more about than you do – and don't roll your eyes when I am talking to you!'

'For fuck's sake, I didn't!'

'And don't swear!' Her mum was screaming now and it sent a jolt of anxiety through her six-year-old veins.

'I can't do anything right!' her brother yelled.

'You can. You can do lots right, and one of the things you can do right is to stop smoking that noxious stuff with your friends.'

'It's not noxious – it's less harmful than a cigarette. They've done loads of research.'

'Christ, Joe! Do you think I know nothing about the world? Give me some credit. You think you're inventing smoking dope and drinking with your mates, but you're not! You're just doing what every other fifteen-year-old who is going off the rails has done for ever.'

'I am not going off the rails!'

'You are missing school, Joe! I know you are. I never see you study or do your homework, and smoking drugs is only a small part of it for me. All of these activities are wrapped in dishonesty, which is not how you were raised. It's the crowd you hang around with and your lack of direction, this is what bothers me.'

'Oh not this again! You've never liked my mates!'

Anna heard Joe stomp across the floor, then the sound of his bedsprings flexing.

There was a moment of quiet. Anna heard a new tone to her mum's voice now and it helped her tummy unknot a little.

'I love you so much, Joe. I can only keep telling you that I love you because it's the truth, but I am scared for your future. I fear that smoking weed or whatever you want to call it is a stepping stone towards other drugs, other habits, and that scares me more than I can say.'

'I'm not stupid!'

'I know, but I have seen intelligent people fall into the grip of drugs and it destroys lives, it takes away all the things that you have every right to expect – a job, family life, a future.'

'You are talking about my dad, right?' Joe asked, quieter now.

Her mum evaded a direct response. 'You are not stupid, Joe. You are smart and brilliant and that's why it would be such a terrible, terrible shame to see all of your wonderful potential go to waste.'

Anna didn't hear what Joe said next as his words were reduced to a whisper.

Her mum came back into the kitchen and reached for the padded oven glove in the shape of a crocodile's head. It usually made her laugh, especially when her mum snapped it at her, but she didn't feel like laughing right now. Anna watched as her mum opened the oven door and removed the two slightly overcooked sponges, laying them on the cooling rack that sat on the plastic tray with red and orange flowers hand-painted on one side.

'Is... Is Joe all right?' she whispered.

'Yes, he'll be fine.' Her mum braced her arms against the sink and stared out of the window at the brick wall of the neighbouring property. Their eyes were, as ever, drawn to the green streak of moss that glistened against the orangey bricks and the leaky old pipe above it. 'God, I hate this room. It's so dark. I dream about having a kitchen with a big wide window overlooking a garden, and I'd have it open all of the time, with a lovely breeze coming in and the scent of flowers filling the place. Wouldn't that be lovely, Anna?'

Anna got the impression she wasn't expected to reply to that. 'I did it, Mum. I got as far as S for salt.'

Her mum nodded, still avoiding her gaze. Her shoulders straightened a little. When she eventually spoke, she sounded weary.

'It's a good distraction, Anna, my alphabet game. You should remember it. When your thoughts are too loud, or you feel afraid or you just want to pass the time, you can go through the alphabet and find things to match the letters. By the time you get to Z, things have usually calmed a little, or you will at least have taken the time to breathe.'

Anna stared at her mum's slightly bowed back and then at the rust-coloured sponge cakes that she no longer felt like decorating. She knew there was not going to be a wedding today after all. Reaching her hand up her back, she yanked at the pillowcase, pulling it from her head and letting it fall onto the chair.

Her tummy rumbled, but she knew this was not the time to ask about the sausage and chips she had been promised for her tea. Instead, she ran to her bedroom, returning with her rough book and a fistful of felt-tipped pens, some with the nibs pushed up inside the casing, though this fact was only revealed when it came to using them.

Anna sat herself in the big chair and laid her pens in a faded rainbow on the table, then opened her book. It was chockfull of doodles, pictures, words and lists. Her mum smiled at her over her shoulder before busying herself at the sink. Anna stuck out her tongue and began:

deer fifi fox
> *my nam is anna cole I six I yam yor mummy*
> *not yor mummy now but in lots of time*
> *my techr is missrs jacksun she is very nis but smels like ham*
> *i did a blu skwid*
> *my brother is nam joe and he bigr than me*
> *my mummy is karen she is reelly reelly good singr*
> *she sings al the time.*
> *I wil rite you letas and you read them when you ar big.*
> *anna cole*

Two

Anna never did get to have her wedding breakfast with Joe. By the time she'd turned seven he'd left home and it was just Anna and her mum in their little flat in Honor Oak Park. Without his presence, the place lost some of its sparkle, but was also a calmer place, quieter. She missed him of course, but what she didn't she miss was the screaming rows or hearing her mum sobbing into her mug late at night in the kitchen. Sometimes he would turn up unexpectedly – at school, in the park, at home when her mum was out shopping – and those were the best of days. He'd invent mad games for the two of them to play, or he'd take her to the cinema. They went to see *Herbie Rides Again* and he bought her popcorn and sweets *and* chocolate. It was more than she could carry, let alone eat. They had stuffed their faces and laughed, as they stared up at the big screen.

There was a small part of her that loved having her mum all to herself at home. Birthdays were especially good. When she was eight they had planned on going for a picnic up on One Tree Hill where there were lovely views over the city. Rain and an icy cold wind put paid to that, so instead they made a tent in the lounge and ate sandwiches and cake sitting under a sheet with nothing more than a torch providing an eerie light. They lay on their tums and spoke in whispers. Despite her initial sadness at missing out on a day at the park, it turned out to be one of the best birthdays she had ever had. And on the day she turned nine, they made it up to One Tree Hill with a Tupperware box full of ham sandwiches, two bottles of orange Panda Pop and a packet of Fondant Fancies. They spread a blanket on the grass, but instead of admiring the view, they looked at each other, reminiscing about their tent in the lounge adventure the year before.

It was now a few weeks after her ninth birthday and for the first time Anna had been allowed to take her brand-new Snoopy rucksack into school with her. Other than that, it was an ordinary day and she was sitting through an all too ordinary history lesson.

She softly kicked her school shoes against the desk leg and watched the trillions of dust particles swirl and settle in the sunlight that filtered through the high window. It bothered her, this reminder of the dust soup she was forced to inhale. If she thought about it too much it made her feel quite sick, the idea that these teeny tiny specs were bits of everyone and everything around her. Joe had told her this when she'd met him in the library and had pointed out the dust patterns, although the idea of breathing in bits of all those books hadn't been quite as disgusting. It had been a lovely afternoon – he'd made the books come alive! It hadn't seemed to worry him that people stared at them as he boomed character voices and acted out scenes. She loved him more than ever at moments like that, giggling in the reading corner, lost in *The Last of the Really Great Whangdoodles*.

She sighed now and looked around the classroom. Try as she might, she couldn't block the thought from her mind. Her eyes journeyed from the less than fragrant Paul Brown, who, as if on cue, scratched his greasy, toffee-brown cow's lick, to the bored-looking stick insects in the sparse tank. She tried to hold her breath, not wanting to let any of their dusty stuff get inside her, but her chest fluttered and her head felt a little fuzzy, so she had to give up.

Miss Hillyard was reading aloud from the textbook on her desk. Its spine was worn and its pages flattened – just like all the other books she used in their class. It was as if each one of her study aids knew exactly what was expected of them. Her round glasses sat on top of her nose and were attached to a gilded chain that looped across her pudgy pink cheeks. All her clothes had flower patterns on them, as if she was trying to make her chubby self look more feminine, and her blouses and scarves came in a range of garish shades.

Miss Hillyard's lessons always struck Anna as a little pointless. All twenty-eight members of her class had the same textbook open in front of them and they were perfectly able to read the words for themselves, even if some were slower than others – again she looked at Paul Brown, who was now ferreting about inside his nose, no doubt for a snack. She shuddered, turning her attention back to Miss Hillyard.

Being slowly dictated to always constituted the majority of Miss Hillyard's lessons, as if she was a baby and not a sharp-minded nine-year-old. She followed the words on the page from beneath eyelids heavy with boredom. It was a struggle to keep her thoughts anchored on the topic. If only her teacher could adopt Joe's method of reading, they would all be much more engaged. Miss Hillyard's drone was like a fuse to any other thought, sending ideas and images into her brain that exploded like fireworks.

What might they be having for tea?

Had her potted lemon tree, sitting proudly on the windowsill in the sitting room, sprouted anything of interest?

And she hoped her mum had remembered to return her library book! The idea of it being late or, worse, getting a fine, made her heart skip a beat. Though if her mum had forgotten and *Danny, the Champion of the World* was still on her bedside table when she got home, she would probably, no definitely, read it all over again before bedtime.

She tried to focus. Sitting up straight now, she pushed the points of her dark, chin-length bob behind her ears. What Anna craved was to hear the details behind the facts in the textbook. Did Miss Hillyard agree that women were brave to fight for the vote, to actually die for something they believed in? What did the husbands and children left at home think when the women they loved were frogmarched off to prison? Who got their tea then? But, as ever, her perfectly formed questions faded on her tongue like snowflakes, disappearing before she got up the nerve to ask them.

She had always been this way – 'quiet with a busy head', as her mum put it. Sometimes she didn't speak for hours at a time and it was only the croak to her voice and the stutter in her throat that made her realise that the lively conversations she'd been having had all happened inside her head. Chitchat and laughter were the preserve of the popular girls, girls like Natasha Collins and Tracy Fitchett, the ones with a gaggle of friends who moved as a gang and laughed to order. *Yes, that's why I'm quiet!* The thought resonated. *It's because I don't have anyone to talk to. There is no one listening...*

Even though it was only a little after 10.30, Anna felt a wave of sleepiness wash over her. The red laminate door of the classroom creaked open. Glad of the distraction, every child in the room lifted their head and swivelled their eyes towards the school secretary. Miss Williams's nose twitched nervously as she knocked on the doorframe, even though she was already standing with one foot in the classroom, as if testing the water.

'Yes?' Miss Hillyard boomed in her direction.

Miss Williams blinked quickly.

These types of interruptions were rare but not unheard of. They usually ended with the secretary handing a slip of paper to the teacher – a last-minute reminder about a dental appointment or a surprise fire drill, or, occasionally, something far, far more important.

None of them would ever forget the day a year ago when a flustered, arm-flapping Miss Williams had banged on several classroom doors to inform them that a man had turned up in the playground and was giving out flyers for a circus that would be performing in Dulwich Park for the next ten days.

Anna, like many of her classmates, knew there was little chance of actually going to the circus, but that didn't matter because there was something remarkable about the man in the red velvet coat with shiny buttons and gold braiding on the epaulettes. He had a small monkey sitting on his arm! An actual monkey! In the playground of their school in Honor Oak Park! A tiny monkey! And it was dressed in a little red coat just like his.

Naturally, a crowd swarmed around the little fella. The staff were seemingly at a loss, unsure whether to order them all back inside or encourage this rare encounter with wildlife. This was Greater London, 1977 after all – how often did they get to see a wild animal like this in the neighbourhood, and not just any wild animal, but one wearing a natty red coat? The bolder pupils called out all kinds of questions to the man with the dapper moustache.

'Can I hold him?'

'Does he bite?'

'What's his name?'

'Where did you get him?'

But Anna wasn't one of them. As was her manner, she stood quietly at the back and gazed at the small, bony head of the little animal, no bigger than a golf ball. She watched his pale brown eyes dart knowingly around and his nimble fingers peel the husk from a peanut shell before popping the kernel into his narrow mouth. While everyone else whooped, cheered and yelled, the monkey looked up above the hubbub and caught her eye. For a second they looked at each other, really looked at each other, and there was a flicker of recognition between the two of them. Anna immediately recognised in the monkey a fellow creature who had a lot on his mind. In the monkey's gaze she saw the same sort of sadness and frustration that she saw every time she looked in the mirror and wished she were the type of girl who travelled in a gaggle with the likes of Natasha Collins. She related to his unhappiness. She knew she would likely never tell another soul about this exchange – she would be disbelieved as well as ridiculed – but she would never forget it. The encounter had ended with the little monkey briefly raising his eyebrows, and this too she'd understood.

My life's not perfect, but it could be much, much worse...

She smiled now, watching Miss Williams creep forward with silly theatricality, as if she were invisible, recalling suddenly that the little monkey had been called Porthos, named after one of three musketeers. Joe had told her this too. He knew all of their names, including the fact that most people mistakenly believed d'Artagnan to be one of the trio, which he wasn't. He was the fourth musketeer, hanging around on the edges, trying to prove himself, desperate for an in. This had been their conversation as they'd strolled along Margate seafront at sunset. Joe had jumped onto the prom wall and mock-challenged Anna to a duel. She had stood poised, en garde, her knees bent, holding her candy-floss stick out like a sword, while Joe raced nimbly around her, flourishing an imaginary dagger before admitting defeat, leaping off the wall and falling to the ground in an exaggerated death scene.

Anna grinned now at the memory and her gaze strayed across to Natasha Collins and Tracy Fitchett as she wondered if they knew about the fourth musketeer. It was only then that she realised Miss Williams and Miss Hillyard had stopped whispering and were both looking in her direction. Her classmates appeared to be following their lead and were looking at her too.

Anna's cheeks burned with embarrassment and her stomach dropped with the beginnings of fear. There was something in the softened smile of Miss Hillyard and the nervous swallowing in the school secretary's throat, which told her that whatever this interruption was about, it was nothing good, nothing as frivolous as a monkey in the playground but something far, far more important.

★

The room was part office, part waiting room and smelt of cleaning products. Not the sweet-scented variety that sent a whoosh of peach or lemon up your nose when you walked into the bathroom – this was more chemical and a little unpleasant. Anna let her gaze flick briefly towards the woman who sat in the corner with a novel in her hands. She had heard her sigh twice.

'How are you doing?' the woman asked for the fifth time.

And for the fifth time Anna nodded and looked into her lap, wishing she had a novel in front of her. *Danny, the Champion of the World* would do. Not that she could read anything right now. She felt too... She felt too...

She reached below her hair and pushed at her ears, trying to clear them. She felt as if she was underwater. Everything, even the woman's voice, was muffled.

'Remember, when your thoughts are too loud, or you feel afraid or you just want to pass the time...' Anna heard her mother's voice in her mind. And she began.

A...

A... answerphone. I think that's one on the desk, either that or it's a cassette player, but I'm going to let it count.

B...

She let her eyes rove the crowded, sagging shelves built into the alcoves of the room.

Books. Easy.

C... clock.

She looked up at the industrial-style timepiece on the wall. *3.15. How long have I been here? A long time. Don't think, just keep on doing the game.*

D... desk.

Her fingers drummed on the tabletop and she tried to count the stain marks left by dozens of tea and coffee mugs. Her tummy hurt and she couldn't stop clamping her teeth together until they ached.

I want my mum! Where are you, Mummy? I need you right now!

The part-glazed fire door opened slowly and the smiling doctor woman she had spoken to before poked her head inside the room.

'How are you doing, Anna?' she asked kindly.

Anna couldn't bear to look back up at her. *I don't know how I'm doing. I'm trying not to think. I just want Joe. Where is he?*

The doctor exchanged a look with the woman in the corner and carried on talking without waiting for an answer. 'We are still trying to get in touch with your brother and as soon as we have, I will come and let you know. Can I get you a drink or anything to eat?'

Anna shook her head.

Please, Joe, please hurry up and get here soon. Please...

'Righto.' The doctor tapped her fingers on the doorframe. 'Well, Julie will stay with you of course, and I will be back as soon as we have more news.' She smiled as she closed the door slowly.

I can't think too much.

I can't think about it.

E... envelope.

F... filing cabinet.

G...

★

Anna didn't remember falling asleep with her arms cradling her head on the table, but evidently she had. She came to at the sound of the door opening, and there he was. Like magic, sprung from thin air.

Her relief at seeing Joe was so acute, it was as if a knot had unwound inside her. Her tummy ache was replaced with the need to visit the loo and she felt her bones go all soft. Her throat started to close up and her tears spouted as she scooted the chair along the polished grey linoleum and jumped up. Running around the table, she crashed into her skinny big brother. With her eyes closed, she locked her hands behind him and held him tight. The large silver-eagle buckle of his leather belt bit into her. She buried her face against the flat of his white T-shirt and inhaled the familiar plasticky smell of his faux leather jacket and the sweet, woody scent that she associated with him. She felt as if the weight of his hand on her shoulder was the only thing anchoring her and stopping her from floating up around the ceiling.

'It's okay, Anna Bee. I'm here now.'

Even though it had been months since she'd last seen him, all it took was him using her family nickname and she felt a million times safer. He was her family, her brother. He knew things that no one else did, he shared her memories. He knew about the alphabet game, and he knew how their mum called her Anna Bee so that with their surname, Cole, added on, she became ABC.

He put his thin arms around her briefly, then gripped her shoulders and bent down to look her in the face. There was a red tinge to his eyes, a crop of spots on his chin and dark, bluish crescents at the top of his cheeks.

'She…' Anna tried to say the words out loud, tried to make it real. 'She…'

'I know, Anna Bee. I know. It's okay. You don't have to say it. They told me when they called and I am so sorry.'

He wiped his nose with the back of his hand and she saw a new little tattoo on the skin between his thumb and forefinger. It was a tiny pot of ink with a little dagger poking out of the top. She ran her finger over it and her brother smiled despite his tears, revealing a gap where a front tooth used to be. This only made her more sad. Yet another piece of Joe was now missing.

He didn't get it. She wanted, no, needed to say it.

'She died, Joe. She just died. I… I said goodbye to her before I went to school. She was standing at the worktop making toast, and "The Things We Do for Love" was playing on the radio and she was singing along.'

Anna could hear it now in her head. She pictured her mum and herself in the rain, in the snow, holding hands.

'And I thought I would see her when I got home for my tea like I always do and then they came and got me from my history lesson to say that she died. She died, Joe.'

Her eyes searched his face for confirmation that this was real, that she wasn't going mad. Because there was still the faint possibility that she had gone mad and even though that would be bad, it wouldn't be nearly as bad as her mum being dead.

'I don't know what to do now,' she whispered. It was a struggle to get the words out.

'You don't have to do anything. I'm here and I'll come back to the flat with you and we'll just have to take it one step at a time. How does that sound?' He gently cupped her chin with his beringed fingers.

Simply knowing the next steps pacified her a little. As long as she was with her big brother, she could get through the rest of the day.

'She… She died in the bathroom. The policeman told me her friend Maura from up the road knocked for her so they could go shopping in Catford and she looked through the letterbox and saw her on the floor. They said she had a heart attack.'

'Yes, that's what they told me too.' Joe straightened and took her small hand into his.

She might have been nine and he eighteen, but at that moment they were once again six and fifteen, disorientated and wandering around Margate trying to find their mum as the light faded and the roar of the funfair lost its thrill and became something scary instead.

Again she pushed at her ears, still unable to shake off the feeling that she was underwater.

'I guess it's all right to take her home?' Joe said. 'Do I have to sign anything?'

'No, you can go. Of course,' the doctor said. 'Everything's in order and you're her next of kin, so that's as good as it can be, in the circumstances. She's had quite a day.' The doctor turned towards Anna. 'Anna, I'll be checking in on you, talking to your GP, and I want to say how very brave you've been today.' She smiled with her lips tucked in.

'Can we go now?' Joe spat, looking anxiously towards the door.

Anna noticed he used his angry voice when talking to the doctor. It was the same voice that had shouted at their mum the last time she'd seen him. 'You can shove it!' he'd yelled, a line of spit dangling from his bottom lip and his wide eyes darting to and fro. 'I came here for help and again you can only nag me! I like to think that if ever I have a son, I'll be there for him instead of giving him nothing but shit!' He had paced up and down then, running his fingers through his hair.

'A son?' her mum had shouted. 'You are only my son when you need something, Joe! I've told you before and I can only tell you again: get clean, come off the drugs and I will help you all I can. But that's the deal. You need to be clean, otherwise it's not fair on me and it's not fair on Anna. We can't do it any more!'

Anna had wanted to shout out, 'I don't mind, Mum! I would rather have Joe home and on drugs than not have him home at all!' but she didn't. Instead, she'd stared at the telly, the one they'd bought to replace the one that had gone the last time they'd been burgled. Her mum had cried and decided not to tell the police. She said there was no point, she said that she knew who'd robbed them and that to get the police involved wouldn't help anybody.

Anna took a breath and looked at the doctor.

'My... My mum...'

'Yes?' The doctor and the other two people in the room all cocked their heads, as if what she might have to say was of huge importance.

'My mum doesn't like dark places or small spaces. She likes the window open and she likes a breeze.'

Julie started whimpering in the corner. The doctor shot her a look.

'Okay.' The doctor nodded. 'Thank you for letting me know that.'

*

Joe reached into the pocket of his skin-tight jeans and pulled out a pound note. He paid the taxi driver while Anna stood by the front gate.

'Have you got your key?' he asked.

She looked up and was almost surprised to see him standing there. In her head, she'd gone back to that morning, to when she'd closed the gate behind her and stopped a little way along the path to pull up her socks. She remembered doing that but very little else afterwards, until she got to school. How was she to know that the last ever image of her mum would be of her standing at the worktop with the butter knife in her hand, waiting for the toast to pop?

Her mum had blown her a kiss seconds before Anna shut the front door and, as always, Anna had caught it and pressed it to her cheek.

Wasted seconds. If she'd known it was going to be the last time she'd see her, the last time she'd hear her voice, she would have clung to her, buried her head in her chest like she had when she was a baby, and she would have told her all the things she needed her to know.

I love you, Mum, more than anyone else in my whole life and more than I will ever love anyone, ever, ever.

I can only go off to sleep if I can hear you washing up in the kitchen or watching the TV in the front room because then I know that you're close by.

It was me that broke Nanny's vase and hid the broken bits behind the ironing board in the hall cupboard. I didn't want to get in trouble and I'm sorry.

It didn't matter to me, Mum, that it was just you and me, or you and me and Joe. Even though Tracy Fitchett says having a dad is the best thing in the world because he takes her swimming and she can jump off his shoulders into the pool. I know, Mum, I know that you are the best thing ever and you are better than two dads or even three dads.

And last of all, I miss you every day when I am at school. I miss you now and I always will. I miss you so much I feel like there is nothing inside me. I'm like an empty Easter egg. And I feel like I might break.

'Anna!' Joe called gently. 'Have you got your key?'

She tried to answer him. Tried to say that there was a secret key tied to a piece of green ribbon in the bottom of her new Snoopy rucksack that their mum had put there with the instruction that it was to be kept for 'just in case'. But she couldn't talk. Her teeth chattered and her limbs were trembling. It was the coldest she had ever been.

'It's okay.' He laid his hand on her back. 'We'll get you inside and you can wrap up in a blanket on the sofa and I'll make you soup or something to eat and we can put the fire on.' He gulped, as if these tasks might be beyond him, and the idea that Joe might not be able to do things made her feel scared, made her shakes worse.

'Do you have a key, Anna Bee?' he pressed.

She handed him the rucksack and watched as he rested it on the low wall of the small yard that housed the metal dustbins of the house that had been divided into three flats. Theirs was on the ground floor, at the front of the building.

Joe went first, pushing open the front door and peering ahead. She followed, letting her hand trail along the wall of the narrow hallway, feeling the dips and bumps of the spongy, flowery wallpaper beneath her fingertips. She wondered what it must have been like when the ambulance men carried her mum out into the street. She wondered if people had gathered to watch.

Joe went straight to the kitchen and switched on the overhead striplight, which flickered and buzzed as it came to life. It wasn't yet dark, but the kitchen was always gloomy, no matter what time of day or month of the year it was.

Anna walked forward on jelly legs until she reached the bathroom. The door was wide open. Their best towel, a large blue one with a frayed edge, was folded neatly on the floor under the sink. She squatted down and could clearly see an indent in it. It was like a pillow – a pillow for her mum's head. Maura must have put it there for her.

Anna stretched out her legs along the cork floor tiles until the bottom of her brown school shoes touched the avocado-coloured side of the bath. Slowly she lowered her body and carefully placed her head in the dent in the towel, exactly where her mum's head must have been. Closing her eyes, she gave way to the tears that flooded out from deep inside.

When she was very little she'd worried about her mum getting kidnapped and thrown over the side of a boat, just as she'd seen happening in one of Joe's favourite films, which she'd watched illicitly from the doorway in her nightie. More recently, she'd pictured kissing her mum goodbye when she was very old, her hand poking out from a lacy bed jacket as she sat propped up on a ton of pillows, an image Anna had borrowed from the wolf in *Little Red Riding Hood*. This had been enough to reduce her to tears – the thought that one day her mum would die.

But the end of her mum's story had come much sooner than she could ever have imagined. This was where she had died.

Right here on the bathroom floor with her head on their big blue towel.

Anna curled her legs up towards her chest and let her howls echo through the flat. Joe raced in when he heard her sobs and he too dropped to the floor and cried along with her.

'Where is she, Joe? Where is my mum?' she managed, her mouth contorted.

'She's… She's with you. She will always be with you,' he croaked.

'I want her to cuddle me! I want her to cuddle me now!' she screamed. Her legs kicked out against the flimsy bath panel. The thuds were quickly matched by thumps from the floor above.

'Fuck off!' Joe shouted up towards the ceiling.

Anna was briefly stunned into silence by his outburst and waited for her mum to shout back her reprimand. But there was no Mum to tell Joe not to swear. No Mum to cuddle her when she needed it the most.

No Mum ever again.

Anna felt desperation rising inside her, filling her up. She pictured it like a dark thing, solidifying in her veins and internal organs, weighing her down.

They stayed there together for what might have been hours, Anna lying on the bathroom floor, Joe leaning against the wall, both crying, both wanting to be in the place where their mum had drawn her final breath.

Eventually it got cold and Anna padded off to her bedroom and slunk down between the covers. With her torch providing a spotlight, she opened her rough book, flicking the pages until she found a space. In black felt-tip, she wrote some lines, crossed them out and started again:

Fifi and Fox
  ~~I havent writen to you for a long~~
  ~~dear Fifi and Fox I thouht I should tell you~~
  ~~hello Fifi and Fox I am very sad and you will be too. My~~
~~mummy~~
  I am so sad my heart hurts all the time.
  I cant rite now. I dont know what to put. I will try soon.
  Anna Cole

Fat tears fell onto the page in splats, smudging the ink. Anna held the book to her chest and lay back on the pillows. She turned her face into the cotton slip, one her mum had washed a thousand times, and inhaled the fading scent of washing powder.

I don't know what to do without you, Mummy. I just don't know what to do. I can't think straight and I am so tired, but my head is too busy for me to go to sleep. I wish you were here to make it better.

Three

Living with Joe was far from easy. Even though the authorities deemed him a responsible adult, it soon became clear to Anna that he was anything but. The most capable member of the household was definitely her. But that didn't make her love him any less.

In the early days following their mum's death she was too numb to notice anything much. It didn't really bother her that the bed linen wasn't changed or that the greasy sheets rucked up under her as she twisted and turned in the throes of her frequent nightmares. She didn't make a fuss when she found that the bread bin was empty bar a few old, green crumbs or that the milk in the fridge had turned thick and sour. All these things seemed irrelevant when just remembering to breathe took such a lot of effort. Trying to figure out how to 'be' when sadness and exhaustion sapped all her energy was demanding enough.

Eventually, though, the fog cleared a little. Her body and scalp began to itch and she started to notice the disgusting state of the flat. It was then that she began to panic.

'I'm... I'm hungry, Joe,' she would whisper, standing in the doorway of the sitting room, which had been commandeered by her brother as his own, his old bedroom now overflowing with dirty clothes and rubbish. It bothered her less than it should. She had no desire to spend any time in the sitting room anyway, not now she couldn't snuggle up on the sofa with her mum. Not now her mum was gone from the flat for ever.

Joe's dirty, reclusive behaviour was the side of him that she found hardest to understand. She couldn't reconcile it with the boy she loved so much. His grimy jeans were heaped on the floor by the side of the chair. The tile-topped coffee table had been pulled up against the sofa and was littered with long, thin strands of tobacco, cigarette papers, empty bottles of Woodpecker cider, half-crushed beer cans, blackened spoons that looked like they'd been dropped in the fire, and strips of tinfoil. There were needles and egg-smeared plates nesting on old newspapers, along with crumpled, empty cartons of John Player cigarettes and Gold Top milk bottles with rings of cheese growing inside them. The heavy red curtains were permanently drawn, making day and night almost indistinguishable.

On days when Joe was relatively with it, he would shrug off the stinky sleeping bag in which he was permanently draped, ruffle her hair, light a cigarette and shuffle into the kitchen. A morning smell lingered on him no matter what the time of day – Anna much preferred it when his teeth had been cleaned and he had showered. With his bare feet sticking to the floor, eyes half closed and gripping the countertop for support, he would heat up a tin of soup and pour it into a mug for her. Anna would take the soup into her bedroom and sip at it from under the duvet, screwing her eyes shut and imagining she was hiding from her mum, who was humming a tune in the kitchen or chasing a spider across the lounge ceiling.

On the bad days, Joe would lie immobile on the sagging sofa, letting out a strange half hum, half groan, his eyes flickering behind their lids, showing that he had heard but was unable to respond. Once or twice he didn't acknowledge her at all and it was at these times that her fear threatened to suffocate her. With her heart beating in her throat, and picturing the large blue towel that she now kept under her bed, she'd creep into the dark room with its sour air smelling of all things adult and she'd slowly reach out her hand and cup it over his nose and mouth. Relief at feeling his breath against her palm was always sweet and instant. Moving slowly backwards, she would coo, just as her mum had done, 'It's okay, baby, go back to sleep...' before closing the sitting-room door. Supper on those nights would be anything she could forage from the back of the cupboard: a couple of soft crackers, a handful of stale cereal, spoonfuls of cake mix and in one instance the hard sticks of spaghetti that she didn't yet know how to cook.

At least there was a hot school meal waiting for her each lunch-time and for this she was extremely grateful, wolfing it down under the snickering gaze of Natasha Collins, Tracy Fitchett and their crew. She'd overheard them commenting on her once-white blouse, now grey, and now they laughed at her urgency to get the food inside her.

'Don't worry, Anna, no one is going to take it away from you!'

She looked up only briefly, with her loaded fork poised, noting their expressions of disgust.

'Fucking weirdo!'

It was strange how she felt only the vaguest flicker of shame, where once she'd have been overly concerned with fitting in. Now their taunts bounced off her. She was hungry and she was sad. That was it. The fact that she couldn't join in with their high-pitched chats about *Grange Hill* and who they currently fancied was just not important. Anna's needs were more immediate. She had lost her mum, and on top of this she carried the secrets of her home life. She was wise enough to know that if the truth about Joe came to the attention of the wrong person, her life might be further turned upside down. All that mattered was staying with Joe, keeping him close.

Anna continued to adore her big brother and she soon learnt how to take care of the two of them. She managed to keep the kitchen in slightly better order and she found out how to boil spaghetti. This, with a squirt of tomato ketchup – both ingredients picked up from the Spar shop – kept their tums full on many a cold night.

Joe occasionally went missing and those were the scariest times of all. She would lie there in the flat, alone and awake, too frightened to sleep, twitching at every sound that crept beneath the door or floated through the window. Even an immobile, unconscious Joe on the sofa was better than no Joe at all.

Peeking her head into the sitting room after two days on her own, her stomach bunched in anger when her eyes fell on the gap where the TV used to live. Worse still was the bare mantelpiece, once chockfull of her mum's favourite ornaments like the china robin perched on a gold-painted branch, and the ceramic red rose inside a glass cloche, which had been her mum's small way of having a garden inside. She'd loved finding quirky little objects in charity shops, but now they were all gone. Joe had even sold the pictures on the walls; in their place sat sooty rectangles that seemed to taunt her. Saddest of all, though, was the sight of the shrivelled brown trunk of her once thriving lemon tree. For Anna this was too much: another beautiful, living thing now turned to dust.

And then, not long after she turned thirteen, it happened. The very thing she'd been dreading most of all, the fear that had been gnawing at her ever since that most horrible of history lessons. In April 1981 Joe didn't come home at all.

E... echoey.

F... Father Patrick.

G... God. God. God, help me! God, please help me. I'm scared and I miss my mum and my brother so much it hurts.

H... hymn book.

I... I... I don't want to be here.

J... Joe... Oh Joe! No! No! No! I can't believe it. What am I going to do now? What am I going to do?

Standing in the April sunshine, Anna folded her arms around her tiny chest, wrapped in the formal navy sailor dress she'd found at the back of her mum's wardrobe. Hollow with grief and loneliness, she eyed the strangers who'd come to the service at St Stephen's. A young woman with severe eye make-up was wailing loudly at the edge of the path. Anna noticed her shiny red T-bar shoes, at odds with the mood of the day; she liked the splash of colour they brought. The woman had very large top teeth that sat proud of her bottom lip. Beside her stood a man with an intricately fashioned beard and sunglasses. He was chewing gum. He pulled down his black leather cap, then patted the young woman's back. The woman looked up, saw Anna and immediately came over, drawing her into a tight hug.

'You're Anna!' she managed.

Anna nodded from within the woman's grasp.

'Joe was...' The woman paused and sniffed. 'Joe was brilliant and I loved him.'

Anna stepped backwards and looked into the stranger's face. A stranger linked to her by their love for Joe. 'Were you his girl-friend?' she asked.

The woman looked briefly in the direction of the man in the leather cap. 'Sometimes.'

'Ruby!' the leather-capped man called.

R... Ruby Red Shoes...

Ruby kissed Anna's cheek and squeezed the top of her arm before returning to her friend. Anna felt an inexplicable desire to run over to her and stay with her. This stranger in red shoes had loved Joe! Ruby continued crying, more quietly now, and Anna watched as she rammed her knuckles into her mouth, trying to stifle her sadness.

Anna's own eyes were dry; her grief was too huge and too private to be shared with these people she didn't know. But she wondered, not for the first time, if she should be making more noise. As her mum used to say: *quiet with a busy head.*

She was surprised how few people were there for Joe. During the service she'd kept her eyes glued to the altar and she'd assumed that the sniffs and whispers from the pews behind her meant there was a large crowd. But now that they were all outside, she could see that there were about fifteen people at most. She didn't know who they were, but she was glad they'd made the effort. Like Joe, most of them looked a bit down on their luck, a bit grimy, a bit broken. The fact that they had bothered meant a lot. She knew how hard it was for Joe to rouse himself on a bad day, and that Ruby and others had managed it sent a ripple of joy through the churn of her thirteen-year-old gut. She hoped Joe had known how much he was loved.

Don't be stupid, Anna, if he'd known how much he was loved, he wouldn't have jumped.

She took a deep breath and shook her head, desperate to erase the image that filled her mind.

I'm sorry, Joe. I know it's my fault. I shouldn't have made you give me the music box! I hope you know that I'm sorry, and if I could go back to then...

She glanced round at the random group of strangers, the last link to her big brother, and knew it was unlikely she'd ever see them again. This brought a new burst of sadness; its tendrils snaked around her gut and pushed deep into her bowels. Within minutes they would all disperse and she would be on her way up the motorway to a city far, far away, one she could only just pinpoint on a map. Her new home.

Home... It would never be home, just a place to rest her head until... Until what? It was too much to think about.

'Are we all set then?'

The question, which came from Aunt Lizzie, caught her off guard. It was only the fourth or fifth sentence her aunt had ever spoken to her directly. She remembered her at her mum's funeral, remembered Joe pointing her out, skulking near the back with a lace handkerchief pressed to her face, seemingly reluctant to engage with them further. Now, as then, disapproval came off her aunt in ripples. Anna noted the impatient twitch to her fingers as she fidgeted with the handles of her Margaret Thatcher handbag. It was hard to imagine anyone more different from her mum.

Anna stared at her and gave her customary nod.

*

The car was a little too warm. Despite the sunshine of the April day, the heating was cranked up high in her uncle's shiny, pale blue Rover. She saw his hand skirt the pale wood veneer dashboard with something close to affection.

Anna didn't feel the need to cast a final glance at the school she wouldn't be going back to. It didn't occur to her to say goodbye, in fact she barely looked up as the car wove its way through the streets she had lived in her whole life. She hardly dared let her eyes drift to the corner shop, afraid she might see her mum coming out of the green door with her shopping basket on her arm and a smile on her face as she handed her younger self a little white paper bag full of mixed penny sweets. 'You're such a good girl.'

Anna's heart used to lift with joyful anticipation of the sweets, which would last the rest of the day if she was careful. 'Did you get Joe some?' she always asked, blinking, hopeful.

'No,' her mum would say, running her finger along Anna's chin. 'I got him this!' And she'd hold up one of his favourite music magazines, which always made Anna's face split with happiness, knowing Joe hadn't been left out. That was just how she liked it: everything done fairly.

Not that there'd been much that was fair about her life in the past four years. Anna scooted the tears from her cheeks with her outstretched fingers, hardly able to picture one let alone both of the people she had loved.

'Are you okay in the back there, missy?' Her uncle's voice pulled her into the present. His accent would take a bit of getting used to. Birmingham. Berr-minngg-gamm. Even today, on the saddest of days, she took a little warmth from his jolliness. He had crinkles around his eyes that suggested kindness.

Her aunt answered sharply on her behalf. 'Of course she's okay, Alan. It's not been five minutes since you asked her last!' This was accompanied by an almost imperceptible tut.

'It's quiet where we are.' Her uncle carried on, undeterred by his wife's rebuke. 'But there's a lot of history. Do you like history, Anna?' he asked gently, as if he understood that today everything needed to be done slowly.

She was trying to formulate a response when her aunt again interjected. 'She doesn't want to hear about that today!' she said sharply.

'I was only going to tell her about the motor industry, the pride of the Midlands. This very car was manufactured not five miles from its parking spot in our driveway. Isn't that something?' He squeezed the steering wheel, making his leather driving gloves squeak, and tilted his head to make eye contact in the rearview mirror.

'Good Lord, Alan, do you think she, or I for that matter, wants to hear your trivia when we've just had to sit through that funeral!'

From the tone of her voice, it was crystal clear to Anna that her aunt hadn't come to the funeral out of love for Joe, or her mum, or her. She felt a deep flash of dislike for the woman and not for the first time wished Aunt Lizzie hadn't bothered turning up, wished she hadn't decided to take Anna into their home, for whatever reason. An image of Ruby Red Shoes floated into her mind. '*Joe was brilliant and I loved him.*' She heard Ruby's beautiful words and added her own. *I miss you, Joe. I miss you so much. I wish I could tell you that I'm sorry...*

'We should talk about something more uplifting,' her aunt said, looking out of the window as if this was where inspiration for a suitable topic might be lurking. Turning her pink face towards the gap between the seats, she smiled as she asked, 'What do you think her dress is going to be like? I can see her in a fishtail, with a lace veil and a train that goes on for miles.'

Anna stared at her. *Dress? What dress?*

Her aunt sighed again, whether with impatience or disapproval it was hard to tell. 'The wedding dress!' she said. 'Lady Di's! Good Lord, the wedding of the century. I would have thought it's all you young girls could think about. A *proper* princess marrying her prince – now there's a fairy tale if ever I've heard one, a true love match, it's so obvious. I bet she'll make a stunning bride. My friend Shirley and I were going to travel up for the day, camp on the Mall, but to be honest, after today's shenanigans, it's more than put me off. I think I'll just get out the best tea service and wave a flag in front of the telly.'

Anna sank further down against the upholstery. On top of everything else, she had also apparently managed to spoil the royal wedding for her aunt.

Turning her head to the left, she pictured her mum sitting next to her on the back seat. She was wearing her favourite white T-shirt with a rose pattern on the front and her faded jeans. Her chestnut-coloured hair was loose about her shoulders. She looked pretty. Anna placed her hand on the grey leather piping and watched as her mum cupped her palm over it. She smiled at her briefly, taking comfort from the contact that flowed between the world in which her mum resided and her own.

It seemed like hours later that the car pulled into a cul-de-sac where lawns were small and neat and children's bikes were propped against garage doors. A white dog barked from an open porch and two little girls played jump rope on the raised kerb.

Anna sat up straight. Her heart was beating fast.

'Here we are then, love. I know this must all feel very strange for you today, but it will get easier as you settle in, you'll see,' her Uncle Alan spoke softly.

Her first impression of the house was that it was like a box or a cell. There were no surprising curves or patterns, no porches or fancy windows, no shutters or adornments of any kind. It was almost fully detached, except for the room above the garage, which was connected to a similar room above next-door's garage. The whole road was like that, with the houses linked together in a row.

Uncle Alan drove the car onto the narrow concrete driveway and ratcheted the handbrake. Her aunt Lizzie scrambled awkwardly to release her seatbelt as she waved to a man arranging a brown tent on next-door's front lawn. 'That's Mr Dickinson,' she said eagerly. 'He takes minutes at council meetings, which is a very important job. He's party to all sorts of sensitive information – you've got to be quite the keeper of secrets to work for the council in that capacity.'

Anna swallowed her lack of interest and watched her aunt heave herself out of the car.

'Hello, Mr Dickinson!' Aunt Lizzie waved coyly, reminding Anna of the way girls in her class acted when they talked to a boy they fancied.

She noted the irritated flicker that passed across Mr Dickinson's face. He returned the wave nonetheless.

'We've just got back from London.' Her aunt hovered with

her wide bottom pushed against the car door, waiting for Mr Dickinson to respond. She continued regardless. 'We've just buried my nephew. A terrible business.'

Anna felt a trickle of ice in her veins. She didn't want her life discussed in this way, casually, as if it was just a piece of gossip. A film of sweat formed on her brow.

'Oh.' The man looked more than a little embarrassed. 'I'm very sorry to hear that.'

'Well,' Aunt Lizzie continued, 'he wasn't without problems. Drugs. Like his father, I'm afraid. My sister, she…'

A… *Aunt Lizzie.*

B… *blue.*

C… *car.*

D… *died. Joe died.*

Anna listened, her blood pumping loudly in her ears, as her aunt paused and then after a snort of laughter added, 'Let's just say she never made very good choices. We've brought our niece back to live with us. But don't worry…' Again she let slip a small laugh. 'She's a different kettle of fish. Wouldn't say boo to a goose and is rather bookish.'

'I really must…' Mr Dickinson resumed unfurling his tent.

'Going somewhere nice?' her aunt pushed.

'Yes.' He spoke with his head down, thus ending the awkward conversation.

Anna looked over her shoulder, squashed her face against the seat leather and peered out of the window of the fancy car, trying to figure if it would be possible to walk back to London and how long it might take. She could sleep in the shed at her old address that belonged to the middle-floor flat. She could sleep in the park in the gap under the slide. She could find Ruby

Red Shoes and ask if she could live with her. She could sleep anywhere, anywhere other than here.

Uncle Alan opened up the hatchback and gave her a little wave. With her mouth hidden by the seat and just her eyes peeping over the upholstery, she felt like a wild creature submerged in a river. She didn't bother trying to find a smile. Her uncle lowered his hand. He hauled her large suitcase from the boot, across the path and into the hallway.

'Out you pop!' he called over his shoulder.

She followed slowly, knowing that once she was inside, that would be it, she'd be there to stay.

'Shoes off!' her aunt instructed, slipping her own small, chubby feet from the beige, heeled court shoes she'd teetered about on all day.

Anna stepped out of her navy blue pumps and looked down at her toes. She wiggled them against the biscuit-coloured carpet. She thought about a morning not long before her mum had died when they'd been outside by the little bin store, shoving last night's potato peelings and an old newspaper into the metal bin. Her mum used to take her time over chores like that, relishing the chance to be outside. Suddenly, caught by a gust of wind, the front door had slammed shut.

'Oh no!' her mum had screeched, rattling the handle and pushing on the door with the flat of her palm, as if this might encourage it to miraculously spring open. 'I'll have to go and get Maura's Dave.' She snickered. 'I never thought having a friend whose bloke had been inside for breaking and entering would be so useful!'

'What's breaking and entering?' Anna had asked.

Her mum had stared at her, blankly. 'You haven't got any shoes on!' she said, pointing out the obvious.

Anna had wiggled her toes against the stained, cracked concrete, feeling the cold seep through her thin socks.

'Right, hop on!' her mum commanded, gesturing at her own feet. Anna had duly hopped on: facing her mum and placing her feet on top of her slippers, they gripped each other's forearms. It was in this dance pose that they sidestepped down the street, laughing until tears rolled down their cheeks, ignoring the quizzical looks of people at the bus stop. Anna knew she'd never be as happy as she had been that afternoon, walking all the way to Maura's house, clinging on to her mum for dear life and giggling fit to burst.

'You might want to go up and see your room,' her aunt said, nodding towards the ceiling as she shrugged off her wool coat. 'Your cousin will be back from youth club soon. Funny how you've never met.'

Anna wasn't sure how she was expected to respond. She trod the open stairs slowly in her stockinged feet, taking in the magnolia-painted woodchip wallpaper and the three small prints that hung symmetrically at the top of the stairs, pictures of ladies in crinolines each holding a lacy parasol at a different jaunty angle.

Uncle Alan had placed her heavy case on the end of a single bed in a small room at the top of the stairs. The bed was narrow but fancy, covered in a lacy counterpane on top of a pink duvet; a matching valance skirted the carpet.

'Shall I close the curtains?' he asked as he reached up towards the abundance of peach-coloured faux water silk that hung at the window.

'No!' She reached out her hand, aware that she had raised her voice. 'I... I don't like the dark and I don't like small spaces. I like a breeze.' She whispered the last few words, curling her hand against her chest, seeing a burst of anxiety in her uncle's eyes.

'Righty ho.' He coughed. 'We'll have supper and then we can help you unpack, how does that sound?' He pulled a white handkerchief from the pocket of his brown suit trousers and dabbed at his red face.

'Thank you,' she managed, her voice no more than a squeak as she dug deep and tried to mask the thoughts that raged. *I don't want to unpack because that means I'm staying here and I don't want to stay here!*

'Ah, that's a good girl!' He smiled. 'You get settled, love, make yourself at home, and I'll give you a shout when supper's ready. Jordan is looking forward to meeting you. He's a good lad.' He walked towards the door. 'And just for the record, Mr Dickinson takes minutes in meetings about extended opening hours for pubs or whether someone can close a road for a street party or not. The way your aunt speaks about him, you'd think he works for MI6. Still, I expect you're not really interested in all that right now.'

Anna waited until he'd left the room before sitting in the small space on the bed next to her suitcase. She knotted her fingers through the gaps in the lace counterpane and listened to the muffled stream of conversation in the kitchen below. She couldn't make out any words, which was probably just as well.

The room was sparsely furnished, apart from a pink velour chair and a white melamine dressing table placed between two built-in wardrobes on the opposite wall. The wardrobe handles and mirror frame were all picked out in gold.

'What would you say about this room, Joe?'

'Looks like a granny room. Probably smells of piss!'

'I miss you,' she whispered, as fresh tears fell. 'I don't want to stay here. I don't like Aunt Lizzie and I don't like this house. I want to go back to London.'

She laid her hand on the suitcase, knowing her mum must have touched the exact same spot at some point.

She leant back against the wall and sobbed quietly.

Pressing her palms against her forehead, she screwed her eyes shut, as if trying to hold her thoughts together. 'How could you do this to me, Joe? You knew that I was already as sad as I could be, and now...' She gasped again, trying to steady her breathing. 'I love you and I miss you, but I am mad at you too. You were all I had, Joe. You were everything, my brother.'

'Tea in ten minutes!' her aunt called up the stairs.

Anna wiped her eyes and sat up straight. She unzipped the suitcase and began rifling frantically through her clothes and possessions to find the thing she was looking for. With a sigh of relief she placed her hands on the shiny surface of her notebook. She held it briefly to her chest, before gripping the pen. Raising her knees, she rested the book on them.

Hello Fifi and Fox,

I was sitting on my bed thinking about you, which I haven't done for a while now. This is going to sound weird, but you are all I have now.

I like that no one knows about you apart from me and Mum. It's like even though she isn't here, you are still our secret thing.

I wanted to tell you that you will never have to worry about anything because I will always be there for you to talk to about anything that is worrying you.

And if I can't be there for you to talk to, then I will make sure there is someone else for you to talk to because when there is no one to talk to it can make you feel very lonely. You can talk to each other or I will find someone that will listen to you.

Like if you don't like sweetcorn there will be someone you can tell so you don't have to eat it and pritend you do.

I am so sad that my whole body hurts. My whole body.

I told you long ago that you would not meet my mummy Karen and now you will not meet my brother Joe, the one I told you about, my big brother.

He died too.

But don't worry about this.

Most people don't die and you will be fine.

When I am older I will teach you the alphabet game, it really helps, and I will take you to the seaside and you can eat as much ice cream as you want and I won't even mind. And when you come home I won't make you take your shoes off in the hall and I won't make you eat sweetcorn if you don't like it.

And make sure you don't take drugs. Don't ever take drugs. Please don't do that. I will make everything better for you.

Anna Cole

Anna sat back and thought of the million ways Joe had made life better for her when he was having one of his good days. He used to come home bouncing with energy and optimism and present her with a box full of goodies – mismatched odds and ends of used make-up, a white embroidered lavender bag. Best of all had been the music box, covered in red leather and with a worn brass lock. When she lifted the lid, a skinny ballerina with a melted face had popped up on a tiny spring. She was wearing a white net tutu and had a painted-on bodice. She pirouetted on a little stick to the sound of 'Für Elise'.

That music box... He'd wanted to get rid of it, but she'd pleaded with him. *'Please, Joe! Please can I keep it!'*

Her tears came again.

She made herself look round the room to distract herself.

L... lamp.

M... mirror.

N... nightstand.

O... ornament.

P... pillow.

Qu... qu...

'Anna, your tea's ready! Ham, egg and chips, don't let it go cold now!'

She jumped at the sound of her aunt's yell and stood tall, trying to stem her sobs. She concentrated on breathing in a normal rhythm, ignoring the way her heart thudded in her ears.

Quiet.

Quiet – apart from Aunt Lizzie's shouts. It's so quiet – no street noise, no buses. I don't want to feel this sad, it makes me tired all the time. I don't want to go and have tea with them. I don't want to meet Jordan.

I wonder how long I can be here before something cracks.

Four

It was a rare hot day in late May and summer was peeping its head around the corner. Anna lay on her front, stretched out on the square of lawn in the back garden. She'd hitched up her burgundy school skirt so that the sun could kiss the backs of her legs, and she'd looped her shirt under her bra so her midriff could get the same treatment. She'd been at her aunt's house for just over a year now, but it was still a novelty to have access to an outside space that wasn't a busy street. She thought of all the things she and her mum would have done had this been available to them during her childhood. She wondered how different her life might have been if Lizzie had been the sister that had followed her unreliable boyfriend to London; if Lizzie had fallen in love with Michael the cabbie who was married to someone else; if Lizzie had had to watch helplessly as her son got drawn further into his all-consuming drug addiction.

We'd have had a paddling pool for sure and we would have had picnics whenever we wanted to. I'd have played catch with Joe and we would have built things like forts or castles out of boxes... I know you would have planted flowers, Mum, and I would have picked some for you when they were tall and put them in a jug on the kitchen table. We could even have had a party out here! That would have been so cool. But best of all, I'd have liked you to have had what you wanted: a garden to look out over, with big windows thrown open to let in the scent of the flowers.

'This is the life!' Jordan settled back in his deckchair. 'I think it's the ultimate decadence, having the time to lie in the sun and crisp up, don't you?'

Anna gave some thought to what represented ultimate decadence to her. The answer came quickly. Ice cubes. Ice cubes were for her what glamorous characters on TV had in their drinks and what wealthy people on holidays abroad chucked into their cocktails. She pictured the loud, rattly fridge in their Honor Oak Park flat, with its rusting freezer compartment in the top that was just big enough for a packet of fish fingers and a couple of ice pops. To have the room for a tray of ice cubes would have been quite something. Imagine using up that space and energy just for a little cube to make your drink cooler – what a thing!

'Look at you, smiling away to yourself! What are you thinking about, Toots?' Jordan reclined in the deckchair, blowing smoke rings up into the sky from between lips coated in a sticky pale pink gloss.

'You should stop smoking – it's bad for you.' She squinted at him, evading the question, still finding it hard to share her private thoughts on such personal matters. She scratched her head with the end of her pencil, then went back to making notes in her geography textbook.

'And you should start!' he replied drily, adjusting the foil-covered flap of cardboard that he was holding in place under his chin. 'It'll make you look cool and interesting.'

She eyed the foil contraption. 'Remind me why you're doing that again?'

'It reflects the sun's rays so that I get a tan under here as well as everywhere else.' He ran the backs of his long fingers under his chin. 'And just to be doubly sure of a good result, I've given my face a little coating of cooking oil.'

Anna rolled her eyes and smiled at him. 'Jordan, you need to revise. You're in the middle of your O levels.'

'Darling, I couldn't give a shit about them. As soon as I've saved enough, I'm getting the hell out of here and going to New York, where I shall be discovered, and the next time you see me it will be with my name in lights on Broadway.' He stretched his arm skywards, sliding it up against his cheek, bending his fingers and tilting his head, as though he had just finished a dance number.

'It's what they are going to discover that bothers me,' she quipped.

Jordan took a deep drag on his cigarette and blew the smoke in her direction.

'Urgh!' She flapped her hand in front of her face. 'Disgusting!'

'What are you revising anyway?' he asked.

She ran her fingers over the text. 'I'm learning about how the earth's crust, its shell, is divided into tectonic plates and how they have shifted over the last two hundred and fifty million years to form continents and mountains. Isn't that incredible? Two hundred and fifty million years...' she whispered. 'And humans have only been here for a blip of time in comparison. We are so insignificant.'

'Speak for yourself.' He giggled.

'I think I already know that our little lives don't mean much, not in the great scheme of things.' She chewed the end of her pencil.

Jordan lowered his foil and sat up in the chair. 'Because you've lost people you love.' His eyes misted.

Anna nodded, paying little heed to her cousin, who was of an emotional temperament. He cried when he heard Barbra Streisand sing and had sobbed so loudly in the cinema when they'd snuck in to see *An Officer and a Gentleman* that an usher had come over and shone a torch in their faces to see if he required any assistance. She had felt acutely embarrassed, knowing this was code for 'pipe down'. Jordan, however, had thanked the usher for her kindness and taken the proffered tissue.

'I can't imagine what you've been through, Toots. You know I love you, don't you?'

'I do. Now please shut up so I can read this,' she answered flatly, rereading the paragraph in her book. She was well used to his effusive outpourings of love and devotion.

'But I also admire you.'

'Jord, thank you, but I need to revise and so do you! Your mum will flip out if you don't get the grades you need for college.'

'I'm not going to college. I've told you – I'm going to New York!'

'*I* know that…' She looked up at him. 'And *you* know that, but you still haven't told your parents. And so why not hedge your bets and do a bit of revision?'

'You are such a nag,' he yelled.

'I nag because I care.' She smiled at him.

'You know, you might be a bit less judgemental if you did smoke and drink.'

'Thank you, for that.' She twitched her nose at the acrid smoke that lingered, recalling the scent of Joe, his body swilling with chemicals and alcohol. She often wondered why her brother had chosen that path, whether he was just built that way, whether he was subconsciously trying to replicate the life of his dead-beat dad. It got her thinking about her own dad and whether she might be unknowingly emulating some of his behaviours and choices. Did Michael have a fascination for the alphabet, for example?

Probably not, you weirdo.

'Anyway, you can talk!' Jordan sniped. 'Or rather, you can't talk. You really shouldn't let my mum boss you around. I worry, Anna, that if you don't find your voice, someone else will always speak for you, and then you won't ever change their opinion or let them know the true you and that would be a tragic waste. You have a lot of good things to say.'

She considered this truth, but, yet again, felt a distinct lack of desire to tell her cousin just how powerless she felt. Yes, she was fond of him, grateful for his friendship, but this was not her family home. Her aunt and uncle felt like caricatures of people she only vaguely recognised. She had nothing in common with them.

Even after a year of being there, everything still felt temporary, from her old-lady bedroom to the school she attended, and she suspected it always would. She was alone, even in a crowd, bent out of shape by what she'd been through, with a deep ache in her chest and a veneer of sadness coating even the most positive of experiences.

She knew her presence in the house made everyone tense. Just the previous week she'd overheard her aunt say exactly that – and more. She'd been tiptoeing down the stairs when she heard her aunt and uncle talking in the kitchen.

'I don't know what I was thinking,' her aunt said. 'I wish we hadn't bothered. I can't stand even knowing that she's up there over our heads, cluttering up my lovely spare room.'

Anna had immediately turned back up the stairs and faced the landing. But if her aunt didn't want her in her bedroom... She turned and faced downstairs again. She'd only be in the way if she went into the kitchen, plus it would mean having to face her aunt. For a full minute, Anna turned this way and that, at a loss what to do, tears fogging her vision. Absolutely no one wanted her and there was absolutely nowhere she wanted to be. She was trapped.

The doctor had asked if she was depressed. She had stared at him. Yes, she was depressed! She began each new day with tears and an overwhelming feeling of sadness. But the despair that engulfed her was so much a part of her now that it had become her normal.

Did she want drugs, the GP had asked, reaching for the prescription pad, pen poised before she'd had time to respond.

She had actually let a snort of laughter leave her lips. 'Drugs? No, thank you. I'll pass.'

Anna had learnt that the only way to survive without her mum and her brother was to try not to think about them. But this brought wave after wave of guilt when they sneak into her thoughts, as if compartmentalising her grief was somehow cheating. She tried to focus on her school work, and she kept herself to herself. There was an unspoken agreement with her classmates that they would ignore her, the new girl, and she would do the same to them; it was far easier to remain aloof than to try and break into the long-established friendship groups. Besides, being openly friendly would only invite questions about where she'd come from and why. God forbid that any of them should try and make her their project.

The worst moments were when she woke in the middle of the night and for a split second didn't know where she was. The bedding and the smell of the room were still unfamiliar and her first thoughts were always to call for her mum and then Joe. When realisation hit that they were gone, her grief would suffocate her, squeezing so tightly she feared she might stop breathing. 'I miss you, Mummy. I miss you so much,' she would whisper into her pillow, crying as silently as she could for fear of waking her aunt and uncle, who slept down the hallway on a squeaky four-foot-six divan.

'How come you're so clever?' Jordan asked, taking another long drag of his More Menthol.

'I'm not.' She stared at the diagram, a cutaway of the earth's crust. 'I just like to read and I have a good memory. But I'm not clever. My grammar is terrible and my spelling could be better.'

'Well, I think you're clever.' He smiled.

'Maybe I'm just clever compared to you.' She snickered.

'Oh, without a doubt! I start to read and then spot something shiny and my mind takes me wandering. I'm like a magpie, a magpie with the concentration span of a goldfish. I'm a magfish.'

'Or a goldpie.'

'Oh. My. God.' He gasped. 'You might just have come up with my Broadway stage name! I'm picturing it right now, in lights!' He ran his palm in an arc above his head.

They both chuckled.

'Only me!' Aunt Lizzie called loudly from the back door, as she always did.

'Fuck!' Jordan hurriedly wiped his mouth with his fingers and stubbed out his cigarette on the grass, throwing the butt into the neat flowerbed behind him and fanning his face as he exhaled a wisp of blue smoke. He tossed the foil contraption to his cousin.

'There you both are!' This was another of Aunt Lizzie's irritating sayings. She always made it sound as if she'd been searching for them for hours and that this was the last place she'd looked – even when they'd just walked in the door after school – implying it was a massive inconvenience to her. 'What are you doing?'

'Revising.' Jordan held up his cousin's textbook as proof. Anna noted that he'd dropped his voice to a lower register.

'Good boy!' Aunt Lizzie clapped, as if Jordan were six and not sixteen. 'Do you want me to test you?' She started down the steps to the back patio, clearly uncomfortable in the heat.

'No need, Mum, I'm just learning about Teutonic platters and how they have shifted over the last two hundred years to form mountains and rivers – it makes me feel that we are all so insignificant.' He sighed.

'Oh, Jordan, you are a little thinker, that's for sure. Take after your Grandad Cole.'

Jordan nodded at his mum with his lips tucked in.

'And what about you, miss? Think it might be an idea to hit the books? Getting a tan is all well and good, but I think you need all the qualifications you can get, don't you?'

Anna nodded, unsure of what to do with the homemade tanning aid in her hand. There was so much about her aunt's comment that bothered her, but it felt easier to say nothing. It seemed not to occur to her aunt that Jordan's grandad was her grandad too. There was also the implication that Anna needed qualifications because she had little else to recommend her. True, she wasn't one of the great beauties – she pictured bouncy, blonde Tracy Fitchett, who hadn't entered her thoughts in quite a while – and nor did she have the support network of a loving family that others enjoyed, but even so.

'Well, I'll go and get the tea on.' Her aunt bustled back inside, then poked her head out through the door again. 'Ooh, I meant to say that I bumped into Mr Dickinson earlier, taking the bins down. He had his niece with him – she's staying for a week. Do you remember Ulla? She was quite sweet on you, Jordan, if I remember rightly! You could do a lot worse. Her uncle has a very responsible job, party to all sorts in those council meetings.'

Jordan smiled and nodded at his mother before she retreated into the kitchen.

Anna sat up and untucked her shirt from her bra. 'I take it back, Jord. I think you will do very well on Broadway – you're a good actor.'

'I know.' He winked at her.

'Phew it's hot.' If her aunt said it once, pumping the front of her purple crimplene blouse as she set the table then pulled the chicken pie from the oven, she said it a thousand times.

Anna watched as droplets of sweat ran down her aunt's neck and disappeared into her voluminous cleavage. She looked down at her own flat chest, inherited from her mother, and wondered how two sisters could look so different. True, she and Joe hadn't looked anything like each other, but they'd had different dads. She curled her tongue inside her mouth – Joe hadn't been able to do that either, of course.

'Jordan has been studying most of the day, haven't you, my lovely?' Aunt Lizzie said.

'I have indeed.'

Anna caught his eye and smiled into her lap.

'I told him he takes after his Grandad Cole, a little thinker.'

Uncle Alan made a harrumphing noise and Anna imagined his irritation at the implication that none of his genes had made their way into his son. Aunt Lizzie often claimed Jordan as her own – 'my boy', 'my Jordan'. She felt sorry for her uncle and wanted to tell the kindly man that he made her stay there a little better than it otherwise would have been. She hoped he knew this.

'What do you mean by a thinker?' Jordan asked as he rested his arms on the tabletop.

'Elbows off the table!' his mother shouted.

Anna, Jordan and Uncle Alan all immediately pulled their hands into their laps. Jordan waited for his mother to turn her back and made another face at Anna.

'Well...' Her aunt ladled the new potatoes into a tureen and used her thumb and a sharp knife to slice a knob from the corner of the butter pack, plopping it on the top of the spuds. 'He had a very good job in the sorting office.'

Uncle Alan coughed, but they all pretended not to notice.

'Everyone knew him,' she continued, undeterred. 'He was well respected, loved in our street and the neighbourhood. And the reason he was so respected was that he read books. Lots of books.'

'Books, you say?' Jordan asked with fake interest, intended purely to make his cousin laugh.

A giggle rippled from Anna's lips and Aunt Lizzie shot her a look before continuing.

'Yes! Great thick books on all kinds of subjects, from the

railways to the war. He loved to read and because he read, he knew things other people didn't.' She placed the steaming tureen on a raffia mat in the centre of the table.

'What things?' Jordan's interest seemed a little more genuine this time.

Anna was also enjoying hearing about her grandad. It was good to know where her bookish nature came from.

'He knew how to repair every sort of engine, didn't matter what it was – lawnmower, boat, car, you name it.'

'My... My brother was good with anything mechanical too. He must have got that from Grandad Cole.' Her voice was small, too quiet for the words to be easily deciphered, but for Anna it felt like a stepping stone towards speaking up. She felt it was important to remind her aunt that they were all from the same bloodline, and it was lovely to be talking about Joe.

Her aunt gave a single shake of her head as she took up her seat at the top of the table. 'My dad also knew enough to say that your mother shouldn't go gallivanting off to London. He knew that all right.'

'Lizzie!' Uncle Alan admonished, his tone more forceful than usual.

'Well, it's true and there's no harm in saying so.'

Anna watched as her aunt dipped her chin to her chest. She remembered her cousin's words from earlier. She didn't like the thought of never having her own voice. Ignoring the quake of nerves in her gut, and after a second or two to summon the courage, she spoke. 'I think... I think my mum was very brave, actually. She must have felt like I do now – she didn't know anyone and didn't know what was going to happen next, but she did it anyway. That must have taken courage.'

Jordan looked at her with something akin to pride.

'Brave?' Her aunt did her usual laughing/tutting thing. 'Nothing brave about leaving two ageing parents to worry themselves sick about your welfare without so much as a goodbye. Nothing brave about that. Selfish is what it is! Who do you think it was had to clean up after her when everything went tits up?'

Anna noted her aunt's embarrassed glance at Jordan after the unusual slip-up in her language.

'I'm guessing you.' This came out a lot more sarcastic than she'd intended.

'Yes! You guess right! And I'll thank you not to be so clever in my house. It was me all right. Me that carried on as though nothing was amiss, ignoring my mother crying into the early hours. And my dad…' Aunt Lizzie paused and swallowed. 'My dad lost his sparkle and I wanted to shout at him, "I'm still here! I'm still here, Dad! I didn't go!"' She patted her matronly chest. 'But that would have been pointless. Karen, the baby, had gone and that was that. I don't think my mother ever really recovered. She died young.'

'Like my mum,' Anna reminded her, feeling a jolt in her chest at hearing her mum's name, which was almost never spoken.

'Yes, just like your mum.' Aunt Lizzie gathered up the napkin from under her dessert fork and wiped her eyes. 'They looked alike, were alike.' Her aunt eyed her across the table. 'You're like them too.'

Anna couldn't decide whether her aunt thought this was a good thing. She knew she had the same physical shape as her mum, but her face was different; she was pointier than her mum, in nose and chin. She bit her lip. 'I don't want any tea. Thanks.' She thought it best to retreat to the safety of the bedroom, fearing her presence would only inflame things. The tense atmosphere and look of discomfort on Uncle Alan's face was more than she could bear.

'Of course you don't.' Lizzie sniffed. 'As I say, just like your mother. Nothing was good enough for her either. Couldn't wait to leave home. Desperate, she was, and if it hadn't been to follow Billy What's-His-Name, that awful boy, there would have been another. She'd have hitched her wagon to anything just to get away, just to spite my poor mum and dad, who worked so hard, and they bloody idolised her! They deserved better!' Her voice cracked. 'She was selfish. I mean... London! That's no place for people like us.'

Anna's mind reeled. She stood from the table, glancing at her aunt to see if she'd finished or whether there was more to come, unsure if it would be ruder to stay or to go. So many questions bubbled inside her, but she knew that fanning the flames might only make things worse for everyone.

'Can I ask you something?' She held onto the back of the chair while her aunt again sniffed into her napkin. There was no answer, so Anna asked anyway. 'Why did you bring me here?'

'Why did I bring you here? What a thing to ask! How can you be so ungrateful!'

'Liz!'

'No, I'm sorry, but she is, Alan! I cook for her, I do her laundry—'

'And I am grateful, but I don't understand why you do it when it feels like you don't want to. You are so...' She tried to find the phrase that best summed up how she felt. 'Off with me.' Now that Anna had started speaking up, it was hard to stop.

Aunt Lizzie's mouth fell open. 'Off with you? What exactly do you mean by that, young lady?'

'You… You always make me feel like I'm a guest that should have gone home a long time ago and it's a horrible feeling because I can't go home. I'm stuck here.'

'That's not the case, lovey. Not at all.' Uncle Alan's face flamed with embarrassment. This sort of exchange was very rare in their house.

'It is the case, Uncle Alan. I heard the two of you talking in the kitchen the other day. Aunt Lizzie sees me as a nuisance. It's as if I'm a bad smell that everyone wants rid of.'

'Well, will you listen to that? Stuck here, you say? Do I need to remind you that you are in a rather lovely link-detached home with your own bedroom, not a prison! And to think I spoke out, said I'd have you because she…' Her aunt's voice cracked. 'Because she was my sister. What would people have thought if I hadn't stepped up?'

Anna stared at her. It still didn't make sense to her. If her aunt had never liked her mum and clearly didn't like her, then why make them all suffer? She glanced over at her cousin, who looked close to tears. This she found upsetting. Lovely Jordan. 'If it wasn't for Jordan…' she began, smiling at him.

'Oh, here we go. "If it wasn't for Jordan…"' Her aunt sniffed up her tears and mimicked her niece's London accent. 'Don't think I haven't noticed the way you've muscled in on him. Good Lord, if you weren't related… Well, I hate to think what you might try. You are more like your mother than you think!'

This was too far below the belt, even for her aunt. Anna was livid. Her breath stuttered in her throat as she searched for a reply.

'That's ridiculous, Mum!' Jordan shot back. 'And, actually, for your information—' He drew breath.

'For your information, he's going to New York!' Anna cut in sharply, knowing this was not the time for any big announcements about Jordan's sexuality, not with emotions already running so high. She kept her eyes locked on her cousin's. 'He's going to finish his O levels and go to New York. He's a brilliant actor.' She smiled at him.

'New York?' her aunt screeched, throwing her napkin onto the table. 'What a bloody ridiculous thing to say! Why would you want to leave us? Has she put you up to this?' She stretched out her arm across the chicken pie and buttery potatoes, pointing at Anna lest there be any doubt who she was referring to.

Anna and Jordan exchanged a look. Jordan sighed and shook his head. 'No, Mum, she hasn't. I thought of it all by myself.'

Anna slowly turned and made her exit, treading softly on the stairs. She perched on the edge of the bed, listening to the back and forth between the three still sitting at the table. She was now quite adept at making out the subtle rhythm of words through the floorboards, made easier when those words were exchanged at volume.

It had been quite an evening. No matter what came next, the damage had been done. Her eyes were drawn to the suitcase nestling under a fine mat of dust on top of the wardrobe.

I do think you were brave, Mum. You didn't know anyone and you didn't know what was going to happen next, but you did it anyway, you ran away...

And it was in that second that she knew the answer.

'Twelve months, three weeks and four days.' She spoke aloud. That was how long she had lived in that house before something cracked.

Five

Anna hoped that Jordan would understand when he opened his tin and found her note, a hastily written IOU to cover the four £5 notes she'd taken. She also hoped that the line of kisses she'd placed under her name might show him how much she loved him.

'Single or return, love?' the driver asked as he peered at her through the bottle lenses of his glasses.

'Single.' She smiled and handed over three of the notes, certain that she would not be coming back.

Having placed her case in the rack at the front, she took a seat at the back of the coach and waited impatiently for it to leave Digbeth bus station. The royal blue velour upholstery was thick with the residue of cigarette smoke, which she knew would cling to her clothes and hair. She flicked shut the little silver ashtray in the back of the seat in front, hiding the squashed brown dog-ends that lurked there.

Ducking down with her knees raised, she looked up sharply at every shout, every yell, in case it was the police, charged by her aunt to locate her and drag her back to the neat, link-detached box where she had to leave her shoes by the front door. It was unlikely, however. She'd thought this first bit through carefully, building on the plan that had started to germinate on the night of the big row in the kitchen. Her aunt and uncle would be out at work the whole day, and Jordan would be at college until late afternoon. No one would know she'd gone missing for at least seven hours. Time enough to make her way to London and to Waterloo, where she could put the next bit of her plan into action.

Anna felt a whoosh of joy in her gut as the half-full coach pulled out of the station. She was glad of her anonymity and happy to be travelling. She curled her legs beneath her on the seat, reached into her bag and pulled out her notebook.

Fifi and Fox
This is very important.

I want you to know that there are some people who will treat you badly and it is not because you have done anything wrong. It is because of something that you don't understand going on inside them. It could be anything. They might be sad or angry and you will never know if it is you or something else that has made them that way and so you must try not to think about it too much.

Overthinking never helps. Trust me, I should know.

Even when people are mean, there is always someone who isn't, so you need to stay with that person. Find the kind ones, the smiley ones and talk to them and they will make everything feel better, I promise.

I have a lovely cousin, his name is Jordan and he makes me laugh. He's funny. You will meet him one day and he can be your uncle. Actually, I'm not sure what he'll be to you if he's my cousin. He might be your cousin too. I'll have to check.

I want you both to be able to tell me anything, anything at all. I want you to talk to me about anything that's bothering you or anything you're thinking about. Like I used to be able to with my mum. You will never have to lie to me or be afraid. Because I will be your mum and that is what mums should do, I think.

I'm trying to be brave like my mum. I'm going home, back to London, where people talk like me and where I'm not such a freak. My mum went to London on her own when she was young and now so am I. And even though I might be alone when I'm there, I actually won't be because my dad lives in London – my dad! I've decided to go to the taxi rank at Waterloo and wait there for him. I have this feeling that if I see him and he sees me, we'll immediately know that we're related. I'll get into his taxi and he'll take me to his house and he'll make me toast and we'll sit on his sofa and watch Wogan *together. We can have a proper chat and catch up on all the things we need to know. We've got a lot to tell each other. I've been thinking about him a lot. I want to know what his favourite things are and I want to know what he looks like. And I want to see if he can roll his tongue like me.*

Anna X

★

'Love, we're here.' The old lady who'd offered Anna some Mint Imperials from a crumpled white paper bag earlier in the journey was now nudging her shoulder, waking her as the other passengers alighted into the bustle of Victoria.

'Thank you.' Anna smiled meekly, a wave of fear replacing the excitement that had filled her earlier. It was dark and busy and the reality of her situation began to hit home. She had very little money and nowhere to go. With her suitcase by her side, Anna looked at the road sign and saw that Waterloo was only one and a half miles away. She could walk that easily.

What she hadn't banked on was having to drag her suitcase along the crowded pavements, nor that being tired would make the job a lot harder. It was a whole hour later that she finally reached the arched entrance and ornate pillars that she recognised as being the front of Waterloo station. Anna remembered the many times she and her mum had run up those steps, rushing for a train or chattering excitedly about the day they'd had. She gripped the handle of her case once again and began the long trudge up to the concourse.

'Goodness me, can I get that for you? It's almost as big as you are!' A curly haired man in a suit and a mackintosh and with a briefcase in his right hand smiled and grabbed her suitcase, lifting it with ease.

'Thank you.' She whispered her gratitude as the kindly man loped up the stairs, taking them two at a time. He placed the case on the top step and waited for her. 'Where are you off to?' he asked with a smile.

'I'm... I'm meeting my dad here.' She gave the response she had rehearsed on the coach and looked down at the tens of black cabs sitting in the traffic below, waiting to ferry their passengers all over the city and beyond.

'Is that right?' The man gave her a funny sideways look that made her think he knew she was lying, then glanced left and right as if checking the coast was clear. He took a step closer and let his head hang forward so that she could still hear him even though he'd dropped his voice. 'I don't believe you are meeting your dad, young lady. Am I right?'

She stared at him. Her mouth moved, but no words came. What should she say and how could he tell?

He laughed. 'Thought not.' He ran his tongue around his teeth and over his gums. 'How about you come with me and I can get you something nice to eat and you can earn some cash and it'll be real quick.' He reached out and stroked his hand along her upper arm.

Anna shivered and jumped back. Grabbing her case, she moved as quickly as she could into the crowd. Her stomach churned with fear and her tears fell. She felt sick as she repeatedly looked back over her shoulder, but the man seemed to have disappeared.

Closing her eyes briefly, she wished that when she opened them her mum would be on the concourse, waiting with tickets in her hand, smiling at her... She felt the thump of disappointment when this didn't happen. Her gut ached. She gazed at the throng of people around her, all of them staring up at the departure board, waiting to jump on trains to places like Epsom, Bournemouth or Strawberry Hill – places where they had someone waiting for them. And then up popped a train for London Bridge, where she knew she could make a connection to Honor Oak Park.

Home.

Only it wasn't home. It was the shell of a memory, an echo of a former life, now gone. Her strength caved with a sick, hollow feeling.

The crowd began to thin and Anna made her way to the taxi rank. Her heart raced as she leant against the post with the 'Taxis' sign above it. For what seemed like hours she studied every driver who pulled into the layby, watching as they opened the passenger door or helped their fare into the back with their cases or shopping. A black man, an Indian man, a man with red hair, a bald man, a very young man, too young to be her dad, another one, Italian, laughing loudly, a happy man, gesticulating wildly. They came and went, but there was no one she felt drawn to, no one who seemed like her dad.

Occasionally one would smile at her and she smiled back, wondering… One man jumped from his cab and as he loaded a box into the boot he looked towards her. 'You all right there, treacle?'

She nodded. 'I'm waiting for my dad. He's a cabbie.'

'Oh right, wha's'is name?' The man paused, holding the door handle, clearly eager to get going but also wanting to chat.

'His name's Michael.'

'Michael what?' He laughed. 'About every other bloke on this rank is Michael, Micky, Mike, Mick – take your pick!'

'I'm not sure,' she managed. 'But he definitely drives a cab.'

The man shook his head as if she was having a laugh, then jumped into his taxi and switched off his yellow 'For hire' light.

Anna continued to watch the procession of cabs, but she began to realise that spotting a man she'd never met and who didn't know she was looking for him was a lot harder than she'd anticipated. Her stomach rolled with hunger, and tired-ness made her body sag. She slid down the post and sat on her suitcase, trying to think of what to do next, where to go. Another hour passed and she knew that Aunt Lizzie and Uncle Alan would by now know she was missing. She hoped Jordan wasn't too mad about the money.

A cold draught circled her ankles and snaked up inside her clothes. Bit by bit her legs and then her bottom and then her arms began to freeze. Her teeth started to chatter. The roar from a group of drunks in suits caused a plug of fear to rise in her throat. She watched them teeter left and right along the pavement, arm in arm, singing and shouting as they went. What if the man with the briefcase or someone like him returned? She knew she couldn't stay there much longer, but where could she go? A new wave of panic engulfed her.

'Anna!'

Anna registered her name being called but knew it had nothing to do with her. No one here knew her or her name. She ignored the shout and continued staring at the taxi rank, rubbing her arms and stamping her feet to try and get warm.

'Anna?' The voice was nearer now, and this time it was a question.

She swivelled her gaze and there in front of her on the tarmac, wearing a ratty fur coat, black patent over-the-knee boots and with her hair dyed white blonde, was none other than Ruby Red Shoes.

'Ruby!' Anna leapt off her case with a rush of energy and threw her arms around the woman. Joe's friend! Relief flooded through her.

'Hey, little Anna!' Ruby stroked her hair and held her close. 'What are you doing here, baby?'

Ruby smelt how Joe used to smell. It was familiar, troubling and comforting all at the same time. Anna looked up into the face of the woman with the large teeth who had added a splash of colour on that unbearably grey day. She noted the way her eyelids drooped, were almost closed, and recognised the fixed smile and vacant air of someone who was usually high.

'Ruby...' she whispered.

'It's good... to see you, Anna,' Ruby stuttered. 'I think about Joe a lot.'

To hear his name was wonderful and painful in equal measure. 'Me too.' Anna screwed her face up, trying to hold her tears in check.

'What are you doing here?' Ruby asked. 'Who are you with?' She glanced repeatedly over Anna's shoulder, like she was waiting for someone.

'I'm not with anyone. I kind of ran away.' She paused. 'And now I'm not sure what to do next. I'm just figuring out what to do.'

'You're on your own?' Ruby bent low and looked her in the eye. She sounded concerned.

'Yes, but I'll be okay.' Anna dug deep for a reassuring smile.

Ruby shook her head. 'No, you won't. This is no place to be by yourself, trust me. You have to go home, Anna!' Ruby nodded slowly. 'You have to go home, tell a policeman, tell someone. But please go home. You shouldn't be here all alone. Take it from me.'

'No!' Anna hadn't meant to shout, but there was no way she was going back to that cul-de-sac. 'I can't.'

'S'not safe for you, baby. S'not safe for any of us, you know?'

Anna pictured the man in the mackintosh from earlier and her heart thudded. 'I don't know what to do, Ruby. Can I come home with you?'

'This *is* home, baby! This is it!' Ruby threw her arms wide and laughed with her head back.

Anna cursed the tears that gathered. Ruby reached for her packet of cigarettes and lit one, then took a step closer. Anna could see the grime on her skin, the small matted knots that peppered her hair. This was not how she remembered Ruby Red Shoes, not at all.

'Jesus, Anna, if I had any more to offer you – a place to stay, a cup of tea, a chair – then I would take you there. But things are…' She placed her fingernail between her teeth and ripped it from the nail bed, still glancing over Anna's shoulder every few seconds, as if she was being watched. 'Things are complicated. Plus I'm working.' She sighed, shrugged her shoulders and gave a sad, sweet smile.

'Where are you working?' Anna asked. 'Couldn't I come with you? I promise I won't make a noise, and then I could go with you after work?' She blinked.

'Oh, Anna.' Ruby smiled her big toothy grin. 'I would love to spend a day, just one day, inside your head.' She reached out and ran her fingers through Anna's lank fringe. 'I need you to take care of you and I need you to go back to wherever it is you've come from because, trust me, anywhere is better than here. Anywhere.'

'You don't know what it's like—' Anna began.

'And you don't know what *this* is like.' Ruby spoke firmly, interrupting her. 'And I hope to God that you never, ever find out. Joe would not want you out here. Joe would want you safe. That much I do know.'

What do you know? Joe met Aunt Lizzie and Uncle Alan at Mum's funeral and he thought they were arseholes. He would understand.

She watched Ruby walk back through the station, feeling the last of her optimism evaporate. She looked around and decided to find a place to spend the night – a bench, a corner, there had to be somewhere she could curl up with her suitcase. It was as she was dragging her case away from the taxi rank that two policemen approached her, one talking into his walkie-talkie and the other speeding up a little, as if sensing that she might run.

Fat chance with this suitcase.

Looking past them, she saw Ruby skulking in the shadows. Ruby had told on her!

Ruby lifted her hand and gave a small wave. Anna turned her back, ignoring the gesture and swallowing the bitter tang of disappointment. She'd thought Ruby was her friend. Some friend.

Six

'Everyone!'

Anna looked up from the table where she sat tapping the biro against her teeth, trying to remember how to work out the long-division problem in front of her. It was an issue. When she was in the classroom she understood everything that her patient maths teacher, Mrs Brownlee, explained, but once she was back at Mead House and trying to do her homework, her mind went blank. The constant background chatter of the care-home recreation room made it hard to concentrate. And her thoughts often wandered, filling her head with images of her mum trying to teach her her times tables all those years ago. *'Concentrate, Anna Bee! Come on! Repeat after me: one times seven is seven, two times seven is…'* As a consequence, something that had seemed pretty simple only hours earlier, under the beady eye of Mrs Brownlee, now left her feeling completely flummoxed. The mustering call from Junior, one of the care-home workers, was therefore a welcome distraction.

Anna glanced up and stared at the girl standing next to Junior. She was new, and she looked angry. She had rage in her eyes and a restlessness to her stance. Her fingers danced on wide thighs wrapped in faded spray-on jeans. She kept looking towards the exit, as if trying to work out how to escape.

Anna remembered being in the same position a year and a half ago, newly arrived at Mead House and very frightened. But Anna hadn't been angry like this girl – she'd been quietly resigned, almost indifferent by that point, scarred by her aunt's rejection of her and embarrassed, if not wholly surprised, that she hadn't managed a single night as a runaway. When she was eventually brought to Mead House she'd understood that her fate was sealed and that this was where she would stay until she turned eighteen – in care, in Leytonstone, east London.

Some of the detail around that time was a little sketchy, but she remembered being driven to a police station, remembered feeling furious with Aunt Lizzie for having reported her missing and furious with Ruby for having scuppered her plans to break free. But now that she was older and more streetwise she could see that Ruby had acted with love. She'd been right, Waterloo station was no place for her. Ruby had saved her, really, and Anna wanted to thank her and tell her that she was sorry she hadn't waved back. She kept an eye out for Ruby whenever she was up town, lovely Ruby Red Shoes, but she hadn't found her yet.

Social services had picked her up from the police station and the next day Aunt Lizzie and Uncle Alan came down to London and they all sat in a meeting somewhere in Marylebone. Her aunt could barely look at her and her mouth was pursed so tight it was no more than a dot. Anna remembered how horrible it had felt that these people, however well-meaning, were the people making decisions about her life. Her life! People who didn't know her, didn't know her mum or Joe, didn't know the first thing about her. She'd felt like a passenger, with no say over what happened next. *I was carried along like sticks on a river. And it felt horrible.*

It was agreed that allowing her to stay in London, her home city, was in her best interests. That was at least something, Anna had to admit. The simple truth was that her aunt didn't want her because she didn't like her and that was that. The only one who cared was Jordan. He'd phoned his mum and had insisted on talking to Anna, sobbing snottily and theatrically down the line. 'Anna!' he'd sniffed. 'No, Anna! Please come home!'

'I can't, Jord. I just can't, but I will miss you.'

'I will miss you too. You have to write to me, okay?'

'Okay.'

She said a stilted goodbye to her aunt, holding herself stiffly inside the insipid hug she offered. Uncle Alan avoided eye contact and patted his ruddy cheeks with his white cotton handkerchief, looking flustered. For Anna this was worse than if he'd remained impassive – did he really have nothing to say? At least Jordan had tried.

'Try and look at this as an opportunity, Anna,' her aunt said as they stood beside the shiny blue car in the car park. 'I think it's best for everyone that we set you on the right path now. It would be harder for you to come home with us and get really attached. I tried, Lord knows I did, but to have you run away was really the last straw. I was beside myself.'

There was a quiver to her aunt's chin, but Anna had noted the lightness to her step and wasn't about to credit her with any genuine change of heart. She stared at her, speechless, counting the seconds till she would be out of her life for ever.

'Everyone!' Junior shouted his call to attention this time, snapping Anna's attention back to the present. His deep, booming,

South African baritone had the desired effect. The younger kids stopped chasing each other around the sofas and one of the older boys even looked up from the TV screen. 'Can I grab your attention for a moment?' he asked, letting his gaze sweep the room until all eyes were on the girl.

'This is Shania.'

'Sha-neye-aar!' One of the younger boys repeated her name with a feminine lilt, which made his mates laugh, as he'd intended.

Anna saw the flare of Shania's nostrils and watched her fingers form tightly balled fists. Her fury, she could see, was ready to surface at the slightest provocation.

'I want you to all please make Shania welcome and show her what a lovely bunch you are.' Junior smiled. 'Anna, Shania will be sharing with you. Her stuff's being taken up now.'

'I don't want to share with her!' Shania growled. 'I need my own room!'

Anna cocked her head in confusion. She'd assumed that the girl, who looked to be a couple of years younger than her, about fourteen, would be grateful to have her as a roommate. She kept her space tidy and was known for being quiet and without too many unattractive habits. She had assumed – wrongly, as it turned out – that it would be her prerogative to feel put out at having to share her room with this feisty newcomer.

'I've already told you that's not possible, Shania, but you will have your own space and Anna will, I'm sure, be the very best roomie. Anna?'

'Yes?' She was aware she'd been staring.

'Would you please take Shania upstairs, show her where she'll be sleeping and sort out some drawer space?'

She noted Junior's subtle wink, an attempt to get her on side, she suspected, and show her that he considered her ready to take this responsibility. He needn't have worried. She was happy to show the girl upstairs, and she felt for her. Being the centre of attention and being talked about had probably made Shania feel even more uncomfortable. She closed her maths book and gathered her things under her arm.

Shania followed her up the stairs, stomping her feet angrily. She didn't respond to the smile Anna cast over her shoulder at the bend in the stairs. This didn't bode well.

Anna pushed open the door to her room – their room. 'This is your bed.' She let her hand trail in the direction of the second bed, only six feet away from hers. It had been freshly made and the books and clothes that she usually stored on the mattress had been cleared away.

'Just so you know, I'm not staying here.' Shania sat down hard on the bed with her arms folded across her chest. 'So don't bother!'

'Okay.' Anna sat on her own bed. She instinctively understood that it wasn't worth challenging Shania.

'My mum's coming to get me. Or my dad,' Shania added, with little conviction. 'In fact, if my dad finds out I'm here, he'll go mental! He'll come and get me, and it will all kick off, and my mum better fucking hide then.' Shania ground her teeth, her breath coming in quick bursts.

Anna stared at the heave of her roommate's wide back, watching as she tried to contain all the emotion that threatened to overflow. She knew how that felt, like all the stuff inside you only just fitted and if you weren't careful your actual self might shatter and everything would come spilling out. And if that happened, it would be very, very hard, if not impossible, to put yourself back together.

'Well…' Anna took a breath. 'Until your mum or dad comes to get you, you can have the top two drawers of the chest.' She pointed at the unit against the far wall. 'And half the wardrobe. There are spare hangers. I don't have that many clothes. And you can use my lamp if you like.' She ran her fingers under the delicate loop-fringing that edged the brown velvet pleats of her bedside lamp. She liked the way it tickled her fingertips.

'I told you…' Shania turned and looked at Anna with her eyes blazing. 'I'm not staying here!'

Anna nodded and sat back against her pillows. She felt unable to leave the room, held hostage by the girl's distress, desperate for the tension to ease. 'Don't cry, Shania. It'll be okay.' She whispered the mantra that had got her through many a lonely hour.

'Shut the fuck up! I am not crying!' Shania yelled.

It was a full ten minutes later that Shania too sat back on the mattress, her head resting on the padded headboard. She looked round at the room. 'I *know* it will be okay, but you don't know what I've been through!' she almost shouted. 'Things have been shit! My mum's got a new bloke who is a bastard, and my dad…'

She paused, angry and embarrassed at the tears that spilled down her round cheeks. 'My dad's in the nick, but he didn't do anything wrong!' She was emphatic, despite not being able to look Anna in the eye. 'It's just a mix-up and when it gets sorted he'll come here straightaway and get me out and he will kick off big time, I'm telling you! And my mum's boyfriend and his shitty daughter better watch out then. So you might think your mum and dad are cool, but I'm telling you, my mum and dad are way cooler. They are brilliant. They are totally brilliant. They love me and we always do loads of good stuff together. And they buy me whatever I want. I don't even have to ask, they just turn up with clothes and presents for me all the time!' Shania turned onto her side and did her best to make her crying silent.

'That sounds nice.'

'It is nice!' Shania yelled.

'You don't have to keep shouting at me, Shania. I haven't done anything wrong. I have given you half of the wardrobe and the two biggest drawers and I said you can use my lamp and it's *my* lamp. It wasn't here when I arrived. I got it from the market.'

Shania spun around and looked at her. Anna saw her shoulders relax and her face soften a little, glad that her kindness had had the desired effect.

'I want my mum and dad to come and get me.' Her tone had lost its aggression now. She sounded younger and she sounded scared. 'I want her bloke to move out of our house. I want to go home. I want to belong somewhere or to someone.'

'I know. And I'm sure they will come and get you when they can. You probably won't be here for very long.' Anna tried out a smile.

Shania nodded, but her sigh told Anna it was more in hope than agreement. 'How long have you been here?' she asked, wide-eyed.

'Erm...' Anna looked up towards the corner of the room as if that was where a calendar hung. 'Nearly two years.'

'There's no way I could stay for that long. It's total shit here!' And just like that, Shania was back in angry mode.

'It's not that bad really.' Anna tried to control the tremor to her voice, blotting out the image of the blue towel with an indent in it, folded and placed underneath the sink on the bathroom floor.

'I don't care what you say, this could be a palace or a mansion, but I'd still rather live with my dad! Or my mum if that shithead moved out. Wouldn't you?'

'I've never met my dad. He drives a black cab, but I don't know much about him. Except that he can curl his tongue like this.' She gave Shania a demo and the girl almost smiled.

'You are fucking weird.'

'I know.' Anna smiled at her.

'That's shit you don't know anything about your dad,' Shania offered with a flicker of empathy.

'I know,' Anna repeated. 'And my mum is dead. And my brother is dead too. So there's only me left. No one to ask about anything.'

'What would you like to ask them?' This had apparently caught Shania's interest.

'Erm...' It was Anna's turn to hesitate. She laughed. 'God, there's so much and now I can't think of a single thing!' *What was my dad's surname? Did I ever meet my grandparents? Do you know how much I love you, Mum?*

Shania stared at her, waiting.

'Okay, so if I could ask one question...' Anna thought for a few moments. 'I'd like to know what my first word was!'

There was a beat of silence. Anna could see Shania digesting this information.

'Why does it matter what your first word on earth was? Surely it's your last word that's more important?'

Anna looked at Shania and smiled at her wisdom. 'You know what, Shania, you're right! I'd never thought about it. I might not know how I began, but I can shape how I finish. Is that what you're saying?'

'Kinda.' She shrugged.

'I miss my family. I miss them every day. My mum used to make me feel better just by being around. She knew how to take away my worries and she knew what I was thinking without me saying anything. And not having her here is really tough. I know what you're going through right now, but at least you can see them.' Anna offered this as some sort of balm.

Shania seemed to consider this. 'The fact that you can't see yours is really shit,' she whispered.

'Yep. It is.' Anna looked down and picked at a loose thread on the duvet cover. All the bedding at Mead House was the same standard-issue linen, doled out from the communal pile. Nothing was yours at Mead House, everything belonged to the care home. You just used it while you were there, while you were passing through.

'I think you're lucky.'

Anna thought she might have misheard. 'Lucky?'

'Yes.' Shania nodded.

Anna swivelled round to face her.

'The way you talk about your mum, she sounds brilliant.'

'She was.'

'And she died. She didn't want to leave you and you didn't want to leave her.'

'No.' Anna's fingers moved to her chest, where the pain was most intense.

'But my mum...' Shania drew breath, her words delivered slowly. 'She only lives three miles from here. And my dad's a twenty-minute drive into Essex when he's out. So close really, but... they just don't want to see me. They didn't die, they just gave up on me. Changed their minds.'

Anna knew better than to rebuff this with platitudes. Shania was too savvy for that. Instead she let her talk, guessing that she didn't confide this sort of thing in many people.

'They split up when my dad went inside. I couldn't believe it when my mum let her dickhead boyfriend and his daughter move in. It was like she didn't miss him at all and I was gutted. She made a new family and it seemed to happen really quickly.' Shania scratched at a mark on her jeans. 'And I suppose I'm a reminder of him. I get sent back and forth between my mum's house and my nan's. I sleep on the floor of my cousin's room at my nan's, and at my mum's I sleep on the sofa cos the dickhead's little girl has got my old room. I am like this big bright piece of a jigsaw that doesn't fit anywhere in the picture, so that's why I'm here. She told me it would only be for a little bit, but I don't believe her!' She punched her thigh in frustration.

'That's really shit.'

'I know,' Shania mumbled, falling back on the mattress.

Anna turned on her side, and both girls lay this way, in silence, looking at the Artex swirls of their shared ceiling, lost in their own shit stories, until they were called down for their tea.

★ ★ ★

The two girls gelled. Anna quickly warmed to her roommate, who was a lot funnier and kinder than she liked to let on. Despite the fact she was incredibly messy and very loud, Shania made her feel a bit less lonely. They had heartfelt conversations in the dark and during the day would do each other's hair and make-up, dancing to Radio 1 and going to jumble sales on Saturday afternoons. Shania wasn't the touchy-feely type, but it was obvious to everyone at Mead House that she looked up to Anna.

Now however, on her eighteenth birthday, it was time for

Anna to move on. Tomorrow she'd be leaving Mead House and setting out on her own. There was to be cake and a little speech from Junior downstairs in the recreation room at five o'clock, but before that all she really wanted to do was sit quietly in her room and have a bit of time to herself. She sat on her bed and got out her pen and writing paper.

Hello Fifi! Hello Fox!

Well, just so you know, writing to you makes me smile. Every time I finish a note and place it in my expanding wallet file, I am most impressed by my dedication. Looking back at the letters I've been writing to you since I was six, I can see that my spelling and writing in some of them was really poor, but the pictures I did are pretty cute! The one of me sitting in a crane is my favourite – I've no idea what I was thinking, but maybe I wanted to be a crane driver when I was seven?

I wonder if you'll ever get to read these? And whether you'll think it's lovely or just creepy that I was only a tiny girl myself when I started to think about the family I wanted to have one day. Obviously I had no idea then that I'd lose my own family so soon, but having you as my future family has really helped, in a funny way.

I love that I was with my own mum when I started writing you letters, and I love that she adored your names as soon as I told her! I so wish I had a treasure trove of letters from my mum! Oh my God, that would be incredible! And from my brother, too, though he was a bit of a hopeless letter writer, so…

I do miss him. I miss him every single day. It makes me so sad to think of the waste of Joe. I am getting close now to the age he reached and that's weird because he was my big brother and yet in a few years I'll be older than him. He will always be twenty-two, but he won't be my big brother any more. He would have been a wonderful uncle, and I am sure a wonderful dad too, if he'd given himself the chance.

Oh dear, I'm crying now. There's been a lot of tears recently. I am leaving Mead House tomorrow, and while I am excited, it feels scary leaving behind what has been my home and my family for nearly four years. Not that care can ever be a substitute for proper family life, not really. I still wonder how my mum's sister could have pushed me away so easily – I could never allow any child I knew to be put into care, not without a fight, but that's for her conscience to wrestle with.

Anyway, there's going to be lots of adventures ahead, I hope. And I especially hope that they're going to include a husband and you two little ones! To get to hold you will be my greatest moment!

Signing off, my little Fifi and Fox.

I wonder why I always say Fifi and Fox and never Fox and Fifi? I guess because it's the way I've always said it.

Anyway, really going now.

Anna (your future mum!)

I think if anyone ever found these letters, they would think I was totally nuts! X

Anna knew her eighteenth birthday would be a big deal, but she was still a little overawed when Junior made his grand entrance into the recreation room.

'Okay, okay! Quiet, everyone!' He glanced round, taking in the kids lounging on the sofas and the others lying on their tummies on the rug, chins in palms, watching TV.

Anna settled back in her chair as they all made their way over to the scruffy table in the middle of the rec room. It was dappled with dots of stubborn plasticine in a rainbow of colours and doodles from a thousand biros and felt-tipped pens. That not one of the sixteen kids needed to be asked twice was testament to Anna's popularity at Mead House. Everyone knew what was coming next, but even though there was a general rolling of eyes and the odd sigh at the predictability, there was still a buzz of excitement at the diversion. And why wouldn't there be, at the prospect of chocolate cake?

Someone flicked the wall switch and the overhead striplight went out, plunging them into semi-darkness. One or two of the younger kids gave a mock scream.

'Haa-ppy birthday to you!' Junior began singing, holding out the rectangular chocolate tray bakes that he was balancing in each hand.

The kids joined in, some of them more tunefully than others. Anna didn't care how good their singing was, it just felt lovely to see the younger kids so excited. It was never going to be the same as having a birthday with their mum or dad, but at least it was something. She remembered the way her mum used rush into her bedroom with a whoop of joy. 'It's your birthday, Anna Bee! Wake up! Wake up, my baby girl!' And she'd flop down and wrap her in an enormous hug, trapping her inside the duvet and smothering her face with kisses. Anna always woke up way before her mum's arrival, but she always played along, pretending to be asleep, knowing this was part of the fun.

Today, as on every birthday, Anna thought of her dad, now the only person on the planet other than her cousin Jordan who might have some interest in this milestone day. But of course he might not. She didn't know how much he knew about her. It was a continual frustration that there was no one she could ask.

She hadn't given up on her quest to find him, despite the abortive attempt at Waterloo station. Quite the opposite, in fact. Her longing for him coloured everything. She was certain her life would be better with her dad in it. If her mum had loved him, then she knew she would too. She just needed to track him down. So she'd come up with a careful strategy, which she deployed at least twice a week, often dragging a reluctant Shania along to assist.

She would wait at any busy junction, or wherever she saw a convenient stopping point, and hail a cab. If, as it got closer, the driver was revealed to be a woman, she would simply step back and wave it on, much to the driver's annoyance, and the same if he was not the dark-haired, white-skinned man of her imagination. If, however, he did look right, she'd wait for him to wind down the window and ask 'Where to?' and then she'd reply with 'What's your name?' Some answered, and one or two were even called Mick or Michael, but they weren't him. Others told her to 'Clear off! Bloody idiot!' and one even threatened to call the police for wasting the time of a working man. She wasn't sure this was actually a crime, but it had the desired effect and she laid off her search for a few weeks.

'Happy birthday, dear An-nnaaaa!' The song reached its crescendo with some of the kids going for a falsetto finale for comic effect. 'Happy birthday to yooooo!'

She bent forward over the large square table. Taking a deep breath, she held her hair flat on both sides and moved her head from left to right, blowing out the candles.

'Make a wish!' came shouts from the floor. 'Make a wish!'

Anna closed her eyes and thought hard. Should she wish for a wad of cash, a new suitcase? No. *I wish… I wish… my dad would come and find me.*

The light was flicked back on and the two chocolate cakes were divided up, overseen by a couple of the girls, who monitored the cutting to make sure everyone had an equal-sized piece. For kids for whom life had been anything but orderly and fair, these small things felt important. They were important.

Junior raised his slice of cake, nestling in a paper napkin in his palm. 'Happy eighteenth birthday, Anna! I can't believe how fast time flies, it feels like only weeks ago that you arrived on our doorstep, looking a little lost, a little afraid.'

She stared into her lap. *I wasn't a little lost, a little afraid – I was completely lost and absolutely petrified.*

She blinked now, sitting at the table in the recreation room on this her last night at Mead House, trying to quiet her thoughts, concentrating again on Junior's words.

'And yet here you are, nearly four years later, Anna, and you're about to leave us and go out into the big, wide world.' He nodded at her. 'You have always set yourself apart by your hard work. The way you study and apply yourself is inspirational, and yes…' He raised his free hand. 'I know this is not the time or place for us to reopen the great university debate – you have made your decision and I respect it. Reluctantly!' He gave a small laugh.

She smiled at him. Her mind was indeed set; she was certain that the single most important thing she could do was to find a job, earn some money, secure a roof over her head and grow from there. It was all about self-reliance. The last few years had taught her that it was vital that she never be in a position where she had no home and no income. University, no matter how attractive a proposition, would only delay putting this safety net in place. University was for other people, not girls like her.

Junior's tone was now sincere. 'We shall all miss you.'

Anna looked at the nodding heads of the other kids around the table. She saw them – and herself – as being like the dented tins left last on the shelf, the ones no one really wanted because they didn't know or care what wonderful things might be contained within.

'But it's important you know that we are here if you need us. And please come back for tea – I promise your name won't be on the rota for dishes.'

Everyone laughed.

'Thank you, Junior. For my cake. For everything. I shall miss you all too.' She crumpled the napkin in her palm.

'As ever, a girl of few words.' He smiled at her.

Quiet with a busy head…

'A *woman* of few words now, if you don't mind!' Shania, her friend and roommate, shouted.

'Yes, good point. Here's to Anna!' Junior raised his cake slice as a toast.

'To Anna!'

'Anna!'

'Anna!'

The other kids, her family for the last few years, followed suit, holding what was left of their cake and toasting her last day in care.

An hour later, Shania sat on her bed, watching Anna rummage through a rectangular plastic sandwich box. She pulled out several small earring studs and began trying to match them up into pairs, which she then laid on top of the notebook on her bedside table. They looked shiny and tempting as they sparkled in the lamplight.

'Tell me again where it is you're going?' Shania asked, unable to disguise the huff to her voice.

'A flat near the Barbican. It's a flat share with a spare room, or rather it was a spare room, but now it's my room.'

'So who are you sharing with?'

'I'm not exactly sure, but I've met one of the girls and she's a nursing student. She seemed nice.'

'Sounds boring.' Shania picked at the pearlescent pink nail polish on her long fingernails. Then she bit at a loose end and began yanking the varnish off in thin strips with her teeth.

Anna smiled. 'You think everything is boring.'

'That's because most things are boring.'

Anna laughed. 'You can come and stay with me. Get a pass and I'll be your guardian for the weekend.'

'Ooh, you can buy me vodka!' Shania perked up at this prospect. 'You should definitely have a party!'

'I hate parties.'

'How would you know? You never go to any!'

'Ha, ha!' Anna finished sorting through her bric-a-brac jewellery. As well as the earrings there were a few strings of brightly coloured beads, a couple of narrow bangles and a large plastic daisy ring. Next she turned her attention to her clothes. A white melamine unit now sat between their beds. The top two drawers were hers and the bottom three Shania's.

'So tell me about the job.'

Anna's face lit up. 'I'll be working for a company on Victoria

Street that organises coach holidays. They drive all over the place – France, Spain, even up into the Alps. To start with I'll just be stuffing brochures into envelopes, sticking labels on them and shoving them in the post. They send out hundreds and hundreds every week, apparently.'

'Sounds—'

'I know – boring!' Anna cut in and they both laughed. 'And you're right, it probably will be to start with, but it's what it can lead to that I'm interested in. Who knows, I might go and work in sales or another department.'

'Jesus, Anna, you haven't started the job yet and already you're planning your promotion!'

She smiled at her friend's exaggeration, carefully pulling the wonky drawer front and easing it along the runners, not wanting to have to fix it again, before extracting a small stack of folded T-shirts and placing them in her old grey case.

'If there are any clothes you don't want to take, I'll have 'em,' Shania said.

Anna nodded, keeping her eyes low, not wanting to be drawn on the fact that Shania's plus-sized frame hadn't a hope in hell of fitting into her titchy tops. 'You can have half of my earrings and any jewellery you want.' She nodded towards the shiny haul on the bedside cabinet.

'Really?' Shania beamed.

'Yes, really. I mean, you borrow it all the time anyway.'

'Thanks, mate!' Shania gave her a double thumbs-up. 'I can wear them when I see my dad.'

Anna nodded, sticking to the strategy she'd adopted for the whole two years they'd been rooming together, not commenting on the fact that in all that time Shania hadn't had a single visit from either her dad, her mum or her mum's shitty boyfriend. The one Christmas card that had showed up, a year and a half ago, still sat in pride of place on the windowsill. The red tones had long since faded to orange, the edges were now curled and the bottom had suffered a little water damage, but Anna knew it would never be put away.

Shania had wasted no time in prodding through the costume jewellery with her fingernail and was now admiring the three pairs of earrings she'd selected. 'God, I hope I don't get some cow to share with next. I couldn't stand it!'

'I don't think you were that keen on me when you first moved in,' Anna reminded her.

'True, it took a bit of getting used to, having to sleep with the bloody curtains open and your lamp on.'

'I can't help it. I don't like the dark.' Anna had never confided in Shania exactly why they had to sleep that way, but the truth was that whenever she was in the pitch dark she always pictured her mum in her coffin and how she would have hated that. She remembered how her mum had loathed small, dark spaces, and she felt the same way. Just the thought of it was enough for her heart to miss a beat and her palms to go clammy.

'But it turned out you were all right,' Shania said, pushing the second of two bright blue glass studs through her earlobes. Twisting her head, she gazed at her reflection in the strip of mirror on the opposite wall.

'They look lovely.' Anna nodded in her direction. 'I shall miss you, Shania. I love our chats before we fall asleep. You make me laugh and you're kind.'

'For God's sake, girl, I've got a reputation to uphold – don't you go telling everyone that I'm kind and funny.' She sucked her teeth.

'You're all talk.' Anna folded a red corduroy skirt from the drawer and placed it with the rest of her belongings. 'Everyone knows you're a softy.'

Shania studied her friend. 'It's funny when you think about it, because you look timid, you're pale and quiet, but you have a core of steel. You're one of the strongest people I've ever met. Nothing fazes you. I've hardly ever seen you cry and you never back away from anything. People wouldn't necessarily know by looking at you, but you're brave, unbreakable.' She giggled. 'Do you remember that time you saw a contender, a guy you thought might be Michael, driving a cab on the High Road, just under the bridge, and you jumped out in front of him, calling and going nuts. Banging on the bonnet. "Stop the cab! Stop the cab!" And he slammed on his brakes and wound down the window, wondering what the emergency was, and you said, cool as a cucumber, "What's your name?" God, I thought he was going to run you over! You are class, Anna, pure class.'

Anna paused in her task and turned to look at her friend sitting on the duvet with everything she owned shoved into cardboard boxes under the bed, beyond happy with her gift of cheap blue earrings. She took in their drab little room. Despite the camaraderie, and the stability it had provided for her over the past few years, it was indeed a shit way to live.

'That's not true, you know.' She swallowed. 'Yes, I'm quiet, but I'm not brave, not really. I've just learnt to not make a fuss – and I really want to find my dad. As for unbreakable…' She ran her fingers over the grey suitcase, now a little saggy in places, its surface scratched and the zip having a tendency to spring apart. She walked over to the dresser and picked up the white paper napkin with the smears of chocolate and the remaining crumbs of her birthday cake. Unfolding it, she held the square open and showed it to her friend. 'You can't break something that's already smashed. It would be like trying to put this cake back together. You can't. It's gone. And that's me.' She scrunched up the napkin and threw it into the bin. 'I got broken when I was nine and my mum died. And then my brother died too and those fragments were crushed to dust. So you're right, nothing can break me because I'm already broken. I'm dust.'

'I don't think you're dust, Anna. I think you're brilliant. I don't want you to go.'

'You'll be okay, Shania. I promise.'

'I'm scared,' she whispered.

Anna thought about the angry girl of two years ago and how such an admission would never have left her lips. 'I know, but there's no need.'

'When you go, who's going to look out for me?'

'You, Shania, can look out for yourself. You can. And I won't be that far away.'

'I want my kids to be like you.' Shania paused, as if considering this. 'I want you to be their godmother so you can teach them all the stuff you've taught me.'

Anna smiled. 'That would be the biggest honour ever.'

'Not that I'm planning on having any just yet!' Shania tutted.

'Glad to hear it. Only two more years and you'll leave here too. Time will fly by, you know that. And when you do leave, you have to work hard, Shania. You have to work harder than anyone. Make a life. Get a job, any job, even if you think it's boring.' She smiled. 'It's really important that you find a place to live and keep working and keep saving. And don't ever, ever take drugs.'

'Might be a bit late for that!' Shania pulled a face.

'Okay, don't take drugs again,' Anna said, with a small shake of her head. 'I mean it. They ruined my brother's life.'

'My dad's too.'

'Well, there you go. Promise me.'

Shania rolled her eyes. 'I promise.'

'And remember what we spoke about that very first night? How it doesn't matter where you start in life, it's where you finish that counts – it's not your first word but your last that defines you. And you can be anything you want to be. It's up to you.' She sat down. 'And you know what...?'

Shania looked up.

'I feel really sorry for your mum and dad.'

'Don't. They're arseholes!'

'But I do. They might be arseholes, but I feel sorry for them because you are fabulous and they didn't get to fall asleep with you for the last couple of years and I did. Their loss was my gain.'

Shania sniffed away the tears that threatened and changed the subject. 'Oh, this came for you.' She reached under the notebook on Anna's bedside table. 'I nearly forgot! Looks like it might be from Jordan.'

Anna studied the New York postmark and the familiar handwriting, then ripped open the envelope. 'You're right, it is from Jordan!' She grinned as she pulled out the pink, glittery card.

Happy birthday, darling! Eighteen? How did that happen? I wish you were here and we could drink cocktails and go out for steak! Not that you'd be legal, but since when did that stop me doing anything? Still waiting for my big break. Still doing terrible waiter jobs. Mum still hasn't forgiven me for abandoning her, still writes weekly, asking if I've met a nice girl and when can she meet her. Incidentally, I have! Drum roll, please! She's called Andrew and works in construction, but I take my cue from you again, oh wise cuz – all in good time and I think telling Mum face to face might be best. Anyway – eighteen! So you can now drive a truck, get married, join the army, oh and have all kinds of sex! (I have only done one of these and can heartily recommend it! And I'll give you a clue, it wasn't driving a truck.)

Anna laughed out loud.

I send you nothing but love, Anna, and can't wait to see you again. And I also can't wait for you to see me on a big screen in your local Odeon while stuffing popcorn in your gob… I can but dream. Do you remember my meltdown when we went to see Officer and a Gentleman? Still not recovered! Happy, happy days.
Love you, Birthday Girl!
Goldpie xx

Anna folded the card back into the envelope and placed it in her suitcase. She thought briefly of her sour-faced aunt and dopey uncle, and, just like with Shania's parents, felt a wave of pity that they were missing so much of their wonderful boy's life.

'I will see you again, won't I?' Shania almost whispered the unthinkable.

'Of course you will, you dafty!' Anna jumped off the bed and hugged her friend tightly.

Seven

'And the bathroom.' The estate agent pushed gingerly on the door and stood back, as if what was in there might be contagious.

Anna poked her head inside the space and decided he might be right. It was more of a cubicle than a room, but it would suffice. Nothing a good scrub couldn't cure. A loo, a sink and a narrow shower, what else did she need? The main thing was that it would be hers, all hers!

'The living zone is along the corridor and there's a spot for a bike in the basement if you need it.'

'Thank you.' Anna answered in her customarily succinct way, laughing on the inside at even the idea of her on a bike. Cycling was one of the skills that, growing up poor in a city, and then without parents, had evaded her. Ditto skateboarding and swimming. A patient teacher had once tried to rectify the latter, but Anna was a girl who relied on instinct and nothing in her instinct told her it was safe or natural to trust water with your weight, hence her tendency to panic and remain vertical, a neat trick in itself.

She chuckled all the way back to the office. 'Living zone'! In reality, this was a long, narrow room with a sink and a camping stove on the worktop at one end and a double bed and a ward-robe at the other. It was lit by two bare bulbs, which she was sure she'd bash every time she walked beneath them. The layout not-withstanding, the 1960s refurb was close to where she worked, saving on precious commute time and, crucially, she could afford it. That was really the only thing that mattered.

In her mind she began the process of decorating, seeing her living space evolve over time with the addition of fancy storage containers for tea, coffee and sugar, and a pretty duvet cover. Excitement bubbled in her throat at the prospect. She wished her mum could see her, wanted to make her proud.

'Well? How did you get on?'

'I took it!' She hunched her shoulders at Melissa, the other secretary on the floor, and smiled broadly.

'Good for you! Will there be a housewarming?' Melissa asked brightly, her heavily made-up eyes sparkling at the thought. Melissa loved a party. The sassy, statuesque American had only recently arrived from Boston. She had confided that her father, a dentist, had decided the only way to calm his daughter's hedonistic appetite was to send her to a capital city on the other side of the pond, with a fully charged AmEx card and no super-vision. In the words of Melissa herself, 'I know, right! Go figure!'

'No!' Anna laughed, shaking her head. 'There's just about room for me in the place – it would be a very cosy housewarming.'

'So when are you moving in?'

'Week after next if my references come through.' Anna's thoughts turned to the shared flat in the Barbican where she'd been for the last three years, since moving on from Mead House. She couldn't wait to leave the place. Night after night she stayed holed up in her tiny bedroom, keeping herself to herself, trying to avoid the slovenly students she shared with and impressing the landlord with her politeness and the potted herbs she tended on the small balcony. He was a keen gardener. She was confident he'd give her the reference she needed. 'It shouldn't be a problem.'

'It'll be nice living and working in Fulham.' Melissa had told her more than once that her own commute from the office to the end of Lots Road, a mere fifteen-minute walk, gave her time not only to really wake up, and to grab a coffee, but also to check out the talent en route.

'Girls?' Mrs Glacier called from her office, which was set to one side of the open-plan area where they worked. 'Might I borrow you?' Her tone was pleasant, but there was no mistaking this was a direct order.

Mrs Glacier had hired Anna on no more than a whim and she would for ever be grateful. Working for the legal firm was a world away from the dingy travel company where she'd stayed for far too long, stuffing envelopes and cleaning up, underpaid and underappreciated, while girls far less able than her answered the phone and got much better money. Now, when her morning alarm rang, she smiled as she reached over to switch it off and begin her day, excited about what lay ahead. It was for her a huge achievement to have secured an office job, to be stepping into a skirt and blouse and not a T-shirt and jeans. For the first time in her life Anna felt like she was on her way. All that was lacking was someone to share her achievements with, someone to hug her in congratulation, a warm body that would bring its own special type of comfort.

She and Melissa walked quickly into the office that Mrs Glacier shared with Mr Pope. He looked after all the post going in and out of the lawyers' offices, doing his rounds twice daily with a three-tiered wire trolley whose compartments bulged with envelopes and packages of all shapes and sizes. Some were held together with fancy red wax seals, others with looped ribbons over brass buttons. Most of these were hand-delivered and signed for and much emphasis was placed on the careful processing of these vital legal documents.

This was a large part of Anna's new role: the sorting of incoming mail at the desk before passing it on to Mr Pope, along with answering the phone. 'Good morning. Asquith, Barker and Knowles, how may I help you?' This greeting changed to 'Good afternoon' after the first stroke of midday, of course. And Anna never got it wrong. In fact, she never got anything wrong; she was diligent and industrious, because she was a girl who needed her job and who knew that without it her life might just unravel.

She was also tasked with keeping the diary for the partners, a most responsible job. In a large red leather-bound book she noted appointments and meetings, using pencil to allow for the alterations that were all but inevitable, given the busy lives of her employers. She booked taxis, restaurant tables, hotels and flights, made sure the birthdays of the partners' wives and children were marked, nipped off to buy cards and gifts 'From your loving husband/father' during her lunch hour and without protest. She typed up letters and minutes, thinking once or twice of the boring, balding Mr Dickinson, '*a council minute-keeper... a very responsible job... quite the keeper of secrets...*', which made her laugh.

'Right, girls.' Mrs Glacier clapped her neat hands together. 'We are taking a leap into the future!' Her eyes shone behind the lenses of her spectacles. 'We are going to get you both a computer.

One to share to begin with, to see how we all get on. It'll be on a table by the side of your desks and you can take turns.'

'What will we do with it?' Melissa asked.

Mrs Glacier pushed her glasses up onto her nose. 'Well, you will be able to type letters and labels and such forth and then print them out.'

'So, like we type on the typewriter, but then you have to print them out? Rather than have the letter in your hand instantly?'

Anna looked at her colleague and had to agree that when she put it like that it made very little sense. They were both proficient at typing documents in triplicate with strategically placed carbon paper between the sheets.

'I quite understand your reticence, Melissa. And I have to confess that it does seem to be a tad of a step backwards, particularly when we have a system that works well and has worked well for decades. Ha!' She gave a short laugh that sounded a bit like hysteria. 'But who are we to stand in the way of progress? The partners have made the decision and apparently Mr Asquith has seen computers work very well in other practices.' She adjusted her glasses again, before leaning forward conspiratorially. 'Between you and me, I can't see them catching on. I think it'll be a fad, but we do need to show willing. Okay?'

'Okay.' Melissa pulled a dissenting face. This was a girl who had her father's AmEx card in her purse, so she was free to make faces, knowing that her life would definitely not unravel if she lost this job. It was another lesson for Anna that having money, security and the safety net of a loving family gave you the sort of choices that she was denied.

'Yes, Mrs Glacier.' Anna walked back to her desk and scrolled through her Rolodex. She was searching for the number of the

courier who was to deliver the books Mr Knowles had bought
and needed taking quite urgently to Kingston Polytechnic in
Surrey, where his daughter, Olivia, was studying to be a teacher.
Lucky Olivia. Anna knew Olivia's grades had been woeful compared to her own.

'Computers?' Melissa drew her from her thoughts. 'I bet they
get rid of them within six months.'

'I know, right?' Anna laughed, adopting her friend's favourite
phrase.

* * *

Anna let her eyes sweep the room to make sure all appliances
were switched off before locking the door of her little flat and
securing her satchel bag over one shoulder and diagonally
across her body. She skipped the three flights of stairs to the
front door and on the way out checked the little pigeonhole
for mail. There was rarely anything more exciting than junk in
there, but she did get the occasional letter or note from Jordan,
living the dream while waiting for his big break in New York,
which always brightened her day. His communications were as
comedic as they were informative.

> *You would not believe what I saw in broad daylight…*
> *And he looks at me as if I have just crawled out from under*
> *a stone and says, 'Darling, not in those shoes!'*

She would replay the snippets in her head, hearing his theatrical
tone and picturing his wild gestures. How she loved him.

Anna stepped out into the bright blue sky of a crisp spring day.
A light breeze fanned her face. She untucked the white points

of her shirt collar to sit outside of the rounded neck of her yellow cotton-knit jersey and pushed the ends of her dark bob behind her ears. Her style was developing nicely; she read magazines, committing to memory the outfits she liked, and copied the looks worn by the shiny girls who dated the lawyers at work, wanting to look like them. Wanting to be like them. It was important to her that she shake off the mismatched hand-me-down chic that had been her style since her mum had died, reinforced by the clothes she was given at Mead House, which had come largely via a charity box. She thought, as she often did, of Shania. It had been a while since she'd seen her and she hoped she was happy on this lovely day.

'Morning!' a voice called from the fruit and veg stall opposite. The red-and-white-striped awning and its table piled high with tempting produce appeared like magic at five o'clock every morning on the kerb outside her flat, then disappeared again before she got back from work a little after six in the evening.

She lifted her hand and smiled at the tall bloke in the denim shirt and fingerless gloves. His fair hair was cut shorter at the back, leaving the fringe and top a little longer, in the style favoured by Jason Donovan. She noted he was nice-looking, smiley. Not exactly Jason Donovan, but close.

He held up a shiny red fruit. 'How about an apple?' he called, in a cockney accent that was marginally broader than hers.

She smiled, decided not to engage him any further and walked briskly along Fulham Broadway towards work. The temptation to glance over her shoulder and see if he was looking was strong.

'What are you looking so happy about?' Melissa asked as she removed her three-inch-high Buffalo platform trainers and slipped her feet into a pair of heeled court shoes, the style suggested and approved by the partners of Asquith, Barker and Knowles.

'I think I might have just had someone flirt with me.'

Melissa sat forward, fully focused, eyes wide. 'What do you mean, you "think"? Surely you'd know!'

Anna bit her lip. 'Not really. I'm not very good at this stuff.'

'Have you had many boyfriends?'

She looked skywards and mentally counted the liaisons, encounters and drunken fumbles that constituted her unfulfilling love life to date. 'Not really. Not what you'd call proper boyfriends. I've never been that fussed. I'm quite a private person, but I've had a few, you know… I suppose… hook-ups.'

'Hook-ups? You dark horse! How many hook-ups are we talking here? Less than four? More than ten?' Melissa's eyes lit up. 'Please tell me more than ten! It's true what they say, it's always the quiet ones!'

Anna laughed. 'They weren't one-night stands, if that's what you're driving at. I just…' She rolled her hand, trying to find the right phrase, one that didn't make her seem like she was either too picky or a slut. 'I just haven't ever met anyone I wanted to get serious with.'

'So how many?' Melissa pushed.

''Bout six.' She looped her satchel over her head and placed it under the desk, then took her seat. 'I don't know why I said "about six". I know the number – it's exactly six.'

'None that were keepers?'

Anna sighed. 'No. Some of them were nice, some of them not so nice, but none of them set my world on fire. I think maybe I'm setting my expectations too high.'

'How so?' Melissa paired her platform trainers and placed them under her chair.

Anna shrugged. 'I don't know, I guess I always feel excited to meet someone new and I love that energy, all the possibilities of what might happen, but then we go out and I look at them and listen to their stories and I feel a bit bored and I try to picture myself sitting with them night after night and I panic, knowing I definitely don't want that, and so I might see them maybe once or twice more and then I go quiet and hide.'

Melissa let out a loud guffaw.

'Morning, girls!' Mrs Glacier called from her office. This was her way of telling them to settle down and crack on with the job. Loud guffaws were not what was expected of the front-office staff at a firm such as this.

'God, Anna, I can't believe that's your thought process! You don't have to get engaged, you just need to have a good time!' Melissa whispered. 'And luckily for you, I am an expert in good times.' She winked.

'I know I don't have to get engaged!' Anna tutted her reply, remembering her mum's advice that it wasn't vital to get married. 'And actually the bloke this morning was nice, good-looking, and he seemed as if he might like a good time. He works on the little market near my flat and he tried to give me an apple.'

'Eeeeee!' Melissa squealed and bunched her fists up under her chin. 'This is so cool! It's like Adam and Eve, him tempting you in with his fruit.'

'I'm pretty sure it was Eve who gave Adam the apple.' Anna smiled, knowing how much Melissa's education had cost and wondering how they had missed that basic fact.

'Potato, potarto.' Melissa batted away the words with her hand. 'The important thing is he made a move!'

'I guess. I mean, I think he did, but he might have just been being kind.'

Anna opened the diary, wanting it to at least look as if she was working should Mrs Glacier pop her head around the door.

Mr Knowles, the youngest partner, a tennis player with a loud snort of a laugh, arrived at the office. 'Good morning, ladies!' He gave a mock bow.

'Morning, Mr Knowles.'

'Good morning,' Melissa chirped.

The two watched him disappear into his office.

'You are on fire today! Did you see the way he looked at you?'

'Mr Knowles? Don't be so ridiculous!' Anna felt her cheeks flame. 'He's at least fifteen years older than me, and married, and eeuuuw!' She shuddered at the unpalatable thought. 'I think Apple Boy is more my type.' She smiled at the admission.

'If you like him, you need to respond, make the next move.'

'Do you think so?'

'Yes!' Melissa slapped her forehead in despair. 'That's like dating 101!'

The phone rang and Anna lifted the receiver, rolling her eyes at her friend's suggestion while simultaneously wondering to herself whether she had the confidence to do just that.

'Good morning. Asquith, Barker and Knowles, how may I help you?' she asked with a certain frisson to her tone.

The following morning, Anna blotted the thin application of nude lip colour on a square of loo roll and studied her face in the mirror fixed to the wall of her tiny flat. She had draped it with fairy lights and liked to look at the delicate orbs reflected in the glass as she fell asleep. Not only did she find the dappled spray of soft light a comfort, but it was these little touches that to her mind made the place feel homey. She tried to re-create the feeling she remembered from their flat in Honor Oak when her mum was alive. The way the surfaces in the kitchen were always clutter- and smear-free and how the bleached net curtains fluttered in and out of the open windows like angel wings.

She sat on her bed and tried to steady her pulse. If she was going to get up the courage to talk to blonde-haired Apple Boy, she needed to order her thoughts. Nerves made her mouth dry.

Supposing she had completely misread the signals? Supposing he was just a chirpy market trader who had a wink and a wide-mouthed grin for every potential customer? Such thoughts did little to bolster her confidence. She walked to the window and peered down at the top of the stripey awning.

A... apple.

B... blonde.

C... cute.

D... do it! Do it, Anna! Make a move!

She grabbed her satchel and slung it over her head, gathered her keys and locked the door.

E... every stair is taking you closer.

F... fuck! There he is!

G... grinning. He's smiling at me.

H... heart. My heart is racing.

I... I like the look of you, Apple Boy.

J... just do it! Do it, Anna, for God's sake.

K...

'Here she is!' He smiled at her, giving the impression that he'd been waiting for her, and, just like that, her mind cleared. She abandoned the alphabet game and stood in front of him.

'I'm Ned.' He was grinning now. She noticed the slight warble to his voice, as if he didn't do this very often, suggesting he too was more than a little nervous.

'Anna.' She smiled back. 'I'm Anna.'

And that was all it took: a tiny ounce of confidence, a big smile and the offer of an apple.

Anna and Ned fell into step with ease and by their third date were nattering like old mates, holding hands as they walked along the street and saying goodbye with a peck on the cheek, confident that they'd be seeing each other again very soon.

'You like him!' Melissa squealed.

'Sssshhh!' Anna put her finger on her lips. 'I don't want everyone to know!'

'Why not?' her friend yelled.

'Because!'

'Because nothing!' Melissa laughed. 'We need to celebrate.' And she began to sing, loudly and to no recognisable tune. '"Love is in the air..."'

Anna covered her eyes in embarrassment as Miss Glacier came into the foyer.

'That's as maybe, Melissa, but we are a legal practice, not a lonely-hearts club, and I would appreciate it if you could keep your singing to the absolute minimum.'

'Sorry, Mrs Glacier.' Melissa nodded contritely.

Anna glanced across at their boss as she swept past and was gladdened by the wink she gave her, followed by the merest hint of a smile.

★ ★ ★

Ned reached across with his big hand and took hers.

'Remind me why I have to do this again?' Anna tilted her head to one side and screwed her eyes shut.

'Because they're my mates. Because you and I have been seeing each other for seven and a half weeks, and because it's important to me. They're important to me!'

'They don't want to meet me, they just want to see you, which is understandable. You go ahead.' She flicked her hand towards the entrance of the pub. 'I honestly don't mind! Go and have fun. I've had a long day and—'

'I'll stop you right there. I've had a longer day, so you can shut up about that. You're not getting out of this!' He pulled her towards him and kissed the top of her head. 'I want to show you off.'

'God knows why.' She inhaled deeply. 'Supposing they don't like me?' And there it was, the real reason, her fear of rejection forever lurking close to the surface.

'Then I promise you we never have to see them again.'

Anna pulled a fake smile and followed her brawny beau into the Red Lion.

'Oi oi!'

'Whatto, Ned!'

'It's the boy!'

The shouts came from around a rectangular table near the window. She felt her gut churn with nerves.

A...

Before she had a chance to begin, Ned pulled her by the arm and held her fast, gesturing over her narrow shoulders. 'Okay, now listen carefully as there'll be a test later.' He pointed to each of his mates in turn. 'Tug—'

'Why Tug?' She wrinkled her nose.

'Don't ask!' The stocky boy raised a half-finished pint and accepted the cheers from his friends.

'Nitz.'

'I was seven!' Nitz shook his head in mock humiliation and ran his hand over his balding pate.

'Johnny, Naz and Bono.'

They waved, winked and smiled respectively.

'Bono?' she queried, taking the seat opposite Naz and sliding her legs under the sticky table.

Bono looked at her sheepishly. 'Because these lot are bastards. And if I was you, I'd head straight back out that door and keep running!'

Anna made to leave, much to the delight of Ned's friends.

Bono continued. 'I once, in my teenage years, suggested we raise money for something I'd seen on the telly, I can't even remember what it was, some terrible disaster, and I thought it might be an idea to have a collection or something. My so-called mates started calling me Mother Teresa, and that stuck for about a year, so as you can imagine, in comparison, Bono is actually better.'

'Because you wanted to do a good thing for charity?' She laughed.

'As I said...' Bono sipped his pint. 'If I were you, I would run for the hills.'

'So what's your real name?' she asked.

The group again tittered into their glasses, nudging each other, waiting gleefully for the punchline.

'Yeah, Bono, what's your real name?' Tug said.

He sighed and bit the inside of his cheek. 'My real name is Maurice.'

The lads laughed loudly, repeating the word 'Maurice!' in case anyone hadn't heard.

Anna smiled at him. 'I can see why you prefer Bono.'

The eruption of laughter around the table, along with the smile on Ned's face, told her that she needn't have worried about being liked or fitting in and that she would definitely be seeing this motley crew again.

When they finally left the pub a few hours later, sauntering out, with Ned's arm around her shoulders, Anna could sense his happiness. It delighted her to think this might be because of her.

'I like your friends,' she admitted.

He exhaled with what sounded like a sigh of relief. 'And they liked you. Told ya.'

'Yes, you did.'

'I can't wait to meet yours.' He tightened his grip.

Anna flushed with embarrassment. 'I don't... I don't have a whole tight-knit bunch like you do.'

'Most people don't – lucky, aren't we?'

'Yes, you are.'

'It's cos we never left. We went to school around the corner, grew up here, all our mums are mates and now we all work here too. But you moved around a bit, didn't you, so it's different.'

'Yes. Very different,' she whispered. She'd been deliberately vague about her background.

It was only as Ned steered her along an alleyway and through the back of the housing estate with the high-rise blocks that she realised they weren't going the normal way to her tiny flat.

'We're taking a very funny route.'

'Not unintentionally.' He swallowed.

'What do you mean?'

Ned hesitated and turned to face her. 'I figured that as it's been a night for introductions, it might be good to get them all out of the way.' He nodded, holding her gaze, gauging her reaction, and licking his lips with a suggestion of nerves.

'You've lost me?'

'There are a couple of other people I'd like you to meet.'

'What? Now? It's nearly eleven o'clock! We can't just turn up unannounced when people are getting ready for bed.' She laughed.

'It's fine, really. I—' Ned didn't get the chance to finish his sentence.

'You coming in or what?' a man shouted from the open front door of a ground-floor flat across the pathway. The hall light shone out onto the concrete apron.

Anna turned to stare at the man. He was in his fifties and was dressed in dark trousers and what looked to be a stripey pyjama top.

'Just a minute, Dad!' Ned held up his hand.

'Dad?' she squeaked. 'You live here?'

'Oh there you are, love!'

She turned again, this time at the sound of a female voice. Ned's mum, unlike her husband, had made no attempt to disguise her nightwear. She was wrapped in a pink towelling dressing gown, beneath which hung the hem of a lace-edged floral nightie.

'Hello, love! I'm Sylvie!' She waved, holding a cigarette up between her fingers.

'Hello.' Anna looked from one expectant face to the other. She was backed into a corner. This was happening.

As she crossed the threshold, a blanket of nostalgia threatened to swamp her. She was in a proper little home that belonged to a family and it felt lovely. She could hardly bear to look at the shoes lined up under the radiator in the hallway. Warmth and love danced in the air, embracing her too. The ache for her mum and her big brother hit her with such force she was almost winded.

She followed Ned into the cosy lounge and sat back on the burgundy leatherette sofa, resting her head against one of the crocheted cream antimacassars. She couldn't imagine wanting to be anywhere else.

Damping down the emotion that threatened, she let her eyes wander the narrow mantelpiece above the gas fire, the shelves in the alcove and the strip of tiles that sat on the floor, a buffer between the carpet and the fireplace. There were ornaments and knick-knacks everywhere. Woven china baskets with crude pottery flowers and dust filling every crevice, a minute wooden plinth with a brass ship's wheel, several thimbles with the names of the places where they'd been bought inscribed on them in gold script, a glass cloche over a faded silk rose, like the one her mum had, and a whole selection of china, glass and wooden angels.

'I can see you looking at all my bits and pieces.' Sylvie smiled at her. 'I love all me ornaments. Most of them were my mum's.' She crinkled her eyes. 'He keeps saying he's going to have a clear-out, but I've told him he'll 'ave to clear me out first!'

'Don't start her off, Anna! She'd have the whole bloody place covered in bric-a-brac if I let her, and I wouldn't mind, but none of it's worth a bob!' Ned's father, Jack, gave a throaty chuckle, which soon turned into a wheeze.

'I told you, it's the antiques of the future!' Sylvie shouted.

Anna sat on the sofa in the small, square room with Ned by her side, enjoying the obvious affection with which his parents ribbed each other.

'Now…' Sylvie took a step forward and tightened the belt on her dressing gown. 'What can I get you, love? Cup of tea, cup of cocoa? It's too late for coffee.'

'Oh no, I'm fine, thank you. I don't want to keep you up.'

'Keep us up! Don't be daft! Cocoa or tea?'

'Cocoa would be lovely.' She couldn't remember the last time someone had made her a cup of cocoa.

'Stick the kettle on, Jack,' Sylvie instructed. Jack duly wandered off in his slippers. 'Now, what you gonna have to eat?'

'Oh, really, nothing!' Anna placed her hand on her stomach. 'Cocoa would be lovely, but it's a bit late for me.'

Sylvie continued as if she hadn't spoken. 'I've got some leftover chicken, or I could make you an omelette – I've got cheese, ham?'

'No, thank you, that's really kind, but nothing for me.' Anna smiled.

'Just toast then?' Sylvie stood poised with her hands clasped in front of her.

'Nothing. I'm fine, thank you.'

'I think we're okay for food, Mum,' said Ned.

'Jack, bring the biscuit barrel!' Sylvie yelled.

Jack returned seconds later with a mini wooden barrel complete with studs and brass-effect metal strips.

'Help yourself.' Sylvie removed the lid and held the barrel out to her.

Anna felt obliged to dip her hand in and was delighted to pull out three custard creams, her favourite.

'That's my girl.' Sylvie's grin told her that she'd done the right thing. 'So, where do you work, Anna?' Sylvie plonked herself down in the chair beneath the picture window.

'She works for a firm of solicitors,' Ned answered on her behalf.

'Ooh er, clever girl!'

'Not really.' Anna felt herself blushing but was secretly chuffed that Ned's mum thought her job was something to be proud of. It felt wonderful. She took a bite of custard cream. It was soft.

'I wish you'd try and talk Ned out of his latest venture.' Sylvie tutted. 'Up all bloody hours of the day and night, filling the house with gone-off strawberries! Fruit and veg – what a thing! I told him he'd be better off doing the painting and decorating like his dad.'

'I've told you, Mum, I don't want to do painting and decorating. I like what I do,' Ned shot back.

'Well, we'll see 'ow you feel when it's cold and dark and snowing.' She winked at Anna. 'We'll see how happy you are being up in the middle of the bloody night looking for fresh bleedin' pineapples. While your dad is snug as a bug with a paintbrush in his hand, heater on, radio playing, cup of tea.'

'My dad's a black cab driver.' Anna didn't know where the words came from or why they'd popped out there and then. It might have been the three glasses of white wine she'd consumed earlier or the fact that this room reminded her so powerfully of her mum that her guard was down.

'You never told me that!' Ned said with obvious surprise.

She shrugged.

'Well, there we go. We know a few cabbies. What's his name?' Sylvie asked.

Anna felt her mouth move, but no words came out. She didn't know what to say.

'His name's Michael,' she eventually whispered, knowing what would come next.

'His surname, love? What's your dad's surname?' Sylvie asked. 'Jack might know him – he knows everyone!'

This time she had found her voice. 'I don't know.'

She saw the crinkle of confusion appear on the bridge of Sylvie's nose.

Jack came back into the room. 'Here we go, darlin'. Lovely cup of cocoa.'

He bent down and held out a plastic tray with red and orange flowers hand-painted on one side. Anna almost did a double-take. The tray was just like the one her mum had had, the one they'd cooled cakes on and eaten their tea off in front of the TV. The one Joe had wrecked by resting a cigarette on the plastic and leaving a puckered black hole in it. She'd quite forgotten about it until that moment. It must have been thrown away with all the other stuff in the flat.

'Thank you.' She took the mug into her hands, balancing the remaining custard creams on her lap and cursing the tears that threatened to spill.

Eight

Ned sat on the edge of the bed and stretched his arms behind his broad back as he yawned.

'I hate you having to get up so early,' Anna mumbled, sitting up and rubbing her eyes. 'I feel like you don't get enough sleep. In fact I feel like *we* don't get enough sleep.'

'Did my mum tell you to say that? Gawd, even after I've been at it two years she's still nagging me about giving up the stall. I wish she'd give it a rest. But I'll tell you what I told her – I'm fine. So don't worry.' He squeezed her foot beneath the duvet. 'I didn't mean to wake you.'

She yawned again. 'It's hard not to in this tiny space. You only have to turn over or fart and I'm awake.'

'I'll only admit to one of those.' He grinned at her and slipped his arms into his padded plaid shirt. 'But you're right, it is a tiny place. I'm sick of keeping everything I own in a plastic box. My clothes are permanently in a suitcase, it's like I'm on the shittest holiday in the world!'

'Thanks a bunch.' She sniffed.

'I don't mean with you! Every minute with you is five bloody star. I mean if I turned up on holiday and was given this place,

I'd probably ask to be moved. And so...' He turned to face her. 'That's what I'm doing. I'm asking you to move.'

'Oh not this again.' Anna lay back against the wall and briefly pulled the pillow over her face.

'Yes, this again. You can't hide. We need to get a bigger place. We've stuck it out long enough – it must be more than a year since I properly moved in, isn't it? And I can't even have the lads over. Can you imagine inviting them in and asking them to sit on the bed and we all have to budge up to make space!' He gave a wry laugh. 'And now you've had your promotion, plus the stall is doing well, so we can rely on my income a bit more and maybe try and find somewhere nearer my mum and dad. They'd love that – you'd never get rid of them!'

'I'd be the size of a house.' Anna pictured Sylvie beating a path from her front door to theirs in her slippers at all hours of the day and night, bearing an endless procession of food. She'd grown to really love Ned's family over the past couple of years, and she was in no doubt that the feeling was mutual. She liked to think of Sylvie and Jack as being like a pair of comfy socks, because they made everything feel a little bit better. So she was surprised at her reaction to the future life Ned was painting. It sparked a leap of fear in her chest, but she couldn't quite put her finger on why.

'I think we should stay here.' She looked around the walls, prettified by framed postcards and additional strings of fairy lights. 'I know it's not perfect, but it's so affordable that, God forbid, if ever I lost my job and couldn't get another, I could still pay the rent for quite some time, just out of my savings.'

'Oh, Anna, you don't have to worry about that stuff. First of all, you'll never lose your job. Everyone knows they just love you there, Madam Senior Receptionist! And secondly, I have a job too and I can look after you.' He looked at her sincerely and pushed his fringe from his eyes. 'You're not on your own any more. You've got me.'

'I know, and that's lovely of you to say, Ned, but it's really important to me that I can take care of myself.'

'You need to let me in a bit more, Anna.'

She stared at him, knowing that this request, however reasonable, might just be beyond her capabilities.

Making her way along the street just outside work, she caught sight of Melissa coming in the opposite direction and waved. They both sped up and met by the glass lobby on the ground floor.

'What's up?' Melissa asked.

'Why do you think there's something up? I haven't said a word yet! Good morning, by the way.'

'How long have I worked with you?'

'Erm, about two and a half years?'

'Exactly. And for all of that time I have sat right by your side for at least eight hours a day. I know your every mood.' Melissa arched an eyebrow and gave her an appraising stare. 'And I can tell by your body language and your expression just how you're feeling before you have said a single word.'

'That's a bit worrying. So what's my body language and expression telling you right now?' Anna pulled a face and stuck out her tongue.

'Ah, that's another thing, Anna. You can joke, but you can't hide how you're feeling – you're one of those people who wears their feelings like a large hat, visible to everyone. So come on, talk to me. We're not leaving here until you do.' Melissa folded her arms across her chest, as if this might emphasise her point.

Anna exhaled and looked into the middle distance. 'I'm having…' She swallowed, regrouping her thoughts. 'I mean, I am starting to think…' Again she paused. 'I think I might be tired. That's probably it.' She forced a tight-lipped smile.

'Come on!' Melissa grabbed her by the wrist and pulled her in the opposite direction, towards the front door.

'Where are we going? We've got to get to work!'

She looked back over her shoulder as Melissa headed purposefully along the street. Anna, tethered to her via a clamped hand, trotted in her wake. They came to a halt at a bench set back from the edge of the road next to a litter bin scrawled with graffiti and covered with cement-like lumps of gum.

Melissa sat down and patted the bench next to her. Anna followed suit.

'I don't think you're happy and I don't like it. You're my best friend and I want you to be happy.' As was her manner, Melissa cut to the chase.

'I am.' Anna avoided her gaze.

'No, I don't think you are,' her friend repeated. 'I think you are happy enough, but that is not enough, if you get my meaning.'

Anna smiled weakly. Ironically, she did get her meaning. She hid her face in her hands, letting out a long sigh. When she sat up and removed her palms from her eyes, her words flowed.

'I think I might be having doubts about Ned.'

Melissa nodded, seemingly unsurprised, and waited for Anna to expand.

'Not so much about him – he's great – but it's a million tiny things.' She paused.

Melissa nodded sagely. 'It always is, honey.'

'He was talking about how much his mum is bothered by his early starts and he was trying to reassure me that he's fine and I stared at him and I realised that I didn't care that much and I know that makes me sound like a terrible person!' She buried her face in her hands again.

Melissa yanked her wrists so she could see her face. 'You are not a terrible person, just an honest one.'

'Oh, Mel, he keeps asking me to move into a bigger flat with him and he says he wants to look after me more.'

'The bastard!'

'I can't even joke about it. He's lovely, I get it, but…' Anna stared at the traffic rushing past and chose her words carefully, words that would mean a change of direction for her, a new start. 'I don't think he's for me, not long-term and I don't think I'm for him, not really.' She grimaced. 'And I feel so bad because he is lovely.'

She looked up at Melissa, who gave a thin-lipped smile.

'I already know this, honey.'

'What do you mean, you "already know this"?' She pulled her head back on her shoulders and knitted her brows.

'Ned is beautiful to look at and sweet. But I see the way you dumb down when you're with him and I have a suspicion that you've fallen for the whole package.'

'In what way?' Anna asked, conscious of her defensive tone.

'I mean that you love his friends, who make you laugh, and his parents, who make you cocoa, and his beefcake bod that protects you and keeps you warm through the cold, dark nights, yada yada…' She raised her hands.

Anna stared at the graffiti on the litter bin – *JW Luvs DS. The*

Selector – anything rather than let her insightful friend see the flicker of recognition cross her face. 'I don't know if I love him.' She whispered the words aloud for the first time and felt a stab of guilt in her chest.

'That means you don't love him,' Melissa stated flatly. 'No one in love, in true, deep, committed love, has ever said that. If it's right, that thought does not occur.'

Anna sighed and closed her eyes. Melissa was right. She did love the whole package, his welcoming parents, who were always so pleased to see her, his mates, who included her in their ribbing, but as for spending the rest of her life with Ned? She pictured their evenings, him watching the TV and her reading a book. They never had any discussions about anything other than their respective days. She wasn't knocking him, his intellect or his job, no way! She admired him and liked him very much, but it was something more than that. There was no spark. No excitement about the future, and there was so much that she had never told him, as if a sixth sense told her there was no point.

Her mum's advice, *'you'll know if he's the one'*, was always there at the back of her mind. She didn't share her mum's conviction, but if she was honest, in her heart of hearts she did know that Ned wasn't the one.

'I can't stand the idea of hurting him.' She shivered at the prospect.

'I know, but the longer you let it go on, the more he will be hurt. The kindest thing is to do it fast, like ripping off a Band-Aid.'

Anna nodded, feeling sick at the prospect. 'Come on, we've got to get to work.'

'Yes, good point. The senior receptionist is a total cow, wouldn't want to get on the wrong side of her!' Melissa reached over and kissed her friend and now boss on the cheek.

Over the next few days Anna tried and failed several times to find the right moment to talk to Ned. It seemed he was always either rushing in or rushing out, or one or both of them was on the point of falling asleep.

Excuses, Anna. Excuses.

She shook her head to rid it of this truth and lingered in the supermarket aisle, wondering what might be quick and easy to make for their tea. It was tricky with only two rings on the worktop stove, but they managed. Admittedly the menu wasn't that varied: pasta and sauce, sauce and pasta, soup, baked beans... She stopped. Something had caught her eye. Staring at the boxes of ready-made cake mix, she selected one for a Victoria sandwich, transfixed by the image on the front.

This was what her grief did, even all these years later. Without warning, it hijacked the most mundane of moments and was powerful enough to make her body fold and her tears spout. She could almost smell the two halves of sponge baking in the oven – her wedding cake. She could hear her mum and Joe arguing in the next-door room. Her memory of that day was still acute.

Anna slowly placed the box back on the shelf and wiped her face with the sleeve of her jumper pulled over her hand. She'd lost her desire to shop for their evening meal. She'd make do with whatever was at the back of the cupboard, or Ned could go out for chips. Again.

'What's the matter?' Ned sat up on the bed the moment she walked through the door. 'Have you been crying?' His face was creased with concern as he hurried over and wrapped her in his arms.

With her head resting on his broad chest, she inhaled the scent of him. It was a nice place to be, a nice, safe place, but Melissa was right: it wasn't enough.

She pulled away. 'Yes, I've been crying. Thinking and crying and knowing that you and I have to talk and kind of wishing that we didn't have to – if that makes any sense. But we do need to talk, Ned. We need to talk about our future.'

And just like that, she'd found the moment. It was now.

She bit her lip and shrugged free from his grasp. Walking over to the bed, she sat on the far side of the mattress. He lumbered over, blocking the light with his frame, before pulling the chair from the two-person table so that he could sit facing her. She had hoped, rather cowardly, that he would sit on the other side of the bed, as far away as was possible in their cramped living zone. That way she might have avoided having to look into his beautiful face.

'I think we should get married.' His words were like a jolt of electricity fired into the air.

Anna couldn't help the gasp of shock or the startled expression that shot across her face. 'What?' She wrinkled her nose.

Ned leant forward, resting his forearms on his thighs. 'I've been thinking about it for a while and Dad said I should get on with it and he's right. Mum's hinted too. I know you have a problem with the thought of leaning on me and I get it, I do, but you need to get over that, Anna, and I think if we got married, then you wouldn't feel so bad about me supporting you, supporting us. Plus I love you.'

'Oh, Ned.' She let her head flop down to her chest. 'I want to talk about how we can split up in the best way possible and you ask me to marry you?'

'Split up?' he repeated, his mouth hanging open in surprise. 'Is that what we're doing, splitting up?' He rubbed at his chin with his palm; she could hear the graze of stubble against his calloused hand.

'Yes.' She nodded, her tears pooling again. 'I'm sorry.'

Ned sat back in the chair. His breath was coming fast. 'Shit.'

'I'm sorry, Ned.'

'Stop saying you're sorry.' His voice had turned sharp. Anger and embarrassment now lapped where only minutes earlier there'd been love and a rosy future. 'Fucking hell!' He raked his fingers through his hair, stood up and walked to the window as if he needed air. He flung open the latch and she too welcomed the cold breeze that poured in. 'I didn't see that one coming.'

He breathed deeply and she figured he was trying to clear his head. This she understood as hers was a muddle of thoughts too. Guilt far outweighed the relief she had imagined she might feel.

'Is there someone else?' he said bitterly.

She shook her head. 'No. No one else.'

They were both silent for a beat or two, wondering whether this was better or worse.

Anna tried to clarify, knowing she owed him that much. 'I just don't feel the way I should. You are lovely, Ned, your whole family is lovely, but that's not a reason to get married.' She stood and made her way over to him, thinking that to hold him might make them both feel a little better.

He dodged her grasp. She felt the flat shrink even further, becoming quite claustrophobic.

Ned scooted past her and gathered up his plastic box from the floor, into which he threw a small pile of clothes, his motorbike magazines and two bottles of cologne from the windowsill.

She sat back in the chair he'd just vacated. 'I also think—'

'Can you just shut up!' he snapped. 'I don't care what you think! I don't want to hear your bullshit excuses or reasons. So don't bother. Christ, Anna!'

She was stunned into quiet, watching as he whipped along the hall and into the bathroom, gathering his toiletries and towel before hurling them too into the box. She knew his behaviour was fuelled by hurt and wasn't a true reflection of his normally calm nature. Finally he put on his trainers and stood with the box in his arms. He looked back at her, his face contorted, whether in sadness or anger she couldn't tell.

'You are fucking weird and I put up with your weirdness because I loved you, but you really are fucking weird.'

He balanced the box on his thigh, turned the latch, then slammed the door behind him in one final act of defiance.

She sat staring after him for a full ten minutes, processing what had just happened, too frozen to cry or shout or laugh, replaying his words over and over. '*You really are fucking weird.*' The worst of it was he didn't know half of her weirdness, didn't know that she used to flag down cabs to try and locate her dad, didn't know about the alphabet game, didn't know she wrote to her imaginary future children, didn't know her at all, not really.

'*I put up with your weirdness because I loved you.*'

'And I guess that's just it,' she whispered into the ether. 'I don't want to be with someone who has to put up with me.'

She lay back on the bed feeling nothing but emptiness. Not a feeling that was alien to her, but it had been absent for a while.

She pictured the granny bedroom at her aunt and uncle's and let her eyes now sweep the flat.

A... *apple. That's how this started.*

B... *bed.*

C... *closet.* She looked at the wardrobe door, which was still open. Its empty hangers rattled.

D... *duvet.* She ran her fingers over the relief of the pattern and pictured Shania sitting on the single bed while she'd packed up ready to leave Mead House. She missed her old roommate. 'I hope you have your own duvet now, Shania, not a standard-issue institutional one. I hope you're making your mark, flying high, working hard.'

When the alarm buzzed her awake at seven the next morning, her first feeling was one of dread at the prospect of having to walk past Ned's stall on her way to work. Should she smile, say something, try to make him feel better? Or just hurry past with her head down? She cursed the fact that it wasn't raining, thinking how convenient it would have been if she could have hid under her brolly, but it was a rare bright day, with barely a cloud in the sky. She took a deep breath and craned her neck out the window – forewarned was forearmed, after all. He wasn't there! No red-and-white awning, no chirpy cockney patter, no handsome smile. She was gladder than she could have imagined. Lovely Ned was no longer her lovely Ned. She hurried into the shower, got into her smart clothes and set off for work.

Back at the flat that night, she leafed through her file of letters to Fifi and Fox, lingering on one she'd written just a few months back. She smiled ruefully at how happy with Ned she'd sounded and at the little hint she'd included about Sylvie and Jack possibly becoming her babies' grandparents. It was time to write an update.

Hey Fifi and Fox,

I have been thinking recently that there is always a temptation when your life moves on to remove any evidence that shows you walking a wrong path or making choices that just didn't work out. Like erasing the name of the boy you used to fancy from your pencil case. I've decided not to do that and I'm leaving my letters to you about Ned exactly where I placed them in the file.

I think it's important, this record of my history, waiting for you.

Ned is a really good person, but I didn't love him, not in the way you need to if you want to stay with someone and make a life together. He thought I was weird and I realise that my life is weird compared to his. This I think is the biggest reason why we couldn't stay together. How could Ned, with his loving mum and dad, his cosy life, his great mates, how could he possibly understand what it's been like for me? How could someone like him get my need for quiet, my need for independence? I am shaped by my life experience and yes, that might be weird, but it is what it is.

I know that leaving Ned moves having you two in my life a little further out of reach and that's the biggest sacrifice of all. Don't imagine I've stopped thinking about you – I think about you every single day! I just need to find you the right dad. We don't need riches, or a big house, so long as there's proper love. That's what's important. The things I want for you are things

I can already provide, like goodnight kisses on the forehead, a warm bubble bath for you on a cold day. And if you ever get sick, I will wrap you in a duvet and hold you tight on the sofa, feeding you tomato soup!

I think about my mum, who made decisions that didn't bring her happiness, not in the end. She chose badly, some would say, and I don't want to do the same. So this has been a good lesson for me. Sometimes things don't work out as you expect them to, but that shouldn't stop you trying or going for it! In fact, the more you try, the more likely you are to fail and the more you will learn.

So try lots! Fail at lots! That's okay. It will all be taking you in the right direction.

This much I know.

Love, Mummy x

Nine

Melissa was on the phone, the receiver cradled beneath her chin while she furiously scribbled notes and nodded. 'Yes, of course, Your Honour.'

Anna grinned at her. She was really laying it on thick. They exchanged a brief knowing look as Anna strode past.

Work had been a lifeline for Anna over the past four months. She'd really thrown herself into her job, determined to keep herself occupied and give herself as little opportunity as possible to dwell on thoughts of Ned and what might have been. It wasn't always easy, though. On a couple of occasions she'd left work and had found herself making her way to Jack and Sylvie's house, envisioning a cup of tea and a bowlful of fruit crumble and custard, before reality caught up with her tired mind and she remembered that she was no longer part of that world. No longer Ned's bird, as they used to affectionately refer to her. And she had to admit that while she didn't necessarily long for Ned any more, she dearly missed being part of his family.

Anna stepped inside the walk-in stationery cupboard and scanned the upper shelves, trying to locate the lever-arch box files she needed. She searched the floor, looking for the small rubber-footed stool she usually stood on.

'Well, this is cosy.'

'Oh! Hello.' She gasped at the sound of Mr Knowles's voice. He'd caught her unawares and was now blocking the door. She felt her cheeks redden and her heart race, partly due to being in such close proximity to a man of Mr Knowles's status, a partner no less, but also because he seemed to take up all the air and as ever she hated being in a small, dark space with no window.

'Need some assistance?' he asked jovially.

'I'm just looking for the... the little stool thing so I can reach the top shelf.' She pointed at the files lest there be any doubt about the spot she was referring to.

'I can help you there.' He smiled at her and took a step closer.

Anna's pulse quickened. She was very uncomfortable with the lack of space between them and with his unfamiliar, slightly lecherous tone. She tried to move backwards and cursed the metal racking immediately behind her. There was no escape.

Don't be ridiculous, Anna! She tried to calm her flustered thoughts. *You're imagining things. Mr Knowles is old and married. He's only being helpful.*

Mr Knowles lifted his hands and placed them on the shelf above her head, either side of her shoulders, almost pinning her there.

She tried to speak but couldn't find her voice. Fear had rendered her mute.

'Actually, Anna, I think you'll find that, like most chaps, the top shelf is one of my favourites.' His left eyebrow lifted in suggestion.

Anna's stomach bunched with fear as he slid against her,

pushed his arms up and reached for two of the files she needed. Slowly he drew away and she felt... She felt... his body against hers.

'There we go.' He breathed out slowly and she could smell something spicy on his breath. 'And be in no doubt,' he continued, 'that I am on hand for whenever you need something.' He ran the tips of his fingers over her neck. 'You only have to shout. Or ring.'

She shuddered with revulsion and hoped he didn't misconstrue that for anything else.

He left the cupboard and closed the door quietly behind him.

Anna thought she might be sick. She quickly walked back to her desk, wary of drawing attention to her distress and not wanting to engage with Melissa, not until she had figured out what to do. But mainly she wanted to put as much distance as possible between herself and Mr Knowles.

Grabbing her handbag from the back of her chair, she tried to make it seem casual as she dashed across the office, down the stairs and out of the building. It was then that her tears came. She placed a shaking hand over her mouth and swallowed the bile that rose in her throat.

'Anna?'

She whipped her head around and there was Nitz, in his overalls splashed with plaster.

'What's the matter?' He put a hand on her arm.

She shook her head and wondered where to begin. 'Nothing. I'm okay.'

'You're clearly not okay, girl. Let's get you a cup of tea.'

Grateful that someone had taken control, she let herself be guided around the corner to the café she knew the lads liked to frequent. She was instantly relieved that Ned wasn't in it. She stared at the grimy surroundings, focusing on the ketchup splats on the wall and the grease-encrusted glass pot of salt with rice grains nestling in the bottom, placed in the centre of the table next to a wipe-clean menu that essentially listed egg, bacon, fried bread and sausage in any number of combinations.

Nitz arrived back at the table with two mugs of strong tea and sat down opposite her. 'Get that down you.' He nodded at her drink and sipped at his own.

'Thank you.' She felt her breathing calm a little.

'Are you upset about Ned? Is this what it's about? We was all really shocked, you know. Thought you and him were going all the way.'

She smiled, embarrassed to have been the one to dump his mate and just as flattered that he thought her worthy of him.

'It's not that. I, er... got into a bit of a situation at work.'

'Situation how? Have you nicked something, got caught?'

'No!' She laughed as best she could through her distress. 'As if I'd nick something!'

He winked. The diversion had done the trick, her voice had found its natural rhythm and she was, on the outside at least, a little calmer.

'I've worked for this man for a while now – Mr Knowles. He's one of the partners. I even buy his daughter's textbooks and his wife's birthday cards.' She shook her head. 'And just now, he... He cornered me in a cupboard. Urgh!' She wrapped her arms around herself and shivered.

'Did he hurt you?' All humour had disappeared from Nitz's voice and his eyes glinted with fury.

'Not really. He just...' She looked at the pine wall cladding, avoiding his stare, not knowing how to express what had happened without using words that might mortify them both. 'He sort of...' Again she faltered. 'He rubbed himself against me and made it very clear that he wanted more.' Her face burned and the words were sour on her tongue.

'Dirty fucking bastard!' Nitz snorted angrily.

'I thought I was going to be sick. He's a big bloke, Mr Knowles, old, really. Oh God.' She again fought the desire to vomit.

'That's so out of order. Want me to 'ave a word?' Nitz looked her in the eye, his voice low, a thick vein on his neck standing proud.

'No! No, definitely not. I can handle it.' She wasn't sure this was true, but above all else, she needed her job. 'Promise me you won't tell Ned!'

'I'm on my way to his house now, as it 'appens.'

'Please, Nitz.'

'You can't let blokes like him get away with pulling stunts like that!'

'I need this job! I need it.' Her lip trembled.

He seemed to be weighing this up. 'All right, Anna, 'ave it your way. I promise I won't tell Ned.'

'Thank you.' She took a sip of tea and felt sad at the thought that Ned might not even care.

That night she hardly slept, kept replaying the event in her head, wondering if she was in any way responsible – had she given Mr Knowles the wrong impression, however inadvertently? She worried about seeing him at the office, not that she had any choice in the matter. He'd turned her place of work, a refuge of sorts, into something quite different. She doubted he'd have the faintest idea about the effect his behaviour had had on her.

With sleep proving evasive, Anna lay in bed thinking about a night not long after Shania had arrived at Mead House. It was a Thursday and as she dozed fitfully through the early hours she became aware of a hand under her duvet, stroking her skin. She kept very still, hoping it was a dream, before opening her eyes to see an agency night warden, a stranger, looming over the bed with his finger on his lips, as if instructing her to be quiet. She had let out a small scream, which woke Shania.

'Get the fuck off her and get the fuck out of here!' Shania had yelled, loud enough to wake the whole floor.

The man had left, thankfully, and was dismissed by Junior the next day. Junior had been concerned and apologetic, but they had no idea how many others the creep had taken advantage of. It was vile and it made her aware of her vulnerability, her lack of protection. She thought about her evening at Waterloo station and the man with the briefcase who'd made a beeline for her. This incident with Mr Knowles had made her realise that though she was now twenty-four, in some ways not much had changed.

Anna showered and chose her most demure skirt and blouse. She even omitted to put on the little make-up she usually wore and tied her shoulder-length hair into a ponytail. A different person might have called in sick, but Anna was a woman who had lived one step away from homelessness and knew that compared with having no roof over her head, being cornered by Mr Knowles in the stationery cupboard was a snip.

She arrived early, hoping to be busy and distracted by the time everyone else turned up. Her heart sank when she saw that

Mr Knowles was already at his desk. She looked round at the door and it was in that second, as she debated whether to go back outside and wait for Melissa to arrive or whether to front it out, that the phone on her desk buzzed. She walked forward and could see it was his internal line. Her stomach churned. Mr Pope wasn't in yet and other colleagues wouldn't make an appearance for at least twenty minutes.

'Yes, Mr Knowles?' She tried to hide the shake to her voice, still ridiculously conscious of needing to be polite to this man who paid her wages.

'Might I have a word?' He coughed to clear his throat.

'Yes.' She put the phone down and walked to his office, calculating how loud she would have to yell if it came to it and what she might be able to grab in self-defence if necessary.

She knocked and entered, as was customary, but she left the door wide open. The moment she saw him, sitting behind the desk in his grand leather chair, her heart skipped a beat. Mr Knowles, esteemed partner, was sporting a nasty black eye. His cheekbone was yellow and blue and his eye a little bloodshot.

Anna opened her mouth to speak but didn't know what to say or where to start.

Mr Knowles coughed again. 'As you can see, I had a rather unfortunate incident when I left the office last night.' He avoided her gaze.

Nitz! You promised me!

'Over twenty years in the legal profession has taught me not to believe in coincidences and so I am quite sure this is something to do with our little tête-à-tête yesterday. Would I be correct in that assumption?' He lifted his chin, as she'd seen him do when interviewing clients.

'I...' Anna swallowed. 'I don't...'

'Let me help you out.' The lawyer knitted his fingers in front of him on the shiny desktop. 'I would of course have much preferred a sharp word from you than this.' He winced a little, seemingly in pain. 'As it is, we shall chalk it up to experience on both our parts. And I think it best we say nothing more about it.' He picked up his glasses and popped them on, then selected a sheaf of papers to study, as if that was that.

Anna straightened her shoulders and found her voice. 'Actually, I would like to say one more thing about it.' She spoke through lips dry with nerves. 'You did make me feel very uncomfortable. Scared, even, and it was horrible.'

He glanced up. 'I...'

'And I did confide in someone that it had unsettled... that it upset me.' Her voice cracked.

He blinked, rapidly.

'But I don't know who did this to you and I didn't ask anyone to do this to you. Quite the opposite, in fact. But... But,' she continued, 'my ex has a hot head and I guess—'

'Your ex?' He interrupted her. 'No, Anna, this was not done by your ex. I was assaulted by a woman in her mid sixties with a foul mouth and wearing slippers.'

Anna bit her lip, unable to hide the smile that lifted her cheeks. She let out a small, nervous laugh. *Sylvie... Oh, Sylvie! Someone was looking out for me! You!*

He lowered his papers and sniffed. 'Well, I'm glad you can find an element of humour in this whole debacle.'

'I really don't,' she replied soberly.

'You have always been...' He scrutinised her, as if searching for the right word. '... agreeable, friendly, and I guess I thought you might…' He paused again. Apparently twenty years in the legal profession wasn't helping with his vocabulary right now.

Anna held her ground, standing tall. 'Please don't assume you know me, Mr Knowles. You don't. You don't know the first thing about me or where I have come from or where I am going.'

There was a second when he held her gaze and seemed to shrink a little beneath it.

'That'll be all.' He nodded towards the door.

She stared at him, knowing she would indeed keep the secret. But she also knew that her time at Asquith, Barker and Knowles had come to an end. She needed a new job. A new start.

That evening, Melissa insisted they go into town and see a film at the Odeon Leicester Square. It was a good call. *The Bodyguard*, proved to be exactly the distraction Anna needed, she bundled up her coat and left the theatre in good spirits, despite having bawled into a tissue for the last twenty minutes of the movie. It made her think of Jordan. After Chinese noodles in Soho, Melissa jumped in a cab back to her boyfriend Gerard's house, singing the title song loudly out of the cab window, as she left. Anna laughed to herself, as she walked down to Embankment Tube station.

She had politely refused her friend's offer to share a cab, not willing to go into the reasons at the end of a such a fun night. The truth was she hadn't wanted to risk opening old wounds. It had been a month now since she'd conclusively decided to give up her desperate search for her elusive cabbie dad. After Ned had walked out, she'd had a bit of a blitz, going to different parts of the city of an evening, walking, and thinking that if only she could find Michael, he might be the key to what lay ahead, a sort of model perhaps for the man who might replace Ned. Someone who might make it seem sunny, even in the rain. She began finding herself in unsavoury places at unwise times – at 1 a.m. at the back of King's Cross station, at midnight on a dark side street off the Old Kent Road. It was when she got followed one night and had to run for it, she made a pact with herself: she would stop searching, it was pointless, too hard and failure in the task only made her feel low. She decided that she wouldn't so much as look at a black cab for the foreseeable future.

As she made her way towards the Tube, past the entrance to the church of St Martin-in-the-Fields, a voice called from a nearby shop door. 'Can you spare some change, please?' The request was familiar, but there was something about the woman's voice that made Anna look twice.

'Can you spare some change, please?' the woman asked again.

Anna stopped and stared at the figure huddled on an open sleeping bag spread out on the shallow step of a vacant shop. The shadowy figure was wrapped in a grey blanket, with her hand hanging limply down and clumps of an unkempt Afro sticking out at all angles from the top of her head.

Noticing that Anna had stopped, the woman reached towards her, her expression blank. 'Spare some change for a cup of tea, please? Please?'

Anna bent down and stared into the woman's gaunt face. Her eyes were bloodshot, her skin looked scarred and her teeth were brown. But beneath the grime and the vacant expression, it was unmistakeably the face of her old roommate, Shania.

'Oh!' Anna felt the swell of tears in her throat and something close to panic in her chest. 'Oh no!' She spoke slowly, studying the face that was now just inches from her own. 'Shania! Hello. It's me. It's Anna.'

'Could you spare me some change, please, and a fag if you've got one?' she asked, seemingly unable to recognise Anna.

'Do you remember me? It's me, Anna. We shared a room.' She spoke gently, trying to coax her into remembrance, but Shania stared right past her.

'Canyousparesomechangeplease...' she mumbled as her head lolled on her neck. Her pupils disappeared momentarily as her eyes rolled back in her head.

'Hang on a minute.' Anna stood and opened her bag. Fishing for her purse, she pulled out all of her cash, a little over forty pounds. 'Here you go.' She bent down again and rolled the notes into her friend's outstretched hand. Then she slipped a piece of paper with her name and telephone number into Shania's pocket, hoping she might find it when she was more with it.

'Thank you,' Shania managed, her head tipped back, her mouth now slack.

'Let me... Let me get you to a hotel, let me get you some help!' Anna held her arm, trying to think of what to do.

'Don't touch me!' Shania barked, recoiling and shifting into defence mode.

Several passers-by slowed and stared. Not that Anna cared. She wanted to do something for her friend, her friend who had promised she would stay off drugs.

'I'm sorry, I'm sorry. I won't touch you.' She took a step backwards with her palms raised. 'I just want to help get you somewhere to stay tonight. Shania, please.'

'I got somewhere to stay tonight. Fuck off! Don't touch me!' Shania was shrieking now and kicking out.

Anna stood up and glanced up the street, unsure whether to stay or go. She didn't want to draw any more unwanted attention to Shania, but...

'Go on! Fuck off!' Shania yelled loudly as she shifted backwards on her filthy sleeping bag.

'Okay. Okay, my darling.' Anna blew her a kiss and walked away, sobbing.

As she sat on the Tube back to her flat, her mind whirred through memories of the days they'd had together at Mead House, the dressing-up, the blue glass earrings she'd left her, the flagging down of dozens of cabs in the search for Michael, the fruitless waiting for Shania's dad to come and rescue his daughter. She cried noiselessly into her hankie, sad for the life her friend now found herself living, so far from what either of them had hoped for. Anna ground her teeth. *You deserve so much more, Shania. My funny, kind, friend. That could have been me. It could have been me and I promised you I'd have a party, but I never did. I never did. And I'm sorry.*

Ten

It had been hearteningly easy to find a new job. Anna had signed up with a recruitment agency and was over the moon to find herself in demand. It was a massive boost to her fragile self-esteem. A glowing reference from Mrs Glacier had paved the way for success, and after several interviews, she was offered three different positions. The one she opted for was at a financial firm located in a beautiful listed building called Villiers House on Cheapside in the City, not far from St Paul's Cathedral. She liked the fact that the building was occupied by lots of different companies – there was a real buzz about the place – and she liked the people she worked for. Not that she really understood what they did all day, something to do with buying and selling money. One thing she understood perfectly was her role as receptionist, responsible for answering the phone, greeting guests and running errands for the brokers. After nearly three years in the role, she was a dab hand at it.

No longer having Melissa by her side all day had been a wrench, but they still saw each other every few weeks. In fact Melissa had called just the other night, reminding her that she and her husband Gerard were having a dinner party this coming weekend. Anna knew that she'd be introduced to several of Gerard's available, art-loving buddies, with whom she would have zero in common, but it was a night out and she'd get to see her mate, who, newly married, was now a lot less available than she used to be. Anna understood of course and was delighted to see her friend so happy. She smiled now at the memory of Melissa's father crying as he walked up the aisle last year with his little girl on his arm. Melissa told her afterwards that they were tears of relief – for a while he'd feared she might hop back across the pond and become his problem once again, something neither his retirement fund nor his nerves could take!

Anna shook her head and returned to the book she was reading, keen to devour all she could of *Captain Corelli's Mandolin*, which everyone was raving about, before she reached her Tube stop. The lengthy commute, from Parsons Green to Mansion House, was another of the good things about her City job. It had allowed her to re-establish her reading habit and to digest what she'd just read on the short walk to Villiers House. She had forgotten just how lovely it was to dive into a book. One of her abiding memories of her mum was watching her sitting on the sofa with her legs folded under her and a book held inches from her nose, completely lost to a story. She took comfort from the knowledge that her mum had had these happy, happy moments too. Anna walked across the beautiful tiled lobby floor of Villiers House and hopped into the ornate lift, ignoring the slight shake to the cage as she pressed the brass button for the sixth floor. Soon after she started working there she'd developed a routine for dealing with the confined space. Standing close to the doors, facing them, she pictured the wide window in the kitchen of her imagination, the one her mum would have loved to have stood in front of, feeling the gentle flower-scented breeze on her face. With her eyes tightly closed, she played the alphabet game while looking out in her imagination.

A... *air.*

B... *blue sky.*

C... *chirping birds.*

D... *daisies.*

E... *endless fields of grass.*

F... *fields of endless grass.*

G... *grass in endless fields.*

The lift stopped and as the doors opened with the ping of an old-fashioned bell she laughed to herself at her cheating. She made a mental note that she had got to G, which was where she would pick it up again on her next lift journey.

'Morning!' She nodded to some of the suited men who were crisscrossing the reception area at this early hour.

'Mawninanna.'

These guys were always in a rush, eliding her name and greeting into a single word, and usually doing everything at a semi jog, whether it was going to the bathroom or grabbing a coffee, wary of abandoning their desk for any longer than absolutely necessary, knowing that a minute could make all the difference to the success or failure of a day's trading. It wasn't unusual for them to work through the night or start horrendously early in order to catch the markets in different time zones. More than once she had arrived at work to find one of them asleep with his head cradled in his arms on top of a cluttered desk, the wastepaper bin brimming with sandwich wrappers, noodle boxes and crumpled coffee cups.

Anna walked to the kitchenette by the cloakroom, hung up

her coat and poured herself a coffee from the percolator. She inhaled its deep, earthy scent and smoothed her black skirt over her thick tights before taking up her seat behind the wide, modern desk that ran parallel to the back wall. A vast oil painting hung behind the desk, commissioned by the board to fill the space. In her view, it was total crap and this realisation had made her understand that just because someone had money it didn't mean they had taste. Her nose wrinkled every time she gazed at the splashes, drips and flicks of multi-coloured paint. Not that it mattered much: when in situ, she faced the entrance door and had her back to it. She was ready with her smile as soon as she saw the shadow of an arrival through the stained-glass doors.

Even at this early hour, a small bundle of mail had accumulated. She flicked through the letters, both incoming and those to be sent, sorting them into wire trays: UK-bound ones destined for the Royal Mail, those going further afield to be sent by courier, and post freshly arrived to be distributed internally. Her fingers arrived at a stiff, brown, formal-looking envelope. She turned it over and saw, highly unusually, that it was addressed to her!

How odd. Her forehead creased in anticipation.

The only people who wrote to her were Jordan and his partner Levi, and their letters arrived like magic in the pigeonhole at her flat. She loved the way they always wrote on half the card each or divided the sheet of paper into two with a neat line and then filled their respective section with wonderful gossip and tittle-tattle about their lives in New York, New York. She loved nothing more than to read about their walks through Central Park, trips to the theatre, the weather, good coffee, bad wine, gourmet hot dogs and a million other little snippets that helped her feel connected to her cousin so far away. She thought it was cute and she savoured each neat line, written in ink pen and dotted with hearts and smiley faces. Unlike her Aunt Lizzie, who apparently found nothing cute about the couple at all and had refused point blank to meet the man her son loved, saying she would wait until he was over this ridiculous phase. Anna clicked her tongue against the roof of her mouth. *She'll have a bloody long wait. Silly woman.*

She looked at the postmark: London. That didn't give much away. It was far from the usual milk receipt or buffet menu that arrived folded over, dropped off and left for her consideration. Having taken a sip of hot coffee, she carefully unstuck the envelope, pulled the folded typed white sheets from their sheath and laid them flat on the table.

Anna instantly recognised the language and style of a legal letter; she had handled enough of them in her time.

DEAR MISS COLE,

She was beyond curious, intrigued by the formality, and quickly read on...

My name is Ernest Faversham and I represent the estate of Mr Harper. It is my sad duty to inform you that Mr Harper passed away on May 16th, 1995 after a short illness.

As instructed by my client, I am contacting you in the wake of his death to pass on a letter (attached herewith) in accordance with the last will and testament of Mr Harper.

Please do not hesitate to contact me.

Yours faithfully,

MR E C FAVERSHAM

'What on earth? I've never heard of him! Mr Harper?' Anna spoke aloud as she slipped the covering letter off the top of the sheets of paper to which it had been paper-clipped, squeezing the bulky corner flap between her thumb and forefinger for good measure.

Dear Anna,
Anna... this was my mother's name and that's been a nice thing for me over the years, knowing that her name lives on in you, my daughter.

It was as if the air had been sucked from the room. With trembling fingers, Anna set the paper flat on the table and bent her head forward, almost resting it on her knees, hoping that this might help stop the room from spinning.

'Oh my God! Oh my God!' she whispered, trying to control the shudder to her limbs and the shake to her hands. She slowed her breathing, aware that the hyperventilating was making her feel lightheaded.

'Oh my God!' she repeated.

'Anna?' a voice called.

She looked up to see one of the traders. Marius.

'Do you know where I can find the...?' He paused at the sight of her. 'Are you okay? You look terrible.'

She sat up straight and swallowed. 'Marius, I... I need to go to the loo. Get someone to cover for me.'

Without waiting for an answer or responding to his stunned expression, she grabbed the sheets of paper from the desk and ran towards the bathroom. Locking the door of the end cubicle, she sat on the closed toilet seat and pushed at her ears; it felt as if she was underwater. Leaning back against the cistern, she closed her eyes and concentrated on breathing slowly. It did the trick.

Finally, when she felt ready, she unfolded the paperwork.

Dear Anna,

Anna… this was my mother's name and that's been a nice thing for me over the years knowing that her name lives on in you, my daughter. I don't know how much you know, sweetheart, so this will come as either a shock or a comfort and I'm truly sorry that I don't know which. It's probably a good idea to read this letter with your mum. And if she objects, tell her it's because enough time has passed and my time has been cut short. I know she will understand.

It was at this point that Anna's tears pooled, sad that this man, Michael Harper, her dad, *my dad!*, had pictured her and her mum living a life somewhere together.

I only saw you once, on the day you were born, and even though I knew I wasn't going to be part of your life, I treasured that moment when I held you and your mum in my arms. The three of us together for no more than an hour or so. It is something I have never forgotten and it's one of my most cherished memories.

In that moment, everything felt possible.

They say you can't help who you fall in love with and this is true. You also can't help when you fall in love, and if I could have changed the time and circumstances of meeting Karen, I would have. But this kind of wishing does no one any good, it just takes the edge off any potential happiness. It can send you nearly crazy with thinking and thinking...

If you are reading this then I am no longer with you. That is a strange thought for me. I have wasted too much time on regrets.

'No!' she howled, her tears coming fast. 'I just wanted to see you once!' she cried. 'I just wanted to know what you looked like, my dad!' All those years of scouring traffic jams for cab drivers, looking into every pair of eyes and hoping beyond hope to see her own reflected back at her. She pulled off a length of loo roll and blew her nose, then wiped her streaming eyes so she could continue reading.

Anna! Even writing your name makes me smile. Anna, Anna...

I hope you are happy. I hope your mum forgives me.

I made promises I knew I couldn't keep and no one is more sorry for that than me. I hope good things for your future.

I am proud to think that I have another daughter on the earth, a daughter made in love. A daughter called Anna.

Michael Harper, your dad x

A complex storm of emotions raged inside her. She placed her head in her hands and tried to digest each different bit.

My dad's name was Michael Harper – I know his full name!

I was made in love. He loved me!

He held Mum and me in his arms.

What a wonderful thing!

The longing for her mum's presence was overwhelming. She wrapped her arms around her trunk.

He named me. I am named after my nan on my dad's side!
A family! I have a sister.
He is dead. My dad died. He died before I had a chance…

Back at her desk, Anna stuffed the letter into her bag and did her best to get through the morning. It felt surreal, as if she was floating, operating on autopilot. She tried to stay focused on her chores, but her mind alternately raced and went blank, as she struggled not to vomit.

She sipped at the glass of cold water that Marius had thoughtfully placed within reach. It was during her lunchbreak that Anna retreated, with permission, to the boardroom and with shaking fingers that slipped off the buttons used the telephone on the wide oak table to call Mr Ernest Faversham.

* * *

'Why are you doing this?' Anna asked herself as she stood by the gate at the end of the path leading to a house in Church Road, Croydon.

She tucked her bob behind her ears and flattened the Peter Pan collar of her floral blouse over the neck of her buttoned-up navy cardigan. Her eyes roved across the house, a standard three-bedroomed Victorian terrace whose upstairs curtains were drawn shut. Like all the houses in the row, the front garden had been ripped up and replaced with block paving. Moss had gathered in the cracks and in the space were parked a new white Audi and a slightly dated black cab that had been polished to a high sheen.

My dad's taxi!

Her heart raced at the sight of the steering wheel and seat where he would have sat hour after hour. Despite all her searching, it wasn't impossible that he had one day passed her in a crowded street or even given her a lift. Wouldn't that have been something?

There was a black wheelie bin and a pair of mud-encrusted wellies with a chewed tennis ball resting on the ground between them. *They've got a dog.*

The wall that separated the front path from the next-door house had a collection of large planters dotted along it, some of which had seen better days. An ordinary house. Only it wasn't it was an extraordinary house, it was a house that contained half of her lineage, memories and tales of the man who had fathered her and the nan she was named after. This is what she was keen to claim.

Her gut bunched with dread at what she might find on the other side of the frosted-glass front door.

A... Anna.

B... Be brave.

C... Come on.

D... Door. Knock on the door...

Her pep-talk worked. While her nerve held, she trod the eight steps along the path and rang the bell, knowing her dad must have done the same thousands of times. She let her finger-tip rest on the little white circle, wondering if particles of him still remained there and liking that idea very much. Then she realised that he would of course have had a key. 'Only me!' he might have called out to a family that might or might not have greeted this with the fanfare it deserved, unaware how fortunate they were to have their dad coming home to them every night. What wouldn't she have given for just one night with both of her parents. It was as she was picturing this that the front door opened.

Anna stared at the man in the doorway. He was in his thirties, had the light stubble of a day-old beard and wore jeans and a grey sweatshirt pulled tightly over his wiry frame. He looked nothing like her.

'Go back, Jester!' he shouted.

There was a second when her bones jumped in fear, until she realised with relief that he was speaking to the skinny mutt pushing against his calves. Reaching down, he placed his hand on the dog's flank and steered him backwards.

She tried out a nervous smile. 'Hello, I'm—'

'We know who you are.' His London vowels flattened in distaste as his top lip curled.

Anna's mouth went dry and her legs twitched with the desire to run. Of course, they were expecting her. Mr Faversham had made the arrangements. A mere six months since Michael Harper had passed away, this was how long it had taken the lawyer to locate her.

The man stepped back, allowing her entry. 'Come in.' He looked over her shoulder and closed the front door. 'On the left.'

She followed the nod of his head and glanced at the red carpet on the narrow staircase to the right, the newel post hidden under a pile of coats and jackets. At the end of the hall she could see a galley kitchen; its surfaces were neat and on one of them sat a packet of Bakewell tarts. She wondered if they'd gone to the trouble of buying them for her. Judging by the man's welcome, or lack of, that seemed unlikely. The back door was ajar, but a white net curtain over the glass hid the view of the garden.

Anna walked ahead on legs made of jelly and paused at the entrance to the room on the left. It was crowded with two plum-coloured sofas, a large chair and a massive TV. On one of the sofas sat a solid-looking woman in her fifties wearing a collection of gold bangles, earrings and chains and a cream, lace-covered T-shirt. She had the lined face of a smoker, which made Anna think of Sylvie. This was Sally Harper, presumably.

The woman stood up and held out her hand. 'I'm Sally.'

'Hello. I'm Anna.' She felt Sally's fingers trembling, just like hers, as they shook hands.

'You've met Micky.' Sally nodded at her bearded son. 'And this is Lisa.'

Anna glanced over at the young woman in the large chair. She was wearing black leggings and had her legs tucked beneath her. Her thick hair was twisted into a knot on top of her head.

'All right?' Lisa's greeting, like her smile, was hesitant.

Anna nodded at her. She was older than Anna by a couple of years, she guessed, and had the sturdy build of Sally, but her face was so similar to her own, she found it hard not to stare. She couldn't help the involuntary smile that lifted the corners of her mouth.

'Would you like a cup of tea?' Sally gestured towards the kitchen.

'No, I'm fine. Thank you.'

Sally nodded with what looked like relief. Anna knew then that there wasn't going to be an abundance of pleasantries and certainly no offer of a Bakewell tart. This was a necessary chore to be got out of the way. She heeded the warning signs.

'Sit down.'

Anna lowered herself onto the empty sofa and watched as Micky sat down hard on the seat next to his mother, budging the dog into a gap between them. His protectiveness was striking and she thought of Joe coming to collect her from the hospital all those years ago, speaking with his hands on her shoulders. *'It's okay, Anna Bee, I'm here now.'*

She felt all three pairs of eyes scanning her, no doubt searching for any resemblance to the man they had loved and lost as well as looking for any clues as to what she might be after.

'I know this must be really strange—'

'You reckon?' Micky snorted aggressively.

'Micky!' Lisa glared at him and he immediately sat a little further back on the sofa.

Anna guessed that her arrival had been discussed in detail. 'I...' she began falteringly. 'I know you didn't know anything about this, about me, and I didn't know anything about you. Nothing at all. I didn't know who...' The words failed on her tongue. She figured that using the words 'my dad' might be more than this anxious trio could cope with, and this too she understood. 'I never met Michael. I didn't even know his full name until I got the letter from the solicitor a couple of weeks ago.' She saw a flicker of emotion cross Lisa's face.

'What, your mum never told you nothing?' Micky fired back, sounding doubtful.

Anna shook her head. 'No. She didn't. All I ever knew was that he drove a cab and his name was Michael.'

Sally harrumphed at this and Anna wondered if maybe it was in his cab that her parents had met.

'But, what, she's told you all about it now? How convenient! And what I want to know is why does she think it's all right now he's not here to defend himself?'

'Don't start, Micky!' Sally reached for her cigarettes, her weary tone suggesting they'd been over this many times already.

Anna understood Micky's anger, his disappointment at his dad's big secret, but she hadn't expected to be the recipient of his rage. 'It's nothing do with my mum. It was me who got the letter, as I said.'

'Funny, I think it's a lot to do with your mum!' he cut in, and whether intentionally he not, he bared his teeth.

Anna's unease flared at how quick he was to blame her mum, a person he knew nothing about.

I am proud to think that I have another daughter on the earth, a daughter made in love. She mentally reached for the words her dad had written, a salve for moments such as this and something she would keep sewn beneath her heart.

'My mum died when I was nine.'

She let this sink in. Lisa shook her head in sadness and Sally lit her cigarette and took a long, deep draw, letting wisps of blue smoke drift from her mouth and nose. Her shoulders dropped with what looked like relief. Even Micky swallowed this unexpected nugget of information.

'Where did you live? Did you have a stepdad?' Lisa asked.

'Erm...' Anna cursed the emotion that constricted her throat. There was something about being inside a family home that did this to her, a reminder of what she had lost. 'No. No stepdad. I lived with my brother at first in a flat and then with some relatives for a bit and then in care.' She brushed invisible debris from her skirt and kept her eyes downcast.

'That must have been horrible.' She liked Lisa's lack of guile.

'It was sometimes.' The two exchanged a look. Similar-shaped eyes stared back at each other; mouths set in alignment hid sets of neat white teeth just like their dad's and their Nanny Anna's.

Micky took a breath. His voice was softer now, but his words were less forgiving. 'Sorry to be blunt,' he lied, 'but what are you doing here? What is it you want exactly?'

Anna inhaled and spoke slowly. 'I want to say that I understand you must be shocked, and it's true what I said earlier, I'm shocked too.'

Again he interrupted her. 'Yes, we got that, but I mean what are you after? Half the house? Me mum's wedding ring?'

'Micky, please! For God's sake!' Sally sighed, took another drag and rubbed her temples with the thumb and middle finger of her free hand.

Anna stared at him. 'No, nothing like that.' She bit the inside of her mouth and thought about what she did want. 'I suppose I wanted to meet you because, like it or not, you are my half-brother and Lisa is my half-sister and I don't have any family, apart from a cousin.'

'So what? You think you can come here for Christmas? Pull a cracker and get pissed around the telly? Share a bowl of trifle?' He sniffed and laughed.

'No. No, I don't expect that.' *Especially not now.*

'Good. You need to understand that just because my dad got his leg over, did the dirty on my mum...' His face became contorted and she wondered if he might cry. 'There's no reason for us to have to pick up the pieces of his mistake, no reason why we have to see you or sit here and play happy bloody families!'

Anna found it hard to witness his visceral distress. It wasn't his fault. She knew what it felt like when you'd thought life was going to give you roses and instead it delivered you a box full of disappointment. She chose not to mention her firmly held belief that Michael and her mum had been in love and if circumstances and the timing had been a little different... She also decided not to remind Micky how lucky he'd been to get such a big share of their dad. What wouldn't she have given for twenty-plus years of contact, instead of the measly hour or so when she'd been too young to register it?

'You're right, Micky. I don't know what I expected coming here, but I felt it was important that you knew I had never met Michael. He wasn't deceitful like that and he obviously went out of his way to make sure no one knew about me until he'd passed away. He clearly wanted to spare you that upset for as long as he could.'

'Spare himself more like,' Sally murmured.

With each comment, the air in the room felt more oppressive. Anna decided it was time to leave. A part of her had hoped that her older brother and sister might welcome her with open arms, but this had proved to be yet another instance when she'd expected roses, yet another family that shared her bloodline but with whom she had no connection. She pictured Jordan, the one good thing to have come from her encounter with her aunt and uncle. Was this how it was always going to be? she wondered. Would she ever have a family that she could call her own? Or would there always be that sense that she was like sticks on the river, a passenger in her own life?

As she cleared her throat and prepared to bid everyone goodbye, a stuttered mewling came from the corner of the room. It made her jump. The dog lifted his head from his paws and stared in the direction of the noise. Lisa swung her legs from the sofa. 'Baby monitor. That's Kaylee, my little one.'

'Ah.' Anna smiled at her.

'Come and see her if you like?' Lisa asked casually from the door.

Anna did like. Ignoring the lengthened necks and narrowed lips of Micky and his mother, she followed Lisa up the stairs, conscious of the handrail being a little loose along the wall, which maybe her dad had meant to tighten, letting her palm linger on the painted wood that must have known his touch.

Lisa cooed as she walked into the little room at the top of the stairs. 'Here she is.' She turned to Anna, her face lit with pride. 'She's four months. My dad never met her. I'm sad about that.' She reached down into the cot, lifted the pink bundle, took her in her arms and kissed her round face.

Tell me about it... 'You'll just have to make sure you tell her all about him.'

'I will.' Lisa nodded and kissed her daughter again. 'Her dad's in the army. He's away at the moment, worse luck. We're only kind of together – we keep getting back together and splitting up – but I miss him even so.'

'That must be horrible, him being away.'

'It is.' Lisa held her gaze. 'Sometimes. Do you want to hold her?'

'Oh! Really?' Anna felt a little overcome by the offer, as well as wary of doing it wrong.

'Yeah! Course! You're her auntie after all.' Lisa lifted her elbow and carefully passed baby Kaylee into Anna's arms.

'She's lovely. Happy little thing.' Anna smiled at her niece.

'That's cos she recognises you probably. We look alike, don't we?'

Lisa's words caught her off guard. Anna hadn't expected to cry, hadn't thought that she would be so deeply affected by the feel of the infant, trusting and compliant in the arms of her relative. Her tears slowly snaked their way into her mouth.

'Yes. Yes, we do. God, I'm sorry, Lisa, don't know what's wrong with me!' She masked her embarrassment with a burst of laughter, her eyes fixed on the little one. The unexpected strength of connection to this young woman and her baby left her feeling quite overwhelmed.

Lisa reached out and squeezed her arm. 'Is there anything you would like of Dad's?'

Anna again felt dazed by the generosity of her half-sister, not only in what she was offering but also in the way she'd chosen to say 'Dad's' and not 'my dad's'.

'If it's okay...' She hesitated. 'I'd quite like to see a photograph.'

'A photograph?' Lisa looked at her quizzically, as if she'd expected something quite different.

Anna nodded. 'I... I've never seen him. I don't know what he looks like.'

'Oh God.' Lisa squeezed her arm again. 'Hang on.' She dashed from the room.

Anna walked to the window with Kaylee in her arms. She inhaled the scent of the child and smiled. Realisation dawned. This was when she would feel like she belonged somewhere or to someone. This is what would anchor her to a family – when she became a mum.

She closed her eyes, picturing the way her mum used to look at her when she kissed her goodnight or greeted her in the morning. It was a look that told her that her life was complete, that her child made her happy, beyond happy! And this, Anna now knew, was what she wanted: her own baby that she could love to the moon and back and who would love her in return.

The future father of her child was out there somewhere. The man who would make her world sunny even in the rain and who would give her the family she craved. 'I know you're out there,' she whispered to the strip of sky visible over the muddle of rooftops. Even the thought was enough to fill her with a bubble of excitement.

'Here we go. I've found a couple.'

Lisa took Kaylee and handed Anna two framed pictures, one of which had a photo-booth snapshot tucked into the bottom corner. One photo was of Sally and Michael on their wedding day, a black and white picture that showed his grainy face smiling at his new bride. He was tall and dark and looked so young. The next one was of him on holiday, holding Micky or Lisa on his lap, both of them enjoying a melting ice cream with messy faces. This image sent a flicker of jealousy through her. But the final picture, the little rectangle that had been shoved into the frame as an afterthought, was the one that drew her attention. It was nothing more than a slightly blurred image taken in a photo booth, but it showed her dad staring straight into the camera and it felt like he was looking at her.

'This is wonderful!' She beamed, running her fingertip over his face.

'You can have it.'

'Really? I can keep it?' She hardly dared ask for fear Lisa might change her mind.

'Course you can.' Lisa nodded, watching as Anna peeled it carefully from the frame. 'They'll not notice.' She jerked her head towards the stairs.

'I wish...'

'You wish what?'

'I wish I knew the circumstances of how they met, my mum and Michael. Maybe Micky is right, it was no more than a quick, irrelevant thing, and maybe he only wrote to me because he felt guilty. I accept that I'll never know, but it would make a difference to me.'

'Course it would. I understand that. And if it helps at all…' Lisa lowered her voice again. 'He was a good man, a loyal man and if ever he had had a change of heart, his loyalty, his sense of duty would have been the thing that won out.'

Anna recognised the guts it must have taken to say this and once again felt immensely grateful for Lisa's generosity. 'Thank you, Lisa, for everything.' She walked forward and held her half-sister in her arms. They were both a little awed by the enormity of this new chapter in their lives. 'I can't tell you how much this picture means to me.'

'Will I see you again, do you think?' Lisa asked, quietly.

'Of course you will,' Anna answered with certainty.

Anna sat on the bus with all sorts of emotions swirling in her head. She held the precious picture in the palm of her hand and stared at it the whole journey.

Michael Harper's dark hair was smoothed back over a high forehead that resembled her own, and his smiling eyes, the same shape as hers, crinkled at the sides with kindness. But that wasn't the main source of her fascination. No, it was his mouth that she couldn't stop staring at. In the photo his mouth was open, his tongue was poking out and it was curled, indisputably curled.

You were right, Joe! This is my dad. My dad, Michael. He has dark hair like mine and he can curl his tongue.

As soon as she got home, she grabbed her plastic wallet of

letters from the shelf in the corner, sat down at the table for two and began to write.

Dear Fifi and Fox,

How can I say this? I have always loved the idea of you, but now I know that I am ready for you! I am ready for you, my darlings! And this thought fills me with so much happiness, I feel I might explode!

I met my niece today – yes, I have a niece! Her name is Kaylee. And as soon as I held her, I knew that what I want more than anything in the world now is to be a mum. Your mum! So get ready, cos I'm properly on the lookout for your dad now.

I can't wait to meet you, can't wait to hold you, can't wait to make you real.

I love you! I love you! I love you!

Mummy x

Eleven

Anna stepped into the street outside Villiers House. One quick glance up and down the pavement and she decided to swerve lunch. The crowds and chaos told her that to venture forth would be more trouble than it was worth. With London hosting Euro 96, the streets were uncomfortably rammed with football-mad tourists, many of them sporting their country's colours and in boisterous, holiday mood.

She sighed and rubbed her stomach, deciding she'd make a fresh pot of coffee and sip that through the afternoon to keep her hunger at bay. She walked slowly across the foyer and into the ancient lift, taking a deep breath, preparing to face the big window of her imagination as usual. She had now resorted to alphabetising the things she saw in the sky *from* the imaginary window: flower varieties, insects in the grass, even the names of her fictional neighbours. It wasn't the easiest of rules: *T – in the sky* – had caused her angst until *Tornado!* had sprung into her mind very early one morning, as she'd visited the loo. Truth was, she quite enjoyed the challenge.

Where was I? My imaginary neighbour's grandsons, that's right…

W... William.

X... Xavier.

Y... Y...

'Hold the lift!' a man called in a posh voice, drawing her from her mind puzzle.

She looked up to see the man reaching out with his brown-paper lunch bag, as if it were a baton he had to pass mid relay. She watched with increasing anxiety as he ran across the ornate lobby and towards the closing doors of the lift cage.

'Shit,' she muttered under her breath, much preferring to ride alone.

Bending forward, she pressed the 'Door Close' button over and over, hoping it would react quicker than he could run. She wanted to spare them both the inevitable awkward small talk that came with being confined together in a lift, or, worse, the embarrassed silence as they each picked a spot in the little cube and stared at it, wondering why it always seemed to take twice as long to shuffle between floors when you were in there with a stranger.

Her repeated pressing had no effect. With the arm of his navy suit lunging through the doors, the running man just made it. He slipped through the gap with precision timing.

'Sorry! I was trying to figure out which button might hold the doors, but they're all a bit worn.' She wrinkled her nose, feeling her face colour as she lied. 'I'm so used to getting in and pressing the floor I need, so I was a bit thrown. I kind of panicked.' She babbled on, over explaining, trying to make her lie sound more truthful and causing her face to colour even more in the process.

'Please don't worry about it.'

He was certainly posh, with the sort of cut-glass accent that always made her feel very conscious of her own blunt London twang. He held up his palm with two fingers raised, as if anointing a subject, and took the spot at the back of the lift, in the corner.

She felt his presence keenly, hating that he was behind her and that she couldn't see him. She wondered if he was looking at her and just the idea of that was enough to cause her shoulders to tense and her nerves to bite.

'Although, in my defence, the whole building is like one of those thatch-roofed cottages – really cutesy to look at, nice to have a pub lunch opposite on a day out, but to live in them is difficult. I've read about them.' *Shut up, Anna! You're just making it worse!*

'I see.' Thankfully he sounded less than interested and she hoped he would get out soon, leaving her in peace for at least the last couple of floors.

Y... Y... Yuri. His grandpa was a space fan, named after Gagarin...

His cough threw her concentration.

'There's no storage in them either,' she wittered on, her eyes closed in embarrassment. *For God's sake, shut up, Anna!* 'Leaky pipes, rats in the roof, low beams!' She raised her palms as if to indicate that the list was endless.

'Sorry...' He paused. 'But were you thinking of buying one?' His tone suggested he was trying to keep up.

'No! No.' She gave a small giggle. *If only.* 'I think my property-buying days are a little ahead of me. I live in a studio/cupboard in Fulham. Shitty but cheap – you know the kind of thing. But I am saving.' She smiled. 'And at my present rate, I should be good to go in about thirty years, given current London prices.'

There was a moment of silence before he decided to speak.

'I'm not sure that's strictly true, you know.'

His voice was beautiful, commanding – a newsreader's voice that wrapped her in velvet and made her think of the finer things in life.

'What isn't?' She looked at him briefly over her shoulder. Closer scrutiny of his face provided a pleasant surprise, a delight! *Nice-looking. Open smile. Short, dark, curly hair. He's tall. Lovely suit. White shirt, silk tie. Kind face, big eyes, long lashes...* She pulled her shoulders back and smoothed her hair around her face.

'I think it most unlikely that all thatched roofs have rats, and besides, I rather like this building,' he continued.

She followed his gaze and looked up at the art deco panelling, imagining it once picked out in gilt, though it was now very faded. 'I didn't say I didn't like the building,' she emphasised. 'I'm just saying I don't think it's easy to work in. It's draughty even in good weather, the wind rattles through the windows and I suspect this lift is one button-press away from plummeting to earth. And in case you are picturing that very scenario, my cousin lives in New York, where they have plenty of skyscrapers.'

'So I believe.' He smiled.

'He told me that it's pointless trying to jump before the lift hits the bottom – something to do with the rate of acceleration and how high you can jump, I don't remember exactly – but it would only help you by millimetres at the most. Apparently.' She spoke quickly, unnerved by the whole subject but smiling at the thought of Jordan and Levi, two of her favourite people on the planet. 'Anyway, it wouldn't be enough to save your ankles from shattering.'

She heard his soft burst of laughter over her shoulder. A nice laugh, not boisterous or irritatingly pitched or snorty or booming, just nice...

'Well, aren't you full of joy?' he said as the lift approached the sixth floor.

She took a step towards the doors, fighting the urge to turn and look at him one more time. She wondered if their paths might cross again and was surprised to realise that she hoped they would. The rumble of hunger in her stomach had been replaced by something else, a mixture of desire and excitement. This lift experience had turned out to be far from awful.

'Is that a south London accent?' he asked quickly.

Was he also trying to prolong their interaction? She turned to him, getting the last look she wanted, and nodded her answer. He had good skin, bright eyes and she felt the flutter of attraction deep in her stomach.

'Thought so. Whereabouts are you from?'

'Oh...' She gave an almost imperceptible sigh, raced through various possible answers in her head, then took a deep breath and decided to stop overthinking it. 'Honor Oak Park originally and then I lived in Leytonstone, so east London too, not just south. You know it?' she asked over her shoulder, waiting for the doors to open.

'No.' He shook his head.

The lift pinged its arrival.

Well, that's that then! Goodbye, Lift Man, lovely posh Lift Man...

Two or three seconds passed and the doors had yet to open. Anna felt a flash of unease and her adrenalin spiked. She banged on the doors with the heel of her palm. *Open! I need you to open now! I'm hot and I can't breathe properly!*

Reaching over, she pressed the button for the sixth floor repeatedly. Nothing happened. She looked over at the man in the corner, trying to hide the flare of panic that threatened and no longer interested in finding him attractive – she needed his help.

'Can you kick them?' she asked.

'You want me to kick the doors?'

'Yes!' She pointed towards them in case he might be in any doubt about which doors she was referring to.

'I don't know what you think kicking them might achieve?'

'I want them to open!' She tried her best to keep the hysteria from her voice.

'I know that. I'm just not sure kicking them is the best policy.' He leant over and pressed the enamelled button with the number six on it.

'Oh, that's a good idea, press the floor and see if they open! Why didn't I think of that?' She slapped her forehead. 'Oh, wait a minute, I did!'

'Do you want me to help you or not?'

'Yes. Yes, I do! But you are not helping!' She raised her voice and ran her palm over her forehead. 'You are only hoping that your button-pressing skills might be superior to mine, but clearly they aren't, as we are still in the lift!'

'What's your name?' he asked quietly.

She took several deep breaths and held his gaze. 'Anna.'

'Anna what?'

'Anna Cole.'

She had to admit that it made her feel better, concentrating on him and the calming rhythm of his voice, his eyes that held hers.

'I'm Theo. And would I be right in guessing that you're not keen on being stuck in here?'

She looked at him and nodded, feeling the dots of sweat on

her top lip. 'I don't…' She took a breath. 'I don't like dark places or small spaces.'

'Okay.' He smiled at her, as if they were chatting in quite normal circumstances, as if they had all the time in the world. 'I can understand that, Anna Cole, but trust me, you have absolutely nothing to feel worried about. These lifts have, er, up-to-the-minute devices fitted, which means that no matter what happens to the doors or the lift itself, it's impossible for it to plummet and impossible for us to get stuck for any length of time. There is an alarm—'

'There is?' Anna tucked her hair behind her ear and cocked her head to one side, listening. This was very, very good news. 'I can't hear it.'

Theo, her lift buddy, smiled. 'That's because it's a, um, silent alarm! It's triggered by a sensor that goes straight to the lift-maintenance company and they will have someone on their way right now to get us moving. So as I say, you have absolutely nothing to worry about.'

'Do… Do they ever run out of air?' She toyed with the collar of her shirt and looked up to the mirrored ceiling, as if the air might be visible and leaking away.

'No. That can't happen.' He spoke gently. 'There are grates that allow air to circulate and the lift shaft takes a feed directly from the street, so it's as good as being outside.'

'Okay.' She closed her eyes briefly and felt her pulse calm.

'Why don't you stand back a bit?' He beckoned her towards the back wall. 'I'm just going to call out through the door and let someone know that we're in here.'

'But the maintenance man is on his way, isn't he? He'll know we're in here, right, like you said?'

'Yes, absolutely, but the people in the building might not know yet, so it's good to let them know too.' He sounded assured. Anna watched as he raised his knuckles and knocked loudly. 'Helloo!' he called.

The returning knock was instant.

He turned to her and smiled. 'See? There are people only feet away figuring out how to get the doors open. We'll be free in no time.'

'Okay. Okay.' She nodded, rubbing her damp palms on her skirt.

Theo leant against the rail that ran round the lift at hip height. 'Are you hungry? I have my sandwich here.'

She watched as he opened his brown paper bag to reveal a paper plate on which sat two thick slices of crusty white bread stuffed with thinly sliced ham and a smear of mustard. Her mouth watered and her stomach growled in response. He took out one of the triangles and bit into it, then handed her the bag.

'Are you sure?' She took the bag from his outstretched hand. It was a very kind thing to do and she was famished.

'Of course!' He nodded, chewing and swallowing his lunch.

'This is good.' She smiled with her mouth full. 'Thank you.'

'You're welcome. I'd have brought napkins and pudding had I known I wasn't going to be dining alone.'

'Oh, cake – you should have got cake!' she enthused, distracted now. 'I do love a bit of cake.' She pictured a Victoria sandwich fit for a wedding.

'So, where do you work?' she asked, daintily nibbling on the crust and popping stray crumbs into her mouth with her finger.

'Top floor.' He pointed upwards. 'The one above you.'

'Oh, the property company? Is that right? I don't really know who does what, it just seems like there are hundreds of blue suits coming in and out all day.'

'Yes, property and land and renovations,' he offered loosely. 'Rooting out rats from thatched roofs, dealing with leaky pipes and rattly windows...'

You're funny. I like that.

'Do you like it there?' She smiled, licking butter, mustard and crumbs from her fingers. Had she been alone, she would have wolfed down the lot in a few bites.

'I like it on some days and on others not so much.'

'What is it you do?'

'A bit of everything.'

'I see.' She rolled her eyes. 'Could you be any more vague?'

Theo laughed. 'And what is it you do on the sixth floor?'

'I'm the receptionist. I answer the phone and put through calls to the brokers and keep the diary and take messages and make tea for visitors, sort the post. A bit of everything.' She looked up at him.

'I get the gist!' He laughed.

'What's taking them so long?' Anna sighed and lowered herself onto the floor, placing the paper plate on her lap, an option she had discounted only minutes earlier but which now seemed like a good idea.

'They'll be working on it.'

'I hope so.' She again took a deep breath and exhaled. 'I think the people who own this building need to spend some money. It's terrible the way they charge inflated rents but don't really care about their tenants. It's the same where I live. I often wonder how much my landlord makes – it wouldn't be too big a deal to get the halls and stairways cleaned. I try my best, but...' She shrugged. 'I bet in the landlord's offices they've got central heating and luxury carpets and draught-free windows, while idiots like us shiver in chilly hallways and get stuck in the lift!' She banged the wall. 'Not that I can moan, our office is totally fitted out – it's beautiful, very modern. Horrible artwork though.'

'Do you like art?'

She saw the optimism in his eyes and knew that she was going to disappoint. She was probably not the kind of girl he usually hung out with – if she had to guess, girls who travelled, visited art galleries, posh girls who grew up in houses where ice cubes were plentiful. 'Not really. I don't know much about it.'

A knocking could be heard above their heads. Her body stiffened involuntarily and she placed her hand on her throat.

'Nothing to worry about, Anna. That's just a signal to us that they're nearly done.'

'Okay.' She believed him and it helped. She liked the way her name sounded on his lips.

'So what took you to Fulham?' He sat down next to her and, far from being awkward, it felt nice, natural, as if they were mates.

'Well, what took me there was a job and what kept me there was a boy, for a while, but now what keeps me there is that I know the place and it's affordable.' She rolled her eyes and shoved the last of the sandwich into her mouth.

'It didn't work out with the boy?'

He was prying, but she didn't mind. She had after all volunteered more information than she would have ordinarily, and she'd eaten half of his sandwich. There was something about being in this bubble…

'It was never going to work out,' she admitted with a note

of sadness. 'He was lovely, is lovely, just not for me. I wish him well, you know?'

He nodded.

'Ned is beautiful-looking and sweet, but there just wasn't that...' She hesitated, searching for the right word.

'Spark?'

'Yeah, I guess so. No spark.' She bit her lip. 'I was going to say chemistry, but spark is good. His parents loved me and that made it harder to end it. They became part of the package and it kind of ropes you in, doesn't it?' She continued without waiting for an answer. 'But we were mismatched in just about every way, really.'

'Ah, he was probably a glass of champagne – exciting, glamorous – but you don't want a glass of champagne.'

'I don't?' She laughed. *This is funny, because you are like a glass of champagne sipped on a veranda in the sunshine! You're like James bloody Bond!*

'No. You want a man who is like a cup of tea.'

Anna stared at him. 'Actually, sorry to disappoint you, but he wasn't that glamorous and I think I might like to meet a glass of champagne!'

Theo shook his head. 'No, you don't. Champagne is for high days and holidays – people don't always have a fancy for it. But a good cup of tea? There isn't a day in the year when it isn't the best thing to have first thing in the morning. A cup of tea warms your bones on a cold day and can bring you close together as you sit and chat. Trust me, you want to find a cup of tea.'

Anna pulled her head back on her shoulders and narrowed her eyes at him. 'Hmmm...' She twisted her lips in contemplation. 'Couldn't I have both?'

Theo laughed. 'I'm not sure.'

She watched, curious, as he surreptitiously placed his fingers under the lapel of his suit jacket and ran his fingers over something bright that looked like it was attached to a little gold safety pin. 'What's that?' she asked, nodding towards it.

'Oh…' He hesitated, then turned over his lapel to reveal a cluster of bright feathers and a shiny red glass bead, all, as she'd suspected, seated on a gold safety pin. She'd never seen anything like it. 'It's a fishing fly.'

'Why have you got a fishing fly hidden on your jacket?' she said in a low voice, figuring that if it was important enough for him to keep it out of sight, there might be a serious reason.

'Well, long story short, someone I cared about, a kind of teacher actually, gave it to me when I was very young and it's a symbol, I suppose, a reminder to look forward when things feel tricky. Something like that.' He shrugged and laughed, clearly trying to mask his self-consciousness.

'My mum did something similar for me,' Anna said. 'The alphabet game.'

'The alphabet game?'

'Yes. It's too complicated to explain now, but I think you're lucky to have had someone like that reminding you of what's important.'

'I was.' He blinked. 'Very lucky.'

There was a second when a needle of embarrassment lanced the promise of more revelations and she decided not to ask anything further. They were strangers, after all.

She scrunched the brown paper bag into a ball and handed it back to him, emboldened, flirtatious and almost forgetting their predicament. He took it and laughed. She wiped her hands on her skirt. This Theo fella was unlike other men she knew. He wasn't the easy, coming-on-to-her type she met in the pub, men like Ned; and nor was he the slick, money-chasing, hardened workaholic type she made coffee for on the sixth floor. Anna realised that for the first time in as long as she could remember she was interested.

'It's strange, isn't it, how someone can appear so out of your league and yet when you get them, live with them, they can lose their gloss a bit.'

'Gosh, what a horrid prospect.'

'I know.' She held his gaze. 'But that was kind of the truth. Once I lived with Ned, I didn't want to end up with him. He was…' She checked herself and smiled briefly, falsely, at Theo.

'He was what?'

She tipped her head back and rested it on the wall, looking up at the ceiling. 'He was not enough.' She stared up at the reflection of the two of them, sitting side by side in the little box. It was a strange environment.

'So if things didn't work out with Super Ned, why didn't you go back to your parents?' he asked.

She noted the 'Super Ned', as if Theo felt he couldn't possibly measure up to someone like that. 'The answer to that question would take far longer than we have, I hope. That is if we ever get out!' She exhaled sharply, nerves beginning to bite again.

'We haven't been here that long.'

'It bloody feels like it.'

'Well, charming!'

They both laughed.

Theo cleared his throat and she felt the weight of his nerves even before he spoke. 'Before we do get out and scuttle off to our respective floors, I wanted to ask, how… how about we go out for a drink sometime?' He concentrated on the balled paper bag in his palm.

'A drink?' She looked at him, excited and apprehensive at the prospect of going out with a posh bloke like Theo, a bloke quite unlike any other she knew.

And then a wave of guilt hit.

'There's something I need to confess and then you can decide whether you still want that drink.'

'I'm listening,' he almost whispered.

Anna patted her legs and gave a small nod. 'I wasn't trying to hold the lift. I was trying to make it go before you made it. I wanted to be in the lift on my own.'

'That's disgraceful behaviour!' He laughed loudly. 'Who would admit that?' He laughed again.

'I like to have everything out in the open,' she explained.

'Well, in that case I might as well tell you that I didn't want you to accept half of my sandwich, never thought in a million years you would – I'm still bloody starving!'

It was Anna's turn to laugh. 'Oh God, I feel awful!' She placed her hand over her mouth.

'So you should.' He smiled.

There was a moment, a second or two when they looked at each other and something occurred, a wordless exchange that gave meaning and weight to the beat of silence. Anna felt a jolt of anticipation.

Just as their eyes locked, the doors began to creak and light filtered into the lift. They were greeted by a smattering of app-lause. The lift was stuck halfway between two floors. They both jumped to their feet and stared at the ankles of their rescuers. The maintenance man dipped down and smiled, holding a jemmy bar. The girl from the lobby had her arms wrapped around a bucket – Anna wasn't sure why.

'Ah, Theo! Just your luck, eh?' The maintenance man reached in with both hands and passed down a ladder.

Theo fed it into the space, propped it along the inside wall and stood back.

'You climb up, Anna. I'll hold the ladder. Bernie will help you at the top.'

'Don't—'

'Don't what? Forget about our drink? Don't worry, I won't.'

'No! I was going to say, don't look up my skirt.' She smiled as she trod hesitantly onto the rickety rungs and was met by more claps from her colleagues and the several people who'd been waiting by the lift. She flushed.

'Are you all right?' Bernie asked.

'Yes, I am, thank you. It could have been a lot worse.'

'It could that.' Bernie sighed. 'An old lift like this one, you never know how it's going to react. You might have been one tiny cog, one little pin away from plummeting to earth.' He whistled, shaking his head and pointing downwards.

Anna's gut churned at the prospect. 'Actually, that can't happen.' She stood tall, smoothing creases from her top before fixing her hair. 'These lifts are fitted with the latest devices that make it impossible to plummet.'

Bernie laughed out loud. 'Who told you that?'

Anna looked at Theo, who seemed to have changed colour. 'He did.'

'I didn't want you to panic,' he said.

She stared at him. 'So is there a sensor that alerts the lift man when someone is in trouble?'

Theo shook his head and wrinkled his nose. Busted.

'The lift man?' Bernie laughed again. 'Best you can hope for is me with me jemmy and Nicola here with her bucket!'

'What is the bucket for?' Theo asked.

'In case anyone was desperate for the loo,' Nicola explained, stepping forward with her pail at arm's length.

'Sweet Lord above.' Anna put her hands on her hips. 'I've a good mind to contact the landlord and give him a piece of my mind!'

'He is the landlord,' said Bernie, pointing at Theo. 'His dad owns Villiers House and it was his grandad's before that.'

'You have got to be kidding me!' She turned to him, trying to recall exactly what derogatory remarks she had made about the owners of the building and feeling her face flush.

'I can assure you we really do look after the building. It's important.'

'So tell me, do you have central heating and luxury carpets in your office?'

'Yes.' He nodded. 'Yes, we do.'

'I knew it!' She thumped his chest. 'Was any of that for real? Or were you just trying to keep me calm? Do you still want to take me for a drink?'

Theo looked at her, an earnest expression on his face. 'Yes. How about after work? I'll meet you downstairs, say 6.30?'

'Sure. I might be a little late as I'll be taking the stairs.' She smiled at him and made her way across the sixth-floor foyer.

★ ★ ★

It was now four weeks to the day that Anna and Theo had had their first date. Anna was sitting at the little table in the corner of the coffee shop, the one where they'd rendezvoused pretty much every evening for the last month. She tapped her watch, narrowed her eyes and made the most irritated face she could muster. 'You're late.' It was difficult to pull off because her joy at seeing him walk towards her across the coffee shop split her face in two. Her smile was wide and instinctive. It still felt surreal that this handsome, suited man was there on her account. *Me! He is here for me! Look at me now, Tracy Fitchett!* The words jumped into her thoughts as her stomach flipped in joy.

'Yes, that's exactly what I need!' Theo sighed and ran his hand over his one-day-old stubble. 'You giving me grief over my timekeeping too.' He pulled a face.

He had given her some idea of the irritations of working for his bully of a dad, but she had yet to admit to him that it didn't sound all bad. After all, he had his own swanky office, guaranteed employment and, as he had once claimed, he was probably the only person who could get away with sliding down the banisters of Villiers House, should the fancy take him.

'Tough day at the office?' She inhaled the scent of him as he sat down opposite. This desire to ingest the smell of him was something new for her. His scent was strongest at his temples and whenever they kissed she gulped down lungfuls of it, finding it quite intoxicating.

'You could say that. I'm afraid I might be bad company tonight.'

'And this would be different from any other night how?' she asked with one eyebrow raised.

I would rather be with you in silence than with the finest storyteller at the top of his game. I would happily watch you sleep. You are all I need, Theo. I want to be next to you, I want to touch you. That is enough.

This was how far they had advanced, able to jest and with no need to be on their best behaviour. The shot of happiness that fired through her veins at the sight of him was just as electrifying tonight as it had been every night since they'd met. She kept waiting to see if that feeling would lessen, checking in with herself after each meeting and at the end of every telephone call. But it hadn't. If anything, the more she saw him, the more she liked him. This was the polar opposite of every other relationship she'd had, where her interest peaked early and was then swiftly followed by a short, awkward descent to goodbye. She remembered discussing as much with Melissa, back before she got together with Ned, explaining how her excitement at meeting someone new quickly turned into boredom and then fear at the prospect of a dull life ahead. This was different. For the first time ever she could clearly picture sitting with Theo night after night, knowing they would never run out of things to say and if they did then silence would do just fine.

Things felt easy. There was none of the game-playing or sub-terfuge that Lisa had informed her was vital in these early days. The two women had sat side by side on Anna's bed with Kaylee napping between them and she had listened, giggling and aghast at her half-sister's advice.

'You have to be cool with him.'

'Really?'

'Yes! Really!'

Anna hid her face in her hands. 'Then I'm scuppered. I have never been cool about anything, ever in my whole life. I am the exact opposite of cool!'

'Well, figure it out! If this bloke Theodopadoodah is as posh as you say, he'll be used to getting everything his own way and having birds falling at his feet, so you need to make yourself different. You can't be like the others – he has to think you're not interested and fight for you.'

Anna doubled over, laughing into her hand, stifling the sound so as not to disturb Kaylee. 'Where do you get your information?'

'You can laugh, but I know what I'm talking about.' Lisa sipped her tea.

'I'm laughing because there is so much that is hysterical about your statement that I don't know where to start!'

Lisa gave a mock humph.

'Firstly, Lis, the idea of him fighting for me makes him sound like my knight in shining armour and I don't need a knight, I want a friend, a lover, someone I can trust. Secondly, he is posh, but he doesn't seem like the kind of bloke who is used to getting everything his own way – he is lovely and kind of flawed, hesitant.' She smiled at the image of him staring at the floor, more shy than cocky. 'Plus I can almost guarantee that I am already very different from any bird he has ever been out with. He's used to Sloaney types, girls with names like Felicity or Mirabelle. And finally, at the risk of bursting your bubble, I'm sorry to say that I think it all might be a bit late. We might only have been seeing each other for a few weeks, but I am as keen as mustard and he knows it.'

'Well...' Lisa drained her mug. 'Don't say I didn't warn you and don't make me remind you of this conversation when it all goes tits up. And don't ever ask for my expert advice again.' She wagged her finger for extra gravitas.

Anna smiled at her. 'Remind me how things are going with Kaylee's dad?'

Lisa made a 'ttch' noise with her tongue against her teeth.

'Haven't heard from him, but I hear he's been seeing his ex, the bastard.'

'Have you tried treating him mean, being cool, making him fight for you?' she suggested.

'Oh sod off, smart arse!' Lisa sank down on the bed with her arms folded across her chest.

Anna scrunched up her eyes and smiled affectionately at the woman she had come to love.

Far from treating Theo mean to keep him keen, Anna revelled in the way the two of them had fallen for each other so quickly and so deeply. They did nothing to hide their mutual joy at being together and she knew that their happiness shone like an aura around them; everyone commented on it. Melissa had teased her, pointing out the colouring of her cheeks when she mentioned him, and Jordan had interrogated her over the phone.

'So, the big question is, have you consummated your relationship yet?'

'God, Jord, that is typical of you!'

'Because it's important! Let's face it, at the end of the day it doesn't really matter what they look like or how well they can wine and dine you, if when you get into the sack you are left feeling a bit bleurgh.'

Anna thought about their time together and blushed. The truth was, Jordan didn't have to worry, she had not been left feeling a bit bleurgh. Quite the opposite: things felt different, felt... wonderful!

'You know what? It is absolutely none of your business.'

'Oh my God! That means you have! You absolute tart. I have never been prouder of you!'

She wasn't about to tell Jordan this, but in solitary moments these days, Anna often found herself closing her eyes and trying to re-create the feeling of peace that engulfed her when she woke in Theo's arms. Her mind had gone all fuzzy and distracted and everything else – food, sleep, friends – had been relegated.

Even now, sitting across from him in the coffee shop, she ached for the feel of his skin next to hers. But he looked exhausted and she didn't want to back him into a corner. 'Shall we not bother tonight, if you're tired?' she said. 'I don't mind,' she lied, looking at him across the table. 'We can go our separate ways if you like, get an early night, reconvene tomorrow after work.' This was their way, to always arrange the next time to meet when they parted.

The way his hand darted towards hers in something close to panic sent a ripple of exhilaration right through her. He held her fingers tightly. 'Or…' He paused, meeting and holding her gaze. 'How about we go to your flat and open a large bottle of wine.'

Going back to her flat had become their thing and he had early on confided that he had never taken a girl to his home in Barnes.

Anna nodded. 'That would be lovely.' She unhooked her hand-bag from the back of her chair and swallowed the firecrackers of joy that bounced in her stomach.

Following him outside into the rain-soaked street, she watched as he shot his arm into the air and called, 'Taxi!' His confident tone and cut-glass vowels echoed like music in her ears; she could happily listen to him all day.

They stood quietly on the kerb as the rain fell around them, Anna with her hair stuck to her face. She looked up at the set of his jaw, his masculine profile, as he stared down cab drivers, waiting to spot the yellow light of an available taxi that would ferry them out to Fulham.

Since getting the letter from her dad and meeting Lisa and the others, Anna had lost her unhealthy obsession with black cabs. But it was still a novelty for her to jump into the back of one without giving heed to the cost. Theo, on the other hand, was clearly comfortable in this mode of transport. She suspected he was someone who had never had to delve down the back of the sofa cushions, squeeze the bottom of trouser pockets in the wardrobe or squirrel around in a bits-and-bobs drawer looking for coins to make up the bus fare. They were worlds apart and yet this didn't feel like a barrier, in fact just the opposite. It felt as if they could talk and talk for infinity and not ever run out of things to say – they had so much to learn about the other. Anna wasn't sure if it was fact or her imagination, but it seemed to her that everything Theo had to say was astute. Each night before falling asleep she would go over what he'd said and spin his words into a glittering spiral that danced above her head.

Finally a taxi drew up in front of them and they hopped in, sitting close together on the back seat with steam rising from their damp clothes.

She nestled into him. 'My dad was a taxi driver.'

'I didn't know that. You don't mention your family much.'

'Well hello, kettle!' She laid her head on his shoulder and felt the quiver of his laughter.

They sat in uncharacteristic quiet as the cab drove out of the City. Theo held her hand and placed their knot of conjoined fingers on his thigh, where it rested comfortably. They stared out of their respective windows, taking in the familiar landmarks that to Anna seemed particularly handsome tonight, seen though the hazy filter of the storm. When she was with Theo everything felt brand-new and fascinating and there was nowhere on earth she would rather be. This in itself was a novelty as she had spent much of her life wishing she was somewhere else.

She turned to look at him and realised that, despite the rain, she felt warm, happy. *You make it feel sunny for me, Theo, even on the rainiest of days.*

When they got to Fulham, they walked quietly up the stairs and into Anna's flat. Anna reached up to flick the light switch, but Theo caught her wrist. 'No, leave the light off, we'll just have the glow from outside.'

'I… I don't like the dark,' she managed.

'Me either.' He laughed. 'But you've got me and I've got you, so we don't have to worry. Not tonight.'

'I don't worry, not when I'm with you. I don't worry about a thing. It's like everything is great in my world and it's the first time I've ever felt that way and I really like it!'

Anna tilted her head to receive his kiss, offered gently, as his trembling hands held her face.

'I… I feel the same,' he began, peppering his speech with light kisses on her face. 'It's like I know everything is going to be okay, because I've got you.'

'You have got me!' She beamed, nuzzling her cheek into his palm.

'There have been times when I was so sad…' He paused. 'No, more than sad – depressed. I have lived with depression,' he said frankly. 'My last term at uni, it was hell.'

'Oh, Theo…' Her heart twisted with sadness that he had gone through this, and she wanted more than anything to help him heal. 'I'm sad you went through that.'

'I think I'm probably still going through it, I don't think it's really left me. Not completely.' He bit his cheek. 'It engulfed me, knocked me sideways. I've come out of that phase, certainly, but it's like something that's always there, lurking just around the corner. I get the feeling it's never very far away.'

She thought of Joe and nodded her understanding.

'But for the first time, I can see light and I guess that's why I don't feel as afraid of the dark.'

She looked into his eyes. 'You don't have to be afraid, not any more.'

Theo nodded. 'This thing that's going on with us, Anna...' He hesitated. 'I don't know what it is, but it's...' He exhaled.

'I know!' She smiled into the darkness. 'It really is!'

They kissed again, and stumbled towards the bed at the end of her tiny living zone.

Early the next morning, she eased open first one eye and then the other and was surprised to find Theo already dressed in his suit and rather crumpled shirt.

'Morning, sleepy head.' He bounced back onto the bed and kissed her.

'Goodness me, you're up early!'

'I need to go home and get showered and changed. Important meeting this morning. I'll see you later.' He kissed her again.

She watched him leave and as he closed the door she did a double-take and stared at her boots. They were not where she had discarded them in haste the previous night. Someone – Theo – had unlaced them and set them side by side against the wall, ready for her to slip into. She pictured her mum doing the same with her school shoes and it brought her to tears that someone, this man, this wonderful man, would want to do that for her. There was something familiar and comforting in his kindness, the sort of simple act that she had missed for the longest time.

She sank back onto the pillows with a feeling of utter peace. Reaching into the small drawer of her nightstand, she extracted a notebook and her favourite ink pen of the moment.

Fifi and Fox,

I have found him. I have actually found him! And I am without a shadow of doubt the luckiest girl in the world!

I have found your daddy and he is WONDERFUL! He is so WONDERFUL! And together we are AMAZING!

And my life is a life I never could have dreamt of. How about that?

Mummy x

Twelve

'So where are we going?' She bounced on the back seat of the cab.

'I told you, somewhere special.' He smiled at her.

'I don't know if I'm dressed right.' She looked down at her work skirt and blouse. These things mattered to her. As ridiculous as it was to place such store in something as frivolous as fabric, without the right clothes for the right occasion Anna felt her fragile confidence ebb. Too often she had been the weird girl in the wrong dress, the unfashionable shoes, the second-hand uniform. She didn't want to feel like that ever again.

'Don't worry, you look perfect.' He stared out of the window and she caught a hint of nerves, surprising after ten weeks.

It wasn't until the cab drove over Hammersmith Bridge that the penny dropped. Theo was taking her to his home! Anna sat back on the seat, all too aware of the significance of this but trying not to add to the tension. Theo reached for her hand and the two sat quietly, each lost in thought.

Her first impression of Barnes was that it felt like countryside, far removed from the sort of London suburbs she was familiar with. The high street was quaint yet classy, the pub had a traditional-style swinging sign, and there was even a duck pond. The poshness of his street was, if not unexpected, then certainly undeniable. Anna looked up in awe at his magnificent house and for a second considered staying in the cab. He had only ever been sweet and complimentary about her studio flat and yet all the time he had this to come home to. She cringed, remembering the moment she'd made him lie on her bed with his eyes closed, only allowing him to open them when she'd switched on her much-loved strings of fairy lights.

'Ta-dah! What do you think?' she'd said, bounding over to him.

'I think it's brilliant!' he'd replied, obviously humouring her. 'Like living in a Christmas tree!'

Theo now took her hand and guided her along the gravel path that bisected the close-cut lawn, its borders delineated by rope-edged terracotta tiles. The gravel crunched underfoot. The imposing red-brick Edwardian house was three storeys high. The ground and first floors were fronted by double-height bay windows with ornate leaded panes of glass running along the top. There were windows in the roof space too, where the fascia was framed by white-painted fretwork that matched the wood-work on the pantiled roof of the porch. And on the wide, shiny red front door hung a brass door knocker in the shape of a lion's head.

'Are you okay?' he asked, squeezing her hand tightly.

Anna nodded up at him and this was how they stood for a second or two in acknowledgement of the moment.

'Well, here we are.'

'Yes.' She bit her lip. 'Here we are.'

Over the last couple of months they had chitchatted and snog-ged, drinking wine and laughing into the small hours, but right now, on this damp autumnal evening, they were both aware that frivolity and playfulness couldn't sustain them for ever. They needed to make a choice: to let their relationship run its course or to step it up a gear.

They had reached a crossroads. In one direction was the path back to singledom, with all that they had shared getting stored away as a lovely memory; in the other was something altogether more serious.

Anna held her breath and watched as Theo fished in his pocket for his keys then gently pushed open the front door. She peered inside the grand, square hallway with its ornate tiled floor in shades of stone, petrol blue and coffee. A wide staircase stood to the right, turning abruptly on a half landing over her head. He walked ahead and disappeared into one of the rooms. She heard the soft click of a lamp and then a golden glow drifted back to where she stood, bathing the place in a honey-coloured haze.

Imagine growing up in a house like this! Imagine walking down those stairs every day into this beautiful space! It's another world, a different life. The world of girls called Mirabelle and Felicity.

It was certainly a universe away from the Coles' dingy flat in Honor Oak Park. Anna tried to shake off her familiar feelings of inadequacy, but the sense that she was somewhere she didn't belong wrapped around her like a cloak.

Classical music began to fill the air: the deep bass of woodwind instruments, the aching tone of strings and then the lightness of a flute. It made Anna think of gossamer threads looping through the air, rising higher and higher. Her chest tightened; the sounds were unfamiliar but profoundly moving.

Theo popped his head around the door. 'Grown-up music.'

'I should say.' She smiled nervously.

'I am as you know a massive Guns N' Roses fan, but this is one of my secret favourites – Tchaikovsky's *Romeo and Juliet.*'

'Like the book? She regretted the statement the moment it left her mouth. It had made her sound stupid.

'Yes.' He nodded. 'Just like the book.'

'You know what I meant.' She wrapped her arms around her waist. The sweet sounds made her think of summer and meadows and at the same time unbearable loss.

'Just setting a fire. Kitchen's straight ahead.' He pointed to a door at the end of the hallway. 'There's wine somewhere, glasses too! Go seek.' He smiled, tapped the doorframe and disappeared back inside the room.

Anna stepped forward with caution. Reaching around the door, she found the dimmer switch and twisted it slowly until light shone from the two heavy-looking brass and glass lanterns overhead. Her eyes danced over the acres of work surface, the hand-painted cream-coloured doors of the wooden cupboards, the Aga, the vast fridge and the white china Belfast sink. In the corner stood a wide, scrubbed farmhouse table for eight with a pew against the wall and matching chairs opposite. She hovered in the doorway, gazing at the room, the like of which she had only seen in glossy magazines in the doctor's surgery.

Slowly she walked forward, drawn by the large sash window above the work surface. She stood on the tiled floor and placed her hands on the countertop, staring out into the semi-darkness. She could just make out the shape of some sizeable shrubs, several mature trees and what looked a lot like a fancy shed or summerhouse.

As the music built, the image of her mum standing at the

window of their grotty kitchen and staring out at next-door's brick wall loomed large in Anna's mind. She recalled her mum's words, spoken with longing and regret: '*God, I hate this room. It's so dark. I dream about having a kitchen with a big wide window overlooking a garden, and I'd have it open all of the time, with a lovely breeze coming in and the scent of flowers filling the place. Wouldn't that be lovely, Anna?*'

'It would be lovely, Mum, so lovely,' Anna whispered out loud.

'Right, fire's roaring.' Theo rubbed his hands together as he strolled into the kitchen. He stopped in his tracks. 'Oh, you're crying!'

Anna wiped her eyes with the back of her hand. 'I don't usually cry. In fact hardly ever and never in front of anyone, not for a very long time.'

'What's making you so sad?' Theo's expression was a mixture of concern and embarrassment.

'I have a lot to feel sad about, Theo, and this music is—'

'I'll turn it off.' He turned on his heel.

She grabbed his arm. 'No, don't. It's so beautiful. It's making me feel.'

'I suppose that's the idea.' He held her hand. 'Come on, let's go and sit in front of the fire. I don't think there's anything in the whole wide world that a roaring fire and a glass of wine can't make feel better. Please don't cry.'

'You know, Theo, I want to cry. And I should cry.' She no longer made any attempt to wipe the tears from her cheeks. 'I feel like it's time and there is so much I want to say to you.' She stepped forward. 'I need you to *see* me.'

He nodded. 'I need you to see me too. There is so much I want to say.' He thumbed the skin on the back of her hand.

'We are from very different worlds,' she began.

'And I thank God for that.' He leant forward and kissed her gently on the forehead.

'I'm… I'm weird,' she managed, pulling away to look him in the eye. 'I've always been weird and I've had a weird life. A life I want to tell you about so that I don't have to worry about revealing it to you bit by bit. I think that's best, like ripping off a plaster.' She quoted her friend Melissa. 'I need to do it quick.'

Theo pulled her into his chest and held her tightly. 'Weird? Oh God, Anna, you have no idea…'

She lifted her head and addressed the space beneath his chin. 'Okay, here's an example. When I was a kid I had no friends and I used to think that I'd spoken telepathically with a tiny monkey in a fancy red coat that came into our school playground. He… He was called Porthos.'

'Well, okay, I'll give you that! That is fucking weird.'

And between kisses they laughed loudly.

Still giggling at the description of her monkey confidant, they made their way out of the kitchen and into the sitting room. They dropped down onto the invitingly dense pale wool carpet and propped themselves against the wide base of the light blue sofa. Their bare feet rested on the blue and gold Persian rug and a soft blanket covered their laps as the fire blazed and crackled in the grate.

'This is a beautiful room – did you pick everything? How did you know where to start?'

Theo screwed up his face. 'Ah, actually I can take no credit. A friend of my mother's is an interior designer and I gave her the keys and came back to this!'

'Wow!' That was all she could think of to say. An interior

designer? How mad was that, and a little sad that this was someone else's idea, someone else's taste. She wondered what her posturing Aunt Lizzie would make of the grandeur.

'Yes, wow. I mean, all the pictures and ornaments and what-not are from my parents' house or were my grandpa's, but the furniture and all this...' He picked up the edge of the blanket and let it fall. 'This was all carefully put together with a finer eye than mine.'

Theo reached over and topped up her glass with the nicely warmed red wine. 'So come on then, Miss Anna Cole, give it to me. I'm all ears. We have tonight and tomorrow and the day after that if need be. But rest assured we are not leaving here until you have nothing left unsaid. I shall hold you captive. I want to hear all the things that you want to say to me. The whole lot.'

She sipped her wine, which sent a warm, fruity trickle down her throat. 'I meant what I said about being weird.'

'How weird exactly?'

She pulled a face. 'I do this thing.'

'What thing?'

She gave a small embarrassed laugh and shook her head. 'It sounds odd...'

'Don't be shy. Tell me.'

Anna took a deep breath. 'I go through the alphabet and assign objects, people, names, anything I can, really, to a particular letter. I've always done it and it calms me.'

Theo looked at her quizzically. 'Is that the alphabet game you mentioned that time in the lift? You'll have to explain.'

'Okay, so in here...' She looked around the opulent sitting room. 'I might do colours. A... apple green. B... blue. C... cream. D...'

'Damson!' He pointed at the sash on the rather grand-looking military gent sitting astride a horse in the painting above the fireplace.

'Exactly! And I do that until I've worked my way through the alphabet. And I do it a lot.'

'O-kaay, so do you do it out loud?'

She was glad he hadn't laughed. 'Only if I'm on my own, but mostly I do it in my head. And I can carry the puzzle over to the next time I'm in the same situation, so say I'm in the sandwich shop and am doing fillings but am only able to get to E—'

'Egg and cress, of course,' he said.

'Of course.' She smiled. 'Then the next day I'll start with F.'

'Are you doing it now?' he asked sincerely.

'No. I only do it when I need to and I don't need to right now.'

'Doesn't it crowd your thoughts, get in the way?'

She shook her head. 'Not really. I've been doing it so long, it's second nature, and as I said, I don't do it all of the time.'

'I see.' He nodded. 'Why do you do it?'

Anna pictured herself and her mum in their tiny kitchen and Joe raging in the bedroom next door. '*I want you to go round the room with your eyes and try to think of something in here for every letter of the alphabet. Don't worry if you get the alphabet wrong, but do as many as you can! I'll start you off. A...*'

She took a breath. 'My mum told me it would be a good distraction, my alphabet game, and that when my thoughts were too loud or I felt afraid or I just wanted to pass the time, I should go through the alphabet and find things to match the letters. And she was right. By the time I get to Z, things have usually calmed a little and I've taken time to breathe.' She grinned. 'It's even become part of my name! I was just plain old Anna Cole until my mum gave me Bee as a middle name so I could be ABC.'

'It's not the weirdest thing.' He smiled. 'I can give you weirder. Like…' He looked up at the ceiling and exhaled, as if considering whether to confide in her or not. 'When I told you the other night that I don't like the dark, it's a little more than that. I am a grown-up who is very afraid of the dark.' He clicked his tongue and sipped his wine.

'Me too.' She tilted her head at him. 'So I would do the alphabet game to try and distract me from the fear.' She pictured herself under the blanket in the care home, her eyes screwed tightly shut.

'Do you often feel afraid?' he asked softly.

'Less so now I'm older, I guess. My fears are different. I grew up very poor and I grew up mostly in care.'

'I know this.'

She saw his expression soften and liked that he was kind, empathetic. 'Yes, but that's kind of my starter for ten, reminding you where I've come from, setting the tone – so just let me get the rest of it out, okay?'

'Okay.' He pressed his lips together and held up his right palm.

'My dad died quite recently,' she began. Theo placed his hand loosely on her thigh; clearly it was as much support as he felt he could give without interrupting. 'But loss isn't a stranger to me, in fact it's shaped me, shaped everything. I had a nice life when I was really little. Not a life full of stuff or money.' She glanced again at the grand oil painting. 'Things were hard for us, but I didn't realise how poor we were because I was happy and I was loved. I was so loved.' She smiled at this truth. 'But now I'm older I can look back and see the little clues to just how tough it was for my mum. I remember being about five and feeling really mad because she made me eat a lamb chop with cabbage and carrots while she got to have toast and jam. God, I sulked! Pushed that lump of meat and those veg around the plate until she shouted at me, you know, really shouted, and I shoved it in my mouth. It didn't occur to me that she could only afford enough meat for me and my brother Joe.'

She felt Theo's body stiffen beside her, whether through a misplaced sense of guilt or in distaste she didn't know, but one thing she did know, it was important to give him the details, important he knew every bit of her, background and all.

'That's funny really,' he said. 'I don't think my mother ever knew if I had eaten or not. There was more than the occasional night that I went to bed hungry. Didn't know or didn't care. Not sure which. Anyway, go on.' He rolled his hand.

She noted his wistful tone and was saddened by the comparison, unable to imagine having so much at your disposal but not feeding your child. 'So those were my early years in Honor Oak Park: hard-up but happy. Just me and Mum and my brother Joe.'

Her throat tightened at her next words, which were followed by a gulp of emotion. 'Joe died too.'

'Jesus!' Theo shook his head.

'I know, right? I'm a bundle of laughs with my terrible tales of how crap my life has been!' She took another drink.

'I... I didn't mean to imply that. I was merely thinking how bloody awful it must have been for you.'

It was 'bloody awful'. She mimicked his rounded vowels in her head.

The two sat staring into the fire, both mulling over what she'd just said. It was Anna who eventually broke the silence.

'Joe was different.' She pictured him again, this time lying on the sofa under a greasy sleeping bag. 'He was almost the exact opposite of me, born with so much knowledge, happiness and sparkle and yet everything he did and saw seemed to erase a piece of him. And no matter how much we tried to hold him together, we were powerless. And then the last piece in his puzzle was me and that music box and the day the police came…'

Theo pulled away and lifted her chin so she would look at him. It was as if he needed to see her expression to fully get the measure of her words. 'What do you mean? What music box?'

Anna realised she'd been rambling a little. She drained the last of her wine and set the glass to one side.

'Joe was a heroin addict.' She sniffed. 'Actually, by the time he died, he was an anything addict, whatever he could get hold of, but heroin was his first love. Anyway, the police came to the flat and I had a music box he'd given me open on the bed. He only gave it to me because I made him, and if I hadn't…'

She paused, trying to gather her thoughts.

'I won't forget the way the police came into our home, looking around with their heads held high, confident, as if they were the ones who had a right to be there and not me. They picked things up, turned over cushions, poked through drawers, drawers where my mum had had her hand…'

She sniffed up the tears that had gathered at the back of her throat.

'Then they saw the music box and the woman called to her colleague and pointed and he grinned and she laughed and they picked it up and she said, "Where did you get this?" And

I shrugged and didn't know what to say. And the man snorted and looked at me like I was rubbish and he said, "As if we don't know." And they took it and left and...'

She paused to catch her breath.

'I've thought about it a lot, but it was that music box that linked Joe to a burglary where someone had got hurt. I think it was the last straw for him, the thing that tipped the scales. He hadn't wanted me to have it – he was going to sell it, I guess, get rid of the evidence – but I begged and he gave in. And it was two days later that he... that he...'

Her body folded. The wind had been knocked out of her.

Theo bent forward and wrapped her in his arms. 'It's okay, Anna, it's all okay.'

She shook her head against his chest, clinging onto his shirt with her fingers tightly clenched, trying in vain to hold back the tide of distress that she'd kept at bay for as long as she could remember.

'It's not okay, it will never be okay!' She sobbed. 'Joe walked into the house and I told him the police had been and he barely blinked, as if what I was saying was of no interest. He looked through me, like he didn't know who I was, and I tried to use my mum's soft voice that sometimes made him calmer, but it didn't do anything. He was so thin and he smelt terrible and I thought of what my mum would say – "Wash, Joe! And for God's sake clean your teeth." And then I told him they had taken the music box and... that was the last time I saw him. He didn't say anything, but I can see it now, him disappearing out of the front door in just his shirt, and the back of his jeans all baggy because his bum had vanished.'

She took a massive breath and stared at the carpet. 'He

jumped, Theo! He jumped off the car park in town and he died! He jumped and he left me and I was just a little girl!'

Her tears again interrupted the rhythm of her speech. 'I think about him standing there and I wonder what he thought about as he looked down at the streets, the cars, I wonder if he thought of me. If he… If he forgave me. I didn't know the music box was stolen! I begged him to let me have it and I could tell he wasn't sure, but I pushed and he gave in because he loved me, but I should have hidden it. I didn't know!'

Anna gave in to the huge sobs that again rocked her body. She felt Theo tighten his grip around her shaking form, holding her close.

'I don't want to be on my own any more!' She raised her voice. 'I don't want to feel like sticks on the river! Like I'm being carried along, clinging on for dear life and hoping I don't drown.'

'I've got you, Anna. I've got you!'

'I've had enough, Theo. I'm tired. I'm so tired of being sad and being scared and lonely! So lonely!'

He kissed the top of her scalp and rocked her until she fell into a sleep of sorts.

It was an hour later when she stirred. Theo finally let go of her and crept forward on all fours, grabbing logs from the fire basket and tossing them onto the embers. 'I didn't want to move and risk waking you.' He looked back at her and she was touched by his considerateness.

'I'm sorry. I hardly ever, in fact never go off like that. I think it's a combination of wine, a long day and being in this place.' She sat up straight and rubbed beneath her eyes, suspecting there would be more than just a smudge of mascara from all that crying.

'And there was me hoping it was because we were breaking through your shell.' He gave a small snort of laughter.

'I think you know it is that too and I'm just trying to save face.'

'But that's just it, I don't want you to save face. I want you to tell me everything.' He looked at her in earnest.

'God, I think that is just about everything.'

Theo sat opposite her as she wrapped the blanket around her shoulders, clutching it to her from inside her cocoon.

'I've never met anyone like you, Anna. I think you're extraordinary, remarkable. Brilliant.'

'I'm so not.' She sniffed. 'I am just very ordinary.'

'But you are! I know blokes in the army who don't have half your resilience, your strength. Most people would be broken, but not you – you're calm, smart. I want to keep repeating the word "extraordinary".'

She let herself smile at the compliment. 'I can't pretend that I haven't wondered whether it might just be easier to hide behind my grief my whole life, keeping everyone and everything at bay. But when I came out of care...' She bit her lip, thinking of Shania – Shania then, full of life, and Shania a few years ago, homeless and hopeless – and shook her head. 'When I came out of care, I had this... this incredible feeling that I had a choice. I didn't want to be another cliché, a statistic, I wanted to live a life that might be considered a success. I suppose to kind of make up for my mum, whose time was cut so short. I mean, mid thirties, that's no age, is it?'

'No. It's not.'

'And that's sort of how I've been – planning, working, but all the time looking for something.'

'Or someone?' he asked steadily.

She nodded, feeling the bubble of anticipation build in her gut. Was he saying it was him? Was this actually happening? She gulped and decided to just get it all out. 'I've realised that what I need, to… to sort of help heal the things that have happened to me, to my family, is… a proper family of my own.' She studied her fingernails, which needed cutting. 'Kids and everything…'

There was a long pause, during which she heard Theo swallowing repeatedly. Anna mentally kicked herself. She'd pushed it too far. *Stupid woman!*

'I had a pretty shitty childhood,' Theo said, breaking the silence at last and scooting across the rug to sit next to her once again.

'You did?' She laid her hand on his arm.

'Yes. Different to yours, of course, in just about every way. A solid home, a good school, for want of a better phrase.' He snorted. 'I guess from the outside it looked like I had everything, but… My parents were aloof, bloody rubbish in fact. I just wasn't a priority and my father has this knack of making me feel…'

She watched his face contort as he tried to locate the right word. 'Making you feel what?' she whispered.

Theo shrugged. 'Like I'm a fucking idiot, like there's something wrong with me. And he really didn't get it when I became so depressed at uni. No one did, not really. It was… complicated.'

He clammed up then, clearly not ready to take it any further, and Anna understood that she shouldn't press him. She was taken aback by the strength of emotion behind his words, by how deeply inadequate he seemed to feel, and by there being things that he wasn't yet ready to share. He masked it well. Maybe they weren't so different after all...

'They bought you this house?'

Theo pulled his head back on his shoulders. 'Oh yes, they were always good at shelling out, writing cheques, but it's no substitute for the feeling you've described of knowing you were so loved. I think I would have benefitted greatly from having someone who cared enough to teach me the alphabet game.'

'*I* taught you the alphabet game.' She wriggled closer and nuzzled her chin on his shoulder.

'Yes, you did.' He turned and kissed her scalp. 'And actually I did have a mentor of sorts, for a while.'

'Fishing-Fly Guy?'

'Yes.' He smiled. 'I'm glad you remember. He was on the staff at my school, a sort of groundsman, a fisherman. He was a wonderful man. His name was Mr Porter.'

Anna looked up at the unmistakeable sound of a stifled sob, which caught them both off guard. It was a night of high emotion, as if having raised the barrier to let joy and happiness in, every other emotion could come rushing at them too.

'Oh, Theo! Oh, darling!' She turned to him and kissed his face.

'I've been lonely, Anna. Like you. Really lonely and afraid. You are the most wonderful thing that has ever happened to me.' He reached for her and kissed her full on the mouth.

'God, what are we like?' She laughed through her sadness.

'I love you, Anna. I love you.'

She felt her laughter bubble to the surface. He had said it! He loved her! Someone as incredible as Theodore Montgomery loved her!

'I love you too. I do, I really love you!'

They fell against each other, laughing some more, giddy in the moment.

'I always think you get the people in your life that you're meant to. I think we're meant to get each other.' She smiled.

'I think you're right. Two weirdos together!'

'Yes! Two weirdos with the lights left on.'

'I think...' Theo paused and reached for her hands, taking them both into his own. 'I think we'll get married and live here, together, just like this.'

Anna couldn't halt the flow of tears that ran down her cheeks. *I've been so lonely too, so scared and I'm sick of trying to be brave...*

'Yes, Theo. I think we will get married and live here, together, just like this.'

Slowly he stood, pulled her up and guided her by the hand towards the staircase, towards a different life.

There was no way Anna could wait until she got back to Fulham to tell Fifi and Fox her news. She was bursting with it. As soon as the clock ticked round to 10 a.m. the next morning, the earliest acceptable time she could take her coffee break, she whizzed out to the café round the corner from Villiers House and laid her pad out on her favourite table.

Fifi and Fox,
I've never thought too much about material things, never thought it was that important. I figured if I loved you enough and made you laugh every day then that would bring you

happiness (and me!). But I have to say that now I know that I'll be able to get you all the things I didn't have, it feels wonderful.

I don't mean ponies and gold, but you can eat meat every day and have new clothes bought just for you, and travel! Oh, the things we can do together and the places we will see...

Your daddy is called Theodore Montgomery and he is a wonderful gentleman and I love him! I never ever want to lose this brilliant, brilliant happiness that I have right now – it makes my head spin so much that I have to hold onto something so I don't fall over! I am in love with Mr Theodore Montgomery and he loves me right back and he is going to be the best dad in the whole wide world.

And oh my goodness, when I get to hold you in my arms and gaze at you in the way my mum used to look at me, then I will begin a chapter in my life that I have been waiting for longer than I can say. My family! My very own little family!

I want to be a mum; I want to be your mum. I want to have a noisy house full of people who don't leave before they're ready to, people who need me as much as I need them, people who are happy to be in my company – people who love me.

My Fifi and Fox, I will always love you and I will always make you feel like there is nowhere in the world that you'd want to be other than by my side .

I love you, I love you, I love you. I love the world right now and all because I am loved by my Theodore Montgomery.

Mummy x

Thirteen

'So when you say a small wedding, how small are we talking exactly?'

Anna glanced over at the very elegant Stella Montgomery, her future mother-in-law, trying to decipher the tone of her question. She noted how Stella exchanged a knowing look with Perry, her husband, who was pushing ice cubes from the back of the plastic tray into the ice bucket. Even so, Anna couldn't contain her bounce of excitement. She wriggled on the chair at the kitchen table and pushed her hair behind her ears. She decided to ignore any negative nuances Theo's mother hurled in her direction; she would paper over the nastiness and stay focused. This was after all her wedding they were talking about and she was determined to feel like a princess for the day.

'We are talking very small, absolutely tiny!' Anna indicated the tininess with her hand, closing her thumb and forefinger together. 'I mean, we're not going to elope or anything like that – although that would be the smallest wedding possible, just the two of us. Can you imagine?' She laughed, tilting her head in Theo's direction and smiling, trying in as polite a way as possible to let her future mother-in-law know that an elopement could be on the cards and might even be preferable if she didn't play ball.

Theo winked at her and in that flash Anna felt fearless. This is what he did for her!

'I mean, it's difficult for me. I'm sure Theo has filled you in, but I have no family who would come to my wedding, apart from a cousin in New York and a half-sister who might come for some of it if she can get a babysitter. Her on/off fella's in the army, on tour a lot, so things are a bit tricky.' She raised the china cup to her lips and blew onto her tea to cool it a little.

'Quite.' Theo's mother reached out and took the gin and tonic from her husband's hand, grasping it keenly, as if it were much-needed medicine. 'So should we be thinking about sending out save-the-date cards? We are already terribly unprepared if, as you say, it has to take place this year.'

'It's not that it *has* to be *any* time, but we want it to be this year.' Theo spoke up.

His mother sipped her gin and tonic and smiled thinly over the top of her glass. 'Yes, of course.'

'How hard can it be?' Anna placed her cup of tea on the table. 'We book a registry office, have a glass of wine and a slice of cake somewhere with flowers in a jam jar on the table, hopefully in a room with a reasonably nice view, and that's it! Job done!' She dusted her hands and laughed again.

Theo smiled. She knew he loved her plan to keep it simple. The two had laughed as he'd described the dozens of embossed, gold-edged invitations that invariably lined his parents' mantelpiece during the wedding season. Each one near identical and, according to him, sent by a bride-to-be who would be half starving herself ready for the big day. They'd be summoned to some far-flung place or to a fading country house, with each bride trying to outdo the other right down to the smallest detail. Theo had given an involuntary shiver at the thought of it all. And Anna had pictured all the birds called Felicity or Mirabelle, who, in her shoes, would be flapping over the minutiae, picking colours, tasting dishes, practising hair and make-up, fretting over flowers and managing to turn the lovely occasion into something quite stressful.

'Stella, I think if you get into the swing of it and accept that it's not going to be a traditional wedding, then you will really enjoy it!'

'Oh my dear, I think I have already understood just how untraditional the whole affair will be,' Theo's mother offered without the hint of a smile.

'We were thinking of a lunchtime do at the Marriott County Hall. They have a room for private dining with a view out over the river to the Houses of Parliament.' Anna had loved the room on sight, thinking it was one of the nicest she had ever seen. Grand yet cosy, a neat trick. And what would her mum and brother have thought of her sitting like a princess in the middle of London with a view of Big Ben? It would be quite something. She thought of Shania and hoped she wasn't still wandering the capital's streets but had found somewhere safe and good. Somewhere really good. How she would love for Shania to have been at her wedding too.

'A hotel?' There was a beat of silence to allow Stella's disapproval to land. 'Well, I am sure that will be lovely.'

Theo picked invisible lint from his trousers, clearly irritated by his mother's tone. But Anna simply beamed, reminding herself that she was to ignore anything negative – this was her wedding day under discussion and she was marrying Theodore Montgomery! Nothing else mattered, not really. 'It will be.' She nodded enthusiastically. 'The menu is fab – we're going to go for roast beef with all the trimmings, including Yorkshire puddings. And then berry cheesecake for afters.'

Another look passed between Stella and Perry, which Anna again understood to mean they didn't approve of her choice in this either. She had to remember to smile and to resist reminding them that for some people meat was still an unaffordable luxury. Roast beef with all the trimmings would do very nicely.

'Of course, you don't have to come, Mum, if you'd rather not.' Theo spoke levelly, and his delivery was cool. 'That'd be absolutely fine.'

His comment surprised Anna, though she had to admit to being a little thrilled by it. It spoke volumes. *I pick you, Anna Bee Cole. I pick you over and above everyone. I am on your side.*

'What a thing to say!' she said loudly, then tutted. 'Of course your mum has to come! She's the mother of the groom.'

'Theo's only teasing.' His father winked.

'I wouldn't miss it for the world. Roast beef in a hotel sounds delightful.' Stella raised her tumbler towards her future daughter-in-law. 'It will be memorable.'

'Are you inviting any of the Vaizey boys?' Perry asked Theo, cutting in before he could react to Stella's sweetly offered barb. Turning to Anna, he added, 'That was his school – Vaizey College down in Dorset. Mine too, actually. Fine old place. Do you know it?'

'No.' Anna shook her head and thought of the interchangeable comprehensive schools from which she had gleaned her straight As.

'I hadn't planned on doing so, no.' Theo sounded awkward as he walked to the fridge and opened it, seemingly not wanting to face his parents. He'd already told Anna that there wasn't a single person from his school days he wanted present, apart from one. And that person was an old man he had let down a long time ago. *The Fishing-Fly Guy.* Anna could tell that even discussing this period in his life caused him pain and she respected that, knowing how potent memories like that could be. An image of a folded blue towel lying on the bathroom floor floated into her mind.

'Well, should we invite Becks on your behalf? He was your housemaster, after all, for so many years,' his mother trilled.

Anna couldn't understand how they didn't get it! She watched Theo's shoulders sag and heard his sigh. He closed the fridge door with a little more force than was necessary and turned to the three of them, who were all looking at him.

'No, I don't want you to invite Mr Beckett.'

'That's a damned shame,' his father growled. 'He always enquires after you.'

'Does he now?' Theo gave a snort of laughter. 'Good to know!'

'Don't be so tetchy, Theodore. You've always been funny about him, about school in general, and it's such a beautiful place. Daddy loved it there, didn't you, darling?'

'I did indeed.' Perry nodded, puffing out his chest and gripping his glass of whisky, as if his wife's words were a personal accolade.

'Well, I didn't.' Theo bit his lip and Anna hated the sadness she saw in his eyes, a brief insight, perhaps, into how he might have felt when he was so depressed. 'I didn't love it there. In fact I hated every second of it. And as for your friend, Mr Beckett, he was a complete shit to me. Not that he was the only one – most people there were shits to me – but he was my housemaster and he was supposed to be looking out for me, but he didn't. Not at all.'

Anna felt a flutter of anxiety in her gut. She hated that even talking about school evoked such a reaction in her man, hated that he was uncomfortable. At the same time she was more than a little shocked that her future in-laws seemed so unaware of this. She thought of her mum, always interested, placing her hand on her shoulder. '*How are you today, my beautiful girl? How was school?*'

'That's a tad dramatic!' Theo's father laughed. 'You can't tell me that all six hundred boys treated you badly! I think you're rather overegging the pudding!'

'You would, Dad.' Theo held his gaze. 'And funnily enough, I seem to remember Mr Beckett saying something similar.'

Anna hopped up from her chair, walked over to him and took him in her arms for a long, tight hug. 'I think someone might have a touch of pre-wedding jitters.' She stood tall and kissed his cheek. 'My handsome, clever man.'

He looked at her and smiled. She watched his face soften, as if comforted by her attention. And she was glad.

* * *

Anna's plans prevailed, a cosy room in the Marriott Hotel was duly booked, and roast beef with all the trimmings ordered. The guest list was modest, and on Anna's side it was positively diminutive, but that didn't matter at all because so long as Jordan was there, she didn't mind if no one else on her side turned up. For his part, Jordan was ecstatic at the prospect and announced that he would be coming to stay with her several days ahead of the big day.

'Holy guacamole! You have got to be kidding me!' Jordan shouted with an obvious New York twang, which he had almost perfected. '*This* is where you live?' He placed his hand on his chest and turned in a circle in the hallway, taking in the ornate cornicing, the tiled floor, the wide staircase that promised grand rooms overhead.

'Yes.' Anna folded her arms and rubbed the tops of her shoulders. 'Although I'm still like "Waaaagh!" every time I come in the door. It's very different from my little studio. When Theo isn't here, if I hear a noise I jump out of my skin! I love it though. Feel very lucky.'

'I should say! God, it's beautiful. But he's lucky to have you and any place you are in is infinitely more wonderful because you are in it, never forget that.' Jordan swept forward and enveloped his cousin in a hug before kissing her hard on the cheek. 'I have missed you, Miss Anna Bee!'

'And I've missed you! I love, love getting your letters. Shame Levi couldn't make it.'

'Yes, poor darling, he was keen to come with me – we both wanted to visit Kensington Palace. I sent flowers of course.' He placed his hand at his neck, as if overcome by the death of Diana, Princess of Wales. 'I simply can't believe it, Anna, can't believe she's gone. And the way those boys walked behind the coffin, oh my God! I don't mind telling you, I sobbed from start to finish.' He fanned his eyes, as if this could prevent more tears from coming. 'Diana was everyone's princess, but I felt like I knew her, felt connected to her even though we never met – does that make sense?'

Anna nodded. She had gone to Kensington Palace herself to witness the sea of flowers. It had stretched as far as the eye could see, and the atmosphere had been heavy with the sobs of mourners who'd travelled there from far and wide. It had felt important to pay her respects to the woman whose wedding day she remembered – 'a proper princess', as her Aunt Lizzie had called her. 'Yes, I think a lot of people felt the same way.'

They observed a second of silence.

'Plus Levi's been rehearsing for months.' Jordan spoke with new energy. 'A musical based on the work of an obscure Nordic poet – whale music and everything.' He sucked his teeth and widened his eyes. 'Anyhoo, they cut the funding and sadly it's not going to see the light of day. Which, if Levi asks you what I said, is an artistic loss, but if he doesn't then let me tell you the whole production was beyond horrific and I thank you, Lord, for the underfunding of the arts!' He looked up and raised his hands skyward.

She loved that he still had the ability to make her howl with laughter.

'So he's at home licking his wounds and applying for any job he can find. I left him scouring the papers. He asked me if I thought he could masquerade as a plastic surgeon, as the pay is great. I told him there's a huge difference between acting a surgeon and being one. I'm hoping to God he doesn't pull it off – can you imagine? Pity the poor patients of the Lower East Side turning up to find Levi in full scrubs but screaming and fainting at his first sight of a medical instrument.'

Anna laughed. How she adored his theatricality.

'Plus,' Jordan continued, 'being out of work made paying for his flight a little difficult. I only just managed.'

'I told you Theo and I would pay for you both. It means the world that you're here.'

'Oh I know, Toots, and it was so kind of you to offer.' He smiled at her. 'But Levi wouldn't hear of it. Me neither. I had savings, plus I think he might have decided to plead poverty rather than admit he was too scared to jump on a plane across the pond. We drive everywhere...' He sighed.

'Next time.'

'Yes, for sure next time. I do miss him though.' Jordan pulled his mouth into a downward arc.

'You've been together for how long and you still miss him?' She smiled, beyond delighted that Jordan had found such happiness.

'Oh, centuries, but he's my guy, what can I say?' He shrugged. 'And now you've found your guy!'

'Oh, Jord.' Her face lit up. 'I can't wait for you to meet him.'

'Me too. So, come on, what's he like?'

'Oh...' She looked into the middle distance, picturing him. 'He's tall and slim with dark, curly hair that's a little thin on top. He could be cocky because he is so incredible, but he's not, he is kind and...' She paused and smiled. 'He listens to everything I say, like really listens, as if what I have to say is the most important thing. He makes me feel special, clever. I love him!'

'Well, that's a very good job as you're marrying the man in less than three days.'

'Don't remind me, I'm so nervous. God, I'm glad you're here.'

'I wouldn't have missed it for the world.' He kissed her again. 'Family.'

'Yep, family.' Anna chose her next words carefully. 'Talking of family—'

'Don't even go there.' Jordan cut her short, holding up his palm. 'I am barely in touch with them and have no intention of going to see them. Does that pre-empt and answer all your questions?'

'Pretty much, but don't you ever miss them? Think of them?'

'Think of them, occasionally. Miss them, no.' He drew breath. 'There is so much more to being a parent than just the creation part – in fact, I think that's probably the easiest bit. It's what comes next, the support, the caring, the accepting and the helping that's the hard stuff and I'm sorry to say I find it difficult to like people that don't like me. Even if they are my mum and dad.'

'I get that.' She nodded. 'I do.' She pictured herself with Fifi and Fox, knowing she would love and support them no matter what. 'For what it's worth, I don't believe it's that they don't like you—'

'Darling, don't even try and justify it. You can't. Trust me. At the end of the day, I have to accept that my mum is an arsehole.'

Anna hooted with laughter. 'Jordan! You can't say that!'

'Well she is, and a bigoted arsehole at that. I can't change her. I've tried, but it's like jabbing at a bad tooth with your tongue – eventually you just have to go and get the damn thing removed. So that's what I've done. I've removed her and Dad from my thoughts and, as I'd hoped, it's now a lot less painful.'

'Well, for what it's worth, I feel sad for what they're missing out on – you are absolutely brilliant.'

'Yes, I am! Goldpie is in the house!' Jordan threw his slender arm up into the air in his familiar disco pose. 'I am also dying for a cup of tea – what does a girl have to do to get a drink around here?'

'This way.' Anna walked ahead, into the handsome kitchen. Her influence on the decor had been subtle. A glass vase of fresh tulips sat on the kitchen table, a couple of wooden hearts now hung on the door handles, and a natty blue linen dish towel was draped over the rail of the Aga, all adding splashes of colour. And, most importantly, a little lemon tree graced a green glazed pot on the windowsill. It was as yet not much more than a slender twig, but she had high hopes, remembering the one she'd tended in Honor Oak Park, when her mum was still alive.

Jordan, like her, walked straight to the wide sash window, which was raised, allowing the breeze and the scent of flowers to fill the room.

'Oh, Anna!'

'I know.' She stared ahead with her hands clasped under her chin.

Her cousin stood next to her, taking in the profusion of hydrangeas, dahlias and Michaelmas daisies that filled the borders beside the brick path. At the end of the path stood a wooden summerhouse, its roof caressed by a luxuriant weeping willow.

'This is so beautiful.'

'I find it hard to do anything but stare out of this window. The view changes every day and I don't think I will ever get sick of it. It's so therapeutic. If only everyone could have access to a sight like this.'

'So you're still in your job?' Jordan asked as she filled the kettle and set it on top of the Aga.

'Yes. I like it. The brokers are a nice bunch and I've been there quite a while now, plus I get to travel in and out with Theo more often than not.'

'You carry on working when you could be a kept woman?' Jordan boomed with mock disapproval.

'Oh, don't!' She sighed, blushing at this uncomfortable truth. 'I have to admit it was a little weird to begin with, working in the building that my fiancé owns. People were a bit...'

'A bit what?'

'Nudgey, elbowy and whispery.'

'Oh no! Not nudgey, elbowy and whispery! Is there a helpline you can call for that?'

'You can mock, but it was uncomfortable. Theo and I sat down and discussed it and he said I had to either buckle up and ignore it or that I should do something else entirely, take the chance to do something I really wanted to, go somewhere or study and that I didn't have to worry about a wage.'

'That's wonderful. He sounds wonderful.'

'Yep. It's amazing for me to have that freedom of choice.' She took two china mugs from the shelf and lobbed a teabag into each. 'I thought about going back to college and studying, but then my friend Melissa—'

'Loud American you worked with at the lawyer place? Blonde, big gob, no filter?'

'The very same, although if you don't mind, I won't be sharing that description with her.'

'Probably wise.'

Anna giggled. 'Anyway, she reminded me that no matter how hard I study or whatever I do, the goal is to be happy – and I am. I'm happy right now. So I stayed and now the gossip has died down and I'm glad I did.'

'Good for you. Looks like you finally found your voice, Anna Bee.'

'I think I have.' She smiled.

Jordan took a seat at the table as Anna passed him his mug of tea and then sat opposite him.

'So come on, tell me what to expect on the big day! Dancing girls popping out of the wedding cake and a barrel of doves released at the stroke of midnight?'

'Not quite.' She sipped her tea.

'Or perhaps a well-trained bird of prey with the ring on a chain around its neck?'

'What is it with you and our feathered friends? No! No birds, no fuss, no flower girl and no top bloody table.' She rubbed her brow.

'Oh dear, have we touched a nerve?' Jordan pulled a face.

Anna sat back in the chair and tucked her right leg beneath her. 'Things have been a bit awkward with Theo's mum and dad – in fact more with his mum. His dad doesn't seem to say much, just gets sloshed and nods off in the corner.'

'I think you'll find that's only in your company, darling.'

'Thanks.' She giggled again. 'And possibly true.'

'So is it a case of the boringly predictable mother who can't let go of her boy?'

Anna paused before answering, knowing it wasn't that straightforward. 'A bit, I suppose, but it's more...' She clicked her tongue.

'More what?'

'More like she disapproves of the way I do things rather than disapproves of me myself.'

'A class thing?'

'Again, possibly.' She shrugged. 'Our backgrounds couldn't be more different. Theo was rowing for his public school while

I was in care and sharing a room with a girl who nicked from Woolworths.'

'Sweetheart, we all nicked from Woolworths.' Jordan batted the air in front of his face.

She smiled. 'But it's not only a class thing. I feel that from the day we first discussed the wedding, she found the whole thing amusing, the fact that I don't know one end of a length of taffeta from the other and that I don't understand the many rules of formal social occasions. Honestly, Jord, she talks about "the done thing" and "giving the wrong impression" and I sit there like a wally because I have no idea what I'm doing wrong or doing right.'

'What you are doing right is marrying her son and making him happier than he has ever been and if she can't see that or doesn't care then it's time you considered the fact that she just might be a member of the arsehole club too.'

'You might be right, but I hope you're not. I like her. She's not warm and fuzzy, not at all – I mean, she's never going to bake me a cake, take me shopping or phone up for a natter – but I do want to be part of Theo's family, no matter how odd they are. And I don't want to alienate the grandmother of our future kids, do I?' She shook her hair out from behind her ears. 'Do you know, the Montgomerys don't even celebrate their birthdays? Isn't that odd? I mean, even at Mead House we got a cake and had a singsong. And yet these people who could have amazing birthday parties, they just don't bother. As I say… odd.'

'Oh, darling, all families are odd. That's the only thing we usually all have in common. So is Mr Hunk all fired up about being a dad then, ready to give you a brood of little Hunklings?'

Anna hesitated, wondering whether to share her niggle of

concern. 'To be honest, Jord, he's been a bit reluctant to talk about all that just yet. But I'm working on it!' She gave a cheeky laugh. 'Oh, I do love you being here! I get a bit lonely in this big old house on my own. Theo works such long hours – I'm not moaning, I get it, but I do miss him.'

'How about getting a pooch?'

'Do you know, that might not be a bad idea.' She gulped at her tea. 'We have talked about it.'

Jordan gasped as an idea formed. 'We could get one before the wedding and dress him in a little morning suit and a top hat and strap the ring to a cushion on his back!'

'I think that would send my future mother-in-law over the edge.' Anna laughed. 'I have even hinted that I might quite like to elope, just to get her to be a bit kinder, but I don't think she took the bait.'

'Oh, you can't elope! No way! I have new shoes!'

'Oh well, if you have new shoes…' She smiled. 'It's true though, I think my ideal day might be just the two of us in a registry office, wearing jeans and then dashing home for scrambled egg on toast.' She paused, hating the stir of discomfort in her gut. 'I know deep down that while she hasn't said anything specifically, Stella would rather Theo was marrying one of the girls who went to his very expensive boarding school.' *A Felicity or a Mirabelle…* 'Or one whose parents they already know or who at least knows that you should send out a save-the-date for a bloody wedding!'

'I think you're being a tad hard on yourself, and it's understandable that you're edgy – it's a big deal! Your wedding day!'

Anna sat forward. 'It's more than that.' She ran her palms over her face. 'I wish…' She swallowed. 'I wish my mum was here, and Joe.'

'Of course you do.' Her cousin placed his hand on her arm.

'I miss them every day, every single day, but getting married has taken that missing to a whole new level.'

'They'll be with you, Anna Bee, watching over your shoulder. I'm convinced of it.'

She nodded. 'I remember playing weddings with my mum when I was little. I put a pillowcase on my head and pretended it was a veil.'

'Well, again, we've all done that.' Jordan tapped the table. 'Carry on.'

His humour did the trick, and she laughed, forcing down the tears that had gathered.

'And she told me...' She took a breath. 'She told me no girl wants to get married without her mum there. And she was right.'

Jordan held her gaze; no quip this time. He sat quietly, respecting her sadness, and she was grateful.

'I would give anything to have her here, and Joe, or even my dad! I know it sounds ridiculous...'

'It doesn't, Toots, not ridiculous at all. We all want that approval from our mum and dad and all for different reasons.' He squeezed her arm.

'My mum also told me that when I got married, I could have whatever I wanted because I'd be the bride and it would be my special day. She said it would be like being a princess, but I don't feel like a bloody princess. I had to argue tooth and nail just to get everyone to agree that I could have a Victoria sandwich as my wedding cake. It was important to me.'

'A Victoria sandwich?' Her cousin pulled a face of extreme disapproval. 'Jeez! What else – paper plates, faux flowers, cheese and pineapple on sticks?'

'Oh, Jord!' Anna buried her face in her hands.

'You don't have to get married, you know.' He whispered this, as if he sensed it was a shoddy thing to be saying in the groom's house.

'No! No, I really do want to get married to Theo. I love him, Jordan. He's wonderful. Perfect for me. I want to marry him and have my children with him – it's going to be wonderful!' She smiled through her tears. 'I guess the whole thing is making me realise what I'm missing, not having my mum and Joe here, and I suppose at the back of my mind I always hoped that whoever I married, their parents would make me part of the family, wrap me up and include me, like I know my mum would have with Theo.'

'Perfect, you say? Does he have no faults?'

'Oh, he has plenty.' She giggled. 'Not least of all, finding ways to dodge the topic of kids, smoking in secret, and smoking even more when he's stressed. But, you know, I have lots of quirks.' She wrinkled her nose. 'And I'm slowly nagging at him to give up cigarettes.'

'Do you still do your weird alphabet thing?'

She tutted and laughed at his choice of words. 'Do you know, since I've been with Theo, hardly at all. It's as if my thoughts are ordered enough and I'm not scared, so I don't need to.'

'That's so cool.'

'It is.'

'I think…' Jordan began.

'You think what?' She looked up in anticipation.

'I think that despite the fact that it's only four in the afternoon, we need something stronger than tea!' Jordan jumped up. 'Direct me to the wine cellar!'

'There isn't a wine cellar, you idiot, but there are cold bottles of Budweiser in the fridge.'

'That'll do.'

The two polished off two bottles each and were decidedly giddy as they downed the third. An hour and a half flew by and all solemnity had evaporated.

'Do you think my mum still has the hots for Mr Dickinson?'

'Oh my God!' Anna yelled, bending double and laughing loudly. 'Mr Dickinson! I'd forgotten about him. Old Mr Dickinson, he'd be now.' She took a swig of her beer. 'Did you know, Mr Dickinson takes minutes at the council – he's a keeper of secrets!'

They roared their laughter.

'Oh God, my poor dad, always going to compare unfavourably with Mr Dickinson and his shit-brown slacks.'

'I remember your mum trying to pair you up with his niece.'

'God, what was her name?' Jordan drummed on the tabletop with his fingers, his eyes closed, as if this might aid his concentration. 'I know I once went downstairs after having a sex dream about his gardener and my mum was at the door in her dressing gown shouting at me, "Ulla is on the front drive, why don't you go and show her your gangshow medal!"'

'Ulla!' she bellowed.

'Yep, that was it – Ulla!' He took another drink.

'Gangshow medal!' Anna beat the table with her palm, wheezing with laughter. This was one of the funniest images she could conjure.

'Well, all I can say is I hope poor Ulla's taste in men has improved with age. I know mine has.' He shivered. 'That gardener was positively ropey! She probably married someone as dull as her uncle, with job security and a pension, but that man will always know, deep in his heart that it was me she loved first – and I bet he can't do this!' Jordan jumped from his chair, walked to the far side of the kitchen, placed the blue linen tea towel on his head and grabbed the spatula from the hook on the wall, using it as an improvised microphone.

'Don't you want me, baby!' He belted it out, tuneless but loud, oh so loud!

Anna raced to his side and with her arms up over her head did her best sultry backing-singer dance.

She didn't hear Theo come in – Jordan's dulcet tones masked the sound of his key in the door.

She stopped dancing at the sight of him and held her side, trying to catch her breath through her hysteria as Theo stared at them from the kitchen door and threw his keys onto the countertop.

'Theo!' She wiped the tears of laughter from her eyes. 'Oh God, I must have lost track of time.'

'So I see.'

She watched his tight-lipped smile and saw the flicker of irritation on his face.

Scooting around the table, she reached up and kissed his cheek. 'Look who's arrived! Jordan!'

Jordan whipped the tea towel from his head and lowered his arms. He walked forward, stretching out his right hand and shook Theo's with purpose. 'Good to finally meet you.'

It broke Anna's heart that Jordan lowered his voice and adopted a well-honed masculine swagger, losing his dancer's gait and the fey giggle that seemed to accompany his every sentence. *Don't hide, Jordan, my wonderful cousin. I love you just as you are. Be you, always be you...*

*

With the dishwasher whirring and Jordan ensconced in the spare room, Anna made her way across the landing to their bedroom. It was still one of the best feelings in the world, to place her bare feet on the rich wool carpet and not to have to worry about getting splinters from grotty, gnarled floorboards.

'Thank you for supper, it was lovely.' Theo loosened his tie and slipped it from beneath the collar of his shirt, draping it around the neck of his valet stand, an antique that used to belong to his grandpa.

'You're welcome. It's lovely to have Jordan here.'

'Yes, I'm sure it is.' His tone was clipped.

Anna took a deep breath. 'I found it all a bit stressful this evening to tell the truth.' She sat at the dressing table and removed her stud earrings, laying them down in a pair on the glass top.

'Stressful?' He looked at her quizzically as he peeled off his cotton shirt, balled it and threw it against the wardrobe door, where it fell into a crumpled heap on the floor.

Anna shrugged. 'I don't know how to explain it – I guess I felt I spoke to Jord and spoke to you and you both spoke back to me, but you didn't really talk to each other and I was so anxious about there being a lull in the conversation that I couldn't shut up, not for a second. Like a plate spinner who has to keep them all turning.'

Theo gave a snort of laughter and shook his head. 'I think you might be imagining the tension. It was fine.'

He disappeared into the bathroom and she heard him pee and flush the loo, followed by the sound of him cleaning his teeth. Picking up a cotton-wool pad, she soaked it in cucumber cleanser and ran it over her face and up under her chin. She liked how they had settled into each other's lives, moving to each other's rhythms in a harmonious dance as they slid and slotted around each other inside the beautiful space they called home.

She waited until he'd switched off the bathroom light and was sitting on the bed to set his alarm, another part of his ritual.

'So do you like Jordan?' she asked quietly, conscious that her cousin was just along the hallway.

'Yes, of course I like him!' He smiled briefly in her direction and looked back to his alarm clock, checking, as he always did, that it was actually set and that the time was correct.

She didn't want to labour the point but knew it was important to speak her mind. 'It's just that you seemed a bit...'

He sighed. 'A bit what?'

'I don't know...' She spun round on the stool until she faced him. 'I got the feeling he annoyed you.'

Theo scratched behind his ear. 'He didn't annoy me, I just found him...' He exhaled. 'I guess he's not like me or anyone I know.'

'Because he's gay?' She folded her arms across her chest.

Theo actually laughed. 'No! For God's sake, is that what you think? Of course not. What a thing to say to me! I couldn't give a shit – as if that would make a difference!'

She uncoiled her arms with relief.

'No...' She could see that Theo was trying to choose his words carefully. 'I think we have very little in common. He's in the theatre, I work in property. He's in New York, I'm in London. I like rugby, he likes Abba...'

'But you both love me and that's what you have in common, right?'

Theo stared at her. 'Don't make it an issue, Anna. It's not him, he's perfectly nice. It's me, just shit from school and stuff. But you're right: we do both love you. I promise I shall make more of an effort tomorrow morning. I'm tired. It's been a bit of a day.'

'It's always a bit of a day. And it always will be a bit of a day if you're unhappy at work.' She knew that ultimately he wanted to leave his dad's company and do something that he felt would make a difference in the world, wanted to slide from under his father's control, do something he loved.

'That's true.' He looked towards the window and sat up and rubbed his face, before patting the bed, indicating for her to come and get in. 'Okay, I know this is going to sound stupid, but from when I was very small, I always...'

'You always what, honey?'

'I always had this feeling that whenever I turned up anywhere, for breakfast, a party, anything, my parents and their friends would look at me as if my arrival was most unexpected, as if they'd forgotten about me and I was this unwanted extra guest. It made me feel awkward and it made *them* feel awkward and I absolutely hated it. I can remember that feeling even now, and when I got home tonight...'

She moved closer towards him.

'I guess I felt a bit the same. You and Jordan were howling with laughter and dancing and I stood there like a spare part. I didn't know how to join in and it took me right back.'

'I'm sorry. I would never, ever want to make you feel like that.' Her anguish was genuine.

Theo shook his head. 'It's not you. You are amazing.' He kissed her hand. 'It's just another shitty throwback to my shitty childhood.'

'It's behind you, Theo.'

'I know.' He nodded. 'And you're right. I'll take Jordan for a pint, how about that?'

'Thank you.' She beamed at him. 'It's important to me. I don't have tons of friends and obviously no family, so those I do have I have to take very good care of. I can't be casual with my affection towards them, or indifferent, I have to value them and nurture them and not let them down! Because I don't want them to let me down. I need them. Jordan is my only link to my mum and to Joe.'

'I understand, my love. I do.'

'I think he and Levi will make wonderful godparents for our children. Along with Spud of course,' she added hurriedly, not wanting to leave Theo's best friend out of this happy picture.

'Our children? Blimey, let's get the hang of the marriage malarkey first, and then we'll see…' He pulled the duvet up over his shoulders and lay back on the stack of soft pillows.

Anna watched him closely, waiting for a sign that everything was okay.

He turned on his side and opened his arms wide, encouraging her into the space against his chest. She flicked off her bedside lamp and nestled in. She was going to be Mrs Theodore Montgomery and they would welcome their babies and everything was going to be wonderful.

Just wonderful.

Fourteen

'I can't believe I am here!' Anna screamed with excitement, running over the dark wood floor. 'This place is so beautiful!'

Any fatigue from the long journey had disappeared at the sight of their open-sided villa, which was perched at the end of a blindingly white spit of sand and entirely surrounded by aquamarine sea so shimmery it made her gasp. It was simply stunning. She almost couldn't control the childlike enthusiasm that erupted from her.

Despite now in theory being able to travel where and when she wanted to, it was still a rare occurrence due to Theo's work commitments and life getting in the way. And yet here she was! Anna, who had been in care in Leytonstone, Anna, who had not been in the popular set of her school in Honor Oak Park, Anna Bee Montgomery née Cole was in the bloody Maldives! *Look at me now, Tracy Fitchett!*

She danced and twirled with her arms outstretched, letting her fingers linger over the tops of the sturdy, dark teak chairs and dressing tables. Plucking at the gossamer-like white cloth that hung in curtains on the four-poster bed, she bounced joyously on the wide, soft mattress.

She looked at Theo, who was watching her with the twitch of a smile on his face.

'Come on!' She beckoned to him. Skipping into the open-plan kitchen, she grabbed a bottle of champagne that had been set on ice in anticipation of their arrival and lifted it high. 'Not too early, is it?' she asked, flinging open the cupboard to retrieve two glasses.

'Never too early on holiday.' He smiled.

She laughed as her husband unzipped his suitcase and hung up his linen trousers and white cotton shirts.

'Look at this place, Theo! I can't believe we're here! And yes, I'm going to keep saying that until it sinks in!'

Anna popped the cork and squealed her delight as she poured the champagne. She kicked off her sandals and raced outside barefoot in her denim cut-offs to lean against the wooden rails around the deck of their beautiful villa. She bent over and peered down into the crystal-clear water below, following the tiny brightly coloured fish as they darted this way and that. The sun warmed her skin and scattered sea diamonds over the surface of the ocean. She threw back her head and faced the rays like a sunflower at midday.

'Is there a boat?' Theo enquired, lighting a cigarette and coming to stand next to her, staring out at the miles of azure ocean that twinkled in the mid-afternoon sun.

Anna handed him his champagne and turned to him with a look of mock indignation. Her hair, now in a new, shorter cut, fell about her face.

'We have been on this tiny island for approximately twelve minutes. Our own Maldivian paradise, to celebrate our first year of marriage, and you are asking if there is a boat?' She reached out and touched his face. 'There is no escaping from me this week, Mr Montgomery. No working late, no meeting Spud, no going for a run, no paperwork to be done in the den and no watching TV! You are here with me and you are present and this is our time to reconnect. One year is something to be celebrated.'

'I didn't mean it like that. I was just thinking we might go fishing. Catch our own supper.' He kissed her nose.

'Good, because I don't plan on doing much of anything, especially not leaving the villa. We can paddle about and lie in the sun, fish from the deck, eat lovely food and sleep.'

He smiled at her. 'That sounds like just what the doctor ordered.'

'And...' She twisted her fingers into his hair and pulled his mouth down to meet hers, their bodies merging. 'I have a feeling that this beautiful place might be good for us in other ways.' She kissed him again. 'I think this would be a wonderful place to make a baby,' she whispered in his ear, nibbling his lobe when she was done.

Please, Theo, please. Please, please let me have our baby...

She felt his body jolt and her heart jumped in response. It was as if all the soft joy was sucked from her veins and in its place came a hardened, crystalline sadness with sharp edges that cut. He pulled away and she looked in anguish into her husband's face. His mouth moved in silence, as if trying to find words of reassurance and comfort but without making another empty promise. Her tears pooled.

'I...'

'No, please, Theo, don't say anything at all.' She placed her trembling fingers on his mouth and shook her head. 'Just let me be. Just let me think that you might change your mind, that you might make our family complete. Just for today. Let me think it might be possible. Please.'

She almost stumbled, knocked off balance by the wave of distress that hit her at full force, as it sometimes did. Her head dropped to her chest and her tears rolled from her elfin chin. Theo balanced his cigarette in the hand that held his wine glass and pulled her into him with his other hand, holding her tight, as if this contact might be compensation enough.

Anna felt the bitter taste of disappointment at the fact that they had been in this paradisal setting for less than twenty minutes but had already arrived at the exact place they'd left off from back at home. They hovered in an awkward, one-armed embrace, chastened by the realisation that it mattered little whether they were in the Maldives or SW13, there was nowhere on earth they could go to outrun the thing they were trying to escape. It dominated their thoughts, lingered in the wings and cast a dark shadow on the sunniest of days, even here, even now. The debate, and the disharmony that ensued, would continue to lap at their heels like the waves beneath the deck.

They stood on opposite sides of the fence: Anna, growing increasingly desperate to have the baby that would turn them from a couple into the family she craved, and Theo, shying away from the commitment, certain that he did not want to bring a child into a world that for him as a youngster had been cruel and unloving. Anna hated the sadness that hung around him like a mist; she wished he would open up to her and was confident there was nothing as a couple they couldn't handle. If he let himself, she knew he would be the most wonderful dad. She just had to convince him that he really was the kind, loving, unselfish person she knew him to be. Then his fears about turning into his own father would evaporate. She had to believe this was possible, as the alternative was too horrendous to contemplate.

Both sipped the cold champagne, Anna now only vaguely enjoying the sharp, chilled sweetness of bubbles on the back of her tongue but thankful that it would dull the sadness that was filling her up. She pictured Joe lying on the sofa of their tiny flat and not for the first time felt a flicker of understanding at his need to remove himself from the hurt of daily life.

Melissa, and Lisa too, had told her to trick Theo. *'Just do it! Get pregnant!'* But she knew more than most the importance of being in unison when it came to having a child. She thought of her mum, a single mum. No matter the reasons why, her mum had had a hard life, that much Anna knew. Anna was determined never to endanger her relationship with Theo, or the deep love they shared, by trying for a baby without his consent. That trust was fundamental to their relationship and something she prized highly. *No secrets…*

It was now early evening and they lay on the vast bed, letting the warm breeze float over them, content to gaze at the palm trees and the conical, frond-thatched roofs of distant villas. An elegant Maldivian heron waded in the shallows, soon becoming no more than a dark shadow against the orange and pink sunset.

'Do you think there are rats in those thatched roofs?' Theo laughed.

Anna giggled drunkenly and ran her fingers over his chest. 'No, I don't.' She spoke with the slight slur of one who had consumed the majority of a bottle of champagne on an empty stomach and then sipped through a fat straw a couple of iced strawberry daiquiris, brought to their room by a floral-shirted waiter who'd held them raised high on a bamboo salver. She watched the sky continue its rainbow display. 'It's so beautiful, like a painting.'

'It really is.'

There was a beat or two of comfortable silence until she spoke again.

'When I met you in the lift, and when we started dating...' She gave a small giggle; it was still funny to them and everyone who knew them that they had met in a lift. 'I was struck by this...' She shook her head, searching for the right words. 'This air of sadness about you.' Anna rolled onto her side and studied her husband's handsome profile in the dying light. 'You always looked like you wanted to be somewhere else, no matter where we were or who we were with, and when you spoke, you looked at the floor as if what you had to say wasn't of any interest. And you hardly ever smiled.'

He looked to his right and gave a small nod, acknowledging this to be true.

'But I think you have grown, Theo, in the last year. I think you trust me now when I tell you that you are wonderful.'

'I do a bit,' he admitted sheepishly, as if he had no right to be given such a compliment.

'And you *are* wonderful, you know,' she repeated. 'No matter what you went through as a child, no matter how indifferent your parents seem, you really are.'

He kissed the top of her head.

'I was with Ned for quite a while, and I didn't know there could be any other way.'

She felt his body tense slightly. She knew he found it uncomfortable when she spoke about her previous man, but she also knew she needed to soften the stiff upper lip he'd been raised with. Better communication was, she knew, the way forward.

He lay back on the pillow and she continued.

'Ned was like vanilla. Nice enough, but everything was plain, ordinary – boring, I suppose. I watched my true self getting sapped – I was shrinking. I would cry myself to sleep some nights, wondering how I could be that lonely, that unfulfilled, and at the same time questioning why being with him wasn't enough. It should have been enough, and for a lot of people it would have been, but not me. It was as if I knew you were out there.'

Anna traced the shape of his arm. 'And then there you were, Theo, in that lift, and you were a kaleidoscope of wonder! Talking to me and keeping me distracted because you cared enough that I might be scared.'

He raised and kissed her hand. 'I never want you to be scared.' He stroked her fingers absent-mindedly and was quiet for a while. 'I think I know what you mean about Ned, about knowing deep down that he wasn't right. It was a similar thing for me with Kitty—'

'Kitty? The girl you liked at school?'

'Yes.' Theo took a few breaths – a few more than Anna was comfortable with. 'When you came along, it blew any feelings I had for her out of the water. Put things into perspective.'

'I like to hear that,' she admitted, relieved.

Theo sat up. 'Actually, it was a bit more than just at school. Our paths crossed after school as well.'

Anna looked at him and felt a surge of concern that there might be more to this Kitty girl than he had let on. It tugged at her old sense of inadequacy, her deep-seated fear of not measuring up to the Mirabelles and Felicitys she knew would have been part of his circle. 'You can say anything, you know, Theo. No secrets, remember?' She kissed him.

'There is something, actually... Something I probably should have told you a long time ago,' he began hesitantly.

She hated the icy drip in her veins. *Oh no, please be gentle, Theo. Don't destroy our magic, don't hurt me...*

'What sort of something?' she asked, the roof of her mouth dry.

'It's about a child.'

Anna felt the colour drain from her face as her smile faded to something like terror. *Oh my God! Oh my good God!*

'A child that... I have never met or know anything about.'

She placed her shaking hand on her mouth.

All of a sudden the words began to tumble out of Theo's mouth. 'Actually, he's not a child any more – I assume he's older than me – but he's my brother, a brother I have never met. Though I do know his name. Alexander.'

'Your brother?' she asked, her relief written all over her face. 'Blimey, I wondered what you were going to say! You have a brother?'

He looked up at her, his expression unreadable, closed. 'Yes. My mum let it slip when she was rowing with my dad once, pissed of course. My dad has another son. He doesn't know I know and my mum made me swear never to mention it to her or anyone. Only Spud knows.'

'I wish you'd told me. Especially given you felt you could tell Spud but not me – I am your wife!' She raised her voice in indignation.

'I know.' Theo pinched the bridge of his nose. 'I could never find the right time.'

'But the right time is now?' She bent down and kissed his face.

'Yes, the right time is now.'

'Theo, I sometimes wonder about all the things you try to contain – I wish you would let me in more.'

'I'll try.' He kissed her nose.

'I have spent my whole life without anyone watching out for me. I didn't have anyone to love who would love me back, because everyone I have ever loved has left me on my own. And then there you were! And here we are! And I want to look out for you too, I want you to share things with me.'

'I promise I'll try.' He tilted his head and looked at her for several moments. 'Right from the start, you came across as so strong and assured, I would never have guessed that you were afraid of anything.'

'I guess we all wear armour.'

'I guess we do.'

'But what I want to say, Theo, is this. I do want a baby, more than you know. I want a family and I honestly, truly believe it would make our lives complete. I really do!'

'Anna, I just don't think—'

'No, don't say it again, I can't bear to hear it. Please let me finish.' She took a deep breath. 'I've never told another living soul this, but since I was a little girl I have written letters to the kids I want to have one day.'

'You have?' His brow creased in confusion.

'Yes. Not lots, but maybe one or two a year. I know it sounds nuts, but it started as just, you know, a little girl thing, but then it gave me comfort when everything around me crumbled to nothing. It made me believe I had a future, a family waiting for me, and it gave me something to feel hopeful about. It still does, in fact.'

Theo ran his palm over her back. 'I understand that.'

'I even gave them names.' She bit her lip, embarrassment making her more reticent now.

'What are their names?' he whispered.

'They're called Fifi and Fox.'

She was glad he didn't laugh and grateful there was no further interrogation. He seemed to just calmly accept it, which hopefully meant he didn't think she was bonkers. She drew courage from this. 'And the thought of not getting to meet Fifi and Fox breaks me in two.' She placed her hand on her chest, where the pain was real. 'I won't give up on the idea, I can't. And I am very aware that we haven't got so much time when it comes to being young and healthy. Look at my mum...'

She slipped down the bed until her head rested on his chest. He stroked her hair and cooed to her until she felt herself slipping into sleep, but her breathing was fractured by the tears that trickled unbidden along her cheekbone and came to rest on her husband's skin. Saying the words was one thing, but accepting them in her heart was quite another.

In the middle of the night she woke and stared out at the sea, where a wide, low moon lay reflected in the calm water. She glanced across at Theo, who was sleeping deeply. Climbing off the bed, she pulled open the drawer of the teak desk and slid out a sheet of fancy paper embossed with the hotel's name and logo. Creeping barefoot out onto the deck, she sat with her back against the wall of the villa and, embraced by the warm breeze, began to write.

My Fifi and Fox, I can feel you slipping out of reach... I love my husband, I do, but I am desperate for you, my children.

One year into our marriage and still no babies. I have asked. I have pleaded. I don't know what to try next.

I await the day I can hold you in my arms. I think about you more and more and every month that passes makes my longing worse.

Melissa says be patient. I am being patient, I have been patient! And it's easy for her to say with young Nicholas nursing on her lap.

I want to be a mum.

I want to be YOUR mum.

I want it more than anything. All I have to do now is convince Theo that it will be fine.

It will all be fine.

Your mum in waiting...

X

* * *

Having been back in the grey UK for a month, the sun-soaked paradise of the Maldives was already a distant memory. Theo had gone to meet his best friend, Spud, for a drink after work. Spud and his family were moving to the States and Anna knew it was going to be hard for Theo to say goodbye. He and Spud had been close ever since university and Spud was his one confidant. She liked Spud and his wife Kumi, although she found him and

Theo an odd pairing – on paper they had very little in common. Anna laughed softly to herself. 'Hello, kettle…'

She walked along Fulham Broadway, off to Melissa's house for a glass of plonk and a catch-up, hoping to avoid the rain that threatened. She didn't see her friend as often as she used to, not now busy family life claimed more and more of her time. Nursery had brought Melissa a whole new group of friends, women who sipped coffee and shared snacks while their children played happily on the floor. Anna felt awkward among them, no matter how friendly their welcome or well-intentioned their questions. She had managed one coffee morning, sitting with them and smiling benignly as they breastfed their rosebud-mouthed babies and debated the merits of organic versus non-organic fruit and the best way to deal with night-time bouts of croup. She had felt she had little to add and left as soon as it was polite to do so, exiting with a small wave and a promise to see them again soon. Then she'd sat in the back of the cab with a pulse to her womb and a tightening of her nipples.

Anna smiled now at how Melissa had turned into this wonderful mother, thinking of her loud friend who had made her laugh every single day when they worked together right there on Fulham Broadway. She pulled her coat around her shoulders and walked briskly past her old office, still wary of bumping into Mr Knowles, definitely a member of the arsehole club. She thought of Jordan and smiled, then pictured the shiner Sylvie had given her creepy boss. All of a sudden, and without too much consideration, she took a sharp right in the direction of where Ned's parents lived. It immediately felt like the most natural thing in the world to go and visit the couple she had been so fond of.

Anna was confident that Melissa wouldn't mind or even notice if she was half an hour late. She was usually knee-deep in Lego around this time, cooking supper for Gerard with a baby monitor turned up full whack and a large glass of Chardonnay in the hand that wasn't stirring the cooking pot full of sauce from a jar.

She stared at the block of flats with its concrete walkways and the chequerboard of lamplight in some of the windows. There was something rather fairy tale about it and Anna felt a pull of affection for this life, a life that could so easily have been hers. She trod the path to the flat and waited by the front door, thinking of the first night Ned had brought her there, how natural it had felt being among his family, his friends. She smothered the image of Stella fiddling with the pearls at her neck, Perry knocking back Scotch like it was lemonade, and the way they always managed to make her feel like an outsider. The stiff formality of their home was at such odds with the warm, open hearth of Sylvie and Jack.

Peeking though the window into the chaotic kitchen crowded with pans, cardboard boxes crammed with goodness knows what, and tins of food, she saw it was reassuringly just as she had remembered it. She pressed the doorbell and felt the pulse of nerves in her veins. Supposing Ned was there? Well, if he was, she'd say hi and leave... It was as she considered making a run for it that the door opened and there stood Sylvie in her apron and holding a cigarette. It had been a good few years since she'd last seen her, but she hadn't aged a day.

'Come in then! Standing there letting all the heat out!' Sylvie tutted affectionately, as if Anna had been there only yesterday and this was nothing out of the ordinary.

Anna stepped forward and into her arms. It felt like coming home and was the sweetest, most sincere hug she had had in a while. She inhaled the scent of sweet perfume, fried food and cigarette smoke that clung to Sylvie's set, grey hair.

'How's my girl?' Sylvie released her and let her eyes sweep over her form, top to toe. 'You look lovely.'

'I'm good. It's been so long.'

'Cup of tea, darlin'?' Sylvie asked, and just like that Anna remembered her lack of sentimentality, her core of steel and her heart of gold.

'Cup of tea would be lovely. Jack not here?'

Sylvie's shoulders straightened as she filled the kettle at the sink and rested her cigarette on her bottom lip. She reached into her pinny pocket with her spare hand and fished out a bit of loo roll.

'He's gone, love. Last June. Terrible shock. His bloody asthma.'

'Oh, Sylvie! Oh no! I am so sorry.' Anna felt incredibly sad. In her mind she held on to the fantasy that things always stayed just as she'd left them. The realisation that they hadn't was shattering. If the proof were not standing in front of her, she would have been hard pushed to picture Sylvie without Jack or vice versa.

'Well…' Sylvie sniffed as she plugged the kettle in. 'No amount of sorrys is going to bring him back, that's for sure, but I d'narf miss him, the silly old sod!' She sniffed again.

'I bet you do. He was a lovely man.'

'He was.' Sylvie nodded. 'It's the little things I miss. I used to nag him about getting a dishwasher and he'd say, "Dishwasher? You've got me!" and now I do the dishes on me own and it's my saddest time. And I miss his noise in the morning. I used to lie in bed and he'd be up five minutes before me alarm, rattling around in here, clinking cups and running the tap and I used to curse him for waking me up too soon. But oh my good God, what wouldn't I give to hear him now, just the other side of the wall, making me a cuppa before me alarm.'

Anna nodded her understanding. 'I remember when my mum died, and you're right, it was the little things… I always used to tread down the backs of my school shoes and just slip them off when I came home from school and when I woke up the next morning, Mum would always have unpicked the double bows and placed them side by side under the radiator with the backs pushed up and the laces looped outside so they wouldn't get stuck under my foot, all ready for me.' She gulped and stared down at her feet, the memory as vivid now as if it was yesterday. 'When I eventually went back to school after she'd died, I couldn't find one shoe and when I did, the laces were still knotted and I had to squeeze and shove my foot in and I cried. I sobbed because even though I was only young, I knew that this was one of a thousand little things that Mum had always done for me but would never do for me again.'

And then I got Theo and he unlaced my boots for me and set them side by side and I knew he was the one.

'Oh good Lord, will you look at us? Right maudlin pair!' Sylvie sighed. 'Biscuit?' She pulled the dusty wooden biscuit barrel from the shelf and popped off the lid.

Anna took the obligatory two soft custard creams, knowing resistance was futile. 'Thank you.'

The women made their way into the cramped sitting room. The lack of space was largely due to the addition of a large, unwieldy running machine on the rug in front of the fireplace.

'Ooh, what's this then? Are you into your keep-fit?' Anna sidled past the huge contraption, trying not to spill her tea.

'No, bloody thing drives me crackers! Ned's wife, Cheryl, bought it for me, thought it might encourage me to stop smoking – did it buggery! I use it to hang the washing on to dry and when Joan my mobile hairdresser comes to do me hair on a Thursday afternoon, we put my chair on it so I'm up high and Joan can reach easier, it helps with her dodgy back. I've never even switched it on, but I don't tell Cheryl that – she's a kind girl, means well. But would you look at the bloody thing!' Sylvie tutted at it with love in her eyes.

Anna swallowed, forming a picture of Ned's wife, who now had a name – Cheryl. Generous Cheryl, who cared about Sylvie's health. A tang of jealousy bloomed on the back of her tongue; she washed it away with hot tea and a small nibble of custard cream. 'Is Ned okay? Happy?'

'Oh, he's smashing. Here, wait till you see these little bobby-dazzlers.' Sylvie reached over to the nest of tables and plucked a framed photo of two little boys, aged about four and five and both in full Chelsea strips. 'What do you think? That's Ned and Cheryl's boys, Alfie and Archie, they're proper boys, run her ragged, they do, but she worships them. We all do. They get away with blue murder, but I can't resist them! They march straight in here and climb up till they can reach me chocolates, then they put their bloody awful telly programme on and lie end to end on the sofa, like lords of the manor. Oh, they have me in stitches! The things they say! Jack was proper smitten. They miss him. We all do.'

Anna held the picture in her palm and stared at the two little faces, beautiful like their dad.

They might have been mine...

'You all right, girl?'

Anna nodded and handed Sylvie back the picture of Alfie and Archie. 'They look lovely. Lucky you.'

'Yes, lucky old me.' Sylvie let her eyes wander to the chair that used to be Jack's.

'I... I'm sorry I haven't been before and I would have come to Jack's funeral had I known.'

Sylvie humphed, as if this reflection was rather pointless. She reached for the packet of cigarettes on the arm of her chair. 'That's all right, love. It's just life, isn't it? We are all busy, too busy. I heard you got married – Nitz bumped into that American mate of yours. The one with the big gob. I see her around sometimes, usually hear her first.'

Anna laughed and couldn't wait to share this with Melissa. 'Yes.' She ran her thumb over the back of her wedding ring. 'He's called Theo and he's lovely, Sylvie, you'd like him.' She felt the creep of a blush along her neck, a misplaced awkwardness at the fact that she had finished with Ned, however long ago.

'Well, course I would! Bring him with you next time. I'll make him a fruitcake, everyone loves my fruitcake.'

'Yes, they do.' Anna sipped her tea and wondered what the hell she was doing. It was a dangerous game, poking around in the boxes of her past that she had sealed and filed long ago.

'Have you got little ones?' Sylvie asked, taking a drag on her newly lit cigarette and holding the smoke in her chest.

'Not yet,' Anna managed, cursing the sting of tears at the back of her throat.

'Well, you want to get a move on! Time waits for no man and no woman's eggs!' Sylvie laughed and wheezed simultaneously.

'Do you think you and Jack would have been just as happy if you hadn't had kids?' Anna swallowed the remaining half of her biscuit.

Sylvie let out a sound that was part snort, part wail. 'Ooh, now there's a question.' She shook her head at the absurdity of the suggestion. 'I mean, I loved Jack, God knows I did – I do!' She exhaled, blowing blue smoke up towards the yellowed ceiling. 'But a life without being a mum?' She turned down her lined mouth and shook her head. 'I know some women choose that, and that's their right, and some women have no choice and make the best of it. But for me? It's not a life I'd want. I don't know what I'd have done without my littl'uns. And it's not only missing out on kids – I can't imagine not being a nana.'

'I think a lot about my mum and how it was such a waste of motherhood – not that I'm not grateful to her, and she was wonderful to me, but to get such a short space of time at it…' She ran her hand over her face. 'I don't know, Sylvie, I'm probably thinking too much.'

'I guess the thing to remember is that you don't miss what you don't have, isn't that what they say?'

Anna needed air, but she fought the compulsion to run out the front door. She finished her drink and exchanged a warm goodbye, making a promise to come back soon that they both knew she was unlikely to keep.

Sylvie wrapped her in her arms. 'You take care now, girl.' She wagged her finger at her like she was a child. 'Tell that Theo to look after you. Be lucky!'

'I will.' She blew a kiss and trod the path, pulling her collar closed around her neck.

I will be lucky and I will take care, as best I can. But you

are wrong, lovely Sylvie, you can miss what you never had.
I miss my mum being here now that I am grown up, I miss my
brother chatting to my husband, I miss my dad being there for
my birthdays, I miss family Christmases and I miss my babies,
wherever they are…

It was these thoughts that made falling asleep difficult, that
and the fact that she was unconsciously waiting for the sound
of Theo's key in the front door. He and Spud must have made
quite a night of it.

She was in the first throes of a dream when she felt him sidle
under the duvet. She could smell the tang of beer and cigarette
smoke on him, and he was decidedly damp.

'Youokaydarling?' she managed in her half-wakened state.

'I went to Blackheath and got caught in the rain,' he whispered.

Anna took in his words, too comfy to move and too dozy to
ask what he'd been doing all the way out in Blackheath. She
did, however, notice that his movements were a bit spiky and
his breathing uneven, as if something had unsettled him. She
felt him move across the mattress and lie against her crescent-
shaped form, spooning alongside her, skin to skin, with his face
tucked against the warmth of her neck.

'I love you, Anna. I do. I love you so much.'

She smiled as her head sank deeper into the pillow. She flung
her right arm backwards and let it rest on his head. *I bet Cheryl*
and Ned don't have this. We are lucky. We are magic.

'Loveyoutoo.' She yawned before sleep dragged her down.

Fifteen

Anna rushed from Leicester Square up along Long Acre – the excitement of being in the West End for her never waned. It was on days like this that she wished Jordan were closer, knowing he would love to be walking the pavements of Theatreland, staring at the posters, offering a critique of actors he didn't know and looking up in awe at the bright lights, murmuring, 'One day…' under determined breath.

'I miss you, Goldpie,' she whispered into the grey mist of the London morning.

Only last week she had mailed him a picture of their new puppy Griff, part Alsatian, part goodness knows what, chosen from a dozen upturned, expectant snouts pressed eagerly to the viewing windows at the dog rehoming centre.

Theo had bent down in the corridor to admire a spaniel with an appealing bound and an eager little muzzle that was almost smiling. Anna had laughed, watching her man fall in love with the little creatures who needed a home, knowing that to pick one would be a hard task. She figured it was the pretty spaniel that would be coming home with them, but then she turned and saw Griff. Unlike the other dogs, who seemed to understand that they needed to preen and look as appealing as possible, he just lay there with his long brindle snout on his big paws and one ear turned down. When he did deign to look in her direction, his eyebrows lifted at the inner corners, his mouth drooped and his expression was one of pure sorrow.

'Oh! Oh, look at you!' She fell to her knees and placed her hand on the glass of Griff's enclosure. She'd seen that face a dozen times during her stay at Mead House, she knew how it felt to have given up hope, one of life's rejects. *Like the dented tins left last on the shelf, the ones no one really wanted because they didn't know or care what wonderful things might be contained within.*

'Hello! Hello, my darling,' she cooed.

'He's had a bit of a rotten start, young Griff.' The kennel supervisor spoke with resignation. 'He's a bit of a loner and has trust issues. Sure, he's a bit rough around the edges, but he's the type of dog that will thrive if loved enough.'

'I can do that!' she had offered forcefully and without hesitation. 'I can love him enough!'

Theo had stood and reached for her hand, which he squeezed in support. 'Yes, you can.'

The nights she spent lying on the kitchen floor with their new resident, stroking his flank and explaining that there was no need to be afraid, he could stop shaking, no one here was going to hurt him, ever, were starting to pay off. Griff had lost his tremble and had twice now crept close to where she sat on the sofa, pushing his nose onto her calf. This had made her happier than she could describe. Theo had been right: it had helped take her mind off the tension between them, tension that hadn't really gone away since their Maldives trip the previous month.

She eagerly awaited Jordan's response, knowing it would be

blunt and humorous, but also that he would understand the absolute joy she found in a dog like Griff.

Turning sharp left, Anna picked up the pace until she reached the little café in Drury Lane. Lisa was already in situ and had commandeered a booth.

'Sorry I'm late, my train was delayed. Nightmare!'

'More like you couldn't leave that doggy! You are obsessed, woman.' Lisa smiled, having been regaled with tales of Griff during an excited late-night phone call.

'I am!' Anna admitted. 'Completely.'

'How many times did you go back and reassure him you were only going out for a while and not to worry?'

Anna threw her head back and laughed loudly at the accuracy of her half-sister's words. 'More than five, less than ten.'

Lisa rolled her eyes.

Anna looked around the café. 'Where's Kaylee?'

'Well, yes, lovely to see you too!' Lisa tutted. 'You can't even hide your disappointment at it being just me!'

Anna laughed. 'Sorry, it is lovely to see you, I was just expecting to see the little munchkin.'

'Micky drove us up and he's taken her to see the street entertainers in Covent Garden. We've got about half an hour, I'd say, before being an uncle out and about in town loses its novelty and becomes a chore.'

'Oh, she'll like that.' Anna didn't want to waste time talking about Micky, who could still only treat her with contempt. The discord sat between her and Lisa like an unpleasant, sharp thing, which they largely dodged around and rarely mentioned. 'Give her this from me.' She placed a navy paper Gap bag on the laminate tabletop and smiled.

'You shouldn't have! She's a lucky girl. Thank you, Anna. She loves her clothes.'

'My pleasure. I like looking at all the little outfits, so much cool stuff!'

Lisa peeked inside the bag at the pink sweatshirt and the packet of rainbow-striped socks.

'You sounded keen to meet up, everything okay?' Anna's thoughts had spun with all that Lisa might be wanting to say, none of it positive.

'Yes, everything's good. I just wanted to tell you something.' Lisa pushed the bag away and clasped her knuckles on the table-top, as if this required no less than her full attention.

Anna sat forward on the banquette, keen to hear.

Lisa took a deep breath and dipped her chin. 'I remember the day we met, when you came to the house—'

'I think we all remember that day.'

'You said you wished you knew what had gone on between your mum and my dad. Our dad,' Lisa corrected. 'You wanted to know if it was a quick, irrelevant thing, a fling, and you thought that maybe he'd only written to you because he felt guilty or because his time was running out.'

'Yes. I do remember my mum saying she loved him and that maybe if things had been different, you know, different timing...' She felt her blush rise, mirrored by Lisa's own. This was, despite their mutual affection, still a less than comfortable topic. 'But that might have just been my mum's take on things. Her wish, if you like. I mean, I was little and so she was always going to sugar-coat things.'

'I know how that works.' Lisa sighed, referring to her own rather complex relationship with Kaylee's dad.

'What can I get you, love?' The slender waiter in his black waistcoat interrupted them, holding his little grey notepad in the air, his pen poised.

'Just a cup of tea, please.' Anna smiled.

'One cup of tea,' he repeated as he jotted this down. 'And for your sister?' He looked at Lisa and both women beamed, delighted that the connection was obvious to the outside world.

'Same, please.' Lisa drew breath and waited for him to turn on his heel before continuing. 'Well, two things. Firstly, I remembered something that I wanted to share with you. When I was little, no more than four or five, I'd say, I was sitting on the sofa with Dad when my mum came storming into the room and she was mad as hell. Her face was scarlet. She was holding a T-shirt, a pale pink T-shirt with capped sleeves. She shoved it into my dad's face and said, "What's this?" He shrugged and didn't say anything, but I saw him sit up straight, paying good attention but trying not to, if you can imagine.'

Anna nodded. She could imagine.

'And then my mum kind of... well, I don't know how else to put it, apart from to say that she kind of growled!'

'Growled?' Anna tried to picture such a thing.

'Yes, it was horrible. I was really scared. I can still picture her pulling at the fabric with all her might, stretching it thin, gripping it in her hands with her elbows sticking out and baring her teeth until it ripped. And then she really went to town, shredding it and yanking off pieces and flinging them to the floor. And then she calmed a little and was out of breath, and she turned to Dad and said, "It's bad enough you would chuck me over for another bloody woman, but don't you dare bring anything of hers into this house. Don't you dare!" And then she walked out and slammed the door.'

'God, that's awful.' Anna felt a spike of unease on behalf of Sally, who must have been hurting, and also for her half-sister, who had witnessed this very grown-up exchange.

'But it's what happened after she left the room that affected me the most and that's what I wanted to share with you.' Lisa ran her tongue over her lips. 'It was almost like I wasn't there. Dad slipped off the sofa and scurried about on the floor, gathering up the bits of pink T-shirt and holding them to his chest like they were something precious. It was this that struck me more than anything else. Not my mum going nuts, but the look on Dad's face as he scrabbled about, squeezing the scraps of cotton in his hands as if they were bits of dough that he might be able to put back together. And he looked...' She paused and stared at Anna. 'He looked completely broken, distraught.'

'That's so sad.' Anna conjured a picture of the man she had never known performing this desperate, demeaning act in front of his young daughter.

'Here we go, ladies. Two teas.' The waiter placed a cup and saucer in front of each of them and left sharply. The café was filling up and he was busy.

Lisa sat up straight and reached into her handbag. 'Anyway, the point of that story is this: I'd forgotten about it, put it to the back of my mind, until...' She flipped what was clearly a photograph back and forth between her thumb and forefinger. 'This is the reason I remembered the whole thing and I think it answers your question about whether it was anything more than a quick fling for Dad.'

Lisa slid the glossy Polaroid snap over the tabletop and there was her mum staring back at her! Anna felt her tears pool. She had precious few pictures of her mum and to see her face, young, smiling and so full of life was a real gift.

'Oh, Lisa!' she managed, before reaching for one of the scratchy white napkins that sat in a natty plastic dispenser at the end of the table.

'I found it in one of his books that he kept in his bedside cabinet. I'm no great reader and it nearly went to the charity shop, but for some reason I decided to flick through it. And there this was, nestling inside it. And look what she's wearing.' Lisa pointed.

Anna wiped her eyes and scrutinised the photo again. Karen Cole was sitting on a bed, a hospital bed, wearing a pink cap-sleeved T-shirt, and next to her sat a youthful, smiling Michael Harper, her dad. They were sitting squashed up against each other, with every possible part of their bodies in contact, thigh to thigh, hip to hip, heads inclined, touching. They looked happy, deliriously happy. Their joined arms formed a rough heart shape in front of them and there, resting half on her dad's forearm and half on her mum's was Anna, a tiny baby, swaddled in a white crocheted blanket.

The three of us. My parents. My family! This was the moment he told me about in his letter. This was when he held us both in his arms!

'The moment I saw this picture I remembered the T-shirt incident and so in answer to your question, I would say your mum, and you, for that matter, meant a whole lot to him. More than a whole lot.'

Anna cursed the tears that she blotted into the napkin. 'I can't tell you how lovely it is for me to see this.'

'Keep it, of course. It's yours.' Lisa smiled. 'He was my dad and I loved him and I hated how he hurt my mum, for all her faults, but he was your dad too and I don't doubt for a second that he loved you and your mum very much. And being kept apart from you must have been so hard.'

Anna nodded at this truth. 'What...' She sniffed and blew her nose. 'What was the book?'

'Ah, thought you might ask.' Lisa reached again into her bag and pulled out a pale green, cloth-covered edition of *The Jungle Book* by Rudyard Kipling.

'Of course it was.' Anna smiled and ran the tip of her finger over the face of the man in the photo. *My dad, my daddy.*

Having kissed her half-sister goodbye and with the book safely inside her bag, Anna raced back along Long Acre until she found a cab and jumped in.

'Barnes, please,' she managed through noisy tears.

'You okay, love?' the cabbie asked.

Anna nodded at him in the mirror.

'We'll have you home in no time. As I say to my little girl, there's nothing in the world that warrants lots of tears, nothing at all.' He gave a small chuckle.

She pictured a little girl at home waiting for her dad who was a black cab driver and her tears fell even harder. Anna took the book from her bag and placed it on her lap, taking comfort from the feel of it beneath her fingers. She looked out of the window as London rushed by.

She had made supper and was now pacing the kitchen, checking on the steak-and-ale pie in the oven and stirring the mash occasionally to keep it soft and warm. She filled the small watering can that lived under the sink and watered her potted lemon tree. Its stem was thickening and had even sprouted woody arms with dark, glossy leaves, but it was still to bear fruit.

'One day, Griff, we shall pick lemons for our summer drinks from this little plant. Just you wait and see.' She smiled at her puppy, who ignored her. This in itself was progress.

'Come on, Theo.' She wiped her hands on the dishcloth. It had been quite a day and she wanted nothing more than to tell her husband all about it. For the umpteenth time she opened the cover of the book and picked up the photograph, holding it up to the window, studying every aspect of the image that had only been in her possession for a few hours but had already been committed to memory, right down to the tiniest detail. She stared at the lick of dark hair across her dad's forehead, hair that she and Lisa had most definitely inherited. Her mum looked so young and beautiful, holding her tenderly and with an expression on her face that spoke of so much promise.

'Nine years...' Anna shook her head. It seemed unbelievable that this healthy-looking young woman in her prime was only to have nine more measly years on the planet. 'I wonder what you would have done differently if you'd known?' she asked the laughing face with eyes not dissimilar to her own. 'Probably nothing.'

Finally she heard his key in the front door. 'Come on, Griff, he's home!' She patted her thigh and raced into the hallway, to be greeted by a decidedly dishevelled husband.

'Theo!' She reached up and held him tight.

'What's up?' He looked at her with alarm.

'I've had a crazy day.'

'Crazy good or bad?'

'Good! Look at this.' Without waiting for him to settle home, she handed him the picture, cradling the book to her chest.

Theo pulled his head back to focus better.

'It's my mum and dad and me. Can you believe it? The only photograph of us all together, as far as I know, taken on the day I was born. Look how happy they are, look at my mum! She looks so young.'

He scrutinised the image and took his time replying. 'You look like both of them. I can see your facial shape in your father and you have your mother's smile and her eyes, undoubtedly.'

It was the perfect response. She loved that he was as interested in the picture as she was. 'I am so happy to have it, and guess what?'

He shook his head and shrugged, handing her back the photo-graph and slipping out of his suit jacket, which he hung on the newel post at the bottom of the stairs.

'He'd hidden the picture in this.' She held the book out on straightened arms. '*The Jungle Book*. He kept it by the side of his bed and as soon as Lisa mentioned it, I remembered that I'd had a copy too. Mine had a green cloth jacket just like this and my mum used to read bits of it to me. I just know he gave it to me. My mum used to get upset reading it and I could never understand why. But now it all makes sense.' She rushed forward and kissed him on the mouth with uncharacteristic enthusiasm. 'Don't you think it's wonderful?'

'If that's the reaction I'm going to get, then yes, I think it's wonderful.' He laughed. 'What happened to your copy?'

'I don't know.' She wrinkled her nose. 'I don't know where any of my stuff went, not that I had anything of value, just little bits and bobs and a few books, toys and whatnot. I know Joe sold lots of our things to get drugs.' She saw him flinch at this casual reminder of their very different worlds. 'And when I went to stay with my aunt and uncle, I suppose the landlord must have cleared out the flat. Can't blame him. It seems a shame, now I'm older, but at the time I didn't give it a second thought.'

'That's really sad.' He kissed her hair.

'I suppose it is. I am so, so happy to have this – you have no idea.' She again cradled the precious talisman to her chest. 'And I made supper.' She turned around, heading for the kitchen.

'A welcome hug and supper? It's my lucky night, which is good because today's been anything but lucky.' He grabbed a beer from the fridge and twisted the cap with his fingers. 'It's been bloody awful.'

She noted the tension in his back, the way he looked up to the ceiling and sighed, as if digesting bad news. It concerned her, but not as much as his furtive air. 'Why so awful?' Anna pulled the pie from the bottom oven and carried it to the table ready for serving.

Theo sat in his preferred chair and loosened his tie, petting Griff's snout with his free hand. 'Oh, Dad not listening to a very sound business proposal. It makes me so mad how dismissive he is. I just want to do something good with all this money that's sloshing around, you know? Use it to try and make a difference.'

'I know you do, honey.' They had had this conversation a thousand times and she was right behind him. She loved him all the more because of his social conscience and the way he never acted as if he was entitled to what he had. Theo was adamant that he should use his privileged position to try and do something positive for those less fortunate than himself, but his dad was categorically against this. It was a running battle between them.

'I've had this idea to renovate this old warehouse in Bristol into studios. It's perfect, red brick and beautiful. And it would be just right as a sort of halfway house for young adults coming out of care. Like when you came out of Mead House and needed somewhere to go.' He glanced up at her and she nodded back, full of love for him and his big heart. 'I've worked it all out. They could live there while they find their feet. I've had a chat with a woman from Bristol council and she said it was just the sort of venture they'd be interested in supporting. And it's not as if we won't get our money back – it'll just take a bit longer than with some of our other projects. That part of Bristol is ripe for development and once it's renovated, the place will be a massive asset for the company. It's a win-win. But no, he isn't interested. No doubt if it was anyone else coming up with the suggestion, he'd leap on it.'

'It sounds like a wonderful idea. My friend Shania would have loved the chance to go somewhere like that. You remember – the friend I told you about?'

'Yes, I remember of course.' He shook off his jacket. 'I was thinking of her, actually. And you.'

Anna's tears pooled at the memory of her last sighting of Shania, homeless and using. She sniffed. 'Having somewhere to go might have stopped her from... losing it. It breaks my heart, thinking of her out there somewhere. Such a different life to the one I wanted for her.'

'If only wishing was all it took.' He walked over, ran his thumb over her cheek and kissed her lightly, before making his way to the table.

'Yep, if only.'

'*I* just wish my dad wasn't so predictable. It's like he's constantly trying to goad me. Plus he's hired this girl at work and she's...'

Anna held the dishcloth in her hand and paused, disliking the squeeze of discomfort in her chest, before going to fetch the mash from the stove top. 'She's what?' she asked softly, taking in his expression, the reddening of his cheek, the glaze to his eyes.

'She's...' Theo filled his cheeks and exhaled, exasperated. He banged his beer bottle onto the tabletop. 'I don't know how to describe her apart from bloody annoying!'

She took her time at the Aga, collecting herself. Call it sixth sense, call it intuition, but there was something in the way that this girl bothered him that bothered her.

Don't be silly, Anna, she's a girl and he is home, home with you and today is a wonderful, wonderful day...

With supper finished and the dishes abandoned in the sink, the two sat on the deep sofa, staring at the fire that crackled in the hearth. As ever, it held them captive. The smoky scents and the pop and hiss of logs evoked an outdoorsy life Anna had never known, but it still made her think of forests, soil, seeds and fecundity.

Theo leant back into the soft cushions with his eyes closed and his legs stretched out in front of him, crossed at the ankles. 'I can feel you smiling next to me.' He spoke warmly.

'I can't help it! I keep thinking about my lovely photograph and that book. Oh, Theo, that book – I love that his hands

have touched it and that it obviously meant something to him.'
She curled her legs up beneath her and snuggled closer to her
husband, resting her head on his shoulder.

Theo gave a low, slow hum. She recognised this as his pre-
doze state, when to speak felt like too much effort.

'I feel sad for my parents. I could never say this to Lisa,
obviously, but it's awful, isn't it? They both knew they'd met the
love of their life, but they couldn't do anything about it because
Dad was already committed and didn't have a way of escaping
without causing hurt and damage to a whole group of people.'

'Going from what Lisa told you about the T-shirt ripping, I'd
say some damage had already been done.' He yawned.

Anna nodded. 'Yep, I think that's true. But what rotten bloody
luck. They say you can't help who you fall in love with. And I
can't help but think how different my life would have been if
they'd been able to stay together. Losing my mum would have
been just as crap, obviously, but at least I'd have had my dad.
And maybe he would have been able to help Joe too... It's made
me wonder, Theo, what things were like for the baby your dad
fathered, for Alexander. I hope he's having a good life...'

Theo patted her thigh with a hand that grew increasingly
heavy.

'Did you hear me, Theo?'

'I did, but I literally can't think about that right now.'

She watched his eyes close, as if he was willing her words to
stop.

'And it makes me think, Theo, what wouldn't my mum
have given to be in my position, with a man she loves and in
a beautiful home? What wouldn't Shania give to have all the
opportunities that we have?' She inhaled and briefly closed her

eyes too, drawing courage to speak the words that were waiting in her mouth, bumping against her teeth and sneaking around her gums, trying to find the courage to leap out. 'My mum was brave, she had a baby in the most difficult circumstances. No money, no partner, no support, but it didn't stop her, Theo.'

'Oh please, Anna.' He sat up, rubbing his eyes with his thumb and forefinger. 'Not this again.'

'Yes.' She twisted sideways to face him on the sofa. 'This again. What did you think, that it's just going to go away? Because it isn't. I see how much you love coming home to Griff and it makes me think about you becoming a dad and my biggest fear is that I am running out of time!' She cursed the desperate tone to her voice. 'I don't want to run out of time.' She repeated, more softly now, the admission painful.

'I can't keep up. One minute you tell me I am enough, that we are enough, and I feel things have settled, but then you jump right back to this.'

She heard the sharp edge of irritation in his words, slashing the cosy, happy, post-supper feeling that had wrapped around them like a warm blanket only seconds before. Griff, as if disturbed by the change of mood, stood and walked to his basket in the kitchen.

'I can't help it. I guess it's because I can't believe...' She paused, rethinking her phrasing. 'Or, more accurately, my heart and mind can't accept that what you're saying is final. I hope, pray that you will have this lightbulb moment when your doubts and worries disappear so that we can just go for it.'

Theo leant forward with his elbows resting on his knees, now fully awake, his words spoken over his shoulder, no doubt easier without having to see her expression. 'I can only keep repeating the facts to you and hope, no pray, that they resonate, because I have to tell you that I am beyond weary of this discussion. It is exhausting and damaging and it drives tiny wedges between us that I fear will be harder to remove than we might think.'

'Don't say that! Please don't say that! I love you!' She placed her hand on his back and saw him nod. Her heart raced.

'And I love you too, but every time we go back to square one, I wonder if it's enough.'

There was a moment or two of silence, each allowing the enormity of his words to permeate.

'I just wish I understood—'

'All right, Anna!' He jumped up from the sofa. 'I will try and make you understand.'

She shrank back against the seat cushions with a flutter of fear in her chest, unaccustomed to him using this tone.

'I spent night after night in a gloomy, cold school, wishing I was someone else, somewhere else. My life was hell. I was ripped apart each and every day. Bullied mercilessly by those fucking idiots. I was exhausted, afraid and lonely. I didn't have a refuge—'

She opened her mouth to speak. He held up a palm, cutting her short.

'And before you say another word, I know it was similar for you. But I don't know how to be a dad. There's stuff you don't know about—'

'What do you mean, "stuff I don't know about"?'

'I don't know!' he countered nonsensically. 'But I do know I can't bear the idea of a child of mine going through what I went through. I just can't! And my parents would insist that any child of mine went to Vaizey, a family tradition—'

'That's nuts. We can send them to any school we choose!'

'God, you just don't get it, do you? It's not that simple. I work for the company, they own a chunk of our house, they own our car, it's just how it is – we're tied to them.' He was shouting now. 'Vaizey College is part of that. And we can laugh about being weird, outsiders even, and it's all well and good for us now, but it was a bloody difficult path to get here, torturous, and I cannot in all conscience, in fact, I won't, allow a child to walk that path. If it wasn't for Mr Porter, well, I hate to think, but there were times when I tried to think of a way out, and if I could have walked to a high bridge or a cliff edge—'

'Theo, no! Please don't say that. Please don't!' She placed her hands over her ears, couldn't bear to hear what might come next. Instantly picturing the moment Joe left the house for the last time.

'Oh God, Anna.' Theo sank down onto the sofa edge and pulled her hands from the sides of her head, holding them in his own. 'I forgot. That was insensitive of me. I'm sorry, but I'm only telling you the truth. There were some dark, dark times for me.'

She felt the emotion coming through his shaking arms like a current.

'But what if our children don't suffer as you did, what if they have a lovely, happy life, guided by us? What if they go to a local school because they are our kids and we insist on it? What if they go through life as I did for my first nine years, knowing nothing but love and happiness? It was only my mum dying that changed my life, because up until that point it was a good life, a wonderful life!' Her voice faltered. 'Why can't it be like that for our children? Why can't we think of it like that? Instead of the worst-case scenario, let's think of the best.'

'I don't think you hear me, Anna. I don't think you hear what I say.' He released her arms and sat back down next to her.

Both stared at the fire. The ensuing silence calmed them. She mentally regrouped and when she finally spoke, she did so calmly, without the tension that had laced her words earlier. She noted that her husband responded differently. Gone was his visceral rejection of all she said. Instead, he sat with his head tilted and his expression neutral.

'I do hear you, Theo. I do. And I think the most important thing right now is that we keep talking.'

'Okay.'

These two syllables meant more to her than he could have imagined. 'I know that what you went through has clouded your view of the world and that is a shame because we all have choices. I was only nine, and a young nine at that. And I remember sitting in the school corridor and I felt like everyone that walked past knew what had happened and was stealing glances at me. Maybe they did or maybe that was my imagination. It's hard to know. Everything about that time is foggy, as if I was looking at the world through a dirty lens. And even though I was broken, I held the image of my mum's smiling face in my mind and she kept repeating, "It's okay, Anna Bee, you are going to be okay." I even nodded occasionally to show the mum in my mind that I had understood, even though I didn't believe it. I thought I was never going to be okay ever again.'

She looked up, happy that he was listening intently to her. It gave her the confidence to continue. 'I had only known a world of clean sheets, warm blankets, Saturday markets, Sunday fry-ups, hot sunny afternoons, homemade cakes, letters to Father Christmas, hard leather school shoes that you had to break in, gym knickers, bedtime stories, Easter eggs that we gobbled up on the spot, simple birthday parties where we sat under a sheet in the front room eating sandwiches, dancing to the radio, summer day trips to the sea, sweets once a week and a brother who farted on the bus to make me laugh.'

Theo gave a soft snort of laughter. She smiled at him.

'That was my life. Everything about me was average – build, height, looks, intelligence, the lot. There was nothing about me to make anyone look twice, unless you were my mum – she looked at me, looked at both me and Joe, as if we had just floated down from heaven. And the point is, every little experience built a small piece of armour that helped me to survive when things went wrong. And things did go wrong, Theo. Badly wrong. My life changed in ways so huge that my mind couldn't think about it. But everything I had experienced taught me that happy was possible! And that's the magic. I never ever stopped looking for it and then I found you.'

She looked up, shocked to realise that he was crying. He never cried.

'But that's just it, Anna Bee. What if you've got no model for being a good dad, no experience of it at all? What if all you've got to pass on is this feeling of dread and misery and wondering every day whether you're doing the wrong thing?'

Anna stared at her husband, but try as she might, she couldn't find the words that would placate them both. Instead, she leant forward and held him close, letting him cry.

With Theo upstairs taking a pre-bedtime shower, Anna stacked the dishwasher and let Griff out for his night-time wee. 'Good boy, darling.' She smoothed his head lovingly. Switching off the main light, she took joy from the subdued glow of the lamp, much easier on her tired eyes and appropriate she felt for the late hour. She reached into the kitchen drawer and retrieved her notebook and pen. Then she walked slowly to the table and pulled out a chair. It was with a heavy heart that she began to write.

Fifi and Fox,
Here it is.

She paused, feeling a twinge in her chest, sadness manifested, before taking a breath and continuing.

I have never been so close to giving up on my dream of you. Never.

I sit here at the kitchen table, writing with tears trickling down my face at these words. It's a hard thing for me to write, and an even harder thing to imagine. But, like always, I have to try and carry on, find the good, because there is one thing I know with absolute certainty and it's this – if I give in to the deep, cold sadness that lurks inside me, if I submit to the lonely longing for the people who have left me and the things I can't have, then the darkness will take hold. It will fill me right up and it will drown me.

I can't let that happen. Because while I am here there is always hope. Know, my darlings, that life is worth living. Life is worth living! It's up to us what shape that life takes. I had reason more than most to let my life crush me, but I didn't let it. I fought against it. And I will keep fighting – fighting to find the happy in this good, lucky life I have made, this life I share with Theo.

I will keep positive. I won't give up. I won't.

Anna

(I hardly dare write Mummy – it feels a lot like tempting fate.)

She pushed the pad and pen away from her, becoming aware of an echo in her mind. In an instant she was quite overcome by a dizziness that made the room spin. With her palms pressed flat on the tabletop, she straightened up, before placing her hand on her forehead, which felt a little clammy. She took deep breaths and loosened the neck of her jersey.

Anna heard a whisper coming from the doorway.

She turned slowly towards the noise.

Squinting now, as surely her eyes must be deceiving her, she placed her hand over her mouth and stared, shocked, surprised and delighted to see her mum, Karen Cole, standing there with her arms outstretched.

There was a second before she found her voice. 'Oh my God!'

Anna felt nothing but a rush of love for the woman she had missed so much. It was beyond wonderful to see her. She cocked her head to one side to listen to the words her mum was whispering from a smiling mouth, both of them overwhelmed by the joy of their reunion.

She placed her hand at her chest and took a sharp breath as she stood.

'Mummy! My mummy… I've missed you! All my life I've missed you! It never got easier, never.' She pointed towards the open window. 'Look! Look at the garden!' As she turned her head towards the window, she noticed the lemon tree sitting on the windowsill, each branch sagging under the weight of several bright, ripe fruits. She smiled. 'Oh! How beautiful!'

Her mum walked forward and gently took her daughter into her arms, wrapping her in a warm hug that soothed her bones and covered her with a blanket of peace.

'Anna...

'Bee...

'Come with me...

'Darling girl.'

As realisation dawned, Anna felt the swell of panic.

'Oh no! No, Mum, I'm not ready. Not ready at all. This can't be my time! No!' She shook her head. 'I don't want to leave Theo! I love him, Mum! Please!'

Karen Cole placed her hands on either side of her child's head and whispered, 'It will all be okay. Everything will be okay.'

Anna had no choice but to trust her. She felt her body yield in submission, and as she stumbled backwards she took one last look at her beloved Griff.

Falling to the floor, she heard Theo speaking, his tone urgent, but his words were muffled. She felt him gently push the blue tea towel from the Aga under her head.

'Anna!'

She was aware of the note of hysteria to his yell, the last thing she heard before being enveloped in darkness.

Sixteen

Theo was crying loudly. His sobs were interspersed with noisy, stuttering hiccups. This was the sound Anna opened her eyes to.

'Are you still here?' she croaked.

'Yes, I'm not leaving you.' He reached for her hand and kissed her fingers.

'I can't believe you've sat there all night. You should go home, get some sleep. They've run all the tests and I'm fine, Theo. I just fainted.' She swallowed. She was thirsty.

'You didn't just faint – you were unconscious for… for… I don't know, it seemed like bloody ages.' Theo's bottom lip trembled again. 'And you heard what they said – you have an irregular heartbeat.'

'Theo, millions of people have an irregular heartbeat and never even know about it. They only found it because they were looking, if you know what I mean.' She smiled.

'But they did find it and… and… I can't help thinking that you fainted because you were stressed—' A big sob cut him short. 'Because… Because I upset you when we were talking about… babies, and if you hadn't been so worked up… And if I'd been a bit more understanding…' He raked his fingers through his hair and sniffed dejectedly. 'It's my fault.'

She shook her head against the pillow. 'This isn't your fault. I was feeling pants and then, sparko!'

'I was so worried.' He wiped his eyes. 'I am still worried.'

'Please don't be, or I will be worrying about you worrying about me and that won't do either of us any good.' She raised a small smile, wishing the sick feeling in her stomach would pass and that the room would stop spinning.

'We're going to get you the best care, you can see any specialist – we'll make you better.'

'I don't want a fuss and I don't want to see a specialist. I am honestly fine.'

Theo leant in and rested his cheek on her arm, as close as he could get from his position in the chair next to her bed. His words were whispered, intended for her ears only. 'I love you, Anna Montgomery. I love you so much. You mean the world to me. I couldn't bear to lose you. It's you and me against the world, remember?'

'Yep. You and me against the world.' She felt a surge of love for her man.

'I need you by my side, Anna. No one understands me like you do, no one loves me like you do. Without you, I'm not sure I could dodge the puddles of shit – I'd just drop straight in and never resurface.'

He closed his eyes, and she smiled, remembering how on their first date she'd summarised her life to that point: mostly good, happy but with the occasional need to dodge a puddle of shit.

'I'm not going anywhere, Theo, I promise. Although in the

seconds before I fainted, I had the weirdest thing...' She paused and shut her eyes briefly, remembering the encounter.

'What was it?'

'I... I saw my mum!'

'Your mum?' She saw his face twitch in disbelief.

'Yes! She was in the doorway of the kitchen and she was smiling at me.' Anna felt the slip of tears along her right temple. 'It was so lovely to see her, she looked beautiful and she looked happy and I showed her the garden. She always wanted a garden.' She broke off, overcome by the emotion of it.

'Oh, darling. Was it a dream?'

She nodded lightly. 'Like a dream, but—'

'But it's upset you nonetheless. I understand.'

'No, Theo, it hasn't upset me. It was lovely, so, so lovely to see her face and hear her voice. She called me Anna Bee. I'd forgotten what she sounded like and there she was, it was so real...'

Theo grabbed her hand now and squeezed it tight, like he was willing himself to tell her something. She sighed, hoping they weren't going to have to go over everything all over again. It was true, she didn't feel that bad, and she wasn't especially worried about having fainted, but she was still tired and she just wanted them to sit there together, quietly, peacefully. He squeezed her hand again and then a great rush of words came out of him. She had to put all her attention on him just to be sure she wasn't getting the wrong end of the stick.

'So, I've been thinking, Anna, I want to give you what you want, I will need your help, but we should go for it, we should have our baby. Our baby! I decided, last night when you were lying there on the floor, I decided that I'd been selfish and unfair and cowardly and that I couldn't bear not to have you with me and so I made a promise to myself that—'

'Oh, Theo! Really?' She hoisted herself up in the bed and stared at him. 'You mean it?'

'I do.' He smiled. 'We can do it together, right?'

'Yes! Yes, my darling, that's right, we can do it together!' She reached for him and snuggled into his arms, her brain galloping off at nineteen to the dozen. A baby, at last! She'd get Melissa to help with decorating the nursery, and she'd ask Lisa about baby gear, clothes and everything. She couldn't wait to tell Jordan – a godfather, finally! She giggled, unable to contain the absolute joy that was bursting out of her. If fainting on the kitchen floor was what it had taken, then it was a price well worth paying.

She'd just started visualising different sorts of pushchairs when a familiar voice called from the doorway.

'What's going on here then?'

Anna looked over and was amazed to see Sylvie standing there in a stripey red tabard over her white cardigan and with her slippers firmly on her feet.

'Sylvie! What are you doing here?' Anna sat up slightly as Theo let her go, and rested on the pillows. 'It's so lovely to see you!'

'I bumped into that gobby friend of yours—'

'That'll be me!' Melissa shouted from behind Sylvie.

'Yeah…' Sylvie gestured behind her head with her thumb. 'Her, and she said she'd had a message from his lordship.' She now pointed at Theo.

'Hi, I'm Theo.' He stood, polite as ever, and walked over to shake her hand.

Anna felt the smallest flash of unease as her husband met the woman who had nearly become her mother-in-law. But Sylvie's reaction soon put paid to that.

'I know who you are. Hello, darlin'.' She hugged Theo to her. 'Anyway, she'd just got the message saying you'd been taken poorly and she was on her way here and I said I'd come too. I gave Nitz the keys so Cheryl could let the kids in from school. I usually give them their lunch on a Wednesday, and I'd already got the fish fingers out of the freezer. Anyway, here I am.'

Anna looked at Theo, his expression one of confusion, as if Sylvie was speaking another language.

'Would you like to sit down?' He offered her his seat, which she took.

'You sound like a newsreader. Very nice.' Sylvie winked at Anna.

'Thank you. I think.' Theo looked at Melissa and Anna watched the two of them exchange a smile.

'It's lovely of you to come, but I'm fine, honestly. I didn't want to worry anyone.' She had to admit it felt good to know she was this loved, that people were bothering about her.

'Theo said it was your heart?' Melissa looked at her friend with tears in her eyes.

'Don't cry, Melissa. He's just panicking. I'm fine.'

'You'd better stop saying you're fine or they'll have you out of this bed!' Sylvie huffed. 'I know what they're like in here. If I were you, I'd shut up and milk it. I wouldn't need asking twice if someone told me to lie down in clean sheets while they brought me tea.'

'Would you like a cup of tea?' Theo offered.

'Oh lovely, darlin', yes, white none. He's a good boy.' She voiced her approval and Anna beamed.

Yes, he is – and he's going to be a good, good dad!

'Right. White none coming up.' He caught Anna's eye before creeping from the room.

'You can't go around scaring us like that, honey.' Melissa stood at the end of the bed and squeezed her friend's toes inside the blanket. 'Theo sounded beside himself. How are you feeling really? Speak quickly before Mr Panic Pants comes back in.'

Anna shook her head. 'Genuinely okay! Just a bit out of sorts – dizzy, sick, and I don't know... exhausted.'

'Ever been bitten by a tick?' Sylvie asked, folding her arms under her bosom and crossing her slippered feet under the chair.

'A tick?'

'Yep.' Sylvie reached for an embroidered handkerchief stowed up her sleeve and blew her nose. 'Our Colin's Susan went out with a fella from the Lake District – bit of a hiker, bit of a dick-head, actually, but that's by the bye – anyways, he had all your symptoms and turned out he'd been bitten by a tick, had that lemon thing.'

'Lemon thing?' Melissa stared at Sylvie quizzically.

'Yes!' Sylvie nodded emphatically. 'A proper disease with all the symptoms the girl's mentioning.' She pointed at Anna lest there be any doubt as to the girl in question.

Melissa looked at Anna and when she was confident Sylvie wasn't looking she twirled her finger at her temple.

'I don't think I've been bitten by a tick – would I know?' Anna smiled, enjoying the company of two of her favourite people in the world, even if it was in a hospital ward and she was feeling off colour.

'Here we go.' Theo walked in and handed Sylvie a Styrofoam cup of tea.

'You are a poppet.' Sylvie took a sip. 'Here you go, you sit down, Melanie, I want to look out of the window.'

Melissa didn't correct Sylvie but sat in the chair and took her friend's hand. 'You have to take good care of you.'

'That's what I've been telling her,' Theo echoed.

'Ooh, I can see Hammersmith Bridge from here!' Sylvie called excitedly as she stood on tiptoes and peered through the blinds.

'Oh, dar-ling! I got here as soon as I could!' Everyone in the room turned to see Stella, who swept in with her hair just so, lipstick immaculate and her pearls resting on a navy cashmere twinset.

Anna looked at Theo, wondering if there was anyone he hadn't contacted.

'Not lemons! Limes! What am I like?' Sylvie suddenly screeched. 'It's limes disease, or something like that! Lemons, limes, same bloody thing, just a different colour.'

'You have Lyme disease?' Stella placed a hand at her chest, clearly alarmed at the possibility of catching something from her daughter-in-law. She arched a disapproving eyebrow at Sylvie.

'No, no!' Theo addressed his mother. 'She hasn't got a disease, she just fainted and I've been organising tea.'

'Ah!' Stella nodded and smiled knowingly. 'Well, that explains a lot.' She looked at Sylvie and spoke slowly, over-enunciating for good measure. 'I'll have a cup of Earl Grey if you have one, or anything herbal – mint or camomile would be fine. No milk.'

They all looked to Sylvie, waiting for her response at having been mistaken for the charlady.

'You want a cup of tea?' Sylvie asked.

'Yes. Yes, please. Earl Grey,' Stella repeated, shaking her wrap from her shoulders and folding it with her manicured hands.

'If you want a cup of tea, Princess Margaret, you can get it your bleedin' self!'

A couple of hours later, Anna and Theo were enjoying the peace and quiet. All visitors had left and it was just the two of them in the room, holding hands.

'I shan't ever forget the look on your mother's face when Sylvie called her Princess Margaret.' Anna gave a small, quiet chuckle despite her fatigue.

'I think what most offended Mum was that she has met Princess Margaret quite a few times and she's at least a decade younger.'

Anna smiled and yawned.

'You're tired, go to sleep and I'll sit here and guard you. As soon as the doctor comes to say we can go, I'll wake you, I promise.'

Anna closed her eyes and tried desperately to summon her mum, who now loomed large in her mind. Small details of her had faded over the years, but now she was once again able to recall the exact shape of her mouth, the particular way her hair fell over her face. It was so exciting to have this whole new way to remember her. *Mum*, she whispered to her in her head, *you're going to be a grandmother! Soon! Very soon!*

She heard the creak to the door and opened her eyes. It was the consultant, a smiling, curt, officious man in his mid sixties.

'How are we feeling?' he asked as he looked at her notes, held fast by a bulldog clip at the top of his clipboard.

'Okay. Ready to go home.'

'Good. Good.' He flipped the pages and held the clipboard behind his back. 'We have all your test results.'

'Right.' Theo sat forward in the chair and gripped her hand.

'As we discussed earlier, your heart is nothing to worry about at this stage, but with your family history we will keep an eye on it.'

'Thank you.' She squeezed Theo's hand. *See, nothing to worry about.*

'There was something else, however.' He paused. 'I know you mentioned irregular periods.'

'Yes. I've been a bit stressed and I know that can affect them.' She nodded.

'It's a bit more than that, I'm afraid.'

Theo's head shot up, and Anna held her breath.

'We ran some blood tests and your hormones are drastically out of balance. It would seem that you are in the middle of early menopause.'

Anna slowly let go of Theo's hand and sat up in the bed. 'What does that mean?' she whispered.

I know what it means! But I need you to say it! Because I might be dreaming again. Please, God, say I am dreaming again, this can't be happening to me, it can't!

'It means, Anna, that your fertility is coming to an end. Your menstrual cycle is slowing, hence the irregularity of your periods and, along with other symptoms, your fatigue, disturbed sleep, mood swings.'

Theo looked at her. These symptoms sounded familiar to both of them.

'I'm getting older on the inside quicker than I am on the outside,' she whispered as her heart thumped in her chest.

'You are far from old, Anna. Plenty of women go through this at a young age and we don't fully know why. Early menopause can just happen. At thirty it's unfortunate but not so out of the ordinary.'

But why has it happened to me?

'So it means no more periods?' Theo said, looking stunned but trying to find the silver lining.

'No more periods,' she whispered. 'No baby.' *Too late.* She hadn't realised she was crying, but fat tears were clogging her nose and throat and making speech painful. 'Oh, Theo! No... no... baby. Not now. Not ever. Not... with you. Not with any-one.' She sobbed into her sleeve.

The doctor tapped the end of the bed. 'I am very sorry. I shall leave you to gather your things.' He turned and walked briskly from the room.

Theo reached out and took her hand into his. She wanted to pull it away, wanted to retreat, but at the same time she welcomed the skin-to-skin contact. She left her hand where it was.

'Oh, Anna!'

She took a huge breath, forced a slanted smile and wiped away her tears. 'I'm trying to keep it together, Theo, I really am. Because if I give in to all this, I just might crack. I am hurt and sad and scared and furious.' She paused. 'I feel destroyed,' she murmured. 'That's exactly it. I feel completely destroyed.' Her small voice wavered.

'I can... I can only imagine what you're feeling,' he stuttered. 'We will get through this together. Okay?' He reached round and slid his arm across her back, planting a kiss on her scalp.

Anna grabbed at his shirtfront as a loud, loud sob left her throat, and then her sadness boiled over into rage and she screamed, 'No, Theo! Please, no! It's all I ever wanted!' She cried noisily, messily, clinging onto him for dear life. 'I wanted my babies. That is all I have ever wanted! Please, Theo. Oh God! Please, no!'

He wrapped her in his arms and rocked her gently until finally her crying ceased and she felt able to pack up to go home.

He left the room briefly and slowly, wretchedly, she climbed into her pants and jeans, tied up her trainers and slipped her jersey over her head. She slumped back down onto the bed.

Why me? Why? It was all I wanted...

'How are you doing?' Theo whispered when he came back in.

Anna shrugged and bit her lip.

He took up the seat by her bedside and again reached for her hand. 'I meant what I said earlier about making a pact when you were on the kitchen floor, when I thought...' He gulped. 'When I thought I might lose you.'

She turned her head towards him.

'I meant every word – that we should have a baby, that I will be a dad for you, with you.'

Her tears fell quickly and her voice when it came was barely more than a whisper. 'Bit late now,' she managed, disliking the flare of anger she felt towards this man who had left it too long. *Too late.*

'No, my darling! There will be a way. We'll find a way. We could... We could adopt! We could become parents that way – we could do it, we could!' He gripped her, clearly pleased that this might be something they could focus on. 'You know more than most how every kid needs a home. We might not be able to... to have a child, but we can help one. Give one a happy home, just like you've always wanted. We can teach it like your mum taught you – how to be strong, how to survive!'

'Or two.' Anna managed a small smile. Through her tears, through the intense pain that was tearing at her heart, she could just about hold on to what Theo was saying. He was right, they could save a child, or two. 'Two kids.'

'Yes, my Anna. Or two.' He placed his head on the side of the bed.

She watched his mouth move, as if offering up a silent prayer.

Theo went to fetch the car and left her in the hospital waiting room. She barely noticed the comings and goings in and out of the glass doors. Her eyes felt swollen and her body empty, numb. How could this happen to her?

Fifi and Fox, I can hardly bear to think of you, lost for ever somewhere...

'Anna?'

She looked up at the sound of her name and stared at the woman in front of her.

'Anna? It's me!'

It took a second or two for her to recognise the face – older, slimmer, and with new piercings in the nose and eyebrow, but still unmistakeably the face of her old roommate and friend. Shania! It was a shock from the last time she had seen her, a welcome, wonderful shock!

'Oh! Oh, Shania!' Anna stood and wrapped her arms around her friend. There was no one else in the world she wanted to see more – well, no one living.

Shania buried her face in her shoulder and there they stood in the busy foyer, each taking joy from the presence of the other. Eventually they pulled apart.

'Look at you!' Shania ran her fingers through Anna's hair. 'You are all grown up.'

'Not really.' She smiled at the girl she had missed. 'And look at you! You look really well.' She chose not to mention their last encounter, knowing that Shania would most likely not remember it, or at least not want to remember it. 'What are you doing here?'

Shania pointed downwards and Anna noticed the unmistakeable swell of a pregnancy bump. 'Early days, but here we are!'

'Oh God! That is...' Anna swallowed her tears. 'That is amazing! You look so well, you clever old thing.' She detested the musket ball of envy that stuck in her throat, knowing it came from a place beyond her control and not wishing her friend anything but good.

'Less of the old, if you don't mind.' Shania chuckled. 'What about you, what are you here for? Are you sick? You look like shit,' she said with typical candour and a flash of protective concern that Anna remembered from Mead House.

'No, I'm not sick. Just... just going home actually, been having a few tests.' She suppressed the howl that built in her chest, not wanting to do anything to detract from her friend's wonderful, joyous news.

'I can't believe it! My old mate, Anna with the core of steel!'

Not really, Shania. I'm already broken. I'm dust.

'So how can I get hold of you?' Shania asked eagerly. 'I've got to go in.' She pointed along the corridor. 'Plus we have way more to catch up on than we can do in a few minutes here.'

Anna opened her handbag and pulled out one of the fancy cards that Theo had had printed with their home address and number; for the second time, she gave her number to her friend.

'Here, call me here, anytime, please. I would dearly love to see you.' Anna held her close once more.

'I will. I promise.' Shania planted a kiss on her cheek. 'It's good to see you, doll.'

'It's good to see you too.'

Anna watched her friend walk away into the bowels of the hospital, waving until she was out of sight. Theo beeped and she looked out, making her way into the fresh air, her vision clouded by tears and her heart fit to burst.

'It's okay. In you get, my love.' Theo opened the passenger door and helped her slide onto the leather upholstery of his luxury car.

As he nipped round to the driver's side, Anna pulled down the sun visor and spoke to the little mirror and the face that stared back at her. 'I don't think it is okay. I don't think anything will ever be okay again.' She sniffed as Theo climbed back in and revved the engine. 'Did... Did you mean what you said about adoption?' She hardly dared ask.

'I did.' He looked at her earnestly. 'I really did.'

Seventeen

'So, tell me once again.'

It was two months since Anna's fainting spell and emergency dash to the hospital. Tonight she sat at the kitchen table, topped up her large glass of white and took a slug, as if his announcement or more accurately her response to it might require this Dutch courage.

'I've bought the warehouse in Bristol. I did it!' Theo grinned as if he were a schoolboy trying to convince her that his hare-brained scheme might just work. 'I thought about what my dad said, that I should put my money where my mouth is, and I did it!'

'For how much?'

'A little under a million.'

'Wow!'

Anna was torn. Part of her was delighted Theo was finally following his heart, building studios as safe houses for kids straight out of care. This had been his business proposal to his dad all those weeks ago, to buy a warehouse near the docks, convert it into studios and do some good. It all sounded sensible. But part of her was concerned that at this point in time, just as they were starting down the route to adoption, he was risking all of their security, their routine, to buy a warehouse in a city she had never even visited. She hated the thought that this might be the thing that stopped her from becoming a mum. The possibility was more than she could stand.

'And it doesn't have planning permission?'

'Yet. No planning permission yet.' He drummed his fingers. 'That's the critical word, but the potential is huge!'

'And you did this with our money, not the company's?'

'Yes. All of our money, in fact.' He gave a small, nervous laugh.

'And you get mad when your parents don't tell you things? Wow!'

Anna emptied her glass and reached again for the bottle. It wasn't the amount of money that was the issue – that sort of sum never felt real to her anyway. No, her main hurt stemmed from the fact that in spite of telling her constantly how they were a partnership in every sense, Theo had made the decision alone, a huge decision that had the power to affect every aspect of their future. His actions told her in no uncertain terms that neither her permission, approval nor even her knowledge of the transaction was required. It made her feel invalid, like sticks on a river – a feeling she had forgotten of late.

'I know it sounds reckless and seems a bit of a gamble.'

It was Anna's turn to give an uncomfortable laugh. 'Ya think?'

He reached across the table and gripped her wine-free hand. 'It's a beautiful red-brick warehouse with a view over the bend in the river looking down towards the Avon Gorge. The original tilt windows are still in situ and it has two towering chimneys. It reeks of history, Anna! And I can see the finished units in my mind's eye.' He used his hand to draw a line in the air. 'Wide, open-plan spaces with industrial detailing and simple kitchens and bathrooms – somewhere those kids can be proud of. All the floors will be stripped back and we'll use waxed ship's timbers. It'll be loft living on the water with beautiful Bristol as a backdrop. And the beneficiaries will be young people who need the support, people like Shania!' He smiled at her. 'This is the first thing I have done on my own, and it feels good! I know the business, Anna. I know we can make money on this and make a difference.'

'But your dad didn't seem to think so?'

The set of his jaw told her that she shouldn't have mentioned this, but that was just too bad.

'He didn't even consider it because it was my suggestion. You know how he is.' He sat back in the chair. 'If it had come from anyone else on the board or he'd thought of it himself, it would be a different matter. The numbers are solid and I am excited about the whole project. For the first time ever, I am excited about a project, and I would like you to be excited about it too.'

Anna tucked her hair behind her ears and sat forward with her elbows on the table. For most of her life she had been told how to feel, where to live, how to travel, given clothes from a communal box, shipped this way and that, until she'd finally been able to find her feet when she left care. Being part of any decision-making process when it came to her life was very important. 'I will be. I am excited for you, happy you're following your instinct, I get all that...'

'But?' he prompted, rolling his hand, hoping this might bring her to her point quicker. She noted the flicker of irritation in his eyes.

'But we're just about to have our first chat with the agency. Adoption is what we're working towards. That's what we're supposed to be excited about.'

'It doesn't have to be the end of your plans.'

'Our plans, Theo. Our plans.' She spoke sharply, and hated the look of disappointment on her husband's face. 'I just need to let it sink in a bit, that's all, and I hate that you did this thing without talking to me first. I even ask you before buying a pair of shoes!'

'Yes, but you don't have to. You know that. You're free to do as you please, of course you are.'

'I know I don't have to, but I still do. I do it out of courtesy and because I believe in transparency. No secrets, remember?' She took a sip of wine. 'And because at the back of my mind I'm still more than a little aware that our home, our lifestyle is only possible because of your family money and not the few shekels I toss into the pot each month. I guess this action from you enforces that.'

There was a beat of silence.

'Anna, you're my wife! I have never, ever wanted you to feel—'

'And I don't!' She cut him short. 'But that's the difference, I guess. I would never feel like I could do something like that with our money, but you do, you did! And I get it.'

A wave of unease washed over her. Talking about money made her feel uncomfortable. 'What will happen if you don't get planning permission?'

Theo held her gaze. 'I will. You have to trust me on this, Anna. I will show you and I will show my dad.'

'Is that why you've done it, to prove a point?'

'No. I've done it because I believe I can turn a million pounds into three and I can give kids who need it a helping hand, and if I can do it once, I can do it again and again. I thought you of all people would get that?'

'I do, I do. And I love that you want to do something like that, but from a purely selfish point of view, I don't want to do anything that might get in the way of our adoption plans.'

'I need to do this, Anna—'

'I know,' she interrupted. 'To prove you're not the little boy eating alone in the dining hall, the little boy who no one thought would amount to much. The little boy who wants to show his dad what he's capable of. I get it. But you should still have spoken to me first.'

Theo stood up and ran his fingers through his hair.

'I... I need to get to bed, I have an early start tomorrow – I'm getting the first train to Bristol. It leaves at stupid o'clock.'

'Please, Theo, don't just walk out! I want to talk to you.' She hated the desperate tone to her voice. She pictured herself on the stairs at her Aunt Lizzie's house. *No one wants me, I am annoying, weird.*

'I'm very tired, Anna.' He unbuttoned his collar.

'No, you're not! You're just tired of talking to me.'

She cursed the tears that spilled, aware of how quickly their conversation had deteriorated, as if this was always the destination and it was only the route they took that differed. 'We are supposed to be a couple, but it doesn't always feel like it. I'm your wife! It's not just the Bristol thing – there's so much you won't discuss. And it seems to be getting worse. Ever since... Ever since Spud went to the States. Is that it? Is it that now he's not here you can't even talk to me?' She sobbed. 'It makes me feel like less of a person – what am I if you can't even face me, talk to me? I don't want to be confrontational, but it often feels like that's all I'm left with, the only way to talk to you and the only way to get a response.'

Theo sighed. 'I thought you'd be happy!'

'And you can sigh, but it doesn't make the problem go away, Theo.'

'Can't this wait? I really do have to be up very early.' He looked at the floor, and at that moment she hated his cowardice.

'I want to be a mum,' she levelled. 'I really do, more than anything. I want us to adopt! It was your idea and it's the best idea you've ever had, not to mention my only chance now. I don't want to run out of time.'

'We're not running out of time,' he whispered. 'We've started the process, we've got a meeting with the adoption agency in a few days, and I'm right behind you. And if after that things have to be put on hold because—'

'Don't you dare!' Anna raised her voice and it surprised them both. 'Don't you dare throw another reason, another justification into the mix! You can't do that!' Her tears fell freely.

'Don't cry. Please, Anna, don't cry.'

'You think I want to cry? You think I like feeling this sad? You just don't understand what this would mean to me. I can do it on my own.' She brightened as she spoke. 'I've been thinking about it – if you don't want this, then I can do it alone!' She clasped her hands in unconscious prayer. Her next words were slow and considered. 'I don't want to do it alone, Theo. I want you by my side. I honestly, truly believe that once you see a child in our home, you'll feel differently and all your doubts, all your worries will disappear! I am begging you. Please, Theo, let our adoption be a priority…' She let this hang in the air.

'You think it's the answer for everything.'

'What if it's the answer for me?' Her voice was croaky, stretched reed-thin with emotion.

'Then maybe you're with the wrong guy!' he shot back angrily.

Anna felt herself shrink backwards. Her mouth fell open and her fear wrapped itself around her throat, making breathing difficult. Her husband's stricken expression told her that his words had either not been meant or had inadvertently revealed the truth. Either way, she was aghast.

'Don't say that! Don't say that, Theo!' she managed.

'Oh, Anna, I'm sorry!' He leant forward and kissed her hair.

'And I always thought...' She took a deep breath. 'I thought if I loved you enough, I could make you see just what an amazing person you are. I thought if I listened, really listened, you'd understand that what you have to say is always of interest to me. But I've come to realise that there is no such thing as loving you enough to fix you, Theo.' She beat her fist against the scrubbed wooden tabletop. 'It doesn't matter how much I love you. You need to love yourself and I can't make you do that.'

Theo ran his thumb along the pale underside of her arm. 'It's complicated.'

Anna's laughter exploded from her. 'You're telling me! That much I know, but it was never meant to be complicated, it was meant to be easy.' She sat up straight in the chair and collected herself, chugging the remainder of her wine and thinking of all the people who had drifted in and out of her world for whom life had been impossible – Joe, Shania, even Jordan, who lived a half life, cloistered away from his parents. But her and Theo? They could have had the moon! 'And it should have been so easy: we met, we fell in love, we got married, one way or another we should have had kids and stayed together, happy ever after! That's it! Nothing complicated at all!'

'Nothing is ever that simple.'

'Correction, nothing is that simple with you!' She was yelling now. 'Nothing! You turn every event into an excuse for even greater introspection, shutting all the little doors in your mind and your heart. You are so closed in!' She formed her fingers into a tight ball. 'All I wanted was for you to love me and for us to have our babies. That was all. And I thought I deserved you. I really did! Things have always been so shit for me, I thought I deserved you!' Her tears came again, beating a path that was as familiar to them both as the discussion itself. This was what happened: they drank, they fought, she cried and fell asleep and he stayed up and drank some more.

'I cannot bear the idea of a child going through what I went through, but I have said that I will try.'

'God, listen to yourself!' Anna wiped her face with the back of her palm, smearing her make-up across her cheeks. 'I'm sick of hearing it! Why is it always about you? Why is everything about Theo and what's best for you? Do I not count? Do you think because I don't come from money or because I'm common, I count less? Is that what you think? Is that why you feel able to go and blow a million fucking pounds on a shed somewhere without discussing it? Oh, it's only Anna, she won't mind!'

Theo shook his head.

'And you know what, buster?' She jabbed her finger at him. 'You didn't have it so bad. Okay, so you didn't have friends, and your parents are useless, but you weren't on the streets, you were in a real fancy school and your dad collected you in his sports car and whisked you away for foreign holidays. I can hear you telling that to the social worker right now! Poor Theo!' She laughed, but this quickly turned to more tears – this too was part of their routine.

'I don't expect you to understand,' he whispered. 'There's other stuff too. Difficult stuff, but I can't—'

'No, you're right, I don't understand because you can't explain it to me.' She balled her fingers into fists as her frustration bubbled. 'Because I lived with kids who'd come off the streets, kids whose parents were in jail! My mum and my brother died, the only family I had ever known, they died, Theo, and I was only a little girl and I went into care and slept with one eye open, trying to hide from a man who came into my room and put his fingers in my knickers!' She was yelling again now, banging the table. 'So don't you dare tell me how tough you had it because your tuck box ran out or the nanny forgot your name!'

'I don't know how to make you understand what I went through. I don't know what to say to you. I don't know how to make things better,' he said quietly.

'No, Theo, you never do!' She raised her palms. 'And that one stock phrase doesn't mean anything any more, not when you don't do anything to change the situation. They're just words that you hand out like Band-Aids.'

'I can't do this,' he murmured.

She heard his words and felt a stab of fear right through her core. She heard defeat in his tone and it felt as if the room was spinning. It was all she could do to hang on, trying not to fall.

* * *

Melissa stirred her coffee and licked the foam from the teaspoon. 'God, it's good to see you. And lovely to be out in the world of grown-ups!' She looked around the coffee shop.

'It's good to see you too.'

'And as much as I love them, the best bit is having a morning without some little person saying "Mommy! Mommy! Mommy!" fifteen times a minute. I swear to God, I often think about changing my name to something they can't pronounce, like Algernon or Myfanwy.'

'Myfanwy would work.' Anna smiled weakly, finding it hard to see beyond her own sadness and thinking how utterly joyful it would be to hear someone calling 'Mummy! Mummy! Mummy!' fifteen times a minute.

'So let me get this straight – you were gabbling a bit on the phone.' Melissa folded her arms on the table and looked at her friend. 'Theo has blown all your cash on this random building project?'

'That's about the size of it, yes.' She bit the back of her knuckle.

'So what does that mean? Are you having to sell the family silver? Live off beans?' Melissa waved her teaspoon in the air. 'Should you not be delighted that he's got this off the ground?'

'I probably should be, yes.' Anna sighed and rubbed her eyes. 'But what it actually means is that Theo is one stubborn idiot who has taken a gamble with our future, and right now I don't know if we need to sell the house, or whether we're broke or...' She raised her hands. 'I don't know much.'

Melissa squeezed her arm. 'Will you have to quit the broker's and go get a proper, better-paid job?'

She'd gone part time at Villiers House eighteen months ago, but she smarted at Melissa's derisory tone. She was still good at her job. 'Possibly, I really haven't thought that far ahead. We may even have to go and live in a bloody warehouse in Bristol.'

'Where is Bristol exactly?' Melissa asked.

'I'm not entirely sure, but it's up the motorway or across the motorway – I don't know. West. And the worst thing...' She looked up at her friend, trying to keep her emotions under control. 'The worst thing is that this project is a distraction, another reason to avoid the whole adoption thing. It might mean another delay.'

Melissa winced. 'Well, I've already told you what I think – you need to go for it! Fake his signature, lie, do whatever it takes! Do you think Gerard would have smiled and agreed if I'd told him I wanted a big wedding, two kids in quick succession, a dog, a large mortgage on a tiny house with no storage that we can't afford, and that my mom would be coming over from the States to stay for three months of every year? Of course not! He'd have run a mile. You have to be subtle, keep the sex good, make him feel like a king and quietly do exactly what you want to, or rather what you need to.' She winked. 'It works for me.'

Anna actually laughed out loud. 'I think that might work for a new car, but not for adopting a little person. I need him to be invested in it, otherwise it's a no go, at least not for us as a couple. And I don't see why it should be about pleasing him. Plus it's already killing me to have to ask for permission.' She shook her head. 'I just wish it were simpler. I wish he felt differently. But I'm getting desperate. I can't force him.'

She stared at the sugar shaker in the middle of the table. 'We had our initial interview with the adoption agency a couple of days ago and it was a disaster. Theo kind of fell apart...' She hung her head, remembering the awkward exchange where he'd given self-incriminating answers and had done anything but shine.

'Why do you think you would make a good parent?' they'd each been asked in turn.

To which he'd replied, 'I don't...' And then he'd gone all taciturn and rabbit-in-the-headlights, giving one-word answers, acting like exactly the sort of potential father no one in their right mind would go near. She still had no idea why he'd gone so weird all of a sudden, though despite her reservations she was pretty certain it had nothing to do with the Bristol thing.

Anna wasn't quite ready to share with Melissa the full horror of this, or their row afterwards, but she was confident her friend had got the gist.

Melissa banged the table. 'Well, you know what they say: desperate times call for desperate measures and wishing never changed jack shit. It's "doing" that does that.'

'True. It's his birthday next month and I'm thinking of really going to town, making him feel special, a way of wiping the slate clean. I need to do something to try and get us out of this arguing rut. I must admit, Mel, I'm getting close to—'

'Ditching him as the dad and adopting with someone else?'

Anna had been going to say, 'close to giving up'. Her friend's option hadn't entered her thoughts, until now.

She kissed Melissa on both cheeks and waved as they walked in opposite directions along Marylebone High Street. Preoccupied with thoughts of Theo's birthday, Anna wondered if tickets to a concert would be a good idea and whether she should invite his parents over for supper. It might heal the rift with Perry over this Bristol project.

A party! That was what she would do, a big old surprise

party! Sod the expense – it would give them all a wonderful lift. Now, which cake...?

As her taxi back from Marylebone High Street pulled up outside the house, she noticed someone sitting on the wall. *Shania!* With a bubble of excitement in her gut, she jumped out onto the pavement and ran over to her friend.

'Hello! Shania! It's so lovely to see you! You should have said you were coming over, have you been waiting long?' Anna spoke as she rummaged in her bag for her keys.

'Not long, no.'

'Come on, come in!'

'This is pretty nice.' Shania stared up at the front of the house.

Anna watched, with a pulse in her womb, as Shania rubbed the front of bump. 'And that little fella is growing! How far are you now?'

'Nearly four months and, actually, Anna, it's not one little fella – it's two!'

'What?' Anna screamed and grabbed her friend by the arm. *You are so lucky and I am trying to be happy, but part of me wants to cry with how unfair it all is. How I would have loved, loved to get my Fifi and Fox...* 'No way! Oh my God, that's amazing! How do you feel?'

'Tired, nervous, excited – the usual.' Shania shrugged, pulling at the open front of her coat, which had no chance of meeting over her distended stomach.

Anna pushed open the front door and watched as Shania walked in and stared up at the ceiling and the landing above. 'God, Anna!'

'It's beautiful, isn't it?'

'I should say. That bloke of yours got any brothers?'

Anna gave a wry smile, thinking of Alexander, whose name was not to be mentioned, ever, by anyone…

Shania shook her head in awe. 'To think we had to share that little wardrobe and a chest of drawers.'

'I gave you the biggest drawers, even though you were so grumpy!'

'I loved you, Anna. You were the first person in my whole life who wasn't mean to me. The first person who told me I was brilliant.' The two women exchanged a look of understanding.

Anna felt the swell of sadness at her friend's admission. 'You are brilliant. Now come on, let's get the fire going and I'll make us some tea.' She ushered her friend into the sitting room and sat her on the sofa, then put a match to the fire Theo had set.

'This is like a fancy hotel or something in a film.' Shania shrugged off her coat to reveal her thin, bobbled sweatshirt, a little stained with food on the front. She sat back on the deep sofa and Anna saw her expression soften as she settled into it.

'I'll be back in a mo. Just relax and I'll make us a cuppa.' She paused in the doorway and looked back at her friend, remembering her own first time in this grand room, the gateway to another world.

She was no more than a few minutes in the kitchen, making a quick cup of tea and letting Griff out, but when she came back in, Shania was deep in sleep. Anna pulled the soft throw from the arm of the chair and laid it over her friend's large stomach. *There we go, little babies, that'll keep you snug.* She sat back on the sofa and watched the fire jump and dance in the grate, sipping her tea and happy to be in the company of her mate, thinking of the time she had seen her on the street and how her heart had ached for her. Her eyes kept jumping to the shape of her bump. *What does it feel like to have those little ones in your tum? I bet it feels lovely.* She pulled the cushion from under her arm and shoved it up her jersey. Lying back, she looked at her feet over the bump. It made her cry.

Shania slept for an hour. When she finally opened her eyes, for a second she didn't know where she was.

'It's okay, Shania, you're here with me, Anna.'

'Jesus! Did I drop off?' Shania sat up straight, rubbing her eyes.

'Did you ever! You were dead to the world.'

Anna smiled. There was something about a person you'd shared a room with, slept next to for so long, that meant you could be completely relaxed in their company. Even after all this time apart, they didn't have to fill the air with pleasantries or be on best behaviour. She and Shania had cried and laughed together into the early hours, got dressed and undressed in front of each other, shared their meagre possessions and looked out for each other when they needed it the most; being together now was easy, comfortable, familiar.

'That cab driver who dropped you off, did you flag him down and ask his name? Or have you grown out of that now?'

Anna threw her head back and laughed until her tears gathered. It was as funny as it was sad. 'Actually, my dad found me.'

'For real?' Shania asked wide-eyed.

Anna shook her head. 'But we never got our happy ending. I got a letter from his solicitor after he died. And I met my half-sister, Lisa, who is lovely, and my half-brother, who is not so lovely.'

Shania shook her head. 'What was his surname?'

'Harper, Michael Harper.'

'Michael Harper,' she repeated. 'This information would have been very good if we'd had it TEN YEARS SOONER!' she shouted and they both collapsed laughing. 'Now, did I hear mention of a cup of tea?'

Anna giggled. 'I made you one earlier, but I drank it.'

'Bloody typical.' Shania knitted her fingers over her wide middle. 'I am thinking that maybe I should tell Samuel, their daddy.' She pointed at her tummy.

Anna remembered their chat in the hospital foyer. 'Well, that's up to you, but I think it's only fair. It doesn't mean he has to be involved if you don't want him to be, but not to tell him at all…?' She thought of her dad and wondered what might have happened if communication had been different.

'It's a hard conversation to have, Anna.'

'I know it. And you don't have to make a decision now, there's still plenty of time.'

Shania nodded. 'Now, about that cup of tea…'

Anna jumped up and headed to the kitchen.

She returned with a mug of tea and watched her friend hold it between her palms.

'I've never been in a room with a real fire before. It's lovely. I want to keep staring at it.'

'Me too. Hypnotic.' Anna tucked her feet under her legs. 'Shania, there's something I want to say to you. Something I want to tell you.'

'Well, good, because there's something I want to say to you too. You go first.' Shania sipped her tea.

'I bumped into you a while back. A few years ago. You were

on the street, and I gave you some cash and tried to help you, but you weren't very with it. I'd feel uncomfortable if I didn't tell you. But it broke my heart and I've been worried about you ever since.'

Shania turned to face her and took her time responding. 'I'm sad you saw me like that. I know I promised you…'

Anna smiled. 'Yes, you did.'

'Things after I left Mead House were…' She paused. 'They were pretty bad.'

Anna thought of Theo's project. Shania continued.

'I got in with the wrong crowd. Actually, that's not true, I was the wrong crowd. I gave up. I honestly thought my mum or dad might come and get me, invite me home, but…' She shrugged. 'Nothing. They'd just moved on and changed the shape of their lives and there was no space for me. It shocked me. Still shocks me.'

'I'll bet.'

'Drugs were the escape and with that choice everything else collapsed.'

'I know that story.' She thought of her beloved Joe, and Ruby Red Shoes, who she still remembered from time to time.

'I've fought hard over the last few years to get clean, to come back, and I have and I'm winning and I want to stay winning.'

'I am so proud of you.' Anna laid her hand on her arm. 'Really proud of you.'

'Well, I am proud of me too.'

'And now this! Babies!' Anna pointed at Shania's tum.

'Yep, babies. Not planned, but no less loved for that.'

'So, want to talk about their dad?'

Shania raised an eyebrow. 'Samuel's a nice guy. Clean-living, hard-working, but he wasn't for me, wanted to settle down and take me to the sunshine.'

'God, he sounds like a right bastard!'

Shania gave another booming laugh. 'As I say, a nice guy, but he's a bit… boring.'

'God, you think everything is boring!'

Shania laughed again. 'It was more than that. You know me, Anna, I can't fall for promises. I can't be let down again. It's better this way. It was a six-month thing before he went back to St Lucia, but for me it turned out to be a whole life thing! Who knew!'

'You'll be fine, Shania. You've turned your whole life around and you've put up with so much since you were a little girl. This is just another chapter.'

'I guess. I'm scared though, Anna. I don't want to mess this up.' As she sat there biting her lip, she looked to Anna like the teenager who'd perched on the end of the bed all those years ago in Mead House. 'And that's what I wanted to talk to you about.'

'Go on.' Anna sat forward, as if this might require her full concentration.

'When I went for my check-up they asked me who was going to be my birth partner and I felt like it was fate that I'd bumped into you in the hospital, so I said you.'

'Really?' Anna placed her hand at her neck.

'Yes, but only if you want to. There's no one else I'd want by my side when I go through this – I want it to be you, Anna.'

Tears flooded the back of Anna's throat. 'It will be an amazing thing for me to see your babies born and I would be honoured.' She stretched forward and held her friend close. 'Thank you for asking me.'

'Who else would I trust with this?' Shania kissed Anna on the cheek, the sweetest kiss she'd been given in a long time.

They heard the sound of a key in the door.

'That'll be Theo.'

'Will he mind me being here?' Shania prepared to stand.

Anna pushed her back into the seat. 'Of course not! He'll be glad to meet you at last.'

'Hello, you gorgeous boy!' They listened to him great Griff in the hallway and both of them giggled.

'Hey, Anna!' he called.

'In here! With Shania!'

'Oh.' Theo walked in and nodded at the two of them. 'Hi, Shania, it's good to finally meet you. I've heard so much about you.'

'You too.' Anna noted she spoke quietly.

'How's it going with the...' He pointed at her stomach, clearly unsure of the right thing to say.

'It's going great. I'm about sixteen weeks now and I've heard the next bit goes very quickly. And it's twins.'

'Twins? Oh my goodness!'

'Shania's asked me to be her birth partner.'

'Oh, wow!' He smiled. 'What does that mean?'

Anna felt a flip of love for her man, which was a pleasant change to how things had been of late. 'It means that I'm the one who guides her through this pregnancy and I'm the one she calls when we need to do the dash to the hospital!'

Theo looked at her and she could read his thoughts. *Can you cope with this, Anna? Is it too much for you, too painful?* 'I am so honoured, Theo – what a wonderful thing to be asked.' She hoped this would put his mind to rest.

'So you must be excited,' he said to Shania.

'More scared, to be honest. My own mum and dad were pretty rubbish and I've always been a bit scared of doing it wrong. But like it or not, these little ones are on their way and so I've just got to figure it out, you get me?'

Theo nodded. Anna saw the pain of recognition in his eyes. 'Yes, I get you,' he managed, before coughing and leaving the room in search of a beer.

Eighteen

Anna stood outside the bakery in the high street in her jeans and trainers – her busy day required this speedy footwear. It was now five in the afternoon and she knew that if it weren't for the excitement of the evening to come, she'd be feeling more than a little low. She had a lot on her mind. Theo had just resigned from his job, determined to go ahead with his warehouse renovation in Bristol, and that had caused another huge row. The one light in her life was Shania. They'd gone together to the hospital that morning and she'd seen the scan pictures: grainy images of two little lives, tightly coiled end to end in her friend's tummy. It was a miracle.

The planning of a surprise party for Theo's birthday had been a welcome distraction over the last couple of weeks, not only the dashing here and there to execute the million tiny chores that would make the event a night to remember, but doing it all in secret. The vast trays of lasagne were prepped and in the fridge, the white wine was chilled and the red rested. Beers lined the fridge door, balloons waited to be blown up, wrapped presents had been hidden in the spare-room closet and her freshly dry-cleaned party dress hung in her wardrobe, ready to wow!

The large, stiff, white carry-box lay flat on her arm. She smiled, chuffed with the delicate sponge-and-buttercream confection, its hand-piped message artistically scrawled in dark icing: 'Happy Birthday Theo! Ship Shape and Bristol Fashion!' it was a concession of sorts.

Her phone beeped in her pocket; a text from Melissa.

'What time tonight? Looking forward to it. You always go to so much trouble, it makes me feel even more guilty for forgetting Gerard's birthday, again! As if he needs any more reminders of just how crap a wife and mom I am. Nearly left Nicholas on a bus yesterday... I am imagining your tuts right now! It wasn't entirely my fault. Will explain later. By the way it's Myfanwy.'

She laughed loudly and did indeed tut. Yes, she went to a lot of trouble, but knowing how many birthday celebrations Theo missed out on in his youth, either due to an oversight at school or simply because of complete indifference from his preoccupied parents, she always wanted to make the day as special as she could for her man, no matter how old he was. And this year, despite their rows, she was determined to do something extra nice, to show him just how much she loved him. She smiled. Her plan was coming together very nicely.

She made her way home, changed into her party frock and pulled her hair into a ponytail before applying a slick of lipstick. Picking up the cake box, she prepared to decant it onto the cake stand. En route, she grabbed her phone from the countertop, its small flashing icon telling her she had another voicemail. It was a missed call from the birthday boy himself; he must have phoned when she was in the shower. With her free hand, she held the phone to her ear, squinting, as if this altered view might help her hear better...

She played the message again.

And again.

And again.

Anna slowly lowered her phone and looked out to the garden. She pushed at her ears, which felt strange, as if she was underwater. She double-blinked as her mind did what it always did when her thoughts were too loud, or she felt afraid or she just wanted to pass the time. It had been a long while since she'd felt the need to do her game. And right now it had nothing to do with passing the time.

A... *Anna Bee, you'll be okay.*

B... *birthday.*

C... *cake.*

D... *drink. I need a drink.*

E... *ever and ever and ever.*

F... *frightened. I'm frightened.*

G... *God help me.*

The cake, nestling in the box on her arm, seemed now to be an extraordinary weight and her arm cramped. Anna felt as if she was moving in slow motion.

She slid the cake carefully back onto the countertop. It could stay in the box.

She allowed a small burst of nervous laughter to leave her lips before firing off a round-robin text to Melissa, their other friends and her in-laws, explaining in the simplest of terms that the party was now cancelled and sorry for the very short notice.

It was no surprise to her that a call came in almost immediately from Stella. Anna let it go to voicemail and then listened to it. Her mother-in-law's whiny tone was enough to set her teeth on edge.

'Oh, Anna, really? How disappointing! We've gone to a lot of trouble to make sure Rhubarb gets fed and walked early and we've given Mrs Fayad a key to come and walk him for his late-night poo. Is there—'

Anna had heard enough. She pressed delete and resisted the temptation to call her back and scream that she couldn't give a shit about Rhubarb or any arrangements they might have made. Actually, that wasn't true; she did give a shit about Rhubarb, thinking then how she loved him and Griff, as much if not more than most of the arsehole humans in the family.

Family... This is not how I want my family to be. Not what I want at all.

Anna let Griff out for a quick run before filling his bowl with dried food, which he wolfed down as soon as he came back in. She switched on the dim lamp in the cooker hood, preferring to be in semi-darkness. Sitting on the reclaimed pew at the wide scrubbed table with her back to the wall, facing the door and with tears streaming from swollen eyes, she placed her phone on the surface and pressed play over and over and over.

H... hob.

I... ice bucket.

J... Jack Daniels.

K... kitchen roll.

L... lemon tree, still no bloody lemons.

M... microwave.

N... noise.

O... opening the front door.

P... petrified, so scared of what comes next.

Q... quiet, the hush before the storm...

She heard the sound of his keys being dropped onto the dresser in the hall and sat up straight. Her heart pounded, her mouth was dry. Griff gave a single bark and looked to her for reassurance.

'It's okay, puppy,' she whispered, unsure if anything was ever going to be okay again.

Theo slowly eased the kitchen door open. She felt the tiniest spark of satisfaction at the sight of him looking eagerly around the room, expecting a birthday celebration and getting nothing, nothing at all. She watched his smile fade and a look of concern take its place.

Good, you should be concerned.

'What's going on?' he asked, locating her finally at the kitchen table, then looking around the room for clues as to her state of mind but finding none.

'Please sit down, Theo.' Her voice was small, cracked.

He sat opposite her; the scrape of the chair legs over the tiled floor was an irritation.

'What's the matter? Are you okay? Has something happened?'

She glanced at him. It was a stupid question given her obvious distress and didn't warrant a response. She waited until he was seated before reaching over and adjusting the volume on her phone. She let her finger hover before pressing the button to play her answerphone messages.

'You have one message,' the robotic voice informed them.

Theo visibly braced himself and cocked his head, ready to listen. He slid his fingertips towards her hand. Anna flinched as they touched, quickly pulling her hand beneath the table and resting it in her lap. She could hear her heart beating in her ears and the rush of her blood.

The moment the message began, she saw the facts, his terrible error, register on his face; he looked stricken.

'Mate, it's me. It's my birthday, but that's not why I'm calling. I feel like I'm falling apart. I told my dad I knew about Alexander and, well, it didn't go how I thought it might. It's made me think about my situation. I don't ever want Anna to feel how I felt tonight, to find out I have a little girl, a child in this world who doesn't know me... I'm gabbling. Call me when you get this. I need to talk to you, Spud.'

Theo reached out to grab the phone, as if silencing it could spare them both, but it was a little late for that. Anna was quicker; she held the phone in the air and stared at her husband, watching his face. She knew the words of the voicemail by heart, the pauses, the sigh... Her head almost bobbed in time with each word and her lips moved as she mouthed them in her head. She watched him cringe at the sound of his own voice, amplified by the silence around them.

'Anna, I...' He stared her, trying to find the words.

She bit her lip, oblivious to the fresh batch of tears that trickled down her face.

'I don't know what to say to you,' he croaked.

She watched him run his fingers over his face, trying to order his thoughts. Her eyes narrowed and her nose wrinkled in disdain. His reaction was so predictable, so clichéd, it stung as much as the content of his voice message.

How can you not know what to say to me? You must have known this day would come.

Finally she took a breath and when she spoke, to their mutual surprise, her voice was level.

'You have a little girl?' she rasped.

'Yes.' He looked down. 'I've wanted to tell you so many times, but knowing how much you wanted a baby, and knowing I couldn't do that, not with this hanging over me…'

'You're a dad.' She swallowed, shaking her head. This fact would still not sink in. 'Is Kitty her mum?'

He closed his eyes and nodded.

'I knew it.' She bit her lip hard, the pain a welcome distraction. 'I always kind of had this feeling about her, the way you looked when you told me she was just some girl from school, the way you changed the subject when her name came up. You were always so evasive. I just knew,' she whispered, trying to find the words. Calmly, she rubbed her hand across her stomach, indicating that this was where the hurt lay. 'Is she posh? Does she talk like you?'

'Why does that matter?'

'It matters to me!' she shot back angrily. He was in no position to ask the questions.

He gave a single nod and she was glad of that at least.

'How old is your little girl?'

He looked up at her, then immediately looked away. Ashamed, presumably, but she had no sympathy.

'She's ten,' he whispered.

'Ten?' she repeated, her heart racing, each new fragment helping to build an ever more devastating picture. 'Where do you meet her? Has she ever been here?' She hugged the tops of her arms, preparing for the next wave of distress, the one that might finally overwhelm her.

'I don't meet her. I don't see her. She doesn't know about me.' He shook his head. 'Her mum made it quite clear it was a one-night stand, literally, and—'

'Does anyone else know about her? Your parents?' she interrupted, considering the gut-churning possibility that they were laughing at her. It would be more than she could stand: Stella, Perry, Theo and the posh girl from his posh school sharing wine and swapping stories in front of the fire.

'No.' He briefly held her stare. 'No one knows.'

'Correction. Spud knows, and now I know.'

Theo nodded.

'Were you there when she was born?'

'No.'

'Do you love her mum? Do you… Do you love Kitty?' she asked quietly, fearful for the response no matter what it might be.

'No, not at all. I was infatuated with her at school, but no.' He shook his head.

Anna thought she might throw up. 'Do you… Do you still see her?' she squeaked, looking down, preparing herself.

'No.' He shook his head and she heard the slight reverb of laughter in his tone, as if to say, of course I don't!

She swallowed loudly. She thought of Sally Harper and remembered sitting on the sofa in their neat sitting room where cigarette smoke clung to the furnishings and the walls, staring at the woman with hurt etched on her face and in her every gesture. No wonder she'd been cold, and Micky angry.

Anna and Theo sat quietly, on opposite sides of the kitchen table, in close physical proximity but miles and miles apart. She didn't know what to do or say next and was floored by feeling so awkward in her own home.

'I don't have any relationship with either of them, Anna. None at all. And I didn't plan it – it just happened,' he whispered.

'It was long before I met you and I was told in no uncertain terms that I was not to make contact because, unlike you, Kitty knew that I would be a shit father and a fucking useless addition to any child's life!'

Anna shook her head. 'Don't you fucking dare! Don't you dare compare me with some woman you had a one-night stand with who doesn't know you like I do! Don't you dare suggest that it is for reasons *she* came up with that *I* have been denied motherhood! You are my husband!' She hated the squeak to her voice, raw with sadness. 'You've been cheating on me since the day we met.'

'I have not!'

'Yes, you have, Theo.' She was cool now, her voice barely quivering. 'Lying through omission and lying by keeping a secret, a big secret! Do you think I haven't noticed the slow looks of longing and that little twitch to your mouth when something reminds you of someone that isn't me? Do they live in Blackheath, this Kitty and her child – is that it? Is that why you were out there that night in the rain? Why you came back acting all unsettled and weird?'

He stared at her, a spooked expression on his face, as if he'd discovered she'd been reading his mind. 'I don't know where they live exactly. The one time I saw the little girl was on a bus. I… I jumped on the bus because I… recognised Kitty sitting in the window, and then I saw Sophie, but I… I didn't know she was there and it's haunted me every day since!'

'Sophie!' Anna sobbed, planting her hands on the tabletop for support. 'Is… Is that her name? Sophie?'

'Yes.' He nodded, unable to stem his own tears. 'Yes, she's called Sophie.' He could hardly get the words out.

The two sat there, letting their tears flow. When the crying eventually slowed, they sat in silence. It was Anna who broke it.

'My whole life has been like walking uphill on a slippery surface. I couldn't get a foothold, there was nothing for me to cling to, one false move and I'd tumble back to the start, a little more bruised, a little more defeated. And then I met you and I clung to you and it felt wonderful!' Her voice faltered. 'I knew I wasn't your first love, but I honestly believed I might be your last—'

'You are, Anna. I love you, only you!'

She saw the way his fingers reached for the fishing fly secreted under his lapel and felt a flicker of anger. If only he could open up to her, use her as his comforter when things got rough, and not some feathered talisman gifted by the fly-fishing guy of his youth.

'Yes, I know. But that's never been enough for either of us, not really.'

Theo stared up at her, his eyes pleading with her. 'I don't know what to say.'

'So you have said, many, many times, but the thing is you never do and that's part of the problem. In fact it is the problem. You've hidden all this from me and instead you've just kept stalling, hoping I'll change my mind about children, hoping it will just go away if you stick your head under the carpet for long enough. It's all so unfair, so unfair.'

'It's not like that, I...' Theo leant on the table and held her gaze. 'I never wanted to hurt you.'

Anna was surprised by the burst of laughter that fired from her mouth. 'Oh, well, that's okay then. I'll tell my heart to heal itself and my tears to stop falling!'

He nodded acceptance of the accusation and continued. 'I hate that this has happened, but also I'm really a bit relieved—'

'Well, great! How lovely for you!'

'Please don't be like that. I feel like shit, but the fact is, it has happened and we need to discuss it and decide on next steps.'

'What the hell am I going to do now?' She stared into the middle distance, directing the question as much to herself as to him.

'I don't want us to fight,' he whispered.

'No, I know, you'd rather we sat quietly and discussed anything other than what matters. The weather, wine, our next holiday, just like your bloody parents. And I've played along. You think you play with a straight bat, but you don't. You're a liar.'

'I haven't lied to you, Anna. Not intentionally. I might have held back, but—'

'Held back? You have a *child*!' She laughed, wiping her nose with the back of her hand. 'Have you any idea what it's like living with you?' She looked up. 'You have never given yourself to me, not fully. I have tried to be content with the little bits of you that you cast at me like pieces of a puzzle. And I scamper to catch whatever you throw because I love you.' She broke off, crying at this truth. 'I love you so much, but every time you give me a new piece of you, you take away an old piece and I now know that I can never, ever complete the picture of you. Never. And as if that wasn't punishment enough, I find out you have a little girl. A little girl you share with a woman who isn't me, a little girl you phoned Spud to discuss while I was running around trying to make a party for you, collecting a fucking cake!' The sob that now left her throat hurt her physically, clawing at her chest on its way out.

'Anna, I... I wish I had told you. I do! But every day, every month that passed made it seem harder and harder to come clean.'

'Well, bravo, Theo.' She clapped. 'But I doubt you would have "come clean", as you put it, if you hadn't misdialled that number today.'

He looked away and both knew this to be the truth.

Anna stared out of the window at the flash of lightning that cracked the sky. The thunder rolled in, and with it came driving rain that lashed the window and made the garden path glisten.

She saw herself as a little girl, chatting to her mummy in her narrow bedroom in Honor Oak Park.

'The thing that matters most is that you spend your time with someone who loves you very much and who you love right back.'

'But... But how do you know, Mum, if it's the right person?'

'Ah, you don't have to worry, that's the easy bit. It will be someone who makes it seem as if it's sunny, even on a rainy day.'

Anna looked out of the window into the dull fog of the storm and noted that neither inside the house nor outside, was even the smallest glimmer of sunshine. Nothing.

It was gone midnight and Anna was sitting on the sofa in the dark with the throw over her legs. She heard Theo lingering in the hallway before he eventually crept into the sitting room. She glimpsed her reflection in the window and was sad to see the broken, frail face staring back.

'I don't know what's happening, Theo. I don't know if we're ending, and I don't know what to do.'

'I'm sorry, Anna. I love you.'

'Please don't keep telling me that you love me – it's like wiping away the blood after you've cut me. It doesn't help the hurt or excuse the act, not even a little bit.'

She watched him hover awkwardly by the fireplace, part wanting him to sod off and part wishing he would stay close and hold her tight. Griff loped out of the kitchen with his ears low, his eyes searching. He didn't like to hear her sad. She sank down onto the floor and sat with her legs stretched out in front of her, stroking her dog's silky fur and taking comfort from it. It was then that she saw Theo's suitcase in the hallway, through the open door. She looked up at him as her tears fell afresh. She was surprised there were any left.

'I've decided to go to Bristol. I need to see to some things there anyway, and I need to sort my head out. I'm sure you do too.'

'I'm sad, Theo, but I'm not surprised.' Her voice was a harsh croak. 'I've been waiting for this conversation since we went to the Maldives. I think deep down I knew then that we were on a timer.' She now understood fully what this phrase meant.

'You did?'

Anna nodded, ignoring the break in his voice. 'I think possibly since the day we married. I mean, I was never right for you as far as your parents were concerned – I don't speak right, I don't know the wrong and right way to do things and I never went to that bloody school they bang on about.' She gave a false laugh. 'And for someone who cares as much about what others think as you do, especially your shitty parents, whose approval you still crave...' She let this hang.

'Don't say that.' He looked distraught.

'Why not? It's the truth.' She snorted through her nose before letting silence crisp the air. When she did resume speaking, her tone had calmed a little.

'Ned might have been vanilla, boring even, but in a weird way, Theo...' She paused to wipe her eyes.

'What?' He sank down next to her on the floor and again hesitated before taking her hand.

She drew breath, steeling herself. 'In a weird way, that vanilla life would have been much easier to bear. Maybe not as exciting or as grand.' She whimpered at this truth. 'I think I love you too much, Theo, and I think I wanted perfect – the dream, kids.' She shot him a significant look. 'At least I could understand him – his predictability, his transparency. I knew what to expect, but with you...'

She heard him swallow the lump in his throat before he spoke. 'To be able to come home to you has for me always been the best thing.'

'When I met you in that lift,' Anna said, 'I thought you were everything I had ever wanted. I thought you would make me happy and oh my God how I loved you! How I love you!'

'I love you too,' Theo whispered.

'But we are driftwood floating on the ocean, looking for a point of anchor, and you're right, I do want someone who will keep me steady. I thought that someone was you.' She studied his face. 'But I didn't realise you were floating like me. Didn't realise that we were both...'

'Adrift.'

'Yes.' She nodded. 'We are both adrift, each hoping the other has the compass. And I thought that children would be the anchor for us both. But all the time...' She shook her head. 'There was Sophie.' *Sophie, that's her name, his little girl.*

Theo stood slowly and ran his hand over Griff's flank.

'Are you going now?' Her voice cracked.

He nodded. 'I feel like I'm drowning.'

'How funny.' She gave a wry smile. 'Most drowning people seek out a bit of driftwood…'

She watched him unhook his coat from the newel post and ferret in the pocket for his car keys.

He bent towards her with arms slightly open, unsure whether or not to hold her, both of them instantly and painfully aware of how in such a short space of time the boundaries had shifted between them, to the point where her husband no longer felt able to take his wife in his arms and offer comfort.

'Just go, Theo! Fuck off to Bristol or anywhere else!' She jumped up and ran to the front door, holding it ajar, standing with her jaw clenched, waiting until he'd passed.

'Anna, I… I can't be the man you need me to be.'

'So you've said. Many times.' She wiped a stray tear. 'And actually, tonight, for the first time ever, I am starting to believe you.'

She slammed the door, denying him the chance to speak, before sinking to the floor once more and letting her howls of distress rebound off the walls.

In the wee small hours, when she finally made it upstairs to bed, she reached for her notebook on the bedside table.

Fifi and Fox,
I was wrong. The man I loved, the man I love, is not worthy
of being your dad. Not worthy of being anyone's dad. He was
right. He has hurt me. He lied to me.

I am too hurt to tell you why.

I am so stupid, so bloody stupid.

Why me? Why is it always me? If there is a God, what did I do that angered him so much that he saw fit to mess up every single aspect of my life?

I can't even think straight. Can't even think.

I am at a crossroads, in turmoil, and there is no signpost telling me which way to go. It's at times like this that I miss my mum so much it hurts. It still hurts, even after all these years. What I long for more than anything is to feel her arms around me, telling me everything is going to be okay.

Anna

Nineteen

Lisa sat with her handbag tucked neatly by her feet and her back straight, sipping her tea as if she was on her best behaviour.

'So you're here all on your own?'

'Yes. Shania has stayed a couple of nights and it's been nice to have company.'

Lisa rotated the mug in her fingers. 'Theo still in Bristol?'

'Yes, as far as I know. Four months now, feels like a lifetime and yet no time at all. When we talk it's awkward.' She paused. 'I hate how quickly he's come to feel like a stranger.'

'I'm still hoping you guys can figure it all out. You're good together.'

Anna nodded. 'That's what I thought.'

'So, birthing partner, eh? That's a big responsibility.' Lisa clearly wanted to steer the conversation onto a safer topic. 'Does Shania not have a bloke?'

'No. Apparently he was too nice, too boring.'

'Bastard.'

'That's what I said.' Anna watched, amused, as Lisa carefully positioned the coaster and placed the mug on it. 'Don't worry, Lis, just put the mug on the tabletop, it's fine.'

'I always feel a bit nervous here, like I'm going to break something or spill something! This really is some house,' Lisa whispered, raising her shoulders and smiling, as if they were there illicitly and she was wary of being heard.

Anna knew exactly what she meant. Since Theo had fled to Bristol, she felt like a lodger. In his absence, she woke to a sense of unease in her gut, as if she might be accused of trespassing in this posh house by the posh people who lived either side. *Mirabelles and Felicitys.*

'I would hate you not to be able to relax. If stuff gets broken or spilt, no one will care but you.'

'Kaylee would love to have the run of a place like this – so much space!'

Anna smiled to hide the sadness that she would never get to hear the thunder of feet up and down the stairs or answer the door to her child's friends. 'Anyway, having a big house is not all good, there's so much to clean! It's a full-time job.' She pulled a face, trying to make light of her very good fortune.

'You've got a cleaner, right?'

'Yes.' She felt her face colour with the familiar guilt, trying to imagine what her mum would make of her handing over cash to another woman to clean her house. 'You could bring your mum here, you know,' Anna said. 'I need to try and build a bridge with her – it would make everything easier.'

Lisa sighed. 'It would, but I think Micky is the key to that, she pretty much follows his lead.'

'I can see that.'

'I was sorry to hear about Theo's dad – was it expected?' Lisa cocked her head to one side as she waited to hear what Anna had to say. Anna smiled to herself: she did the same thing when she was listening and she wondered if this was something they'd both inherited from their dad.

'No, it wasn't expected, but I suppose it never is, is it? Death. Even when people are ill, their passing still comes as a shock. His mum is obviously upset, though she still manages to make it all about her. I've taken her over soup that was too thin and soda bread that was too salty.' She rolled her eyes. 'I saw Theo at the wake, the first time since he left.' She paused, the pain in her chest just as acute as it had been at the actual sight of him, no matter that she'd known he would be there.

'That must have been difficult.'

'It was.' She nodded. 'It was weird, there were moments of ordinariness, as though we'd forgotten what had gone on and were just our normal selves, and there were moments of pure sadness when I wanted to wrap him in my arms and tell him it was all going to be okay. But I couldn't – there was this barrier.'

Lisa grimaced. 'That's sad.'

'Yep, and, interestingly, when I took her soup over—'

'Would that be the thin soup?'

'The very same.'

They both laughed.

'Stella told me that Theo had taken the business card of a therapist her friend had recommended.'

'Can you see Theo doing therapy?' Lisa sipped her tea and, despite her sister's reassurance, reached for the coaster.

'I don't know. He's so reluctant to open up about things that have affected him. He talks to his bestie, Spud, but as far as I know not about anything that really bothers him. It's such a shame, I just know that if he did, he'd really get something out of it.'

'You still want the best for him?'

Anna nodded. 'I do. I am hurt about Sophie, of course...'
Saying her name had become a little easier. 'But I love him.'

'I know you do, darlin'.' Lisa smiled at her.

'But that doesn't mean I can forgive him or live with him. Love isn't always enough.'

'Tell me about it. I mean, I love Kaylee's dad. The knob.'

'Things still not good?'

Lisa winced. 'I know he's been seeing his ex and where does that leave me? Hardly the best grounds for getting back together. I think I'm better off without him – you know what they say, once a cheater, always a cheater.'

'I guess.' She nodded, thinking of how their dad had cheated with her mum...

Lisa's phone buzzed in her handbag and she reached inside, pulled it out and answered.

Anna could make out the angry burble of the man on the other end, if not the actual words. He was clearly shouting.

Lisa glanced up at Anna and spoke into her mobile. 'I know that, Micky.' She sighed. 'And I will be out when I have finished my cup of tea. Jesus, can you just give us five minutes!'

She ended the call and shook her head. 'Sorry, Anna, he's arrived early to pick me up and you know what he's like.'

'Actually, I don't know what he's like. He doesn't talk to me, remember?'

Lisa ran her fingers through her hair. 'I hate how you two are so far apart. I've had enough, I really have. I mean, for the love of God, we have so few people in our lives, we could all do with being a bit closer, and it's hard for Kaylee, it's her birthday in the summer and all she wants is her family in the same room with a bit of cake and a bloody balloon or two, but that's too much to ask of Micky and it's bloody selfish! It would be so great if we could all just be civil without me feeling pulled every time I want to see you.'

It was a lightbulb moment for Anna. She stood up and grabbed her handbag. 'Come on, Lis, finish your tea. We're going out.'

'Where are we going?' Lisa stood, swigging the last of her drink before placing the mug carefully on the coaster once more.

Anna ignored her. Calling Griff inside, she shut him in the kitchen and marched across the hallway with Lisa following. She slammed the front door behind her and strode towards the purring black taxi cab that sat outside her house. Micky, who was leaning his elbow on the open window, did a double-take then stared straight ahead, avoiding her gaze.

Anna walked round and tried the passenger door.

'It's locked!' He shook his head.

She banged the window. 'Then open it!'

'Not for you, no.'

Anna laughed. 'For the love of God, have you heard yourself, Micky? You're behaving like a child.'

'I can behave however I want, it's got nothing to do with you,' he snarled.

'Actually, it has, because it upsets my sister.' She met his glare.

'She's been my sister for a lot longer than she has yours, so don't start with that!'

'Actually, she's been my sister for my whole life, thirty-one years. The fact that I didn't know about her is another thing.'

'You think you're something special—'

'No, Micky!' She interrupted him with her shout as she ran round to his window and continued to yell at him face to face. 'That's where you're wrong. I do not think I'm something special and I never have! And I'm sick of the way you treat me! It's bloody ridiculous and I'm not going to take it any more!'

'Good, fuck off then and leave us alone!' He jerked his head towards the driveway.

'Oh, you'd like that, but here's the thing, pal, I'm not going anywhere! And what does your fiancée, Tina, think of your weird obsession with me? Doesn't she tell you to get over it, because that's what I would say to Theo, I'd find it so stupid!'

'I don't give a shit what you think!'

'Ah, but you clearly do, otherwise you wouldn't try so hard to be so foul to me!'

'What's going on?' Lisa called, standing on the pavement in a state of confusion.

'I'm trying to talk to Micky, but he's locked the passenger door and won't let me in, so we're doing it this way, through the bloody window!' She sighed her frustration. 'You're right, Lisa, enough is enough.'

'I don't know why you bother with her, Lis,' Micky called to his sister.

Lisa looked at her feet, visibly torn.

Micky continued. 'You might have forgotten what it was like for Mum, but I haven't!' He curled his lip at Anna once again.

'What was it like for her?' Anna stared at him defiantly. 'Go on, tell me!' she shouted, slapping the door with her hand.

Micky took a deep breath and began. 'You have no idea!'

'Try me.'

He looked at her with the familiar snarl to his top lip and took a second or two to phrase his thoughts. 'I'd see her pacing between the lounge and the kitchen waiting for him to come home, smoking and crying and smiling at me, trying to make out everything was okay, and if I asked, "Where's Dad?" she'd just break down again, and I was only small, I couldn't do anything about it.'

Anna felt a surge of pity for the angry child who'd grown into an angry man.

'And all the time he was carrying on with your mum.'

'But that's not *my* fault, Micky! I understand you're mad about it, hurt, but you can't take it out on me, I wasn't even born!'

'Who else can I take it out on?' he said angrily.

'God, why do you need to take it out on anyone? Why do you think it's okay to kick *me* when you're angry? How is it I have become that person?'

'Because it was hard enough knowing that he was doing the dirty on my mum, and then to be grieving when he died and to find out about you! Jesus Christ, have you any idea what that was like?'

'No, I haven't, because you don't tell me, because you don't talk to me. But, you know, the person this really hurts is Lisa.' She pointed over her shoulder. 'And that's not fair because she's the best, she showed me kindness when it was in very short supply and she made me welcome, she became my family!'

'Oh yes, and don't we know it! That's another thing, swanning in and buying your way into Kaylee's life with your fancy bloody presents and Gap clothes and God knows what before scurrying back to your fancy house and your millionaire old man.'

'Micky!' Lisa shouted at her brother from the pavement. 'Don't say that!'

'Why not? It's what Mum and I think. Just like her mother, who lived all hoity-toity up at Honor Oak Park, shagging Dad while our mum cried her eyes out and marched a bloody hole in the carpet! I used to picture you sitting in a castle eating sweets while we sat and waited for him.'

'Right.' Anna felt the rise and fall of anger in her chest. She tried the back door of the cab and when it opened she jumped in. 'Come on, Lisa!' she called to her sister, who trotted over and hopped in beside her.

'Get out of my cab!' Micky shouted, baring his teeth at her through the plastic divide between the front and back seats.

'No, Lisa and I need a cab and you are here so you might as well take us.'

'Get out of my fucking cab!'

'No!'

'Please, Micky,' Lisa pleaded tearfully.

At the sight of her distress, he seemed to calm a little. 'Where do you need to go? I thought we were going home?'

'Tell him to take us to Honor Oak Park.'

'Can you take us to Honor Oak Park?' Lisa repeated her words in a rather farcical manner.

To Anna's surprise, Micky slowly pivoted back round, released the handbrake and pulled away from the kerb.

She held Lisa's hand briefly and gave her a knowing look. Micky steered the cab eastwards, skirting Wandsworth and Battersea, through a light traffic jam in Clapham and across the common, and on to leafy Dulwich, where grand properties lined the roads. Micky sneered at her in the rearview mirror and she looked away, holding her nerve. Eventually they reached Honor Oak Park.

She hadn't expected the punch to the chest as she saw the station entrance through which she and her mum had passed a thousand times, hand in hand, either setting off on an adventure or coming home from one. Micky stopped at the crossing to let several pedestrians pass. Anna looked at the wall to the left and remembered crouching against the bricks, a tense expression on her mum's face as she placed her finger on her lips. '*Stay here for a second or two… It's a game! Like statues. How still and quiet can you be?*'

'You okay?'

Lisa's question drew her back to the now. 'Yes, I'm fine.' She smiled weakly. Sitting forward, she tapped on the glass. 'Can you pull over, please?'

Micky did as he was asked.

Anna jumped out and walked round to the driver's door. 'Can you get out of the cab, Micky?'

'Do it, Micky, please,' Lisa, now standing by her side, added.

Micky snorted his displeasure before ratcheting the handbrake and climbing from the driver's seat. He left his hazard lights on and followed Anna across the road. 'Where the bloody hell are we going?' he snapped.

Anna ignored the question and headed down the road, past the old betting shop, a new coffee shop and the convenience store that had changed its name, before coming to a halt outside a rather rundown house. Rubbish was piled in the tiny front yard where once neat bins had been lined up in a row, ready for the weekly collection. She ran her hand over the low, crumbling concrete wall. Her stomach flipped and her heart beat fast as she pictured Joe resting her Snoopy school bag on it while he rummaged inside for a key. '*Do you have a key, Anna? Anna Bee, do you have a key?*'

'This is our castle, Micky! This is where my hoity-toity mum lived. Not the whole house, just the ground-floor flat.' She pointed at the bay window, glad that the curtains were drawn and she couldn't see into the room that had been both her mum's pride and joy and her brother's prison. 'She bought me and my brother meat, but she ate toast and jam because it was all she could afford. Which suggests she wasn't being supported by anyone. I'm sure no money came out of your pocket, nor food out of your mouth. The kitchen was tiny and gloomy, but she still grew things, lemons in a pot, and a massive cheese plant in the corner of her bedroom. She never had any help. Her parents threw her out, pretty much, when she fell in love with a junkie and moved away, and then she had my brother Joe. And I loved him.' Her voice broke. 'I loved him more than anything in the world. He was wonderful. My mum died when I was nine and they carried her out of that very door.' She pointed, her voice reedy. 'And Joe looked after me as best he could, but he was an addict and I usually went to bed hungry and a bit scared. Joe was a petty thief and he jumped off the top of the car park in Bromley when I was thirteen and that's pretty much when I went into care. And it was horrible, most of the time.'

Micky looked down at the ground, as if he was a little ashamed, or at least touched by her story. Lisa blew her nose.

'So don't you tell me about a hoity-toity life, a life of privilege. My mum would have been in awe of your three-bed semi with a kitchen door out to the back garden. She fell in love with your dad and I believe he fell in love with her and I can only imagine how shit that must feel, but it happened and now they're dead! All of them, Micky, they're all dead! And there is fuck all I can do about any of it and I'm damned if I'm going to let you treat me like a piece of shit because of a mistake your dad made or a choice my mum made. Got it?'

Micky took a deep breath, looked the house up and down, then turned and walked slowly back to the taxi. Lisa stepped forward and held her in a warm hug before planting a kiss on her cheek.

The traffic had increased and progress back west was slow. The three sat in silence, each mulling over the afternoon's events, but despite the revelations, the atmosphere felt a little lighter. The cab crept towards Wandsworth, when Micky indicated and pulled over. He jumped out and opened the back door.

'Come on.' He ushered Anna and Lisa out from the back seat and walked briskly ahead.

Anna looked at Lisa, who shrugged. They followed him into a greasy spoon that was packed with taxi drivers, all sipping drinks from Styrofoam cups and taking large bites from bacon sandwiches served on grease-smudged paper plates.

'All right, Micky?' a stout woman called from behind the counter. 'What can I get you, love?'

'Three teas and a plate of biscuits, please, Dee.'

'Coming right up. Ooh, bringing guests, are we?' She nodded over in Anna's direction.

'Not guests, no. These are my little sisters, Lisa and Anna.'

Lisa threaded her arm through Anna's. Anna's heart was fit to burst.

'Oh, how lovely!' Dee smiled. 'Pretty!' She winked. 'Not like you, you ugly mug.'

Micky grinned at them both. 'Yep,' he said. 'They take after our dad.'

Anna felt happiness dancing on her shoulders. She remembered Jordan's advice, given years ago. '*I worry, Anna, that if you don't find your voice, someone else will always speak for you,*

*and then you won't ever change their opinion or let them know
the true you and that would be a tragic waste. You have a lot of
good things to say.'*

Yes, I do, Jord. Yes, I do.

Back home in Barnes that evening, her heart was still singing
with the pleasure of having made up with Micky. She decided
to call Jordan in New York and fill him in. So many of their
phone calls over the last few months had been sad ones, with
her either ranting about Theo or sobbing about how much she
missed him. It was nice to have some happy news.

Jordan, as predicted, was thrilled for her, though Anna still
couldn't quite picture him and Micky going for a pint together.
Equally predictably, the conversation then moved on to familiar
territory.

'You know, Anna...' Jordan began.

Anna held the phone close to her face and tucked her hair
behind her ears. The line was a little crackly with a delay.

'It's been, what, three or four months now? Do you not think
Theo's sweated enough? Isn't it time you tried to sort it out?
He's your guy, remember. Look how it's gone with Micky, you
finding your voice, making things better. Can't you—'

'Jordan, it's not that straightforward! This isn't a kiss-and-
make-up thing. He kept such a huge secret from me, he deceived
me, for all that time. He has a child, Jord! A little girl.' She
instantly regretted raising her voice. 'I'm sorry, I shouldn't yell
at you.'

'You yell away, I'll just ignore you and retune when you start
making sense.'

That made her smile. 'It's so complicated.'

'But here's the thing.' Jordan sighed. 'It doesn't need to be. There is nothing, nothing that Levi could do that would make me want to be away from him – nothing. And so we would always find a way to work things out. And it's either like that for you and you find a way or...' He took a deep breath. 'Or maybe it's time to start over and tread your own path.'

Anna closed her eyes. 'It's not that easy, Jord. As you said yourself, I love him unconditionally and that's the problem. He's the one! He's the one I want to be married to. But I don't know how to get over this, I don't know how to move things on.'

'He's not as strong as you, Anna. I'm so proud of how you did that thing with Micky, but Theo's more fragile. He's been weak, that's for sure, but is that such a crime, all things considered? And if he's going to therapy that should help him with his depression, if that's what's going on with him. And therapy must work otherwise every single New Yorker I have ever met wouldn't bother with it, but they do!'

She gave a wry smile. 'But what if nothing changes?'

'Then you pack a very large bag, get your cocktail-drinking head on and jump on the first plane over the pond, where I will show you my gangshow medal and Levi and I will make you dance so hard you'll forget why you were ever blue.'

'That'd have to be some dance.'

'Toots, you haven't seen us in action!'

'Thank you. I love you, Jordan. I love you so much.' Her heart brimmed with affection for the man who had made a difference to her life since she was thirteen.

'You get it all back, now stop with the niceness, you've made my mascara run!'

Twenty

Anna set a place for one at Stella's kitchen table and watched as her mother-in-law took up the seat, adjusting the pearls at her neck.

'It's so very thoughtful of you, dear, to cook for me, but there really is no need.' She placed the linen napkin over her lap.

Anna smiled at her. 'I always remember you saying that if you didn't have to cook for Perry then you wouldn't bother, and we can't have that. You need to keep your strength up.' She waited for the microwave to ping, heating up the dish she'd prepared that afternoon.

'Well, if you're going to insist, do you think we could avoid pasta and dairy, as both have a rather negative effect on my constitution.'

Shit. Anna briefly closed her eyes and looked through the glass at the dish she'd chosen for that night.

'Have you seen Theodore?' Stella asked.

Anna noted the studied nonchalance of her tone. She shook her head. 'Not since Perry's funeral. We've had a couple of phone calls, both of them short and to the point. Truth is, I don't really know what to say to him.' It was unusual for her to confide in Stella like this, a woman who had always kept her emotional distance.

'Quite. It's a muddle, no doubt about it. But I do think it must be hard for him, being exiled to a strange city, away from home, and building up a new business. It does feel rather that the poor chap is being punished, and all for an indiscretion committed so long ago, and entirely out of his hands, if that... situation is to be believed.'

Anna turned slowly, the thump of embarrassment in her breast. *So you know too...*

'Theo is not being punished and he's not in exile. He left of his own accord – there was no discussion, as such. He said he needed space and I respect that and actually I think I needed space too. It was a shock to me, still is a shock to me, regardless of how long ago it all happened. And actually, Stella, it's not the "situation", as you call it, that's the problem, it's the deceit, that's the thing that hurts.'

Stella had more to say. 'Well, it is none of my business of course. We only found out very recently, and I know it's different nowadays, but I think it's a woman's lot to turn a blind eye, support where she can, take the rough with the smooth. Why would you want to air your dirty laundry in front of your spouse? Or your child, for that matter. We never did and it worked for us. Perry and I were deliriously happy.' She paused and patted her hair with her elegantly manicured fingers, but Anna could detect no other visible sign of emotion.

Anna pursed her lips. *Deliriously happy, my arse!*

Stella rallied and continued. 'And at the end of the day, no one forces one to live in such a lovely house, paid for, enjoying all the spoils her husband can provide. No one forces a girl to do that, no matter how strong her principles. She can always take it or leave it.'

The microwave pinged. Anna removed the glass dish with her hands trembling inside the oven glove and placed it in front of Stella. 'Do you know, Stella, I think you're absolutely right. It is none of your business.'

Stella blinked quickly, quite unused to being addressed in this way. She lifted her fork. 'Well, this smells delicious, what is it?'

'It's macaroni cheese. Take it or leave it.'

Anna sat with Griff on her lap and stroked his silky ears. 'It's quiet, isn't it, boy? Not that that's a bad thing.' She laid her head back on the cushion and wondered where Theo was laying his head at that moment. 'I bet he misses you.' She smiled at the pooch, who seemed to sigh, indicating that the missing was not one-sided.

'The way Stella spoke to me today... I can't imagine what it must have been like growing up with that. Not the sort of home you'd be happy sharing secrets in, that's for sure. Especially for someone prone to depression. Eh, Griff?' She buried her face in his fur. 'Even I find her attitude hard to handle, and I'm an adult. And the way his dad treated him, no wonder he has no confidence. I'm not excusing it, but I know Joe used to lie because he didn't want to get into trouble. It's cowardly, but I get it. I think Theo backed himself into a corner. I don't know, puppy, sometimes I think my head might explode with it all.'

A... *always love you, Theo.*

B... *believe in yourself like I do.*

C... *can't sleep properly without you here.*

D... don't hide from me, not any more.

E... everything passes, everything.

With darkness pulling a blind on the day, Anna fell into a fitful doze.

A sudden ringing roused her. She sat up. Her neck ached from being bent at an odd angle and she felt groggy. Realising it was the phone in the hallway, she gently shooed Griff to the floor and ran to answer it, having no idea how long she'd been dozing for.

'Anna!'

'Shania, are you okay?' She'd caught the breathless urgency in her friend's greeting.

'I need you to come to the hospital. It's happening. Fuck! It's happening now! And it's happening fast. I'm scared! I'm really scared!'

'Okay, okay, just keep calm. It's all going to be fine.' She hoped she spoke the truth. 'Where are you now, my love?' She tried to keep her voice steady, even though her heart raced.

'In the flat, but they're sending an ambulance. Please, Anna, hurry! I'll meet you there.'

'I'm on my way.' As she spoke, her eyes scanned the hallway, locating her coat, bag and keys. 'Try and keep calm, honey, remember to breathe, and I'll be there as soon as I can!'

In the cab, Anna sat forward on the back seat with the five-pound note scrunched tightly in her hand. Her stomach bunched in nervous, fearful anticipation as she tried to imagine what might await her at the hospital. *I hope I'm not useless, I hope I know what to do! Hang in there, Shania, I'm on my way.* She hoped her words might float ahead and land in her friend's consciousness, providing a pinch of support until she arrived.

'How much longer, do you think?' she asked the cabbie.

He sucked his teeth. 'I reckon another twenty minutes if the traffic isn't playing up.'

'It's a bit of an emergency.' She swallowed.

'So you've said, love. Twice.'

She decided to sit back and try and keep calm. She couldn't for the life of her remember if she'd locked the front door before leaving, such had been her hurry. Her first thought was to ask Theo to check, until she remembered that he wasn't at home any more, and yet again this fact hit her like a thunderbolt.

Finally they reached the hospital. 'Just anywhere here is fine.' She spoke quickly to the cab driver as he pulled up, desperate to get to Shania. 'Please keep the change,' she managed, jumping from the back seat.

She took a deep breath and walked briskly into the foyer, glancing briefly at the seat in which she'd been sitting when she'd bumped into Shania after her own stint in hospital. God, how her life had changed in just a few short months.

She jabbed the button and waited for the lift. Again she thought of Theo, keeping her calm on the day they met, giving her his sandwich... But this was no time for nostalgia. She stepped out onto the fourth floor and was immediately struck by the bustle of activity, even at that late hour. A man stood, leaning his elbow on the windowsill, staring out into the night sky with a mobile phone clamped to his ear. He was tearful. She didn't dare look long enough to ascertain if they were tears of joy or sadness. A man and a woman sat holding hands on the plastic seats of the waiting room. Nearby, a huddle of people young and old, the women in saris and with a toddler darting in and out of their legs like a tiddler in the weeds, were gathered round the payphone on the wall. They were all offering updates, hugging or sniffing the news down the line to the people who loved them. She felt like an intruder, unwittingly encroaching on the most private of moments.

Doctors and nurses crisscrossed the foyer in a purposeful, well-rehearsed dance and a porter wheeling a trolley loaded with what looked like gas canisters wended his way through the crowd with a whistle and a smile. Anna walked to the reception desk and hovered anxiously. She tapped her thigh with impatient fingers, waiting for the receptionist to finish her phone call, knowing Shania was in this building, keen to get to her.

'Sorry to keep you. How can I help?' The woman looked up over the countertop.

'I... I'm trying to find my friend, Shania Bowland. I got the call that she's gone into labour and I said I'd meet her here. I'm her birthing partner.' She held the receptionist's gaze, hoping her explanation was adequate and suddenly anxious that being a friend or birth partner was not enough of a credential for her to gain access.

The woman ran a finger down a list in front of her.

'Yes, Miss Bowland is in Room 16 – follow the corridor to the right and someone down there will be able to assist you.'

Anna jogged along, counting the room numbers as she went, her breathing fast, her heart racing.

'Can I help you?' A smiley nurse approached her.

'Yes, please! My friend, Shania Bowland, having twins? I'm her birth partner, Room 16?' she gabbled, aware that the clock was ticking.

'Yes, come with me. She's doing fine.'

'Good. That's good.' Anna felt some of the tension leave her body. This was great news.

The nurse pushed open the door and Anna took a second to scan the room and get her bearings.

It was neither large nor cluttered, as she had imagined, but small and sparse. The main feature was the bed, which had a large light on a pivot to one side and a low-slung striplight overhead. There was a heart monitor beeping out a steady electronic rhythm, and a gas canister, like the ones being ferried about by the whistling porter, placed by the side of the bed. Both of these were connected via wires or tubes to Shania, who was sitting upright with her legs splayed and a look of terror on her face.

She stared at Anna with huge eyes. Her thick Afro was splayed against the white pillowslip and the voluminous pale green hospital gown, tied loosely around her shoulders, had slipped down, exposing her chest. Shania's lips quivered with relief at the sight of her friend and Anna thought she looked very much like the teen who'd stood with a thunderous expression as she was introduced to everyone at Mead House, only now she wasn't angry but scared. Her vulnerability, however, was just the same.

Shania sat up straight as fat tears fell down her face. 'Anna!' Her voice was muffled, barely more than a croaked whisper.

'It's okay.' Anna smiled, dumped her handbag and coat on the floor and sat on the side of the bed as she took her friend into her arms. 'It's all going to be okay.'

Shania pulled the plastic nose and mouthpiece away from her face and reached for her. 'Oh my God, I am so glad you're here! I was beginning to think you might not come, and I have no one else to call. No one, and it made me think about how sad that is. These babies...'

Anna gripped her hand, damp with sweat, and kissed her

forehead. 'Sssshhh! These babies are going to have everything and everyone they need, don't you worry about that. And traffic, that's why I'm late, but here I am. Everything is going to be fine. The nurse said you're doing really well.' She remembered to keep her voice soft and steady, aware that if she sounded alarmed, it might be infectious.

'I don't feel like I'm doing really well.' Shania paused. 'I feel like shit, and it hurts! And I know it's only going to hurt more and I feel scared about it hurting more!' She screwed her eyes shut as another contraction built. 'And what's the point of doing a bloody plan when it hurts so much that you will just do bloody anything to make it stop!'

'Don't try and talk,' she cooed as she moved onto the chair by the side of the bed. 'Just breathe and go with it. Let it wash over you, breathe and count, and it will soon pass.' She breathed out slowly, and in again through her nose, and out through her mouth, just as they'd practised. 'We have a drugs plan and I know it by heart.'

'I want all the drugs they can find and I want them right now!' Shania shouted.

Things calmed and Shania dozed a little. Anna was glad of the breather, a chance to gather her thoughts.

A while later, Shania woke with a start, agitated and excited. Her nap seemed to have boosted both her energy and her mood.

'They're on their way, Anna! Can you believe it?'

Anna shook her head, as if this news was still surprising to her, despite having had the last few months to get used to the idea. Regardless of telling herself to be brave, giving herself silent instructions not to cry, her resolve melted at the thought of two babies making their way into the world. *Fifi and Fox…*

'Samuel still doesn't know?'

Shania shook her head. 'I couldn't find the right way to tell him.'

Anna recalled Theo saying something similar. 'All in good time,' she replied soothingly.

'Oh God, Anna, here it comes again!'

She watched her friend dip her chin to her chest and bear down, as if she could control the pain that way. Her face was scrunched up in discomfort and her body folded over the vast bump of her stomach. It was a strange thing that rather than feel thankful it wasn't her going through the pain, Anna felt nothing but a sharp blade of envy cutting across her consciousness.

I want to know what that feels like. I wish… I wish…

The machine started to beep a little erratically and the midwife rushed in, talking calmly but working with speed. 'How are we doing?' She pressed a button on the heart monitor and placed her hand on Shania's stomach. 'I think we might need to keep an eye on these two, they're obviously impatient to meet their mummy!'

'It bloody hurts!' Shania managed through gritted teeth.

'Let's get you breathing that gas and air again, my lovely.' The midwife reattached the nose- and mouthpiece over Shania's face and bent low. 'Breathe, my love. That's it, nice deep breaths. We're going to move you down to the delivery suite.' She turned to Anna and gave her a wink that was meant to be reassuring but was in fact anything but.

Shania pulled at the plastic guard. 'I wish…' She panted. 'I wish Samuel was here! Where is he, Anna?' Then she put it back in place and breathed with urgency.

Anna had read the booklets, gone through the plan and played

344

out the scenario in her head a thousand times, but nothing had prepared her for the feeling of utter hopelessness that now engulfed her. Her eyes flew to the window, as if out there in the inky blue night sky, up among the stars, might be where the answer lay. She shook her head, hating her inability to wave a magic wand and make everything better. She thought about Samuel and she pictured Theo. 'I don't know where he is.'

Things again seemed to slow once they were ensconced in the delivery suite. She felt useless. 'Can I get you a drink? Anything?'

'No, I'm okay.' Shania breathed slowly, she looked exhausted. 'Anna…'

'Yes, honey?' She sat forward so their heads were close together.

'I kind of knew you'd seen me when I was on the streets. That whole time for me is like a bad dream and I don't know what was real and what wasn't, but I kind of knew, I felt you…'

Anna patted her arm. 'It's all good now, darling. You don't have to think about that. Just think about these babies, who are on their way!'

'Oh shit!' Shania threw her head back. 'Oh shit!'

'Nurse!' Anna called out, wary of being alone with her if things were speeding up.

And then things went very fast.

Clad in her J-cloth hat and hospital gown, Anna did her best, offering words of encouragement when Shania needed them and smoothing her hair from her sticky forehead. 'You're doing great, I am so proud of you!'

Her friend's responses were guttural, an almost primal reaction to her pain; this was no time for considered replies.

'Here we go,' the midwife announced from where she sat on a stool, her hands poised. 'I can see baby's head.'

Anna's hand flew to her stomach. With splayed fingers she laid her palm on her abdomen, quieting the flutter in her redundant womb. 'This is it, Shania! Here we go, you're nearly there!'

It's okay, Anna, keep it together, you're doing great, you're supporting your friend, keep going! The empty platitudes sounded hollow in her head.

Shania, clearly shattered now, gripped her hand tightly. Her face crumpled again under the exertion.

And then the most incredible thing happened, something Anna would never forget. A new thing, a miracle, and it was as if she'd been caught unawares, as if this event was as surprising as it was magical. The midwife lifted a baby into the air! A tiny, curled, damp baby with a cap of dark hair flat against its head and a squashed nose. Its arms and legs were coiled against its body as if it was none too keen on being taken from the cosiness of the only home it had ever known. It let out a quiet mewl, calling, Anna thought, to its sibling.

'A little boy!' The midwife smiled, her hands reaching down again.

Shania stared open-mouthed at her friend. She looked done in, caught in some kind of limbo between giving in to the sheer joy at the sight of her first baby but knowing that she had to focus and deliver the second. With baby one whisked away, the next fifteen minutes were both easier and harder. Shania's energy was all but spent, but the high of having delivered one son was motivation enough.

And then, just like that, a second little boy was lifted into the air.

Neither could speak for the tears that clogged their throats and noses.

The nurse came over with a loosely wrapped bundle in each arm. Shania reached up and took both of her children, looking from one tiny face to the other with an expression of pure wonder. 'Oh! Oh!' was all she could manage.

One of the baby boys started to move his mouth, as if seeking food, and Shania lowered her gown and laid him skin to skin, trying to help him latch on. She nodded at the other, sleeping infant. 'Can you take him, Anna? I can't quite manage with them both.'

Anna sat back in the chair with the tiny baby in her arms.

She knew that she would never be able to adequately describe those moments. The feel and scent of a newborn in her arms was the greatest gift anyone could have given her. Sadness washed over her, pulling her down to the depths of her longing and holding her captive, making breathing difficult. She thought of her mum, giving birth not a million miles from there, and her dad, hovering illicitly in the wings, waiting for a photograph to be taken, the only photograph, which he would secrete inside a book for his whole life. She thought of Theo, who had not witnessed the birth of his little girl, Sophie, and for all that he had missed out on, and she felt sad. But mostly Anna knew that, no matter what, she would forever miss what she had never had, the feel of a baby growing inside her body and being delivered from it. A body that had played a trick on her, giving up on fertility before she'd had the chance.

'That's Joshua.' Shania smiled in her direction. 'And this hungry little fella is David.'

'Joshua and David.' Anna ran her fingertip over Joshua's rounded, sleeping cheek.

'Your godsons!' Shania reminded her.

'Yes!' She nodded. 'My godsons.' No matter what twists and turns her life might take, these boys would forever hold a piece of her heart. And it was a piece she was more than happy to give. 'Clever you, Shania.' She thought about the night of her arrival at Mead House all those years ago. *Look at you, you belong with these babies, that's home.*

The two women held hands across the mattress, each totally lost in the child in her arms.

* * *

They'd finished lunch and Shania sat back on the sofa and picked up her cup of tea. 'Is that thing on?' She nodded towards the baby monitor on the mantelpiece.

'Yes. You're getting as bad as me – I've checked it twice!'

It was nothing but a pleasure to have Shania and the boys staying with her in Barnes. The arrangement had been hastily agreed just before Shania was discharged from hospital, a temporary measure, until Shania got the hang of life with twins. Anna couldn't bear the thought that they would leave at some point. Getting up to the boys in the night, changing and feeding them, made her happy. She was obsessed. The shared care only served to bring her and Shania closer.

'Ah, silence is golden!' Shania closed her eyes and smiled.

The silence lasted less than ten minutes. The front doorbell rang and Griff barked. 'It's okay, boy, I've got it!' Anna smoothed his head and went to answer the door.

'Oh, wonderful! What a lovely surprise. Come in! Come in!'

'We were passing and Kaylee wanted to come and see the babies.' Lisa kissed Anna on the cheek as she came in with Kaylee in tow.

Anna bent down and grabbed her niece in a brief hug. 'Hello, cutie.'

'All right, mate?' Micky offered his customary greeting and followed them down the hallway.

'Yes, good. Let's get that kettle on.' She kissed him too. The novelty of receiving his affection had still not worn off and she doubted it ever would.

It was as she placed the mugs of tea on the tray that the boys began to cry. Shania put her own tea down – 'No rest for the wicked!' – and hurried up the stairs. Anna was impressed with her natural ability; nothing seemed to faze her. She figured that was one positive of having lived through adversity; it meant Shania was tough, and it would take a lot more than the pressure of being a single mother of twins to test her.

All present gathered on the sofa and the rug in front of the fireplace for the grand arrival of Joshua and David. They shrugged and smiled in eager anticipation.

'Where's them babies?' Kaylee asked.

'Having their bums changed.' Anna winked at her. 'And trust me, you will be glad they did.'

The front doorbell rang again. Griff barked and Anna jumped up.

'It's like Piccadilly Circus in here!' Micky shouted, cuddling Griff on his lap.

Anna opened the door and was a little taken aback to find Stella standing in front of her, the first time she'd seen her since their snippy exchange over the unwanted macaroni cheese.

'Stella! Come in!' She stepped forward and wrapped her in a warm embrace, knowing it was important to erase any embarrassment, to give her grieving mother-in-law a way back.

'I… I wanted to…'

Anna noted her nervous blink and the uncharacteristic falter to her voice. 'You don't need an excuse to come over, Stella, of course you don't. This is Theo's house,' she said without malice. 'I've just put the kettle on, how about a nice cup of tea?'

'Well, that would be lovely.'

'We've got quite a houseful!' Anna smiled, leading her into the sitting room. 'You've met Lisa before.'

'Yes, of course. Hello, dear.'

Lisa smiled. 'Hi, Stella, nice out, isn't it?'

'It is.'

'And this is my brother Micky.' Anna pointed.

'The taxi driver.' Stella nodded at him, clasping her scarf to her neck, clearly ill at ease in a room that was familiar to her, and for this Anna felt another wave of empathy.

'The very same.' Micky waved. 'In fact I've left the meter running outside – it's going to cost her a fortune.' He nodded at Lisa.

'Oh dear!' Stella sat in the armchair and didn't get the joke.

Kaylee curled into her mum's lap and sucked her thumb.

Anna heard the natter of conversation flowing back to her in the kitchen while she made Stella's tea – Earl Grey of course. As she foraged in the fridge for a lemon, her eyes were drawn to her potted tree on the windowsill and there, behind the dark, glossy leaves, hung a plump yellow fruit.

'Oh, Mum, will you look at that?' She twisted it from the branch, held it to her nose and inhaled deeply, before cutting a slice and placing it with pride on the saucer of her mother-in-law's cuppa.

'There we go, Stella.' She set the plate of biscuits on the side table, laughing as Micky dived in and passed two custard creams to Lisa.

'Here they are!'

Everyone whipped around as Shania walked in with the babies in her arms. Kaylee leapt up and raced over to them, staring at the little bundles.

'These, Stella, are Joshua and David, my godsons.'

'Oh my!'

'Would you like to hold one?' Shania bent down and waited while Stella settled her tea on the floor and reached out.

Stella took Joshua into her arms and nestled him to her chest. 'Goodness me.' She coughed to clear her throat. 'I had quite forgotten how wonderful this feels.' Tears trickled from her eyes, which instantly became bloodshot.

'It does the same to me, Stella,' Anna cooed as she sat on the floor next to her mother-in-law, ready to offer physical as well as emotional support.

'Well…' Again Stella sniffed. 'I think these little chaps are jolly lucky to have you as a godmother and hopefully you will have your own here soon, running around. Adoption is the thing for you, Anna. You must be bold, you must pursue it.'

Anna could only nod. It was the biggest vote of confidence Stella had ever given her.

Stella had more to say. 'I was on the phone to Theo this morning, dear, and he asked me to give you a message.'

Anna cocked her head. She was all ears.

'He asked me to tell you that there's a sheet of paper he wants you to look at – it's in his pen box on the desk.'

Anna exhaled, disappointed. A bloody bill, probably. Hardly

the sincere bid for reconciliation she'd half been hoping for. She nodded. 'Righto.'

Stella lowered her voice, obviously not wanting the rest of the room to listen in. 'And you were right, you know, Anna. It is all about the deceit and it should never be about turning a blind eye. The very existence of Alexander troubles me even now, all these years later. Such a waste...' She tucked in her trembling lips. 'But Theo's a good boy, nothing like his father. His... indiscretion was long before he met you, wasn't it, dear? He really is quite different from his father.' She gave another sniff.

Anna placed a hand on her arm. She wasn't sure what had caused this softening of her mother-in-law's shell, but she was thankful for it nonetheless.

Lisa broke the awkward silence that had fallen over the room. 'I must say, Shania, you're looking fantastic. Kaylee's four already, but I'm still carrying pounds of baby weight.'

Stella turned to look at the girl in her stretch leggings. 'Well, if it's weight you want to lose, you should cut out scoffing those biscuits for a start.' She humphed and Anna laughed.

Stella Montgomery was back in the room.

It was early evening by the time all the guests had left. The twins were sleeping.

'What a wonderful day!' Shania almost sang as she immersed Joshua and David's bottles in the sterilising unit.

'It really was.' Anna looked up at the unmistakeable sound of a sob coming from her friend, who had only seconds before seemed so happy. 'Oh, honey, what's the matter?'

Shania leant on the countertop. 'I am so grateful to you, Anna, and I always will be.'

'It's been my pleasure. I love having you all here, you know that.'

Shania nodded. 'And I love my boys, you know I do.' She shook her head. 'But it's not the same without Samuel – nothing is. He is what makes me feel safe, keeps me steady. Boring or not, I want him with me.'

'Don't cry, my love. Come on, no more tears.' Anna walked forward and took her friend in her arms. 'There's only one way to fix this. Now, are you going to call him or am I?'

As Shania made the call in the kitchen, Anna headed up to Theo's study, curious as to what was so urgent about the sheet of paper in the pen box on his desk.

Quietly closing the door behind her, she frowned at the loose papers scattered all over Theo's desktop. She sat in his deep leather chair and ran her hand over the much more neatly stacked files and letters ranged along the shelf to the side. Her fingers wandered over the inlaid lid of the vintage pen box. Opening it, she pulled out a single sheet of paper. She wasn't quite sure what she was looking at until she unfolded it and her eyes fell upon the title: My Anna Bee.

Pulling it free, she lifted it to her face and read with interest.

Here we go, Anna, my first ever attempt at the alphabet game...
   A... Anna.
   B... beautiful.

She looked up – 'What on earth?' – before resuming her reading, running down the list.

C... *courageous, so much more courageous than me.*
D... *determined.*
E... *eager.*
F... *funny.*
G... *gorgeous.*
H... *hopeful.*
I... *interesting.*
J... *jenuine.*

Anna looked away and laughed.

K... *kind.*
L... *lift buddy.*
M... *mine.*
N... *nice.*
O... *open.*
P... *patient.*
Q... *quizzical.*
R... *ravishing.*
S... *sexy.*
T... *trustworthy.*
U... *uncomplicated.*
V... *valiant.*
W... *wife. My wife!*
X... *xtraordinary.*
Y... *youthful.*
Z... *zoofriendly (you do sponsor several animals!).*

She laughed and spoke into the ether. 'That's me, Theo, I am your xtraordinary liftbuddy and I am here waiting for you. I miss you. I miss you, my man who makes it sunny even when it's raining.'

She gathered the dirty coffee cups and empty plates scattered with crumbs that had been collecting by the side of her bed and took them to the kitchen. After popping them into the dishwasher, she sat at the kitchen table, picked up her ink pen and flipped open her writing pad.

Theo's list had filled her with a kind of energy. All was not lost, it couldn't be, not when those were the words he'd used to describe her. She was ready. Ready to fight for their future.

Dear Fifi and Fox,

Life is funny.

You never can tell how things are going to turn out, but that's nothing to be afraid of, in fact that's what makes life exciting!

I sometimes stop and think of how my life was when my mum died and I look at the life I have now and it's like two lives, one so sad and lonely, and the other so full and happy – this life with Lisa, Kaylee and Micky, and my puppy, Griff, and Jordan and Levi, and Melissa, and Stella, and Shania and the twins, all the people that I have around me who love me, and I feel so lucky.

I am so lucky.

I wonder what would Michael Harper have said about today? What might he have had if he hadn't hidden in the shadows and what might I? It's made me think about what Theo is missing, and that's not right. It's not fair.

I don't know what will happen next, no one does, but I do know it's important to remember that I am happy right now. I look over my shoulder, look back at the path that has brought me here, and I realise how far I've come. I feel proud that I didn't fall through the cracks and Theo has played a huge part in that. I miss him. I miss him so much. I want him to come home. I can't wait for him to come home!

So what about you two? Little Fifi and Fox...

I want you both to know that the joy you have given me, picturing you in my mind and clinging to the idea of you when all around me was stormy, well, you've been very important to me. You two have been the anchor when I felt like sticks on the river. You've kept me grounded, given me sanctuary, and for that I will always be very grateful.

Once again I send my desire for motherhood out into the universe. I haven't given up my dream, not yet. Today made me think, who knows, maybe there's an empty corner in the life of a little girl called Sophie, maybe she might like to have a spare mum just like me...

The phone in the kitchen rang. Before answering it, she quickly finished her letter.

I can but hope. There is always hope!
And I do so with love.
Anna X

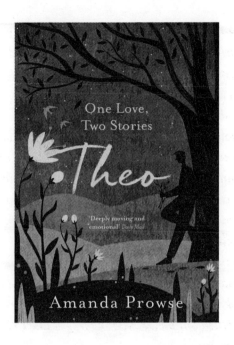

There are two sides to every love story...

Anna Cole grew up in care, and wants to start a family of her own. Theo Montgomery had a loveless childhood, and wants to find his soulmate.

Then, one day, they meet.

Each shows the other how to love. And each shows the other what heartbreak feels like...

This is Theo's story.

Turn the page for an exclusive preview of Theo.

One

Theo felt the swirl of nausea in the pit of his stomach. He swallowed and looked to his right, along the length of the lower playing field, calculating how long it would take to run back to the safety of the building should the need arise. He knew that Mr Beckett, his housemaster, would be watching from his study, peering through the wide bow window and rocking on his heels with his hands behind his back. He pictured him staring, stern faced, monitoring his every move. 'You go immediately!' he'd said angrily. 'And you undertake the task assigned to you. And I want you to think, boy, think about what you have done! Yours is not the behaviour of a Theobald's boy! And I won't tolerate it, do you hear?'

And Theo had gone immediately, trying to ignore the fear that was making him shake and the sting of tears that threatened, knowing that neither would help the situation. He stared at the dark, weatherworn patina of the wooden door in front of him. Even the thought of making contact with the infamous man in the crooked cottage made his heart race fit to burst through his ribs. He'd heard terrible stories about the cranky ogre that lived within. Theo could only take small breaths now and his skin pulsed over his breastbone. Raising his pale hand into a tight fist, he held it in front of his face and closed his eyes before bringing it to the oak front door, tapping once, twice and immediately taking a step back. The wind licked the nervous sweat on his top lip. It was cold.

There was an unnerving silence while his mind raced at what he should do if there was no reply. He knew Mr Beckett wouldn't believe him and the prospect of further punishment made his stomach churn.

Finally, a head of wiry grey hair bobbed into view through the dusty little glass security pane.

Theo swallowed.

'Who are you?' the man asked sternly as he yanked open the door and looked down at him.

'I'm... I'm Theodore Montgomery, sir.' He spoke with difficulty. His tongue seemed glued to the dry roof of his mouth. His voice was barely more than a squeak.

'Theodore Montgomery?'

'Yes, sir.' Theo gulped, noting the man's soft Dorset accent and the fact that he was not an ogre, certainly not in stature. But he did look cranky. His mouth was unsmiling and he had piercing blue eyes and a steady stare.

'Now there's a name if ever I heard one. And how old are you?'

'I'm... I'm seven, sir.'

'Seven. I see. What house are you in – is that a Theobald's tie?' The man narrowed his eyes.

'Theobald's, yes, sir.'

'So you are Theodore from Theobald's?'

'Yes, sir.'

'Well, that's some coincidence.'

Theo stared at the man, not sure if it would be the right thing to correct him and tell him that, actually, it was no coincidence.

The man nodded, looking briefly into the middle distance, as if this might mean something. 'And you are here for MEDS?'

'Yes, sir.' He tried to keep the warble from his voice; it was his first time in 'Marshall's Extra Duties', a punishment that fell somewhere between detention and corporal punishment. He was grateful to have avoided the sting of his housemaster's cane, at least.

'Is this your first time?'

The man, who smelt of earth and chemicals, lifted his chin and seemed to be looking at him through his large, hairy nostrils. They reminded Theo of a gun barrel, but one with grey sprigs sprouting from it. The man was old and looked more like a farmer than a master, the kind of person he'd seen up in Scotland when his father had taken him grouse shooting on the glorious twelfth. He shuddered at the memory of that weekend, having found nothing glorious about it. He hadn't liked it, not at all, and was still ashamed of how he'd cried at the sight of the birds' beautiful mottled plumage lying limply in the gundog's mouth. His father had been less than impressed, banning him from the shoot the next day. Instead, he'd had to sit in the car for eight hours with just a tartan-patterned flask of tea and a single stale bun. There'd been no facilities, so he had to tinkle on the grass verge. It was a chilly day and his shaky aim had meant he'd sprinkled his own shoes. Thankfully, they'd dried out by the time his father returned.

'Yes, sir.' He nodded, sniffing to halt the coming tears.

'Well, for a start, you can stop calling me sir. I'm not a teacher. I'm part groundsman and part gamekeeper. My name is Mr Porter. Got it?'

'Yes, sir. Mr Porter, sir.'

Mr Porter placed his knuckles on the waist of his worn tweed jacket and looked Theo up and down. 'You're a skinny thing, reckon you're up to picking litter?'

Theo nodded vigorously. 'Yes, sir. I… I think so, sir. I've never done it before.'

'Don't you worry about that, it's as simple as falling off a log. You ever fallen off a log, Mr Montgomery?'

'No, sir.'

'It's Mr Porter.'

'Yes! Sorry…' Theo blinked. 'Mr Porter, sir.'

Mr Porter shook his head in a way that was familiar to Theo, a gesture that managed to convey both disappointment and irritation. Again, an image of his father flashed into his head. Theo offered up a silent plea that Peregrine James Montgomery the Third, Perry to his friends, would not get to hear about this latest misdemeanour. Theo had been a Vaizey College boy for a little over three weeks. His father had been not only head of Theobald's House, but also captain of the cricket and rugby teams, earning his colours in his first term. His were big shoes to fill. *'Don't you let me down, boy!'* His father's words rang in his ears like rolling thunder.